MEGA

JAKE BIBLE

D1247938

Foreword

As a writer, you sometimes get inspired and sometimes inspiration finds you. With Mega it was a bit of both. When I was told Severed Press was looking for sea monster novels, I passed on the idea at first, instead, concentrating on Z-Burbia. But the idea mill never sleeps and soon I had a pitch in mind for quite the story.

Pirates. Navy SEALs. Giant sharks.

I wanted to do more than just people on a yacht getting eaten; I wanted there to be substance to the story. And I wanted it to be an adventure thriller, like in the grand tradition of Clive Cussler. Thus Mega was born.

I'd love for this story to continue into other novels, since I've grown fond of Team Grendel and the rest of the crew of the Beowulf. They are like old drinking buddies.

I hope you enjoy the insanity I have put down on paper. I know I enjoyed writing it.

Cheers,
Jake Bible
December 2013

CHAPTER ONE: PIRATES

Saltwater sprayed Abshir's face again and again, as the skiff sped across the choppy waves of the Indian Ocean, but he barely noticed the saline annoyance. His worry was what the water was doing to the AK-47 clutched in a grip that could crush rock. Only hours earlier, his father had placed the rifle in his hands, wishing him well on his first true run, as they stood on the deck of his father's ship.

"You will do your tribe proud today," Daacad Khalid Shimbir said as he handed the rifle over. "Keep ever watchful. Do you know what to ask?"

"Where is the control room? How many men are on this ship? Do you have weapons? Where are the weapons?" Abshir responded.

"That is good, that is good," Daacad laughed, patting his son on the shoulder. "You leave a boy, but come back a man. What do you watch for, never turning your eye?"

"The horizon," Abshir said. "I look for a ship. I yell when I see one."

"And then you listen to Kaafi," Daacad said, "you do what he says."

"Yes," Abshir nodded, "I will honor you, father."

"Yes," Daacad nodded, "you will."

The wind turned and the waves came at the skiff from the other side, an occurrence the men expected. Kaafi, the oldest and most experienced at nineteen, looked back at Najiib who was manning the rudder. Only a year older than Abshir, Najiib had been on seven runs and was the best with the motor by far. He had a knack for reading the water and his smile told Kaafi that all was fine, even as the large raft started to rock dangerously to one side.

"Hold steady!" Tarabi shouted, the fourth and last member of the pirate raiding party. "Don't you know how to steer?"

Najiib ignored him, as most did, and just looked ahead at the clear horizon. At seventeen, Tarabi was a monster and still growing. His neck was as thick as Abshir's thigh, his arms and legs like small trees. His deep, black skin shined in the midday sun, showing the intense definition of his muscles. For a people that were primarily long and lanky, Tarabi was an anomaly; one that Daacad had wasted no time in recruiting. If he hadn't, then one of the other tribal gangs would have. But Daacad had seen the intimidation potential of having a young man Tarabi's size armed with an RPG-7 sitting in a skiff as they pulled alongside a target vessel.

"There!" Abshir said, his eyes catching sight of a vessel far off. "Do you see?"

Kaafi did see. He raised his binoculars and his lips peeled back in what others called his death grin; his ability to smile had left him years ago. "Good eyes. Container ship."

"What flag?" Tarabi asked. "American? Is it American?"

To capture an American ship, or one with an American crew, was the ultimate goal. They could ransom the crew for three to four times the amount of a European crew. Although an American crew would mean possible interference by the US Navy, but that was something they were willing to risk. And why were they out in the Indian Ocean, miles from the coast of Somalia's Puntland region, instead of up by the Gulf of Aden and the many more ships that traveled through there?

The Gulf of Aden had been over pirated and was patrolled by the international members of the Combined Task Forces and Operation Atalanta. Too many gangs had taken too many chances, ruining a good thing for everyone. This was why Daacad had always kept operations close to Hilweyne on the coast of the Mudug region of Somalia. It was hundreds of miles south of the gulf, and despite the highly public taking of the Maersk Alabama and subsequent killing of the pirates by US Navy SEALs in 2009, it had always been a lucrative territory. It presented its own issues such as erratic weather and choppier seas, but on the whole, it was an area pirates dreamed of. And Daacad had no plans on relinquishing a single bit of control.

Abshir thought of his father and about how proud he would be if they could pull off an attack his first time out. His clansmen and fellow pirates would hail him. It would be known that he was worthy to take over for his father when the time came.

The smile on Abshir's face amused Kaafi, for he'd seen it many times on the faces of young, inexperienced pirates. He knew it would last until they got close to the ship. The size of the vessel would wipe that smile right off. And what they might be forced to do once on the ship, would keep that smile away permanently. His had never returned.

"You do not show fear," Kaafi shouted at the young men, "you make *them* show fear. You make *them* wet themselves when we come aboard. The first one to resist gets hit." Kaafi pantomimed with the butt of his own AK-47. "The second one to resist gets shot. Anyone with a weapon gets shot. Do not hesitate. Shoot. Aim for the belly. It may not kill them and their cries for mercy will keep the others in line. Do you hear what I say?"

They all nodded as adrenaline started to pump through their systems. The minutes it took to close in on the ship were the longest minutes of Abshir's life. The ship grew larger and larger as they grew closer. Once they were less than a couple hundred yards away, the ship's claxons started to blare, warning the crew that an attack was coming.

The clock began to tick.

It was assumed someone from the ship would send out a distress call to the nearest Task Force vessel, but Daacad had already done his research and knew the closest vessel was more than four-hundred miles away. It would take that vessel a minimum of eight hours at flank speed to reach them. And they would have things well under control within eight hours. The plan was to hijack the ship, steam it close to Daacad's mother ship where they'd take the ship's crew, and exchange it for a full crew of his own. The container ship would be steamed down the Somali coast to a port that he controlled, while the crew would be taken back to his base in Hilweyne. The ship's cargo would be sold and the crew would be ransomed.

His father's plan in mind, Abshir's finger twitched near the trigger of his AK-47. The container ship was massive and even if it held nothing but grains, it would be worth millions. The crew would be worth almost as much; as he spotted the German flag flying from a pole above what he assumed was the bridge. They wouldn't fetch the same price as Americans, but close enough.

Najiib turned the skiff parallel with the container ship, making sure not to get caught in the wake of the massive boat. Kaafi raised a bullhorn to his mouth and announced, "You will stop! Stop this ship! You will be boarded! Do not resist or you will die! Do not touch your weapons, or you will all die!"

Far above, heads and faces peered over the side and Tarabi waved his RPG about, showing them that he could blow a hole in the hull of the ship if they did not comply. Many of the heads ducked back, but some still watched as Tarabi aimed the RPG at them and put his eye to the sight. That sent them scurrying back from the rail.

"Lower your ladders!" Kaafi ordered. "Do not make me ask again," he looked over his shoulder at Tarabi, "or my friend will sink you!"

Just as Kaafi was about to get impatient, three ladders were dropped down. Kaafi motioned for Abshir to go first. The boy slung his rifle and took hold of the ladder, careful not to lose his footing and fall into the churning waters. If he did, he'd be lost forever, pushed under by the wake of the ship and more than likely, shredded by the huge aft propellers. Abshir climbed as fast as he could, finally getting to the top and over the rail. Kaafi waited for the sign and when it came, he took the RPG from Tarabi and nodded for him to follow. The large young man made it up the ladder in a third of the time it took Abshir and his scrawny arms.

"You follow as soon as I am up top," Kaafi said to Najiib. "Let the skiff go. It will be destroyed under this ship and no evidence will be left."

Najiib nodded, even though he didn't need Kaafi to say anything; it was not his first run and he was well aware of the procedure. But Kaafi was in charge.

He timed the jump perfectly. He positioned the skiff next to the ladder so all he had to do was grab it as soon as he let go of the rudder. With all his strength, Najiib hauled himself up the ladder as the skiff became submerged and then lost. He didn't even give it a second glance as he adjusted his AK-47 and climbed up to join his compatriots.

The others were already moving the plan along as Najiib climbed over the rail and stepped onto the deck. Men held their hands up in the air as Kaafi and Tarabi shouted at them to keep moving and take them to the bridge. He knew Kaafi would rest control of the ship from the captain quickly and then steer towards the rendezvous point. In less than an hour, they'd switch out the crew and then be on their way to the secure port.

"We are to move aft and go below deck," Abshir said. "Find the engine room and make sure no crew is there to shut down the engines."

"Yes, I know," Najiib said, struggling to keep the annoyance from his voice. He was supposed to pilot the ship once the crew was handed over to Daacad, and resented that the man's son was ordering him around like he was the rookie, instead of Abshir.

"Yes," Abshir nodded, "then let us go."

Najiib waited, and then started to laugh. "Aft is that way," he smiled, realizing his resentment was misplaced; the boy was no threat. "Follow me."

Abshir looked over his shoulder at the many huge containers that were stacked row after row upon the deck of the ship, then hurried and followed Najiib aft and to a large hatch that led below deck. It took them a few moments for their eyes to adjust, as they moved into almost total darkness.

"They have cut the main power," Najiib smiled as he pulled a small flashlight from his belt. "But there will be backup power keeping the navigation, communication, and ventilation systems going. Not to worry, I will get this up and going soon. Then we will have full power and can take the ship where we want."

The engine room was several decks down, and Abshir was sweating and out of breath by the time they worked open the hatch and stepped into a cramped, hot room. It smelled of grease and ozone, making Abshir's nose twitch. He tried to stifle it, but the sneeze couldn't be held back. His head rocked forward as he let loose, and he sneezed so loud that he almost didn't hear the gunshot. Sparks flew out against the wall right where his head had been.

But as he felt heat sear the side of his face, he realized someone was still shooting at them. He ran to the side, opening fire with his AK-47, shooting randomly into the engine room.

"Stop that!" Najiib shouted. "You'll kill us both!"

Another shot rang out and it was almost impossible to tell where it came from, as the entire room echoed with the ear splitting bang. Najiib waived his hand, gesturing for Abshir to crouch low. He did and tried to see under the machinery that ran the ship. There, across the room, deep in shadow, but just at the edge of Najiib's flashlight, was a pair of boots.

Abshir smiled and took aim, laying the AK-47 almost flat on the floor. He pulled the trigger and a man screamed, falling flat so Abshir could look directly into his eyes.

"Finish him," Najiib said, "we'll take his corpse up top as an example."

"No! Wait!" the man screamed, but Abshir did not hesitate. All he could think about was the approval of his father. The man's head was ripped apart, a third of it becoming spray against the iron and steel of the room.

"I will have this going soon," Najiib said. "Can you drag him up?"

"I will try," Abshir said as he slung his rifle and made his way to the far side of the room and the bloody corpse.

The man held a 9mm pistol in one hand and something else in the other. Abshir couldn't see what it was in the darkness, so he hooked his hands under the man's arms and began to drag. It was a considerable effort to get the man out of the engine room, and Abshir sighed heavily at the thought of dragging the corpse all the way up to the upper deck. But to quit would be shameful, so he pushed on.

Nearly exhausted, his muscles burning, Abshir finally stepped out into sunlight. He pulled the corpse partially out of the hatch, and then collapsed to the hot steel of the deck, his chest heaving from the exertion. He closed his eyes and turned his face to the sun, letting the heat he had known his whole life invigorate him. He was not one of those people that needed shade, or needed the coolness of artificial air. He loved the sun and the smell of the sea. He was right at home.

After a few moments rest, Abshir opened his eyes and looked at the man's body. He reached out and pried open the man's hand, taking what was clutched inside. Abshir looked at it for a couple minutes as conflicting emotions warred inside him. Finally, he frowned and threw the object away, letting the breeze take it. As Abshir once again lifted the corpse and started to drag it towards the bridge, the thing the man had held –a photograph of him with a woman and two small children- floated through the air and out over the open sea.

"There you are, Abshir," Kaafi said as the teen stepped onto the bridge, nearly collapsing from his exertion. "What do you have there?"

"An example," Abshir said, yanking the corpse over the threshold of the bridge's hatch, "for all to see."

Tarabi laughed loudly and menaced the group of men seated on the deck in front of him. "See that? Do you? That will be you if you don't cooperate? Now, how many more are on the ship? Where are the weapons?"

"Ich spreche kein English. Sprechen sie Deutsch?" a man seated in front of the others asked. "Sprechen sie Deustch, ja?"

"What is that?" Abshir asked. "German?"

"Ja," the man nodded, "Deutsch. Ger-man."

"Parlez-vous francais?" Kaafi asked. The man, the captain of the ship, shook his head sadly. "Nein?"

"Nein," the captain replied.

"Do you speak this?" Tarabi asked, smashing a fist into the face of the man seated directly behind the captain. All of the men cried out in shock. "Yes?"

"Tarabi," Kaafi warned, "you hit when I say so."

"Yes," Tarabi nodded, "I know."

"Do it again," Kaafi death grinned. Another man was hit. Kaafi grabbed the captain by his collar and pulled him across the bridge and into a corner, isolating him from the others. "You speak English. I know you do. I had to learn it and I know you learned it. All ships' captains speak English."

"Nein, nein," the captain replied, shaking his head. "Ich sprechen---"

Kaafi slapped the man across the face, open handed like he'd slap a girl. He did it again and again until the man held up his hands, blood trickling from his lips and nose.

"Okay, okay, stop now, please," the captain said. "Please, no more of the hitting."

Kaafi laughed –a short, dark sound- and stepped back from the captain. "Good, now we are getting somewhere," he said. He looked back at the other men and Tarabi. "Now you can tell me who my friend should kill first. Which one dies now?"

Tarabi pulled a long knife from his belt.

"Nein!" the captain shouted, holding out a hand. "No, please!"

"Then you do what we say and no tricks or lies, yes?" Kaafi asked. "Or they die. Understand?"

"Understand," the captain nodded, "no tricks. No lies."

"And you will call me captain, yes?" Kaafi asked.

"Ja," the captain nodded, "Captain."

"Order your engineer to turn the power back on," Kaafi said.

"You killed him," the captain replied, pointing to the corpse by Abshir's feet. "Kleimer was the engineer."

"You don't have a second engineer?" Kaafi asked. "For a ship this big? I think you do."

The captain glanced to the group of men. Kaafi watched his eyes closely.

"That one there?" Kaafi asked, pointing at a man in the middle of the group. "You. Come here."

The man looked from Kaafi to the captain. The captain nodded and the man got up, carefully stepping away from the leering Tarabi.

"You are the Second Engineer?" Kaafi asked. The man nodded. "And you can restore the power?" The man looked at the captain. "Hey!" He looked back to Kaafi. "Answer my question."

"Ja," the man said, "I can be turning the power on."

"Good," Kaafi said, "then do it."

But the power came on without him.

Kaafi smiled.

"Then I do not need you," Kaafi said and shot the man in the stomach. Blood burst from the wound and splattered the captain, making the man scream. Kaafi laughed and looked at the other men. "Stay in line, do as you're told, and you will be needed." He nudged the dying Second Engineer with his foot. "Try to escape or fight and you won't be needed. Understood?"

All of the men nodded that they understood.

"Abshir?"

"Yes, Kaafi?" Abshir asked, stepping forward.

"Help Tarabi secure the men," Kaafi said, "and have Najiib join me here. We are losing time."

Abshir nodded and smiled, waving his AK-47 at the men, then towards the hatch. They didn't need any more instruction and quickly stood up, their hands on their heads. Single file, they left the bridge with Abshir and Tarabi right behind.

"Come back for the bodies," Kaafi said, "they will stink up the bridge."

"And do what with them?" Abshir asked.

"Throw them overboard," Kaafi said.

"Oh," Abshir said.

"Is that a problem?" Kaafi asked.

"No, just…"

"What? Out with it, Abshir."

"Should they not be blessed?" Abshir asked. "What about their souls?"

"They are Christians," Kaafi laughed. "They have no souls. Into the sea with them."

Abshir nodded. He followed Tarabi out and they secured the men with rope to the rows of pipe that ran the length of the bridge. The sun was boiling hot and would kill the men in hours if they were left like that. But in the time it would take to get to the rendezvous point, they would only be weak and not dead. It would keep them from fighting back if they got any sudden burst of courage.

Once secured, Abshir went back and dragged the two corpses one at a time to the railing. He set his rifle down and squatted, struggling to lift the First Engineer over the rail. After considerable effort, he managed it, and watched as the body tumbled through the air and was lost into the churning wake below.

Catching his breath, Abshir started with the Second Engineer. As he got the body halfway over the rail, something fell from the man's pocket. Abshir, leaving the corpse draped over the rail, bent down, and picked up a brand new iPhone.

"Look, Tarabi!" Abshir shouted, waving the phone.

"Good for you," Tarabi nodded. "What's that around it?"

Abshir studied the case the phone was in. It was hard plastic, but with an orange foam outer shell. He squeezed it a couple times and the foam returned to form each time. "I think it floats," Abshir smiled, "in case it falls into the water."

"Yes, that would be a good place to float," Tarabi mocked. "Now get rid of that body."

Abshir grabbed the man's legs and lifted the corpse again. He nearly screamed when the man struggled slightly, not quite dead.

"Bitte," the man whispered.

Abshir ignored the man's plea and shoved with all of his strength. He leaned over the rail and watched as the body bounced off the hull, sending it flying just to the outside of the ship's wake. The body hit the water and floated away. Abshir watched it as it bobbed face down in the water, the man finally dead from the impact. He wondered if that man had a photograph on him of his family; he should have checked his pockets, but was too startled by the man being alive.

Abshir was about to turn away when something caught his eye. Even all the way up on the upper deck, Abshir could see the shadow of a large shape down in the water. It was huge. Abshir shook his head and squinted, thinking it was a trick of the sunlight playing across the water. But the shape was there and moving towards the floating corpse.

"Tarabi?" Abshir called, keeping his eyes focused on the shadow. "Come see this."

"Are you stupid?" Tarabi asked. "I am watching the crew."

"But---"

"Shut up, boy," Tarabi said, "don't waste my time."

Before Abshir could respond, the shadow became substantial, its mouth, filled with row after row of teeth, broke the surface of the water, swallowing the corpse whole. Abshir jumped back, a small cry escaping his throat, his eyes wide with fear. The thing was gigantic. Bigger than anything he'd ever seen.

"What is wrong with you, Abshir?" Tarabi asked. "You cry like a girl."

"Out there," Abshir said, pointing towards the rail as he backed away, "something out there."

"In the ocean? Really?" Tarabi laughed. "There are many something's out there."

"It was a shark," Abshir said, his eyes wide with fright, "a very large shark."

"Good for it," Tarabi said. "It found some free food."

"It was a giant," Abshir said.

"Like me," Tarabi smiled, "the Tarabi of the sea!" He watched how Abshir shook. "What is wrong with you? Sharks can't fly. Unless you go swimming, it won't get you. But I will if you don't stop being like a little girl."

Abshir nodded. "Yes. Sorry."

He tried to smile at Tarabi, but he couldn't quite do it. The image of the size of that mouth filled his mind. He was not good at math, barely having had any schooling, but he knew sharks well enough to figure out the length of the creature. If he was right, he didn't think the shark would need to fly for its mouth to reach the upper deck fifty feet above the water.

"Go get Najiib," Tarabi said. "Tell him to go to the bridge like Kaafi asked."

"Right," Abshir said absently, "I'll get him."

He made his way to the aft hatch and down to the engine room slowly. He felt better in the cool darkness, away from the rail and the water. He found Najiib walking towards him and he stopped.

"What is the largest shark you have seen?" Abshir asked.

"What kind of question is that?" Najiib replied. "Why ask me that?"

"I saw a shark," Abshir said, "it ate one of the corpses."

"One of the corpses?" Najiib asked, looking up towards the upper deck. "How many men did Tarabi kill?"

"None," Abshir said. "Kaafi killed the Second Engineer when you got the power going again. To make an example."

"Oh," Najiib said. "So what is this about a shark?"

"The one I saw was sixty, maybe seventy feet long," Abshir said. He saw the look on Najiib's face. "No, no, I am serious, Najiib! It was a giant of the sea!"

"There are no sharks that big," Najiib said, pushing past the boy and taking the steps up. "Not even great whites. Maybe a whale shark, but even that doesn't get sixty feet. And doesn't eat corpses. Your eyes tricked you. It was the sun on the waves making the shark look bigger than it was."

"Right," Abshir said, following Najiib up, "you must be right."

"Do not mention what you saw to your father," Najiib said. "He will think you are not fit for runs. Men that cannot trust their eyes cannot be trusted at all. Keep what you said to yourself and I will keep it to myself. Understood?"

"Understood," Abshir said. "But I already told Tarabi."

"He is a fool and your father will not listen to him," Najiib said, tapping the side of his head. "Nothing up here worth your father's time."

"Yes, okay," Abshir replied, "thank you, Najiib."

"Go help Tarabi and I will speak to Kaafi," Najiib said. "And no more monster sharks."

"No more monster sharks," Abshir smiled, feeling silly over what he saw. Of course it hadn't been seventy feet long. That was stupid. That was little boy thinking. And his father didn't send a little boy on a run, he sent a young man.

Najiib was able to adjust the ship's heading and they were at the rendezvous point in under an hour, pushing the engines at full. Abshir stayed by the rail, his eyes scanning the horizon for his father's ship. He purposely avoided looking down into the water.

"There!" Abshir yelled towards the bridge. "I see them!"

Per procedure, Kaafi had stayed off the radio, but turned it on when he got the word from Abshir. He switched channels until he found the one Daacad had given him.

"We see you," Daacad's voice said after they finished their quick greetings. "Bring to full stop and wait. A skiff is on its way to you."

The skiff bounced across the waves as it sped towards the ship. At full stop, the ship didn't produce a dangerous wake, but it was still a trial getting the captive crew down to the skiff. Abshir watched as the skiff sped away, Tarabi seated behind the prisoners with his AK covering them, and headed back to the mother ship. There hadn't been enough room for everyone to go at once, so he waited behind. The skiff would come back with a small crew to help Najiib pilot the ship to the secure port.

Then there it was again: a dark shadow in the water, just behind the returning skiff.

He thought about telling someone, but remembered Najiib's words. If he mentioned a monster shark to anyone else, he'd never be allowed to go out on a run again. He could feel his pulse quicken and watched as the skiff pulled alongside the ship. The shadow continued underneath, lost below the ship.

"Ready, young Abshir?" Kaafi asked, making Abshir jump. "Relax. You have done your father proud."

"Yes, thank you," Abshir said.

Kaafi greeted the men that climbed up over the rail and pointed them towards the bridge so they could join Najiib. He then slapped Abshir on the back and pointed to the ladder dangling over the side to the skiff fifty feet below.

Abshir slung his rifle across his back and swung himself over the rail, placing his feet carefully on the ladder, terrified of what would happen if he fell. More than likely, he would snap his neck from the fall, but that was not what terrified him. What if he didn't snap his neck? What if what was in the water got him?

He took a seat in the skiff and watched the gently rolling waves as he waited for Kaafi to join them. Once in his own seat, Kaafi gave the order, and the skiff turned and headed towards the mother ship.

"What are you looking at?" Kaafi finally asked, worried about the way Abshir stared at the water. "Do you see something?"

Unfortunately for Abshir, he did see something. He tried not to look too scared, but it was impossible to hide it from Kaafi. The man leaned past Abshir and looked into the water. Down below, many feet below he could see a shape.

"What is that?" he asked.

"You see it?" Abshir asked.

"Yes, of course, why wouldn't I see it?" Kaafi asked. "It is huge. And fast."

"Yes," Abshir nodded. "Is it a shark?"

"Could be," Kaafi said then looked harder. His death grin became an actual smile for the first time in years. "No, no, look!"

The shape began to surface, maybe thirty yards from the skiff.

"What is that?" Abshir asked. "That's not a shark."

"It's a whale!" Kaafi laughed. "Look at it!"

The beast surfaced, shooting water fifty feet into the air from its blowhole, and then dove back down again. The men on the skiff all laughed and pointed, excited by such a rare sight.

"What kind of whale is it?" Abshir asked. "Did you see its mouth? Those teeth?"

The whale had opened its mouth briefly when it surfaced, and Abshir was shocked to see two full rows of teeth –one row on top, one row on the bottom- that looked like they were meant for more than eating krill.

"Yes," Kaafi said, puzzled, "I have never seen a whale that big with teeth like that. I don't know what kind it is."

Abshir wished his father could see the creature, he knew a lot about sea life. Then he realized he had something that he could use. He pulled the iPhone from his pocket and turned the video camera on, aiming where the whale had last been.

"Where'd you get that?" Kaafi asked.

"Off the Second Engineer," Abshir said. "Tarabi was jealous. I think he wanted it, but I found it first."

"Good for you," Kaafi said, his eyes scanning the surface of the water for signs of the whale. "There!"

Abshir turned the camera on and aimed it at where Kaafi was pointing. In just seconds, the whale surfaced again, but this time it breached and came up out of the water, half of its body visible as it twisted in the air and then fell back again. The wave it produced rolled towards the skiff and the men didn't realize what was going to happen until it was too late.

The wave hit the side of the skiff, flipping it like a piece of paper. The men went flying into the water, their cries of surprise cut short as they went under. Abshir struggled to get back to the surface and was both happy and dismayed. Dismayed because he had lost his AK-47, but happy because he still clutched the iPhone. It hadn't been the whale's fault they had capsized. It wasn't the men's fault either, since none could have known there would be something so large in the water that day.

The skiff floated upside down and Abshir swam towards it. He reached it and crawled on top of the hull. He checked the phone and the case had kept it protected. The camera was still recording and he almost turned it off when he saw another shadow. Just below where Kaafi was swimming.

"Uh oh!" he shouted at Kaafi. "The whale is below you! Swim! Swim!"

Abshir wasn't sure if the whale would attack a man, but the image of the huge mouth swallowing the Second Engineer's corpse rushed to the forefront of his mind. And that image troubled him. It wasn't the same as the whale. Sure, he was not an expert on sea life, but still he wasn't stupid.

"Kaafi!" he yelled. "Hurry!"

The shadow was coming to the surface quickly, right at Kaafi.

"It won't eat me," Kaafi yelled, spitting sea water from his mouth, "I'm not whale food!"

And he was right, because the whale breached a good forty yards away. This time it didn't roll and splash, but came up and quickly dove back down. When its tail was in the air, Abshir gasped.

Half of its tail had been bitten off. Abshir had no doubt about that, he could plainly see the gouges of teeth marks. But what could do that to a whale so big? His eyes fell on Kaafi and the man looked at Abshir, terrified, then down at the shadow that wasn't a whale, and coming up at him.

The rest of the men had made it to the skiff and they all scrambled up onto it, yelling at each other not to make it roll and sink, while also yelling for Kaafi to swim. They saw the shadow as well.

Their yells ceased the second the shadow was a shadow no more and exploded from the water. Half of them screamed as Kaafi was swallowed almost whole. Almost. When the massive jaws bit down, his shoulders, neck, and head, went flying into the water, blood spreading everywhere.

"KAAFI!" Abshir shouted. "KAAFI!"

The thing fell back into the water and the men clutched at each other, their eyes scanning the waves, looking for signs of its return.

"What was that?" Daacad shouted, pulling his binoculars away from his face, as he stood on the deck of his ship. The men behind him stared out at the water, stunned. "Did any of you see that?"

"I do not believe it," Tarabi said, "he was right."

"Who was right?" Daacad asked. "Tarabi? Who was right? About what?" But the man didn't respond. Daacad looked at the other men and rage filled his features. "Get us over there! Get us to that skiff!"

His order was relayed to the bridge and the ship began to turn and move across the water towards the overturned skiff. But it was too late. Daacad watched in horror as the thing surfaced again, this time lifting the entire skiff into the air and biting it in half. Men screamed, Daacad heard them crying for help, and he was positive one of the voices was his son's.

"Faster!" Daacad yelled. "Faster!"

The creature had submerged again, and when they got to the wreckage of the skiff, it was nowhere to be seen. Daacad, careful not to sound panicked and lose face in front of his men, shouted orders left and right. The wreckage had spread across the water by the time they got there, so a net was tossed out in hopes of retrieving some of it and anyone left alive that possibly clutched to the shattered and splintered boards.

After three passes, all of the wreckage was retrieved, but not a single man. Not whole, at least. When the net was hauled to the ship's deck and opened, an arm slid from under a snapped board. Tarabi was the first to see it, and what the arm's hand held. He quickly picked it up and pocketed what he found, and then waved the arm at the others.

"This is all that's left!" he shouted. "What happened?"

A blow to the back of his head knocked him to his knees, which was not an easy thing to do to a young man Tarabi's size. He got up and spun around quickly, ready to fight, but stopped instantly, as he looked down into the eyes of Daacad.

"Give. Me. That," Daacad snarled.

Tarabi handed the severed arm over like it was made of hot lead and stepped well out of Daacad's reach. The leader of the pirate gang held the arm carefully, his eyes welling with tears. On the inside of the arm, close by the wrist, was a long, jagged scar. He knew that scar. It was from when his son was small and fell from a tree, catching his arm on a broken branch. A wave of anguish washed over him and it was his turn to fall to his knees.

No one on deck moved a muscle until their leader was done sobbing and crying over the loss of his son.

When Daacad was able to gather himself and get to his feet, he looked at Tarabi.

"I want to know what that was," he said. "I will not rest until I do."

Tarabi nodded, and then waited as the man turned away, still clutching the arm, and walked up and into the bridge. He shouted at the other men to get to work and they scattered even though some had seniority over Tarabi. When he was sure no one was watching, Tarabi slipped below. Everyone was on the upper deck, so he was alone when he pulled the iPhone from his pocket. Despite its time in the seawater, there was still blood on it, stuck in the crevices between the hard case and the outer protection of the foam.

He double-checked that he was alone, and then turned on the phone. The video app came up immediately and Tarabi played the last video shot. He watched it over and over, listening to the surprised voices of Kaafi and Abshir as they watched the whale breach. It was on the eighth or ninth viewing that he noticed it: a shadow in the water close by the whale. He could tell by the angle of the sun that the shadow was not from the whale itself, but something just as large under the water's surface. The shark.

He briefly thought of taking the phone to Daacad and showing him the video, but decided against it. Daacad would take the phone from him and keep it for himself. Tarabi couldn't stomach the thought of losing it, not even to his gang leader. It was an iPhone! No, he would keep it for himself. He'd only ever had a flip phone, so he wasn't quite sure how it worked, but he knew a guy back in Hilweyne that would.

There was a lot of activity back in port when the pirate mother ship docked, and Tarabi pushed the phone from his mind as he helped unload the hostages and drove them to the gang's compound on the far side of Hilweyne. They were locked up and hooded so Daacad could make a quick video demanding ransom, or the container ship's crew would be executed.

Once the hostages were secured, and Daacad was gone to tell his wives of the loss of his son, Tarabi took his chance and slipped from the compound. He walked to his destination instead of driving, not wanting one of the gang's vehicles to be spotted and recognized. When he reached his intended destination, a small, rundown hut, he knocked softly on the rickety door. A couple minutes went by and then a small child opened up.

"Tell your father that Tarabi is here," Tarabi said. The child just stared. "Now! Go!"

The child scurried away and was replaced by an angry looking man.

"Tarabi, what is this? Why do you scare my son?" a tall, thin man asked, his black skin marred by pock marks and scars. "And why are you here so late?"

"I have this," Tarabi said, pulling out the iPhone, his smile like a child's at Christmas. "I found it today."

"Give me that!" the man snapped, yanking the iPhone from Tarabi's grip. He started flipping through the settings and checking the apps. "You fool, this can be traced! You are lucky I know how to turn that off."

"Oh," Tarabi said, his face flushed with embarrassment, "I did not know."

"Leave it with me a couple of days and I'll make sure it is safe to give back," the man said. "It'll be like new." He caught site of the blood that Tarabi never wiped off, but didn't say anything. He knew whom he was dealing with.

"A couple days? That long?" Tarabi said, disappointed.

"Yes, I am a busy man," the man said, waving Tarabi off. "I will send one of my children to fetch you when it is ready. Now go away, you have disrupted my evening."

Tarabi thought about showing the man how disruptive he could make the evening, but stopped himself. He really wanted that iPhone. He couldn't wait to see the looks on the other men's faces when he pulled it out for the first time. He'd make sure it was spotless then.

"Fine," Tarabi said reluctantly, "two days. If I do not hear from you by then, I will come back, and I won't knock."

"Yes, yes, I understand," the man said, "goodnight, Tarabi."

The door shut and Tarabi stalked off, his shoulders hunched with slight defeat.

The man inside waited until he was sure Tarabi was gone, and then turned and hurried over to a work bench on the far wall of the hut. His wife and children watched him as he undraped the bench to reveal a bank of computer monitors in various states of repair and disrepair. He pulled a box out from under the bench and searched until he found the right cord, plugging it into a desktop tower.

"Finish eating," the man commanded his family, and they all turned back to their almost forgotten meal, sneaking glances here and there, as the man worked.

He brought up a program similar to iTunes. After a couple of minutes, he'd stripped off and copied everything from the iPhone. He then set it to reset and put it aside as he looked at the files he'd obtained. He shook his head as he scanned through the pictures of a white man and his family, the ship he had worked on, and other various aspects of his life. He was about to delete the files, then saw one was not a still, but a video.

The video came to life and he had to turn the volume down on his computer as Abshir's voice echoed about the hut. He didn't even notice his family crowding around him as he watched the video again and again, stunned at what he saw.

CHAPTER TWO: A PROPOSAL

The man watched the video, his eyes glued to the tablet he held in his hands. He was oblivious to the sounds of the bar around him, despite the fact it was a busy Friday night and the bar was jammed with patrons. The video ended and he looked at the screen, then up at the man that sat across the table from him, back down to the tablet, and then up to the man. He set the tablet aside and took a long drink from the glass in hand.

"That's something to see," the man said with a cultured South African accent. The rest of the accents around him were less than cultured. He flinched as a large woman stumbled by, her beer sloshing from her mug. He had never been much for socializing with the seedier element of his countrymen and countrywomen. Adjusting his tie, he cleared his throat, smoothed the front of his suit jacket and started again. "What I mean to say, is that it's an impressive video. Truly."

"Impressive?" the man across the table laughed. Late twenties, dirty blond hair, bright blue eyes, the man looked like a retired Abercrombie & Fitch model, but in much, much better shape. The black t-shirt he wore accentuated the already defined muscles in his arms and chest. He leaned forward, those bright blue eyes turning to ice. "Impressive? That's all you have to say? It's fucking incredible!"

The muscled man reached out and tapped the tablet. His finger emphasizing each word he said.

"That is the find of the last two centuries, Mr- uh, what was it again?"

"Konig," the man replied, "must I remind you each time, Mr. Chambers?"

"Call me Darren, please," Darren Chambers smiled. "My apologies. I am shit for names. Always have been. I can learn a new language in 48 hours, but can't remember the guy's name that holds my future in his hands. Messed up, am I right?"

Darren laughed. Mr. Konig didn't.

"Anyway, you saw what is on that video," Darren said. "That is what I have been searching for. All these years of research have led me to this point, a single YouTube video uploaded by some anonymous African teenager. At least that's my guess. I gave up a career as a US Navy SEAL to pursue this. I can't have it all fall apart because Stanvelt Banc of Cape Town is annoyed that I'm a little late on my payments."

"Six months in arrears, Mr. Chambers," Mr. Konig said, "that is not little. Nor is your loan. You are compounding late fees and penalty interest every day. Do you know how much that is, just for this week?"

"Do I want to?" Darren laughed. Again, Mr. Konig did not.

"186,000 rand, Mr. Chambers," Mr. Konig said. Darren had just taken a sip of his whiskey and spit half of it onto the table. "That would be about 18,000 US dollars. Per week, Mr. Chambers. You are currently in debt for nearly 800,000."

"Rand?" Darren asked hopefully.

"US dollars," Mr. Konig replied.

"Yikes," Darren smiled, wiping at the whiskey that was sprayed on his phone. Just as he set it back on the table, it rang. Again. His Chief Officer had been trying to call him for twenty minutes. He let it go to voicemail, adding to the thirteen others. Unlucky number that.

"But with this discovery, I will be able to pay that loan off in just a couple of months," Darren insisted. "Book deals, speaking tours, exclusives, National Geographic special, at the very least. All I need is just another extension…and an additional fifty grand. That's all."

That did make Mr. Konig laugh. It was a shrill sound and several of the bar's patrons turned to make sure he wasn't having a fit. His face went red with the unwanted attention and he cleared his throat, adjusted his tie (which did not need adjusting), and smoothed his suit once more.

"Mr. Chambers---"

"Darren," Darren smiled. It was a charming smile and one Darren had relied on most of his life. "I think we're on a first name basis, don't you?"

"You can't even remember my last name, Mr. Chambers," Mr. Konig said, the chill in his voice answer enough. "What I was going to say is that there will be no need for an extension." He pulled his phone from his pocket and smiled at what he saw. "As of five minutes ago, your loan account was closed. You no longer owe us anything."

"What...? Wait, what the hell are you talking about?" Darren asked as Mr. Konig stood up and buttoned his suit jacket. "Closed? How?"

"It was paid off by an investor," Mr. Konig said, looking about the bar, trying to find the best way through the crowd to make his exit. No routes were appealing as they all involved having to squeeze past several large groups of drunken Saffers (a term Mr. Konig found derogatory, even if many of his fellow South Africans did not).

"Investor? What the hell does that mean? That's my ship! My ship! You have no right to-!"

"Let me stop you there, Mr. Chambers," Mr. Konig said, "I did nothing. The Stanvelt Banc of Cape Town has been sending you notices for weeks that your boat would be sold at auction at precisely seven in the evening on this date. You did not respond to any of the notices."

"Notices? Auction?" Darren said. "I thought that was just bank threats. You know, empty and just there to pressure me."

"Banks do not make empty threats, Mr. Chambers," Mr. Konig replied. "They do not need to."

"Then what the hell was this all about?" Darren asked, standing and spreading his arms over the table, and then pointing at the tablet. "Why'd you ask to meet if you had no intention of extending my loan? And why'd you ask to see the video over and over…ah, shit."

"We drew straws," Mr. Konig said. "Crude, I know, but none of us wanted to be the one to distract you while the auction was happening. Your reputation does precede you. I am happy that the temper you are known for did not surface this evening. I have a date with a young woman in real estate and would hate to arrive late and in a sorry state."

"Distract me…," Darren said to himself, his face flushed, a vein at his temple pulsed. He glanced at his phone and the notification that the number had grown to fifteen messages. His CO hadn't stopped trying to reach him.

"Right, yes, well," Mr. Konig said, extending his hand, "I am sorry for the circumstances, but I did enjoy the video. I hope you catch your mystery whale, Mr. Chambers. Others in the office have laughed, but I have always believed it to be an adventurous way to pass one's time. When I retire one day, I hope to take to the sea, too."

The man waited for Darren to shake his hand then let it drop when it was obvious it wouldn't happen. He nodded to Darren and started to walk away.

"Hey, Konig," Darren called out. "You liked the video? Here. Take it, asshole!"

Mr. Konig turned and his eyes grew wide. The tablet hit him square in the forehead and he stumbled backwards, his hand reaching back for support, but finding a mug of beer instead. The glass tumbled to the ground and shattered, spraying the former owner of the beverage from toe to chest. Mr. Konig was able to steady himself, but his legs went weak as the splattered man stood up, dwarfing Konig by almost a foot.

"Oh," Mr. Konig said before a large fist hit him in the nose. His blood quickly joined the mess of glass and beer on the wood planked barroom floor.

"You owe me a beer," the man said, as he grabbed Konig by his suit and lifted him into the air. "Now."

"Right, right," Mr. Konig said, his voice choked and slurred from his ruptured nose, "a pitcher even."

"Hey," Darren said as he grabbed the man's arm. "That's my banker. I'd appreciate it if you put him down."

"I could give two foks what you care for, Yank," the man sneered. "Go back to your table and let a couple Saffers work this out."

"You know what?" Darren asked, looking as if he'd comply with the man's request. "I've lived in South Africa for years now, off and on, and I still don't get why you like being called Saffers. Sure, I get it's short for South African, but it sounds too close to Kaffer for my taste."

"I agree," Mr. Konig said, his feet dangling above the floor as blood continued to drip from his nose and off his chin. "Never liked it myself."

"You gonna put him down?" Darren asked as he turned towards his table. "Or do I have to ask you the hard way?"

"The hard way?" the man asked. "Don't know that way, Yank."

"Here," Darren smiled as he lifted a chair and swung it around, "let me show you."

The chair exploded against the man's shoulder and he lost his grip on Konig. The banker tumbled to the ground and quickly crawled under the table he had shared with Darren just moments before. He watched as the man turned to Darren and smiled.

"That is your hard way?" the man laughed, pulling back a fist. "You Yanks need to learn a better way."

"Chambers! No!" the bartender shouted and all eyes turned to the altercation just as the man threw the punch at Darren. "NOT AGAIN!"

The man's eyes went wide as his fist hit air. Darren wasn't there anymore. He hadn't even seen him move. Then his eyes went wider as his side exploded in pain. Then his back. Then his other side. Suddenly Darren was in front of him again. Smiling.

"You'll be pissing blood for a week," Darren said, "just a heads up."

The uppercut that hit the stunned man sent him flying off his feet and nearly out of his shoes. He slammed into the table behind him, obliterating it. People screamed, yelled, shouted, and rushed at Darren, but he just stood there looking at the man lying in the ruins of the table.

"The hard way," Darren said just as he was tackled by three of the man's friends.

Konig covered his head and watched in horror as the entire bar broke out into violent chaos. Darren had gone down under three bodies that almost matched his first assailant, but he wasn't there anymore. The men were landing punches on each other and the floor for a couple seconds before they realized their quarry had slipped their grasp.

Darren made sure to let them know exactly where he was, as he grabbed the top one and pulled him up off the floor. His knee met the man's groin and all that escaped the man's lips was a high pitched squeal and hiss. Darren patted him on the cheek and let him fall back to the ground. The other two pushed up and came at Darren, but he swatted their punches away like flies, sending both men stumbling past him, completely off balance.

A quick kick to each backside sent the men flying across other tables, destroying more furniture and adding to the insanity.

"Gonna stay under there all night?" Darren asked as he bent down and looked at Mr. Konig.

"Behind you!" Mr. Konig shouted.

"Yes, that's probably a good place to be as I clear us a path," Darren said, extending his hand. Mr. Konig didn't take it. "Fine. Be that way."

Darren took two fists to the back of the neck and went down hard on his knees. He shook his head and grimaced at the pain it produced.

"Your hard way is for moffies," the man jeered, "my girl hits harder."

"Oh," Darren said as he dodged the next throw, "where's she at? She should be with a real man, not kak like you."

Grabbing the man's arms over his shoulder, Darren rocketed to his feet, bending them in ways arms weren't meant to be bent. The man screamed as Darren snapped his arms, spun the man about, grabbed him by the back of the head and slammed his face into his knee. Darren smiled at the sound of crunching bone. He let the man collapse to the ground and resisted one last kick in the gut. Just wasn't fair.

"Staying?" Darren asked Mr. Konig. "Fuck if I care."

"Dammit, Chambers!" the bartender shouted at him as Darren ducked and dodged his way to the front door. "You're paying for this!"

"Bill that guy," Darren yelled, giving a last wave as he dashed out the door and away from the brawl that was just getting worse. "He started it."

Darren burst onto the sidewalk and did a quick assessment. Sirens coming fast, curious people heading towards the bar and the commotion inside, traffic slow and sporadic, a taxi up the street on the corner.

"HEY!" Darren bellowed as he sprinted towards the taxi. "TAXI!"

The car slowed and Darren dove into the backseat, staying down across the torn upholstery.

"You part of that, hey?" the cab driver asked, his voice a thick Afrikaans that took Darren a split second to adjust to. "Don't need no dronkie in my cab. Get yourself a new one."

"Ain't drunk, pal," Darren said. "Didn't have time to finish my drink before that started."

"Shame," the cab driver said, "hate to waste a drop. Where ya headed, bra?"

"Table Bay," Darren said, finally sitting up as the cab pulled away, "the port."

"That's extra," the driver said, "not my route, bra."

"I'll pay it," Darren replied, hoping he actually had enough. "Just get me there fast."

Darren leaned back into the seat as the cab sped through the streets of Cape Town, South Africa towards the Port of Cape Town.

"You want me to pull to the V & A?" the cab driver asked.

"Duncan," Darren said, "my ship's there."

Or it was, Darren thought. *Was his.*

"Fuck," Darren muttered.

"What's that?" the cab driver asked.

Darren waved him off and turned to look out the window. His ship, the Research Vessel Hooyah, was his life. He'd left the Navy Seals four years earlier under not the best of circumstances. It was an amicable split, and reflected so in his file, but he'd burned a few bridges in the community when he left. He was considered a candidate for Team Six and it ticked more than a few of his buddies off that he'd walk away from that kind of honor to chase a whale.

But it wasn't just any whale. No, Darren had seen his Moby Dick. Coming back from a mission off the coast of Somalia, Darren had found himself in the water with something that scared the ever loving fuck out of him. Which, being a hardened SEAL, was not an easy task. He'd been only about half a click from the Zodiac that was waiting to extract him and his Team when something bumped him from below. Not one ever to panic for anything, Darren had casually looked down to assess things. He nearly lost his rebreather as he stared straight into the largest eye he'd ever seen. It had been the only time his training had failed him and he'd reacted to his surroundings with anything but cold, calculating analysis.

He got himself together and studied the creature as it rolled past him and began to dive. He estimated it at fifty feet or more. Probably more. He knew his marine life and had never seen anything like it before. He couldn't match what he saw with any whale he knew of. The body was too thick, the tail was too wide, and the brief seconds he'd seen the creature's head, he'd taken notice of a jaw that shouldn't have existed on any contemporary whale.

That meant it wasn't a contemporary whale. It was something new. Or, as he'd find out when he was back aboard ship and had time to research, it was something old. Very old.

He had been hooked from then on.

He told himself that he had to leave the SEALs because the creature had spooked him. It was a millisecond, but enough for a SEAL to question himself. He'd killed men and women; destroyed villages and apartment complexes; wiped out terrorist cells and drug cartels. None of that bothered him, or at least, he didn't let it. But for a whale to freeze him up? Not acceptable.

Or that's what he told himself. It was harder to admit that he was obsessed. He was a SEAL and didn't get obsessed. Which was utter bullshit, since most SEALs lived in an OCD-fueled wonderland of hyperactive intelligence that bordered on insanity. All contained in a hardened discipline of perfect calm and empty headedness. It was a life of contradictions.

So he walked.

It took him a year to get a crew together that didn't think he was completely fucked in the head. With some charm and creative financing, he'd managed to buy a ship and start his obsession in earnest. The whale was out there and he knew it. So did half of his crew. The other half just wanted to believe, and thought it was pretty cool their captain was an ex-SEAL.

But the cool wore off quickly and Darren had gone through more crew members than he could remember. He sure as shit couldn't remember their names. But his Chief Officer stuck with him the entire time. And that was who he called as the cab got closer to the Port.

"You fucking listen to any of those voicemails, oh, Captain, my Captain?" CO Marty Lake asked as he answered his phone. "I'm guessing by the lack of screaming that you haven't."

Chief Officer Martin Hogarth Lake was close to the same age as Darren, but years ahead in wisdom. He kept it all cool when the shit hit the fan, and he made sure Darren could have his freak outs when the frustration got to him. He never let the crew think anything but the highest for their Captain, even if it meant dangling one or two over the rail to teach a lesson. Lessons were learned quickly when around CO Lake.

Except for Darren, who never learned his lesson. That lesson being, always listen to his CO. Especially when the man was telling him they were going to lose the ship.

"I don't need to," Darren said, "I got the gist of it from the banker. Motherfucker was there to stall me, wasn't he?"

"If you mean to distract you from the auction that just ended so you didn't turn the bidders into a pile of split fuck? Yeah, that was his job. And he did a splendid job since you didn't even answer your fucking phone."

"Is it gone?" Darren asked.

"What? The Hooyah? Yep. Crew's here though. I'd put you on speaker so you can cheer them up, but they're busy cursing your name."

"What about all of the equipment?" Darren asked. "Our files?"

"Files are at my feet and on flash drives," Lake said. "Don't worry about the research."

"But...?"

"The equipment was purchased with the bank's money, Captain. It was part of the package."

"Fuck," Darren said as he rubbed his forehead. He glanced ahead out the windshield and sighed. "I'm pulling into the Port now. See ya in a second."

He hung up and jammed his phone into his jeans pocket, and then fished out his wallet. Twenty rand was all he had.

"Pull up there," Darren told the cab driver. "Wait for a second and I'll get some cash."

"Oh, no ya don't," the cab driver said as he pulled to a stop, "pay me now, bra."

"Listen, my Chief Officer has cash. I'm tapped right now. Didn't get my change from the bartender because of that fight. Cut me some slack, bra. I won't stiff ya."

"Pay. Now," the cab driver said.

The automatic lock clicked down and Darren stared at it for a second. Then moved. Using his elbow, he busted out the window and pulled himself out of the cab before the driver could protest. The cab driver shoved his door open and jumped out, a long baton in his hand. He leveled it at Darren's chest.

"Now you pay for that too!" the cab driver shouted, the baton almost touching Darren's chest. "Who the fok you think you are, bra?"

"Just put that away," Darren said, his hands up. "I'm gonna get your money. Chill, bra. All I have to do is---"

The baton stabbed Darren in the chest.

"Ya call who ya need to call, bra," the cab driver said, "but ya don't go nowhere until ya pay me."

"Fuck," Darren said, "the hard way. Second time tonight."

"What's that?"

"I said it's gonna have to be the hard way. Sorry."

"No need for that, Mr. Chambers," a man said as he placed a hand on Darren's shoulder. "I'll cover it."

Darren looked over his shoulder at a man about his height of six-two. The man was a couple decades older than Darren, fit and tan; well weathered by the sea, but not aged yet. Dressed in khakis and a polo shirt, the man looked like a golf pro. He gave Darren a smile and took his hand away. Not quickly out of alarm for the look on Darren's face, but out of respect for his personal space.

The man looked at the window and grimaced as he pulled out his wallet. "What'll that cost you?"

The cab driver shrugged. "More than you have in that wallet."

"Assumptions make an ass out of you and me," the man said as he fished out a few thousand rand. He had an American accent and Darren tried to place it, but couldn't. "Here ya go, pal. This should do."

The cab driver carefully took the sheaf of bills and counted them out, his eyes going from the money to Darren to the American and back to the money.

"Will that do?" the American asked.

"Yeah, it'll do," the cab driver said as he stuffed the cash in his pocket and got back in his taxi. He pointed the baton at Darren. "You got lucky, bra. I know how to use this."

Darren and the American watched as the cab pulled away, and then turned to each other.

"I believe he was the lucky one," the American chuckled. "Am I right?"

"Who the fuck are you?" Darren asked.

"Mr. Ballantine," the American said, holding out his hand, "good to meet you."

Darren shook the hand that was offered. "Got a first name?"

"No," Mr. Ballantine said.

"That's bullshit," Darren said. "But whatever. Thanks. I'll get the money to pay you back. You take PayPal? Just give me your email and I'll send it right over."

"We both know that's not true, don't we?" Mr. Ballantine said. "Those rand in your wallet are all you have to your name.

And while Chief Officer Lake may have some cash tucked away in his duffel, he doesn't have as much as I just gave that cab driver."

"How the fuck do you know my CO's name?" Darren asked, his body tensing, ready.

"Relax, operator," Mr. Ballantine asked, "or do you go by Captain?"

"Captain," Darren replied, "I'm not an operator any longer." He looked down the dock and in the direction of the Hooyah. "May not be a Captain any longer either."

"Oh, don't sell yourself short," Mr. Ballantine said. "Captain Chambers it is, and I have a feeling it'll stay that way."

"What the fuck, man? You seem to know a lot about me," Darren said. He could feel a pain start to build behind his right eye and knew a migraine was coming. Fuck. He hadn't had one in months and from the feel of it, it would be a nasty little bitch. "I can't pay you. We've established that. And personally, I'd like you to go the fuck away. You creep me out. Thanks for paying for the cab. Have a good one."

Darren started to walk away, but the American grabbed his arm. Darren's first instinct was to take the fucker down; slam him to the ground and wrench that arm of his out of the socket. But something in the grip made Darren think twice. Both thoughts took all of .02 seconds.

"I think you and your crew need me, Captain Chambers," Mr. Ballantine said.

"Let go of my arm, sir," Darren warned. The American did immediately, but offered no apology. "You don't know what I need. You looked up some shit on Google and now you're trying to do whatever it is you're doing. Whatever you're selling, I'm not buying. Like I said, you creep me out. You have con man written all over you. You even smell plastic, like a fucking Ken doll just out of the packaging. Again, thanks for paying for the cab. See ya later."

"Captain Chambers," Mr. Ballantine said, "you need to listen to me. I have an offer you will want to hear."

"You really want to push me? Is that how you want your night to go?" Darren asked. "Who the fuck are you?"

"Mr. Ballantine," Mr. Ballantine replied, "I already said that."

"Listen, pal, I'm thankful for you bailing me out there, but you can fuck off with the mystery," Darren said. "Tell me who you are or you're getting put down."

"Walk with me," Mr. Ballantine said, gesturing towards the dock that led to what used to be Darren's ship. "I'll explain as we go to meet your crew."

"You aren't meeting shit, asshole!" Darren yelled. The migraine was coming on strong and he could start to see small spots floating in his vision. The lights that ringed the parking lot were like daggers. "FUCK OFF!"

Mr. Ballantine stared at Darren for a second then nodded. "Yes, of course. My mistake. All of my research told me you were the man for the job. Obviously, I did some assuming of my own. I am sorry to have wasted your time."

He held out his hand, but Darren didn't take it. He didn't even look at it, instead keeping his focus on Mr. Ballantine's eyes. There was something in them that Darren knew and recognized. He saw the same look in his eyes every morning when he looked in the mirror. There were a select few in the world that had that look.

"Good evening," Mr. Ballantine said, dropping his hand and giving Darren a farewell nod. "I'd say this is goodbye, but I have a feeling we'll be seeing each other again soon."

"Fuck off," Darren said and started to turn, but headlights lit the two men up as Mr. Ballantine turned away.

The creep level escalated quickly and Darren changed his stance slightly, giving him more stability and also access to the Walther he had strapped to his ankle. The car, a black Mercedes with tinted windows, pulled in front of Mr. Ballantine and the driver got out and came around to open the backdoor for the man. Darren was surprised the driver was a woman -barely five feet tall and looked like she weighed maybe a hundred pounds wet, but didn't make any assumptions about her. The way she held herself told him she was trained. And she wore dark sunglasses at night. That was always a red flag.

Mr. Ballantine gave Darren a brief smile and got in the car. The driver didn't even glance at Darren, just closed the door and resumed her place behind the wheel. Darren watched the car drive off and didn't move until he had counted to thirty and was sure the vehicle was gone.

"Fucking crazy night," Darren said as he took a couple steps backwards before turning and heading down the dock.

By the time he got to the Hooyah, his head was screaming and pounding. Half the vision in his right eye was gone. All he wanted was a dark room, some Percocet, and for the world to fuck off. But the looks on his crew's faces told him he was going to be the one doing the fucking off.

"They just tugged it away," Lake said as he walked up to Darren.

Tall, tan, with close-cropped black hair and deep-set brown eyes, Lake would have been considered dashing, but the scar that ran from his hairline, through the brow of his left eye, across the bridge of his nose, and across his right cheek, made him look like the henchman to an evil overlord bent on world domination. Which Lake was cool with. Kept the crew in line.

"Shit, Marty," Darren said, "I fucked this up royal. I honestly thought the bank would extend the loan. I mean, I showed the guy the video. Shit! Now I don't even have my fucking tablet!"

"Bank took that too?" Lake asked.

"I left it at the bar," Darren said, "classic."

"Care to say a few words to the crew?" Lake asked. "Some words of wisdom? A last farewell? Maybe some ideas on what they should search on Monster.com? I'm thinking 'goose chase expert' might be appropriate."

"Kiss my ass, Marty," Darren said, stepping past his CO to the rest of the crew.

The Hooyah wasn't a large ship by any stretch of the imagination and only took eight men, including Darren, to fill out the crew. Lake stood behind Darren which left six men, their duffels stuffed with their possession and set on the dock at their feet, staring at their former captain. Darren looked them over, gauging their moods and possible anger levels. But all looked more sad than angry, which almost made it worse. Darren could handle the anger, but the looks of defeat killed him.

"I owe each of you an apology," Darren said. "You signed on with me on faith. Faith that I knew what I was doing and that our research would lead to something. Half of you think I'm full of shit, half of you think I'm crazy."

"All of us think that, Captain," Second Officer Daryl Jennings said. Average height and build, with a receding hairline of thinning red hair, Jennings was an unassuming figure. Darren knew better, having found him in an Australian jail (even though the man was as American as the rest of the crew) after nearly taking on an entire dockside bar himself. "Only half of us know it."

Darren smiled and most of the crew smiled with him. "Thanks, Jennings. That makes this easier."

"It ain't easy for me," Boatswain Trevor "Popeye" De Bruhl said. "I don't know shit about working on land. And ain't no boats hiring. I checked."

De Bruhl got his nickname for a very good reason, he looked just like the cartoon character. Short, thin, bald, with massive forearms that were covered in tattoos, De Bruhl even had a one-eyed squint like the real Popeye. He drew the line at the corn cob pipe, though. He hated smoking and had zero problems with snatching a cigarette straight from a man's mouth if it bothered him. Popeye was American born and raised, having lived there for most of his forty-two years on the planet, but both parents were South African nationals, giving him dual citizenship and privileges that came in handy for the Hooyah. Or did.

"I'm going to need a ride back to Mobile," Chief Engineer Karl "Bach" Breytenbach said. "No way I'm walking all the way to Alabama."

Probably the most versatile of Darren's crew, Bach had a way with machinery and anything having to do with boats. His father's family owned a marina close to one of the casinos that filled Mobile Bay in the Gulf Coast. From a young age, Bach had spent all of his free time playing with engines and nautical systems. He could strip, clean, and reassemble an Envinrude E30MRL in almost the same time that it took Darren to strip, clean, and reassemble his Colt M4 carbine.

Even with only one hand.

The hand Bach did have was scratching at the grey stubble on his scalp. Six feet and two hundred pounds, Bach wasn't small, but he had a way of seeming smaller because of the missing appendage. Most people saw him, but looked past, dismissing him because of his "handicap." Their mistake. Bach had spent most of his fifty years hardening the stump at the end of his left arm so that it could pack quite a wallop.

"I'll get everything straight," Darren said, "for all of you."

First Assistant Engineer Morgan "Cougher" Colfer, always at Bach's right hand, nodded, his long, stringy black hair flopping in his face. The Batman t-shirt he always wore was stained with grease and what Darren hoped was ketchup. Darren nodded to him and Cougher nodded back, then buried his face in the crook of his elbow and let loose a goose honk of a cough.

Standing behind Cougher was Chief Steward Beau McWhitt. He just stared out at the night shrouded water of the port, his thumbs hooked into the armpits of his tank top, his biceps seeming to flex and quiver on their own. Darren made a note to ask the kid if he was back on the 'roids. He turned his head and looked at Darren finally, the breeze catching his white-blond hair and blowing it into his baby face. At five feet six, he had the features of a teenage boy, just without the acne, perpetually looking like he was just about to hit his growth spurt. But being twenty-three years old that was a dream left in the past.

"Where's Gunnar?" Darren asked. "Did he already take off?"

Lake turned and nodded down the dock to a figure seated at the far edge, barely seen in the gloom of the night.

"Shit," Darren said, "how bad is he taking it?"

"They took everything, Captain," Jennings said. "Most of the equipment he'd built himself. The guy's fucking all tore up."

Everyone muttered their agreement.

"Shit," Darren said again, "I'll go talk to him."

"He's got his knife," Cougher said, "been flipping it about since the tug showed up."

"Noted," Darren said, "thanks."

They had been friends since well before Darren had enlisted in the Navy and trained to be a SEAL. It was hard for Darren to draw up a memory that didn't have Gunnar firmly planted in it. Childhood friends, they had grown up together in the same neighborhood, their backyards butting against each other. They had competed in everything throughout school, sports, games, cars, everything. They would have competed in the Navy also, both having a love of the sea, but Gunnar chose medical school instead of life as a sailor. He ended up top of his class at Johns Hopkins, and then decided after his residency that he didn't want to be a surgeon and pursued a doctorate in marine biology. Everyone was shocked, but Darren understood.

They had always stayed in touch, talking almost weekly. So when Darren came to Gunnar with his wild story of seeing a creature that couldn't exist, the friends took up where they left off. It was as if the ocean became their new neighborhood and they started to compete in a new way. Instead of sports and cars, they competed with who had the most faith in their mission; who had the most drive to see it through.

Darren was heart stricken to have to tell Gunnar that they both just lost.

"You want to kill me?" Darren asked, sitting next to Gunnar at the edge of the dock. He glanced at the Buck knife Gunnar twirled between the fingers of his right hand like a drummer showing off with his stick.

"Nah," Gunnar said, "too much work. I'm exhausted."

"Me too," Darren said. "Sucking ass is hard work."

"But you're so good at it," Gunnar said, finally turning to look at his old friend. "One might say you even excel at sucking."

"Harsh."

"Wrong?"

"No," Darren said, shaking his head, "I do excel at the suckage."

They looked out at the water, both struggled to bring to words what they felt.

"I'll make it up to you," Darren said, "I promise."

"Don't," Gunnar said.

"What? Make it up to you?"

"Promise," Gunnar said. "It's one you know you can't keep."

"Jesus, man," Darren said, "why you gotta hate?"

"I could stab," Gunnar said as he flipped the knife from his fingers and into his palm, the blade reversed so his thumb rested on the end of the handle. While he didn't do it in a threatening way, the action implied the blade should have been placed to Darren's throat.

Blade games. Another of their competitions.

But Gunnar kept the blade close to his mid-section, and then lowered his hand into his lap, any aggression he had felt floated away on the sea breeze.

"What really sucks is they didn't let me grab my binders," Gunnar said. "I have my drives, so that's good. But all my binders with my sketches are still on the Hooyah."

"I'll get those back," Darren said. "That's a promise I can keep."

Gunnar let out a short bark of a laugh. "Well, then everything is going to be just fine," he said. "Thanks, man."

Darren clapped him on the shoulder and then stood up. "Okay, no more moping. Let's go get shit faced."

"Who's buying?" Lake asked from a few feet away. The rest of the crew was right behind him. "Wasn't trying to eavesdrop, just wanted to make sure you two didn't kill each other."

"Good call," Gunnar said as he took Darren's offered hand and stood up. "Looks like I'm buying. Yay to a trust fund."

"Is that trust fund hiring?" Popeye asked.

"Doesn't work that way, Pop," Gunnar said, "I've explained that to you a million times."

"Then what's the point of the damn thing?" Popeye asked. "It just gives you money? You don't work for it? More like lazy fund."

Half the crew snorted; Gunnar didn't mind, he was used to it.

"Wouldn't happen to have enough to buy a new boat, would you?" Bach asked.

"Doesn't work that way either," Gunnar said, "smart ass."

"So...drinks?" Darren asked. "Who has the van keys?"

The crew all looked at each other, and then looked at Lake.

"Shit," Lake said, looking out into the dark water, "they're on the Hooyah."

"Nice," Darren says, "who knows how to hotwire?"

Everyone raised their hands, including Darren.

"That's why I love you guys," Darren said, then took off running, the migraine easing up finally. "Last one to the van is designated driver!"

The race was a great way to let off steam; all the crew loved a good competition. But it backfired as soon as they hit the parking lot.

"Where's the van?" Beau asked. "Who moved it? I parked it here this morning after picking up groceries."

They all looked at the almost empty parking lot, and then turned to Darren.

"Shit," he said, "I thought the van was paid off."

"Son of a bitch," Bach said, pointing his stump at Darren. "What the hell, Captain?"

A horn honked twice, and then headlights blinked on across the parking lot. The crew watched as a brand new Ford passenger van with tinted windows pulled up in front of them. Ballantine's driver got out, walked around to the side, and opened the double doors, gesturing for them to get in. The passenger's window rolled down and Mr. Ballantine was smiling at them.

"Hello, gentlemen," Mr. Ballantine said, "I figured you'd need a lift so I went and got my van. Care to hop in?"

"Man, you don't take fuck off for an answer, do you?" Darren said, the crew all looking from him to Ballantine and back.

"I said I'd be seeing you soon," Mr. Ballantine said, "and a good thing since you seem to be missing your ride."

Darren just glared, so Ballantine shifted his focus to the crew.

"Who's up for a drink or two?" The men just stood there. "I'm buying. And when I say a drink or two, I mean as much as you can hold."

"I'm in," Cougher said.

"Yep, me too," Jennings said.

They both hopped into the van, giving Ballantine's driver lecherous grins. She ignored them.

"Anyone else?" Mr. Ballantine asked.

"By as much as I can hold, do you mean before I puke or after I rally and start drinking again?" Popeye asked.

"Drinker's choice," Mr. Ballantine said.

Popeye slapped Darren on the shoulder and got in also. He was quickly followed by the rest of the crew, leaving Darren standing on the curb with Gunnar.

"Something I should know about this guy?" Gunnar asked. "Is he going to ass rape me if I get in there?"

"I don't know him," Darren said. "Never saw him until tonight when he started getting all stalker cryptic with me."

"You going to try to touch my swimsuit area?" Gunnar asked Mr. Ballantine.

"Would you like me to?" Mr. Ballantine asked.

The crew all leaned forward and stared at Gunnar.

"Not tonight," Gunnar said, "but I'll let you buy me a drink. I need one. Or ten."

"Whatever," Darren said as he followed Gunnar into the van.

The driver shut the doors and quickly walked around front. She opened the driver's door and pulled herself into the seat in one fluid motion, and Darren couldn't help notice how well she carried herself.

"Where'd you serve?" Darren asked.

"Darby doesn't speak much until she gets to know you," Mr. Ballantine said, turning in his seat so he could face Darren and the rest. "But she has spent some time with the Institute."

"Israel?" Gunnar asked, leaning forward towards Darby. She slowly turned her head and Gunnar quickly backed off, unable to read her eyes behind the dark sunglasses.

"A little time in Mossad," Mr. Ballantine replied, "until I obtained the privilege of her services."

"Mossad is intelligence," Darren said as Darby turned her head back around, put the van in drive, and pulled away from the curb. "You're trained for more than that."

"Yes," Mr. Ballantine said, turning back around also, "she is."

They were all silent for a minute, wondering what they'd gotten themselves into.

***

"There's a bar just up the---," Cougher started to say, but was cut off.

"road and on the left," Mr. Ballantine said. "Yes, I've watched you all frequent it often when in port."

"We are so getting ass raped," Gunnar said.

Mr. Ballantine laughed heartily, his hands slapping the dashboard.

"Mr. Peterson, please," Mr. Ballantine said. "You are not going to get ass raped. I have business to discuss with all of you. I think you'll be quite happy with what I have to offer."

"No ass rape?" Popeye asked.

"Disappointed?" Jennings asked, elbowing Popeye.

"Cram it, dickhead," Popeye said.

The van slowed and pulled into the small parking lot of a bar that looked more like a rundown shack than a drinking establishment. A neon sign in the window blinked erratically.

"The Plank," Mr. Ballantine said, "Quaint."

Darby stopped the van, got out, and opened the side doors.

"Wait here, please, Darby," Mr. Ballantine said, "but keep in touch."

Darby nodded and went back to the driver's side once the van was unloaded of its confused and wary passengers.

"Drink what we want and it's all on you?" Bach asked. "No tricks?"

"What tricks could I pull?" Mr. Ballantine asked. "Drinks on me, gentlemen! Have fun!"

The crew whooped and whistled as they barreled through the door. Lake hung back, but Darren nodded to him and he followed after the rest, leaving Darren, Gunnar, and Mr. Ballantine standing in the parking lot as Darby drove off to park and wait with the van.

"Before we go in I want your story," Darren said. "No more cloak and dagger cocking bullshit. Play me straight or you don't walk away from this parking lot."

"Always straight to the threats, eh Mr. Chambers?" Mr. Ballantine asked. "Not that I disagree. I believe the direct route is always the best. Why waste time?"

"You're wasting mine right now," Darren said.

"Fine, I'll explain," Mr. Ballantine said.

"You want me to go inside?" Gunnar asked.

"No, no, Mr. Peterson," Mr. Ballantine said, "this concerns you as much as anyone."

Darren and Gunnar stood and waited while Mr. Ballantine looked up at the night sky. Just as their patience was about to give out, he looked back at both of them.

"I work for a company that specializes in solving problems," Mr. Ballantine said. "Until now, those problems were strictly of a technological, intellectual, and logistical nature. It appears we are going to branch out into problems a little more…substantial."

"So?" Darren asked. "What does that have to do with us?"

"Well, Mr. Chambers, you have a skill set and a temperament that fits a specific profile I'm looking for," said Mr. Ballantine. "Your skills as a former SEAL make you just what I need."

"For what?" Darren asked, crossing his arms.

"For rescuing hostages and killing pirates," Mr. Ballantine smiled. "Hooyah."

"Yeah, sounds like hooyah," Darren said.

Mr. Ballantine frowned. "I'm sorry, but I thought hooyah meant hell yeah or fuck yeah. Am I mistaken?"

"It also means fucked up, fuck you, and oh shit," Darren said. "I think they all apply."

Mr. Ballantine's smile faltered. He glanced over his shoulder in the direction of the van then looked back at Darren. "Well, that's why I need you. You can set me straight when I get it wrong."

"Listen, I appreciate the trouble you're going through to impress my crew," Darren said, "they deserve a little relaxation after the bullshit I put them through, but they aren't SEALs. Even if I was crazy enough to hear the rest of your spiel, I don't have a Team to do what you need. Not that I want to. I'm out of the guns and ammo game."

"Except for the Walther on your ankle," Mr. Ballantine said.

"Personal protection," Darren said, "and good eyes."

"This isn't just about pirates and hostages," Mr. Ballantine said, "this is also about your research." He looked at Gunnar. "And yours. This is a scratch my back and I scratch yours deal. You sign on and you get all of your equipment back plus almost unlimited funds to continue your search for *Livyatan Melville*. Care to hear more?"

Gunnar and Darren stood there, stunned. Mr. Ballantine's smile returned, wider than before.

"How about we join your crew?" Mr. Ballantine said. "Sit down, have a few drinks, get to know each other on a personal level and then you can decide if you are interested. I don't expect an answer tonight, at least not right now. We have another stop after this."

Darren shook his head, looked at Gunnar, looked back at Mr. Ballantine, and then burst out laughing.

"This is totally fubar," Darren said, "but what the fuck, right? Hooyah."

"Hooyah," Mr. Ballantine smiled gesturing to the door. "After you."

The Plank was fittingly, for a bunch of sailors, a dive. A long bar ran the length of one side and a long counter with stools ran the length of the other side. The crew was seated along the counter, joining the already shitfaced, and apparently passed out, two other patrons. A bored bartender with a large, bulbous alcoholic's nose slammed down a row of glasses and proceeded to fill them with the house brown. The crew cheered while he did it, which briefly roused one of the patrons.

"Shut your poes," the man slurred then lowered his head back to the counter.

"Did he just tell us to shut our pussies?" Cougher asked.

"Just you, Cougher," Jennings said, "since your pussy is always gaping open."

"It needs to air out or it gets stanky," Cougher said.

"We appreciate that," Popeye said, "now grab my fucking drink for me."

"Why do I have to grab it?" Cougher asked. "Get it yourself, bitch."

"How about we take a seat down there?" Mr. Ballantine asked, pointing towards three stools open at the very end of the counter towards a corner with an obviously busted jukebox shoved into it. He grabbed a glass of brown and the bottle from the bartender's hand and just kept walking.

"Oy!" the bartender shouted.

"He's paying," Darren said, picking up two glasses and handing one to Gunnar. "We'll need another bottle."

Gunnar smiled at the bartender as he followed Darren to the stools and a waiting Mr. Ballantine.

"What do you know of *Livyatan Melville*?" Gunnar asked as soon as he sat down. He knocked back the entire glass of brown and tried not to choke. "Fucking hell! That shit is nasty."

"But it does the trick," Mr. Ballantine said, knocking his own back and refilling both his and Gunnar's. "And to answer your question, Mr. Peterson, I know a great deal about that improbable whale. I even know what its skin feels like." He lifted a hand and waved it slowly in the air. "From lip to tail."

"You've seen it?" Darren asked, leaning forward. He hadn't touched his drink yet. "In person?"

"I have," Mr. Ballantine said, draining his glass again. Gunnar joined him. Darren left his on the counter. "I had to throw away my wetsuit after that encounter. Can't get the shit smell out of neoprene. I tried. Too bad since my father had given me that wetsuit for my fifteenth birthday."

"You were just a kid when you saw it?" Darren asked. "That was what? Thirty years ago?"

"Close enough. Sent me on my current career path," Mr. Ballantine smiled. His glass emptied, Gunnar's glass emptied, they were refilled. "Not a drinking man tonight, Mr. Chambers?"

"Not yet," Darren said, "someone has to make sure Gunnar doesn't get ass raped."

"Thanks," Gunnar said, "I appreciate that."

"I am beginning to think this is an inside joke between you two," said Mr. Ballantine. "A reference to your younger days as neighbors?"

"Goes to our grave," Darren said. "Tell me what you saw."

"I will," Mr. Ballantine said. Glass emptied. Refilled.

Mr. Ballantine proceeded to describe almost exactly what Darren had seen those years before. Darren studied the man, looking for the tells, for the signs he was full of shit. Part of being a SEAL, a major part, was observation. There was no such thing as an insignificant detail to a SEAL. He watched Ballantine's eyes, the corners of his mouth, the pulse in his neck. He listened for hesitation, for stutters, for the hollow sound of a story repeated by rote.

Nothing.

Either Ballantine was the best of liars, or he was telling the truth.

"So you've seen it," Darren said.

"Hooyah," Gunnar said, raising his glass.

"Hush, you," Darren said. "You have my interest, Mr. Ballantine. In regards to the whale, but the other part? The problem solving? Not my business anymore. Not my crew's business. We're a research team, not a combat Team. And no way I'm going by myself." Darren lifted his glass, drank it down, and then leaned back in the stool, resting his back against the counter. "Even if I agreed to help, you aren't going to get what you need. And that's a full Team. Combat ready and trained."

"Then you put together a Team," Mr. Ballantine said. Empty glass, full glass.

Darren barked laughter and some of the crew glanced his way. It was his laugh he gave when someone said something stupid. When combined with a bar it usually meant a brawl was close behind. Darren saw them and gave a thumbs up so they'd go back to getting shit faced and not worry.

"Put together a Team? How the hell will I do that?" Darren said. "I'm not exactly welcome in the community. I'd be lucky to get anyone to answer their phones, let alone agree to work with me. I'm the Moby Dick nutjob, get it?"

"Yet, there is one number you could call and it would be answered on the first ring," Mr. Ballantine said. Empty, full. Empty, full.

"Slow down," Darren said, taking the bottle from Ballantine and filling his own glass. "You don't have to prove anything, Mr. Ballantine. You won't impress me by puking your guts out. Or bleeding from your ass."

"This shit'll do that," Gunnar said, his words slurred, "been there, shat that."

"He has," Darren said. "What's this magic number you're talking about? It's news to me."

"Commander Vincent Thorne," Mr. Ballantine said, a wicked smile on his face. He killed another glass and then slammed it onto the counter. "He'll answer."

"Shit, man," Gunnar said as he tried to take the bottle from Darren. Darren blocked him from taking the bottle, but poured him another. "He wants you to call your father-in-law."

"Ex," Darren said, "Ex-father-in-law." Darren set the bottle aside. "And no way I'm calling him. We don't talk much."

"Bullshit," Gunnar said, "you talk to him all the time. Always checking up on Kinsey."

"Asshole," Darren said, "now you're cut off."

"You can't cut me off," Gunnar said, "I'm just getting started."

Darren kicked the stool out from under Gunnar and he hit the dirt coated floor in a heap. He tried to get up and then collapsed, his eyes closed, his head resting on his arms.

"He's always been a lightweight," Darren said. "Reason number sixty-eight why he would have sucked as a SEAL."

"Let's get to business then," Mr. Ballantine said. His eyes were clear and steady despite the amount of alcohol he'd already put away. "You make that call, get Commander Thorne to help put a Team together and I give you all the funding you need to hunt your whale. Once the pirate compound has been successfully raided. That has to be key. If that mission cannot be accomplished, then our time together is done, and I won't be able to help you."

The bartender started to yell as Beau got up on the counter and dropped his drawers. He started to piss wildly, spraying the rest of the crew.

"Jesus," Darren said as he looked at his watch, "thirty minutes? Really?"

"Nice watch. Rolex?" Mr. Ballantine asked. "I thought the SEALs stopped that tradition."

"It was a gift," Darren said, "from Vinny, in fact." The bartender was still shouting, as were the rest of the crew. "I better get them out of here."

"I'll have Darby bring the van to the front," Mr. Ballantine said.

Darren waited for Mr. Ballantine to finish calling Darby before he spoke again. "You're missing one key element to all of this."

"Oh, and what's that?" Mr. Ballantine asked, a smile on his face that said he hadn't missed anything.

"I don't have a boat anymore," Darren said as he walked away.

"Not a problem," Mr. Ballantine said as he helped Darren lift Gunnar off the floor.

"How do you figure that?" Darren asked as they walked Gunnar to the front door. The rest of the crew got the hint and fell in line. There was a considerable amount of bitching.

"I'll show you," Mr. Ballantine said, "if you don't mind taking a little detour before I drop you and your crew off."

"Oy!" the bartender yelled as Cougher and Popeye reached over the bar and snagged a bottle of brown in each hand.

"That'll go on the tab," Mr. Ballantine said. "I'll settle up here if you can handle Mr. Peterson."

"Been doing it most of my life," Darren said.

He walked out and found the van ready and waiting. Darby stepped up and helped get Gunnar into the van, which wasn't easy as the rest of the drunken crew kept stumbling and bumbling their way into their seats.

"Thanks," Darren said. Darby just nodded.

Mr. Ballantine came out of the bar, wallet in hand, and got into the bar. He opened the glove box and tossed the wallet inside. Darren couldn't help noticing the Sig Sauer P226 that the wallet landed on.

"Nice piece," Darren said, "but I prefer the P220. Better stopping power with the .45 rounds."

"If every shot hits the eye, then it doesn't matter," Mr. Ballantine said, "but I tend to agree. It was a gift from a friend." Ballantine shut the glove box and nodded at Darby. "Klipshen Marina, Darby."

She nodded back and drove away from The Plank.

***

The van slowed next to a long concrete block wall and turned into the driveway as an iron security gate automatically opened. Darby steered around a small building then stopped about twenty yards from a private pier.

Darren had a ton of questions and they all caught in his throat. Except for, "What the fuck?"

"Yes, I expected that response," Mr. Ballantine smiled. He wasn't smiling for long as Darren's fist found his cheek, knocking his head back against the side window.

"Mother fucker!" Darren yelled as he lunged over the seat and started to throttle Ballantine.

The man didn't have to time to defend himself before Darren was yanked off him by Darby, her arms braced around Darren's neck.

"I had a feeling that might be a response also," Mr. Ballantine said, rubbing at his bruised throat.

Darren's eyes bulged and he sputtered and spat as Darby slowly choked him out.

"That's enough, Darby," Mr. Ballantine, "I think Mr. Chambers will behave."

Darby gave her boss a questioning look, then complied. Darren lunged at Ballantine again, but Ballantine had managed to get his hand behind him and opened the van door, sending them both tumbling to the pavement.

The crew had frozen when Darren went ballistic, shocked by what was happening. But they quickly regrouped as their captain fell out of the van. The doors were opened and they jumped out, ready to lend a hand. But Darby had other ideas, as she sent first Popeye then Lake and Cougher to the ground. Beau and Bach came at her from opposite sides, but were soon a part of the pile, their lips split and noses pouring blood. Jennings watched her for a moment then smiled, his hands up.

"You win," he said, "I know a losing fight when I see it."

Darby just waited.

"Of course, you never know until you try," Jennings said as he came in fast, a right hook aimed for Darby's head.

The woman ducked and rolled, coming up to the side and behind Jennings. Her fists landed six shots to his kidney before he had a chance even to turn. He went down on a knee and had to put a hand to the pavement to keep from collapsing. He lifted the other hand to ward her off.

"Cool, cool," Jennings coughed, "tried and failed. I got it. Don't fuck with you."

Darby watched him, and then held out a hand. "Exactly."

Jennings took it and gasped as he was pulled to his feet. She nodded at him and then went over and separated her boss from Darren. Despite his training, Darren had taken a few shots from Ballantine and was almost as bloody as the other man.

"You bought the Hooyah!" Darren screamed at Ballantine, pointing at the pier where his former ship was docked. "You fucking asshole!"

Beyond the Hooyah was a much larger ship with the name "RV Beowulf II" on the stern.

"That's my equipment," Gunnar said as he staggered from the van and saw men wheeling boxes and crates to the new ship. "They have my equipment!"

"And we are moving it to your new ship, Mr. Peterson," Mr. Ballantine said, wiping blood from his mouth. "If your captain agrees to my proposal."

"Why would you buy my ship?" Darren snarled. "Why do that?"

"Yeah," Cougher said, "kinda douchey."

"It tied up some loose ends," Mr. Ballantine said. "The transaction cannot be traced back to me or the company I represent. As far as anyone knows, you are out of the research business. Set adrift as so many are when funding has fizzled out. Just another failure in oceanic research."

"But why?" Darren asked. "Why not let us keep the Hooyah?"

"Because, Mr. Chambers," Mr. Ballantine smiled, "you're going to need a bigger boat."

CHAPTER THREE: A TEAM IS BORN

The screen of the phone dimmed, and then went black as former SEAL Commander, Vincent Thorne, sat at his kitchen table, his eyes staring at the rectangle of plastic and glass.

"Not how I thought I'd start the morning," Thorne said as he got up to make some coffee.

Dressed only in a pair of boxers, he scratched at his cotton covered ass while he waited for the water to boil. A man of many tastes, Thorne only drank his coffee from a French press and only black. He'd had enough weak ass, watery crap in the Navy. He didn't plan on spending retirement drinking shit in a mug.

Not that his retirement was on solid ground after the phone call he took. He rubbed the salt and pepper stubble that covered his round head, thinking over the last few minutes of the early morning. The clock on the stove said it was five-thirty, which meant it was twelve-thirty in Cape Town. What, his former son-in-law couldn't have waited another couple of hours?

It didn't matter too much to Thorne, he was used to getting up at the crack of ass, coming instantly awake as soon as his eyes opened. It was from years of service as a SEAL, and even more years as Commander of the BUD/S training program. He rather enjoyed being up before the sun, just so he could sneer at the orange orb as it crested the horizon and say, "I win."

The water kettle began to whistle and he pulled it from the element, pouring the steaming water over the grounds in his press.

He affixed the lid and plunger and then let it steep as he went into his bedroom to throw on some clothes. It was going to be a long day and he didn't want to bother with a shower. He doubted it would be noticed where he was going.

His small apartment was located on the outskirts of Coronado, California, only a couple miles from the Naval Special Warfare Center, and as he looked about at the dusty rented furniture and few personal affects, he shook his head, wondering how he'd gotten there. Not that he was losing his mind and didn't know how he physically got there- a moving company had hauled his stuff from the Naval Center to the apartment complex; he'd followed in his Jeep Wrangler. No, he wondered how he had gone from Commander of one of the most elite military programs in the world, to retired jackass that made coffee while he stood in his boxers. It had only been a year since he'd left the Navy, yet it still didn't feel right, like a shirt that had shrunk in the dryer.

He hadn't wanted to leave the Navy, but he'd been forced to. Not forced out, just left no honorable choice but to resign his post. He was due for retirement anyway, so it had been in the back of his mind for a long time. Yet, the circumstances weren't exactly how he had wanted to go. He thought about that as he picked up a photograph of his family the last time they had all been together.

His son, Vincent Junior, stood in the middle, looking handsome in his Marine dress uniform. He had died three months after the picture was taken, a casualty of the battle in Sadr City. Thorne's daughter, Kinsey, stood with her arm locked in her brother's, dressed in her own Marine uniform. What big brother did, Kinsey always followed. Their mother was at Vincent Junior's side, not knowing that a drunk driver would take her life three weeks after they received the news of young Vincent's death.

That left Kinsey and Vincent Senior as the last of the Thornes. He sighed as he set the picture down, not wanting to think too much about the task ahead. He would hit Northern California, and then double back to San Diego. That would be the hard part. It was why he was going to NorCal first, so he could get reinforcements. He'd taken the job on one condition- his daughter would be a part of it all. She needed it. That was a fact that Thorne knew in every fiber of his body. She hadn't deserved the way she had been treated; neither did he for that matter.

When her brother had been killed in combat, the normally kind and easygoing, yet driven, Kinsey Thorne, lost something. The kindness was no longer there, but the drive was. She wanted in the thick of combat, she wanted to kill, kill, kill. It would be years before she would even get a shot at the opportunity. Not that the Marines were letting women fight on the front lines; no, that was a long way off. It was that the SEAL BUD/S had decided to open the training to women. The Navy was going to be the trailblazers in the gender equalization of the United States military.

And Commander Vincent Thorne was going to oversee the switch.

Kinsey had applied and been accepted right away. She was a perfect candidate and joined six other women at the Naval Special Warfare Preparatory School in Great Lakes, Illinois. Once the two-month prep training was done, she was the only female recommended to move on to the full BUD/S program in Coronado. Not surprising to her father, Kinsey was comfortably in the middle of the pack the entire six-months of training. Also not surprising to her father, was that she passed and moved on to SQT (SEAL Qualification Training).

What did surprise him, was that after making it through BUD/S and the notorious Hell Week, she would risk everything with a stupid mistake. She denied it up and down, and he struggled to believe her, even taking the drastic step of retiring when she was dishonorably discharged. But the evidence was there-amphetamines in her last blood work. She had two weeks left of SQT. Two weeks, and instead of being booted, she would have been the first female in military history to be assigned combat duty. And not as some grunt, but part of the elite SEAL forces.

"Fucking shame," Thorne said to himself as he depressed the plunger on his press, waited for it to settle, and then poured the coffee into his insulated travel mug. He grabbed the duffel bag he'd packed and took a look around the apartment he never considered home. "Fucking shame."

He opened the front door and stepped out into the California morning, ready to hit the road and start the next phase of his life.

***

"Are you fucking high, dude?" Max Reynolds asked as he leaned back against the tall fir tree, a joint in his mouth and a bottle of pale ale in his hand.

"Yeah," the young hippie at his feet said, "totally."

"You dialed in?" Max asked.

"800 yards," the hippie said, "adjusted for elevation."

"And wind?"

"Adjusting for wind is for sucks," the hippie said. "Can I shoot?"

"Here," Max said as he put the joint to the young man's mouth. The hippie inhaled deeply, held it, then let it out, a cloud of smoke drifting above him and the sniper rifle he rested on a sleeping bag in front of him.

"Dude," Max said, shaking his head, "you just gave away your position. What do you do when you exhale?"

"Blow it up my sleeve, let my shirt filter and trap it," the hippie said, bummed he hadn't gotten it right.

"Exactly," Max said. His radio squawked.

"Dude, you sending up smoke signals?" his brother Shane asked over the two-way. "Looks like you're ordering take out from there. Was that a pint of kung pao chicken or a quart?"

"Yeah, yeah, I know," Max said, "he has been duly chastised."

"Good," Shane said, "carry on."

"Dialed in?" Max asked the hippie again.

"Good to go," the hippie said.

"Then break that bitch," Max smiled, putting a set of binoculars to his eyes. He found the watermelon 800 yards away, across the field of cannabis growing in the narrow valley.

The sniper rifle barked and Max smiled as a poof of dust went up about a foot in front of the watermelon.

"Dead on," Max said. "If that was a person, they'd think twice about taking another step."

"Hey, bro?" Shane asked over the radio. "We expecting anyone today?"

"Not that I know of," Max said, "why? What you got?"

"I have movement at your eleven, north end of the valley," Shane said. "I've got a bead on him, but you're closer, so go have a chat."

Max turned his binoculars in the direction his brother had indicated and scanned the area. It took him a while, but he finally found the mystery person. The guy was geared out, for sure. Pro stuff, not weekend warrior or recreational hunting gear. The man's face was covered in a cammi balaclava, so Max couldn't tell age or nationality. He doubted the guy was cartel, but you never knew. Not anymore.

"You have a shot?" Max asked. There was no answer. "Dude, do you have the shot?"

"Huh? What?" the hippie asked, looking up at Max. "Me? I thought you were talking to your brother."

"Dude, you are paying us to train you to protect your fields," Max said. "You now have a target approaching your field. This is go time."

"You want me to shoot at him?" the hippie asked.

"I want to know if you have a shot," Max said. "Get to work and tell me."

Max watched the man progress through the firs, pines, and oaks, towards the field of cannabis. He waited for the hippie to tell him he was ready. And waited. And waited.

"Dude?" Max asked, glancing down at his client. "You're gonna miss your window."

"I have it," the hippie said, "but it's like 1,200 yards. I can't make that shot."

"Not with that fucking attitude," Max said, pissed. He took a hit off the joint and tossed it to the ground.

"Hey, man!" the hippie said. "That's some of the new hybrid! I only have a little left!"

"You won't have anything left if that guy gets to your crop," Max said. "Now tell me you have the shot."

The hippie hesitated then, "Yeah, I have it."

"Good," Max said, "now move."

"What? You don't want me to take it?"

"Fuck no," Max said as he got onto the ground and shoved the hippie over, taking his place behind the sniper rifle.

The rifle was his first: an MK-12, modified with a collapsible stock and switched out receiver from an M-4 so it could go full auto if needed. Not that it was needed out in the wilds of Northern California. Max put his eye to the 32-power Nightforce scope and watched the target for a minute.

"Aren't you going to adjust for distance?" the hippie whispered.

"Already did," Max said, handing over his binoculars, "now shut it and watch."

The hippie quieted down and put the binoculars to his eyes.

"1,200 yards, but he's on a slope, see?" Max said. "The angle will change as he walks down towards the field. Plus, he's moving at a good clip. The guy's in shape."

"So you're leading him?" the hippie asked.

"I am," Max smiled. "Good to know you've been paying attention." Max watched the target. "Because he's moving, and I can't see the ground through the underbrush, I'm gonna give him a kiss."

"A what?"

"A kiss," Max said. "Take some bark off one of those pines by his head. That'll get his attention."

"What if you miss and hit him?" the hippie asked. "Dude, you'll blow his head off."

"Then I won't miss," Max said and slowly squeezed the trigger. Max watched through the scope as pine bark sprayed the man's covered face. "Just a kiss."

The man stopped, looked at the hole in the pine tree, then turned and looked directly at Max's position. Then he flipped him the bird.

"Dude," the hippie said, "the guy is flipping you off."

The guy lifted his other hand and extended that middle finger as well. Then he did a little dance, turned, and yanked his pants down to show Max his bare ass.

"Bro," Shane said over the radio, "see that tattoo? I know that ass."

Max looked at the tattoo on the man's left ass cheek of a gorilla with its middle finger extended. He couldn't help but laugh.

"See if you can find him on the radio," Max replied.

"I already found you two," a voice crackled, "been listening to you for the last hour."

"Hey, Uncle Vinny," Max said.

"Hey, Uncle Vinny," Shane echoed.

"Hello, boys," Thorne replied. "Sorry for the drop in, but something just came across my desk and I thought you'd be interested. Where can we talk?"

"Can we use your cabin?" Max asked the hippie.

"Yeah, sure," the hippie replied, "but what about the lesson?"

"I think you've got the hang of it for today," Max said. "You stay here and come in when it gets dark."

"Oh…sure," the hippie frowned, "by myself?"

"Yes, by yourself," Max scoffed. "What? You need a babysitter?" He stood up and brushed himself off then looked down at his rifle. "Take care of her. You scratch it and they'll never find your body."

The hippie laughed then stopped abruptly when he saw Max's face.

"Right, dude, not a scratch," the hippie said, "not even a smudge."

"Good," Max smiled and picked up his pack. He put the radio to his mouth. "There's a cabin one click over that hill at your two, Vinny. We'll meet you there."

Max handed the radio to the hippie.

"Should I call if I get in trouble?" the hippie asked.

"What trouble are you going to get into?" Max laughed. "No, you call when you're coming in. That way we don't shoot you."

The hippie stared at Max for a minute. "Man, you are too intense. Fucking take some bong hits when you get to the cabin. Chill."

"Wish I could, dude," Max said, "I really wish I could."

Max nodded at the hippie then took off. He was halfway to the cabin when his brother, Shane, appeared at his side. The Reynolds brothers were nine months apart and almost looked identical, both six feet tall, 175 pounds, with yellow-blond hair, green eyes, and freckles across the nose. But there was one easy way to tell the difference between them- Max was missing his left ear and had scar tissue running from his scalp, down his neck, and onto his shoulder. The brothers had fun in the SEALs using their similarity to their own advantage. At least until an IED (improvised explosive device) in Afghanistan changed Max's looks forever.

Shane was allowed to accompany his brother home to recuperate, and when their time was up, they opted out of another enlistment. Max had lost much of his hearing on his left side and had become increasingly jumpy due to stress, insomnia, and the occasional flashback. He preferred not to drive anymore because he saw IEDs everywhere, even in small town Northern California. He once slammed to a halt in an intersection and jumped out of his pickup truck, with his 1911 drawn, and nearly took the head off a co-ed that had dropped her backpack on the curb across the street. Later, he told his brother all he saw was a Taliban fighter, not a hot girl in cut-offs and a tank top.

Shane did the driving from then on out.

But, being Navy SEALs, they couldn't just sit on their asses at desk jobs. While in Afghanistan, they became close with some of the natives, including an older man that cultivated cannabis for a living. Being California boys, born and raised, the Reynolds knew quite a bit about weed. They learned a ton more in Afghanistan. Especially about the business side of it all.

They learned how cut throat the business was quickly, and spent some time showing the farmer how to protect his crops with some simple countermeasures. They spent some time training the man and his sons on how to create a sniper hide so they could watch their crop and spot poachers. The crop had already been raided by poachers twice that year and they were losing their livelihood.

Once stateside again, the Reynolds realized they could take those same lessons and apply them to the medical marijuana growers in Northern California. It may have been legal, but it was still a dangerous profession. The growers not only had to deal with poachers that wanted to rip them off, but the cartels were sending men up to torch fields and root out the competition. Then there were the local corrupt cops that came by to snag some free weed and hassle the growers.

A well placed round between the boots made everyone, from poachers to cartel muscle, think twice about approaching the field.

Word spread and the Reynolds were the new, cool thing in the cannabis culture. Their experience in Afghanistan had paid off, in money and weed, something they acquired a taste for in Afghanistan. Both being snipers, they always looked for a new edge, and weed was it. Contrary to popular belief, weed didn't impair mental or physical reactions. In fact, in the hands of the right person, it boosted both.

The Reynolds began setting records for distance and accuracy while in the field in Afghanistan. They, of course, kept their secret "technique" between themselves. The head shed would not have been happy to find out that two SEAL snipers were as high as the mountains that ringed the Afghanistan border. That wouldn't have gone over well.

"What shit has hit what fan?" Shane asked. "Not like Vinny to drop by."

"You think Sis is okay?" Max asked. Sis was the nickname of their cousin, Kinsey. Not having a sister of their own, they named her that when they were young; it followed Kinsey up through high school, into the Marines, and even at BUD/S training.

"Probably not," Shane shrugged, "that girl is a fucking mess."

"Mostly her fault," Max said, "if you believe what they say."

"What they say is bullshit," Shane replied. "She wasn't on speed. No way. Not Kinsey."

"You ever know Sis to admit failure?" Max said. "I haven't. I wouldn't have put it past her to look for an edge to get by in BUD/S, and then SQT."

"Still don't believe it," Shane said. "Maybe in BUD/S, but in SQT? She was home free."

"You still think it was a conspiracy? The brass refused to let a girl get through and get assigned to a Team?"

"Makes more sense than her taking pills," Shane said.

"I don't know, bro," Max said. "Then why fall apart like she did if she didn't already have a problem? That girl is a walking pharmacy now."

"Like we should talk," Shane said as he lit up a joint and handed it to his brother.

"Different," Max said after taking a hit, "completely different."

"Not to the brass," Shane said. "We got lucky we never had to piss. We'd have been booted before the cup had cooled."

"Jesus, you girls make more noise than a ten-cent whore on a Saturday night," Thorne said from the ridge just above them. "Is this what you teach your degenerate, stoner clients?"

"It's called flushing out the prey," Max smiled as he double timed it to his uncle and gave the man a huge hug. "It worked, right?"

"Hey, Vinny," Shane said as he caught up and got his own hug in, "what the fuck's up?"

"Let's step inside," Thorne said, his eyes scanning the area, "a little privacy is good."

"There's no one out here," Max said.

"That's not quite true," Thorne smiled, "I'll show you when we're done talking." He glanced at the lit joint in Shane's hand. "Still on the wacky grass, huh?"

"What can I say, Vinny," Shane smiled as he took a hit, "I'm a hopeless junkie just looking for a fix. Gonna rob an old lady later and take her pension so I can buy more of the pot and get high. Then I'll go on a murder spree. It'll be crazy, daddy-o, crazy."

"Smart ass," Thorne said.

They all walked into the cabin, taking their sunglasses off in perfect unison. Each took a seat at the small table by one of the dirt crusted windows. The Reynolds watched their uncle and waited for him to start.

"I got a call from your favorite ex-cousin-in-law," Thorne said. "He needs an extraction Team. And he needs it now. I thought of you two."

"Ditcher called?" Shane asked, using the nickname they gave Darren Chambers when he and Kinsey divorced. "What's that bastard need with an extraction Team?"

"He gonna rescue Flipper from Sea World?" Max laughed. "Or has a walrus been taken hostage by a pod of orcas?"

"Pod of orcas?" Shane asked. "You've been watching Animal Planet again."

"Guilty as charged, bro," Max said. "Don't get me started about Whale Wars and Japanese whaling practices, man. Despicable." He looked at his uncle and grinned wide. "Has

Ditcher finally decided to put together his eco-warrior Team? I knew one day he'd get in with the granolas and go native."

"Pot calling the kettle black, don't you think?" Thorne asked, looking over at the large three-foot bong by the wood stove in the corner of the cabin.

"The pot pays for the kettle," Shane said. "We certainly don't do it for the free weed."

"But that is a nice perk," Max said, reaching over and plucking the joint from Shane's fingers.

"Do you mind?" Thorne asked, frowning at the joint. "This is serious."

"So is this," Max said, holding out the joint. "Goes for 5K a pound. That field back there will yield easily over 600 pounds per acre. That's three million bucks an acre. Guess how many acres are in that field?"

"Okay, okay, I get the idea," Thorne said, "doesn't mean I agree with it."

"Twenty-first century, Uncle Vinny," Shane said. "Get with the program. Everyone's smoking dope and getting gay married."

"We would get gay married, but they don't let brothers marry," Max said.

"Except in Alabama," Shane added.

"And no fucking way we're moving to Alabama," Max said. "Plus, I have a medical marijuana card on account of my hideousness."

"And we're not gay," Shane said.

"There's that," Max agreed.

"Boys? Shut the fuck up," Thorne said, smiling. "I always forget how exhausting you two are."

"Then why come see us?" Shane asked.

"Because there are only a handful of men in this world that can shoot like you two," Thorne said. "And as much as I may respect them, I can't trust them like I trust you. And it's Darren that's asking, and he's family."

Despite having divorced their favorite cousin, the Reynolds still liked Darren. It took a lot more than a failed marriage to get on the Reynolds' shit list. Darren was good people and they knew that.

"What's the op?" Max asked.

"He has been approached to put together a Team for a company that solves problems," Thorne said. "That's all I know."

"Not much to go on," Shane said. "You think it's legit?"

"Darren wired me the signing bonuses about an hour ago," Thorne smiled. "I back checked the transaction and it's legit enough. And that is quite a bit to go on, trust me."

"So, no info other than Darren's word? And some lame signing bonus?" Max said, shaking his head. "Not much of a sales pitch to get us to walk away from our business, Uncle Vinny."

Thorne took out a small notepad and wrote down a number then showed the brothers.

"What's that?" Shane asked.

"What you get if you say yes right now and come with me," Thorne said. "Quadruple that per successful op and then add the same amount as a yearly salary if the Team works out."

Shane and Max turned to each other, their jaws hanging open. Max took the notebook and looked at the number, even tracing it with his fingers. He handed it to Shane who repeated the gesture before handing the notebook back to Thorne.

"What kind of pack and prep time do we have?" Max asked. "We'll have to cancel with clients. That's not going to be easy. We'll need that bonus right away so we can issue some refunds."

"Bonus will be wired to your accounts within the hour," Thorne said. "You can make cancellation calls once we're on the road. As for pack and prep, you have an hour once we get to your place. We have to hit the road and be down to San Diego before 2000 hours."

"San Diego?" Shane asked, giving his brother a look. "Why there?"

"Is that where the plane's waiting?" Max asked, hopeful. "Any reason it couldn't wait for us up here a little closer?"

"Yes, the plane is in San Diego," Thorne nodded, "but that's not the reason we're going back there."

"Ah, crap, Uncle Vinny," Max said, "you have to be shitting me."

"This is a bad idea, Vinny," Shane said. "A very bad idea. Does Darren know?"

"It was one of my stipulations for taking the job," Thorne answered. "I need to do something for her."

"She's not trained," Max said.

"Bullshit she's not," Shane said. "She's a fucking Marine."

"She never saw action," Max argued.

"Because she has tits and a twat, not because she can't kick some fucking ass," Shane countered.

"I agree with both of you," Thorne said. "But she's my daughter and I want her on the Team. Plus, it's my job to know who is ready and who is not. She's ready. Once we give her a little kick in the ass. As both of you know, there is no person on this planet faster and more accurate with a pistol. That girl was born a natural."

The Reynolds couldn't argue with that; they knew how many awards and contests their cousin had won over the years. Even with their SEAL training and experience, they couldn't do what she could with a pistol. Put a .45 in her hand and she'd clear a room faster than a platoon with M-4s. But...

"She's a fucking junkie," Max said. "Let's just lay it out there. Even if we could get her to go, she's gonna have to detox. That ain't gonna be pretty."

"We?" Thorne asked. "So you're in? And you'll help get Kinsey?"

Without saying a word, the Reynolds brothers held a long conversation with nothing but eye contact and body language.

"Yes," Shane said, "but you let us handle the detox. We dealt with our share of junkies in Afghanistan."

"Plus, you're her dad," Max said, "you'll crack."

"I'm a SEAL, son," Thorne frowned, "I don't crack."

"You ever detoxed someone?" Shane asked.

"No, haven't had that privilege," Thorne said. "Doesn't matter though."

"Yeah it does," Max said. "Junkies will push every single button you have, then invent buttons and start pushing those. If you aren't prepared for it, you'll end up using along with them before they even get to the hard part."

"I can take it," Thorne said.

"No, you can't," Shane said. "It's like when parents say you don't get it until you have a child. You know that feeling, right?"

"Right."

"Same thing," Max said. "You ever see The Exorcist?"

"Of course. Don't be an asshole," Thorne said, getting annoyed.

"Think of it that way," Shane said. "That demon in her will lie and say anything and everything to get a fix. You won't stand a chance."

"You have to trust us, Uncle Vinny," Max said. "If you want us to help, then we do it our way."

"Or you go get her on your own," Shane said. "Which means never."

"You know we're right," Max said, "or you wouldn't have come to us first."

"Or you would have cleaned her up yourself a long time ago," Shane said. "How was she the last time you saw her? In an agreeable mood? How much money did she take you for? How many promises did she break? How many lies did she hammer you with?"

"Fine," Thorne growled, "I get it."

"Keep telling yourself that," Max said, "but you aren't going to get it until you see it. What time do we need to be in the air?"

"2400 hours," Thorne said, "wheels up a minute past."

"Fuck," Shane said, "that's not going to be easy."

"Never is," Max said.

"Nope," Shane agreed, getting to his feet. "We better move ass."

"What about your hippie client?" Thorne asked.

"We'll call him later," Max smiled. "Didn't you say he was about to have company?"

"Six non-friendlies are almost here," Thorne said. "None spoke English, but didn't look like migrants. Lots of tats and some heavy iron."

"TEC-9s?" Max asked.

"Yeah," Thorne nodded.

"Cartel," Shane said. "Fuck. We can't leave him to those guys."

"Let's make an example," Max smiled, looking at his uncle. "Care to join?"

"I'd love nothing more," Thorne said.

The three men left the cabin quickly and headed back towards where Thorne had parked his SUV. They were only a quarter of the way there when they spotted the six cartel enforcers that had been sent north to teach the hippie a lesson on who owned the weed trade. The men bumbled their way through the woods, crashing through the underbrush without a care for the noise they were making.

"City guns," Shane whispered as he lay on the dirt about one hundred yards above the men. "Idiots."

"You think that may be over doing it?" Thorne whispered as he looked at Shane's rifle- a .338 MacMillan. It was second only to a .50 caliber in stopping power. Although many snipers argued it had the same stopping power with better accuracy. Shane was one of those that argued.

"Yes," Shane said as he squeezed the trigger. The bullet hit the first man, center mass, vaporizing his chest and lower rib cage. Before the man fell, they could see right through him.

Max joined his brother, but with an Accuracy International .300 Win Mag, instead of the higher caliber rifle Shane preferred. It didn't vaporize flesh like the .338, but it came close. Max was a headshot shooter and three skulls went pop in rapid succession. Shane liked the center mass shot, knowing that if his shot was off a little, the target would at least be gut shot and die later. No one came back from a .338 round to the belly.

The cartel men lay dead in the pine needles, their blood pooling around roots and twigs.

"Now we get to work," Shane said, getting up and hurrying down to the corpses.

"Here, hold this," Max said as he handed his rifle to his uncle, "only take a minute."

It wasn't until they were in Thorne's SUV and almost to the brothers' house that he brought up what they did.

"Did you have to flay them open like that?" Thorne asked. "And jam their junk in their mouths?"

"It sends a message," Shane said. "The cartels don't fuck around. That shows them that the owner of that field doesn't fuck around either."

"It'll go two ways," Max said, "they'll see the bodies and think it's not worth the hassle and move on."

"Or they take it personally," Shane continued for his brother. "And they kill the guy. Which was what was going to happen to him anyway, so at least we gave him a fifty/fifty chance."

"You guys are regular heroes," Thorne said.

"Hey, we know what we do and who we work for," max said. "These guys grow weed, they don't cure cancer. We explain to them just how dangerous a life they've gotten themselves into before we take a job. We guarantee nothing except for giving them some mad gun skills; staying alive is, and always will be their job, not ours."

"We're instructors and consultants," Shane said, "not bodyguards."

"So full disclosure up front?" Thorne asked.

"Signed in triplicate," Shane said, "we have a good lawyer."

"Good for you," Thorne said.

A quick prep and pack at the brothers' house and they were on I-5 and heading south back to San Diego. And Kinsey Thorne.

None of the three men kidded themselves that they were looking forward to it.

***

The ones that make it through BUD/S are the top of the top. Not physically, but mentally. Less than ten percent graduate from the program, because less than ten percent have the mental fortitude to take all the pain and fear, roll it into a massive ball, and bury it deep inside themselves. The SEALs weren't made up of men that were the strongest or could run the fastest; SEALs were the men that could outlast the strongest and the fastest and still kick ass.

They were, to an extent, superhuman.

And like all superhumans, they didn't handle failure well. And to a SEAL, living a "regular" life was failure. More than a few fell into the bottle after retiring. Some found harder things. Even though Kinsey Thorne wasn't ever officially a SEAL, she had qualified as one, and was raised by a SEAL father with two SEAL cousins. If it hadn't been for the blood work coming back positive, she would have easily been assigned to a Team.

That made her a hundred times more dangerous than the average junkie.

And not just to herself, but to those that she ensnared in her elaborate junkie plans to stay high.

The scene the Reynolds and Thorne walked into was a perfect example.

"Get up, you lazy fuck!" Kinsey shouted, spittle flying from her lips as she bent over a naked man stretched out on the shag carpet of her dingy apartment. Dressed in only a pair of soiled panties, her normally blonde hair cut short and spiked on her head in various neon colors, Kinsey cocked her leg back and kicked the man square in the gut.

He rolled over and threw up, projectile vomiting against the wall and baseboard just a foot from his face.

"You fuck!" Kinsey yelled as she straightened up and kicked him again (which produced more vomit) then took a long drink from the bottle of cheap whiskey she clutched in her hand. "You'll fucking clean that up now, bitch!"

The knock at her door puzzled her for a minute or two. She couldn't place the sound at first since no one ever came around. The complex's super had learned to stay clear of her even when she was late on the rent. He could have called the police, or had her evicted, but Kinsey had figured out the underage prostitution ring he had been running for years and they came to an agreement. She paid when she could so he didn't look bad, and he left her alone so she didn't blow the whistle on his business.

It was not exactly the honor expected of a SEAL, but Kinsey had never become a SEAL and had made a point to take the SEALs' code of honor and shit all over it. She blamed the whole damn men's club of them for what happened to her. They couldn't handle having a set of tits do everything they could do.

"FUCKING SHUT UP!" Kinsey yelled as she swayed her way to the front door after realizing the knocking wasn't in her head. She looked over her shoulder at her collapsed companion and put a finger to her lips. "You shut up too. Or I cut your nuts off."

She threw the door open and leaned against it in all her glory.

She never expected the fist that slammed into her face.

If it had been an average woman that the fist had connected with, then she'd have crumpled in an unconscious heap. But due to the many substances in Kinsey's system, she just staggered back a couple of steps, barely feeling the hit. It did confuse her, though, and she dropped the whiskey bottle as she shook her head.

"What the fuck, MAN?" she yelled, rubbing her face. "You better run. I'm gonna have to kill ya now."

"Jesus," Max said as he rushed her, "this sucks."

"No one should have to tackle their naked cousin, man," Shane said as he followed his brother. "This shit is gonna give me nightmares."

Max got her around the waist and lifted her into the air, and then came down hard, slamming her into the floor, his shoulder buried deep in her gut. All of the air left Kinsey's lungs. So did the contents of her stomach. Luckily, she'd only been on a liquid diet for the past 48 hours; whiskey and bile sprayed into the air.

"Fuck all," Thorne said as he crossed the threshold, his hand to his mouth and nose, trying to block out the stench. "I didn't think it would be this bad."

"Daddy?" Kinsey called out as soon as she heard her father's voice. "Daddy! Help! These fucks are trying to rape me! They're raping your little girl! And this one is a monster! His face is melting!"

Max started to respond, as he struggled to grab a hold of Kinsey's flailing arms, but instead, he took a shot to the throat and the words were stopped instantly. Luckily, the booze and drugs softened the power behind the shot, or he'd have choked to death right then.

"Fuck, Max!" Shane yelled as he pulled is brother away, checking his neck to make sure his airway wasn't crushed. "Jesus, Sis!"

The mentioning of her nickname made her pause as she recognized the voice, but was unsure of the source. It gave her father just enough time to move in and drop a knee onto her chest. He kept his eyes averted from his daughter's bare breasts, but he couldn't help but look at the rest of her emaciated body. Her skin was pallid and hung from her bones, her ribs poked out, her hips stretched the skin at her waist, her cheeks gaunt and sunken, matching the depth of the dark hollows under her eyes. She had various cuts, scratches, burns, and the worst of all, track marks, covering her arms.

She looked like the walking dead.

But she was more like the fighting dead as she thrashed against her father with a strength that didn't seem possible from such a wasted body. Normally, a skinny junkie wouldn't have been a problem for a trained SEAL, but Thorne couldn't separate the fact that it was his daughter he was dealing with. That slight distraction made him hesitate, which was not the best strategy.

Kinsey brought her knee up and Thorne cried out as his balls were jammed up inside him. It hurt enough for him to lose his grip, which allowed Kinsey to worm out from underneath him. She rolled to the side and her hand darted between the couch cushions, pulling free a large hunting knife. Shane left his brother and came at his cousin, his eyes on hers, very aware of the blade that Kinsey brandished.

"Sis, dammit, knock it off," Shane said. She cocked her head, but he could tell she still didn't recognize him. "It's me, you stupid cow. It's Shane."

"Shane?" Kinsey said. "Who?"

"Your fucking cousin, dipshit!" Shane yelled. "What the fuck, Sis?"

"Disarm her," Thorne said as he stood up on shaky legs, "I'll handle the rest."

"Gee, Uncle Vinny, thanks," Shane said. "I'm glad I get to be the one that disarms her."

Kinsey pushed herself to her feet, the knife steady and pointed right at Shane.

"You get the fuck out of here," she croaked, her voice raw and harsh. "I didn't invite you here. This is my place."

Shane turned so he only showed Kinsey his profile, lessening the target space, while Thorne pulled Max across the room and made sure he would be okay. Kinsey watched it all with frantic attention, her eyes darting here and there without any pattern. With a deep sigh, Shane put his hands up, fingers spread wide.

"Sis, listen to us," Shane said, "we're here to help you. Not fight. No fighting. Fighting is bad."

"I'll kill you," Kinsey said, "you try anything and I'll kill you. I'm a trained killer."

"But not a murderer," Thorne said, looking over his shoulder at his daughter.

"Daddy?" Kinsey asked, her arm dropping slightly, the knife angled more towards the floor than towards Shane. "Daddy? When did you get here?"

"I've been here for a while," Thorne said sadly. "You already told me to stop them from raping you. Which they weren't trying to do. They're your cousins, Kins. That's Shane and this is Max. Your cousins."

"SEALs," Kinsey said quietly, "I wanted to be a SEAL."

Her face dropped and she looked like she would cry, but then it changed in a heartbeat and a look of intense anger and hatred overtook her features. Shane didn't like that look and made his move.

Dodging to the right then ducking low and coming up fast on her left, Shane got under her knife arm and was able to shove it aside as he brought his knee to her elbow. She cried out and dropped the knife, but that just freed up another hand, which she used to rake at Shane's face as he grabbed her about the waist.

"Fuck!" he shouted as Kinsey dug deep gouges into his cheeks.

A scream of deep rage came up out of Kinsey's belly and she went for her cousin's face again, but this time her arms were stopped as her father got around and behind her. He grabbed her by the wrists, bent her backwards, then slammed his elbow right between her gold/green eyes. She stared at him for a split second before those eyes rolled up into her head and she collapsed.

"What about him?" Shane asked.

"Him who? Oh, him," Thorne said, "get that piece of shit out of here."

Shane looked at the man passed out in his own vomit and shook his head. "Fuck him. We'll just leave him."

"I want him gone," Thorne said as he scooped his daughter up into his arms.

At her prime, she had been a solid 140 pounds, and at five feet and eight inches, she had never been considered a small woman. But the person Thorne held in his arms weighed nothing and seemed to have shrunk to the size of a small child. To him, it was like carrying the little girl he used to put to bed after she fell asleep in front of the TV. He carried her to the bathroom, trying not to look at the state it was in, and set her in the tub. He then walked back out into the living room.

"Get him gone," Thorne insisted. "You okay, Max?"

Max gave a thumbs up and pushed himself to his feet. "Yeah...ow," he said, his voice a scratchy croak. "I'll...help, bro."

He grabbed the vomit man's legs and Shane got him up under the armpits, wincing at the dampness. Thorne watched them carry the man to the front door, then turned and walked into the small bedroom. His heart sank as he saw more drug paraphernalia as well as piles of empty whiskey bottles. He wasn't sure if he should be disgusted at all the used condoms that littered the floor, or glad his daughter was using protection.

Yanking a collapsible bag from his pocket, he shook it open and started to fill it with whatever clothing didn't look toxic. He honestly wished for a HAZMAT suit as he waded through the trash and detritus of his daughter's life. The bag was only half-full when he stopped, figuring whatever else she needed they'd acquire later. He was about to leave the room when he saw something sticking out from under the mattress. He went back and retrieved it, surprised to see it was a print of the same picture he'd looked at earlier in the morning.

Except it looked like Kinsey had scratched her face out of the picture. Thorne sighed and let the picture drop.

"Ready?" Thorne asked the Reynolds. The brothers nodded. "Good. One last thing and we're done."

Thorne had a wad of clothes in his hands –some sweats, a t-shirt, a bra- and he handed them over to Shane as he went back into the bathroom. Kinsey was still passed out in the tub and hadn't moved a muscle. That would change quickly. Thorne turned the shower on full blast, leaving it on cold. The spray hit Kinsey in the face and neck and she started to stir, and then started to swat at the water.

"Fuck!" she shouted. "Fucking stop!"

Thorne turned off the water as Kinsey sputtered and wiped the water from her eyes. She looked up at the angry face of her father.

"You'll put on some clothes and come with us willingly, Kinsey," Thorne said, "or we dress you and you come against your will. Do you understand the similarities in your options?"

Kinsey watched him for a moment, her eyes coming into full focus for the first time since the men came through her door.

"I'm getting dressed and coming with you," Kinsey said.

"Good girl," Thorne said as he patted her cheek.

He waited as she pulled herself out of the tub, not offering her any help, and watched as she put on her clothes. Once dressed, he pulled her by her elbow out into the living room.

"Now apologize," Thorne ordered.

Kinsey looked from one cousin to the next and tears welled in her eyes. She wiped her nose with the back of her hand and swallowed hard.

"Hey," she said finally.

"Hey," the brothers replied.

"Sorry," she said.

"Not yet," Max smiled.

"What does that mean?" Kinsey asked, looking at her father. "Where are we going? I'm not going to rehab. They're all full of shit there. I'll break out before dinner."

"Not taking you to rehab, Kins," Thorne said.

"Not conventional rehab, at least," Shane added.

"Got a job to do," Max said.

"And we're late," Thorne said as he guided his daughter past her cousins and out the front door.

Kinsey started to pull back, looking over her shoulder at her apartment.

"I don't have shoes," Kinsey said.

"I'll grab them," Max said. "In your room?"

"No," Kinsey said as she shook her head. "I don't have any at all. I think I traded my last pair for a hit."

The three men, all battle hardened veterans, nearly choked up at that statement. What Kinsey had done to herself was her fault and no one else's, but she was family. And for a time, they had all walked away from her. They looked at each other and silently came to an understanding that Kinsey Thorne would never be allowed to go without shoes again. Or go without the constant support of her family.

As they got into Thorne's SUV, he looked over his shoulder at his nephews. "Glad you took control back there. I never would have been able to get through it."

"He's fucking with us, right?" Shane asked his brother.

"Yes, bro, he's fucking with us," Max nodded.

***

Two hours into the chartered flight was when Kinsey started to sober up fully.

"There has to be a bar on this fucking plane," Kinsey said, her nails digging into the scarred flesh of her left forearm. "You know, with those tiny fucking bottles? I just need something to take the edge off."

"What edge?" Shane asked. "What are you on?"

"Nothing now, asshole," Kinsey snapped. "Sorry, sorry. Just, you know, stuff."

"Crack? Crank? Oxy? Junk?" Max asked.

"It's all junk," Thorne added, a few seats away, his eyes closed.

"I mean heroin," Max said.

"I know what you mean," Thorne replied, opening his eyes and turning his gaze on his nephew. "It's still all junk."

"Yeah, well, when that junk is out of my system," Kinsey laughed, "it isn't going to be pretty. Just give me something to get through the flight. Come on. I'll go cold turkey when we land. I just can't do it while we fly."

"You aren't getting off this plane until we are at the job," Thorne said. "This is your home for the next 48 hours. You start cleaning up as of now. No booze, no junk, no nothing. Got it?"

"No nothing," Kinsey whispered then gave a short bark of a laugh, "story of my life."

Thorne was up out of his seat and in his daughter's face so fast she barely had time to track the movement. Max and Shane got to their feet out of instinct.

"Fuck you," Thorne said. "Fuck you and your fucking self-pity. You have had a good life, Kinsey Marie Thorne. You had a wonderful mother and an amazing brother. And I know I haven't been perfect, but I have always been there for you and I have shown you nothing but love and support. Even when it was only me and I had the weight of everything on my shoulders." He jabbed a finger into her breastbone. "Fuck. You."

He walked over to a wet bar and opened a small fridge, tossing Kinsey a mini bottle of water. She caught it, surprisingly, but just set it aside.

"That's what you get to take the edge off," Thorne said as he went back to his seat. "So settle in and just enjoy the flight."

Kinsey didn't argue. But she didn't open the water either, just folded her arms across her chest and leaned back into the seat. She didn't know where they were going after Miami and she didn't care. As soon as the door opened on the tarmac, she planned on making a break for it. She knew a guy in South Beach that could hook her up. Money didn't matter, not for a California girl like her. Bat her eyelashes and show a little boob and she'd be high as a motherfucking kite by sunrise.

That's what she told herself. But as the plane flew on and the minutes felt like hours, she had to wonder if she'd make it. Did she know the guy's number? He'd have to pick her up at the airport. She would have to have something waiting for her in Miami when they landed. Her skin was on fire and she felt like it was going to split apart and crawl off her body, slinking away into a dark corner of the plane.

"Can we turn off the lights?" Kinsey asked. "It's bright in here."

"The lights are on so we can see you, Sis," Shane replied. "Not about to stay in the dark with you."

"Turn the fucking lights off!" she yelled.

"Leave them," Thorne said, his eyes closed. "Light is good for you. You've been in the dark for too long."

"Fucking show you the dark, old man," Kinsey mumbled.

"Hungry?" Max asked. "There's some peanuts. The salt and protein will do you good."

"Is that what you think after swallowing some guy's load, asshole?" Kinsey snapped.

"You'd know," Max smiled, "I'm guessing you're a bit of a connoisseur when it comes to cum swallowing."

"That's enough of that," Thorne said, working hard not to think about the reality of that statement. "We'll be landing in a few minutes. Shut the fuck up until then."

The pilot came over the intercom just after that and announced their descent. They landed on a private airstrip just north of Miami proper. As soon as the plane came to a stop, Kinsey jumped to her feet.

"I'm gonna stretch my legs," she said as the pilot opened the cabin door, "just for a second."

"Sit," Thorne said as he passed her, pushing her back into her seat, "we're only here to refuel and pick up the rest of the Team."

"Rest of the Team?" Kinsey asked, her nails working furiously at a scab by her wrist. "What Team? Where are we going?"

"Need to know," Thorne said, "and you don't need to know yet."

Max followed Thorne out the door and down the short set of steps.

"Who are we picking up?" Max asked.

"Pilot and a gunner," Thorne said, "used to be HITRON in the Coast Guard, but both got booted after filing a complaint against their chief."

"What'd he do?" Max asked.

"Tried to fuck them both," Thorne said as he spotted two women walking towards them. "They weren't cool with that."

"No shit," Max said as the women, gear slung over their shoulders, walked up and both offered their hands.

"Roberta La Pierre," the first woman said as Thorne took her hand and gave it a strong shake. Five five and 120 pounds, long black hair with widely spaced brown eyes, she was attractive in a way neither men could have expressed. It could have been the way she held herself- confident, secure, strong. "Call me Bobby."

"Bobby, this is my nephew, Max Reynolds," Thorne said. "Max and his brother are our snipers."

"Already have a gunner," Bobby said, nodding to the woman next to her.

"Lucretia Durning," the woman said, shaking hands with the men. "Lucy. I'm the gunner to her pilot."

Lucy was nearly six feet tall, wide at the shoulder, and had a head of shockingly red hair. Her face was covered in dark freckles that showed even in the night. She smiled at Max and gave him a nod- shooter to shooter then frowned as she got a better look at his face.

"Where'd you get that?" Lucy asked.

"IED. Afghanistan," he replied.

"Bummer," Lucy said, "got a brother missing both legs because of an IED."

"HITRON, right?" Max asked, changing the subject. "So you know the .50 caliber pretty well then?"

Lucy lifted the large duffel bag she held and patted it. "Got mine right here."

Thorne looked back and motioned to the pilot that was standing at the top of the plane's steps. He came down quickly and took the bag from Lucy, stowing it in the baggage compartment under the plane. He then came back and took Bobby's bag.

"You said to pack light," Bobby said, "that we'd have access to gear when we landed?"

"That's what I have been told," Thorne said. "I'll tell you the rest on the flight. We have about thirty-six hours of flying to do before we get to our destination."

"Which is?" Lucy asked.

"Cape Town," Thorne replied. "There, we'll meet our employer and get our kits together. If what I've been told is true, then we'll have some time in Cape Town to go shopping."

"Sky's the limit," Max said, smiling broadly.

"Really?" Bobby laughed. "So we can just bop down to the South African Wal-Mart and pick up a MH-65 Dolphin?"

"No need," Thorne said, "one will be waiting for you."

"Sweet," Lucy said, "let's get going."

"Just one second," Thorne said. There was a large crash inside the plane and he winced as everyone else looked towards the cabin door. "There's a complication I should warn you about."

"MOTHER FUCKER! LET ME GO!" echoed from the plane.

"That's my daughter," Thorne said, "she's had some substance issues, but we are getting her straight. The worst is over, though."

"Not even close," Max said. "The worst has yet to come. This is going to be a bumpy ride."

"Always is," Bobby said.

"No shit," Lucy said as the two women walked confidently to the stairs and up into the plane.

"What do you mean the worst has yet to come?" Thorne said. "Sure, she's being a bitch, but we can ignore that."

"Can you ignore the sweating? The vomiting? The diarrhea? That's what's next," Max said. "She will convince you she's dying and you'll believe her because in a way, she will be. We have two objectives on this flight: make sure she doesn't hurt the plane, and make sure she doesn't hurt herself."

"I'm guessing you left off the third objective of making sure she doesn't hurt us for a reason," Thorne said.

"Because we will be getting hurt," Max said. "You know how Kinsey fights. Jesus, she used to kick the shit out of me when we were kids. Now she's a trained Marine and almost a SEAL. I have zero illusions that any of us will get out of this without some serious bruises."

"So maybe the third objective should be not to let her kill us," Thorne said.

"I think that's a given," Max said, then sighed as Kinsey let out a bloodcurdling scream. "Let's get this party started."

The time on the flight was mostly spent waiting for Kinsey to do one of three things: fall asleep, stop screaming, or shit herself before she could hit the head. The Team Thorne had put together quickly bonded over the detoxing of one Kinsey Marie Thorne. They took shifts, making sure someone was awake and watching her at all times, and that someone was awake and watching the person that was supposed to be watching her.

When they landed in Morocco to refuel, Kinsey made a break for it. But was quickly put down by Lucy with a hard punch to the gut. Unfortunately for all, that led to Kinsey evacuating her bowels right there in the cabin. The smell of rancid junkie shit was stuck in everyone's noses the entire second leg of the flight, no matter how much air freshener they sprayed.

The moment the plane was wheels down on the tarmac in Cape Town, there was a mad dash to get outside and into the fresh air. And despite the fact she had a 100 degree fever and looked like death warmed over, Kinsey was the first at the cabin door. Thorne wasn't too worried, since he'd radioed ahead to warn those waiting of what was to come.

"Get me the fuck off this plane!" Kinsey yelled.

The pilot unlocked the cabin door and extended the stairs; Kinsey bolted into the South African afternoon, her face held up to the warm sun. The rest of the Team walked down after her, wary and cautious. A long black van was parked near the plane and Darren was seated in the passenger side, his arms resting on his legs as he watched them from the open door.

"Welcome to South Africa," Darren said, getting up and walking towards them, "you guys are a sight for sore eyes."

Kinsey's breath stopped and her eyes shot open at the sound of his voice.

"Good to see you, 'Sey," Darren said.

"Go fuck yourself, 'Ren," Kinsey replied.

"That would be my job," Bobby said as she walked past them all and into Darren's arms. "Hey there, stranger."

"Hey back," Darren said.

The kiss between them was not meant to be subtle.

"So that's why he insisted on the women," Shane said.

"He insisted because we're the best interceptors in the fucking world," Lucy said, "you'll see."

"This is going to get complicated quick," Max said.

"No fucking shit," Thorne replied as he watched the stunned look on his daughter's face.

"No fucking way," Kinsey said, backing towards the plane's stairs. "Get me the fuck back on that plane!" She then promptly turned and puked all over the tarmac.

CHAPTER FOUR: THE BEOWULF II

The twelve-passenger van wasn't close to full with everyone in it, so Kinsey was given her own bench seat at the back. She curled up on the seat, her legs tucked up against her chest, and closed her eyes, hoping that the pain and nausea would stop. But she knew better. You didn't become a junkie without knowing other junkies. And when in the company of junkies, you meet those that have tried to get clean.

She knew she had a few more days of hell before she'd even get close to seeing the other side.

Which made her wonder why her father had brought her. She could hear the others talking, knew they were driving to a different part of the airfield that held the Dolphin helicopter, which would fly them out to the ship that was already steaming up the African coast towards Somalia. Papers were passed around that everyone had to sign; classic NDAs (non-disclosure agreements) that made sure they didn't talk to anyone about what they were doing.

That was where things got vague. Darren refused to go into detail about the job, just kept telling them that their employer would explain everything once they were onboard the ship. No one liked the lack of intel, but from what Kinsey could make out, the pay was so good none of them really cared. They were professionals and were used to need to know scenarios.

So why bring her? Kinsey kept looping back to that thought, between the shivers and small convulsions that wracked her body.

A small Team was all that was needed and her cousins, with her father, plus Darren and the Coast Guard women, were enough for simple missions. Then there was the driver, some woman that looked to Kinsey like she could chew them all up and spit them out without breaking wind. They didn't need a junkie in withdrawal, fucking things up.

As the van pulled to a stop, Kinsey wished they'd just leave her; let her die in the back of the van and end her misery. The thought of getting on a helo, then on a ship for the next few days made her want to retch. And she didn't have anything left in her stomach to retch.

"Holy shit," Kinsey heard Bobby say as the van doors opened, "that's not a 65-D, is it?"

"Not even a 65-E," Darren replied. "Next gen 65-F. Coast Guard hasn't even seen this model. Our employer has deep pockets and doesn't mind emptying them on us. Wait until you see the Beowulf II."

"What happened to the Beowulf I?" Max asked.

"Good fucking question," Darren said. "Darby? Care to chime in on that?"

"No," Darby said, "we don't talk about that."

"Fair enough," Darren said, cutting off Max before he could ask more questions. "Let's get the gear onboard and lift off. We have some space to cover before we rendezvous with the ship."

"No shopping?" Max asked.

"Everything we need is on board already," Darren replied.

"Can't wait to fly that," Bobby said.

"No can do, baby," Darren responded. "You all signed NDAs, but you haven't signed your full employment contracts or liability waivers. Until then, you are guests. Darby will fly, but you can ride co-pilot and check the panels out."

"Not cool, Chambers," Bobby growled.

"Best I can do until I's are dotted and T's are crossed," Darren replied.

"Sis?" Shane asked. "You awake?"

Kinsey opened her eyes and looked up at the face of her cousin.

"Yeah," she replied as he helped her sit up, "Rip, roaring, and ready."

"Good," Thorne said, pushing Shane out of the way. "Time to get a move on. Hump your ass into that helo and let's go."

"Love you too, Daddy," Kinsey said as she got out of the van, her legs shaky and loose. "Can't wait to spend the next few days with you."

"Weeks," Darren said, "we'll be gone for weeks."

"I thought it only took eight days to get to the target?" Shane asked.

"Yeah, what's this about weeks?" Lucy asked.

"It'll all be explained when we get to the ship," Darren said, "until then, just kick back and enjoy the view. Sun should be coming up any minute now. It'll be spectacular."

"Thank God," Kinsey said as she staggered over to the helo. "I don't know if I can make it without seeing a spectacular sunrise. Woo hoo!"

The gear was transferred from the van to the helo and Darby boarded and started her pre-flight countdown. Bobby got in next to her and assisted so she could learn the differences between the 65-F and the 65-C she was accustomed to. The one main difference that everyone noticed was the helo was painted matte black, and not the usual red and white the US Coast Guard used.

"Wyrm?" Lucy asked, pointing to the words painted on the tail.

"Yep," Darren smiled, "our employer named it. Paint dried on the flight over here." He looked at everyone and opened the side doors. "Gonna be a tight squeeze with the gear, so jam in, folks. And we need to hustle or the ship will be out of range. I'd hate to ditch this bird in the drink before the job even starts."

For emphasis, Darby started the motors and the rotors began to turn and come to life. Everyone hauled themselves inside and got secured. The Dolphin was meant for a crew of four, but could hold up to ten if needed, including the pilot and co-pilot. Meant mainly for short range missions by the Coast Guard, the MH-65 was used by the HITRON (Helicopter Interdiction Tactical Squadron) unit to take down possible terrorist threats to the US, which included drug smuggling. It was fast, maneuverable, and in the hands of the right pilot and gunner, a deadly bird of prey.

Shoulder to shoulder, everyone strapped in and hung on as the helo lifted into the air. Slowly, as the helo made its way east, the sun started to peak over the horizon. Those that had sunglasses handy put them on, the rest squinted. Kinsey just moaned, unable to handle even the sunlight that filtered through her eyelids. She wrapped an arm over her face and leaned her head back.

"Grab some shut eye if you can," Darren said over the com, "we have about two hours of flying before we get to the Beowulf II."

Everyone heard him through the headphones they wore and the SEALs of the Team instantly closed their eyes and were out in seconds. It was a skill all SEALs learned to cultivate: sleep whenever and wherever you could. Lucy looked at the three sleeping men and shrugged, closed her eyes, and joined them. Kinsey was in too much agony to sleep, although she felt exhausted. Her body was numb, yet full of fire at the same time. She wouldn't have been able to explain it even if she wanted to.

Expecting Darren to be asleep with the rest of the former SEALs, Kinsey braved opening her eyes to get a look at him. She regretted it as soon as she saw his eyes locked onto hers. There was so much said in those eyes that Kinsey wanted to scream at him, but that would have split her head open, so she just glared. Or thought she glared, she couldn't tell if her body was obeying. Darren gave her a weak smile, and then turned and looked out the window.

Time dragged on and Kinsey thought she'd go insane from the constant drone of the rotors. Not to mention the intense snoring of her cousins; they were both almost as loud as the Wyrm. Just as she was about to lose her shit and shove her cousins out the doors, Darby's voice came over the com.

"There she is," Darby said, "one minute to landing."

The rest of the Team stirred and stretched as much as they could in the cramped space. They turned and looked out at the ship that was steaming along in the bright blue water below.

"Holy fuck," Max said, "that's a research vessel? Where have I seen that before?"

"Looks like the RV Falkour," Shane responded, "that ship that Google financed."

"Close," Darren said. "It's a sister ship, of sorts, but highly modified for our needs. And about five meters longer to accommodate the extra helipad and the mini-sub on the stern."

"It has a mini-sub?" Max asked. "Cool."

"Yeah," Darren grinned, "I haven't had a chance to get out in it. That'll be part of the training the next few days for some of you." He pointed as they swung around to land on the foremost helipad. "Two full Zodiacs, one on each side, next to the lifeboats."

"Any more bells and whistles?" Shane asked.

"Tons," Darren said, "you'll see. Trust me, you'll fall in love with the Beowulf II as soon as you set foot on the deck."

Darby brought the Wyrm in for a landing and soon the motors were cut and the rotors started to power down. Kinsey was grateful for the reduction in brain-melting noise, but she quickly realized she had a different problem: she'd lost her sea legs and the rocking of the Beowulf II was almost as bad as the rotor noise of the Wyrm.

"Just kill me," she said as she stepped out of the Wyrm, ignoring the helping hands offered by both of her cousins. "You want to help? Smack me in the head and toss me overboard."

"I might let them if you don't stop acting like a pussy," Thorne said as he grabbed his gear. "No wonder you couldn't hack it as a SEAL."

Darren, Max, and Shane froze and looked from Thorne to Kinsey, waiting for the explosion. But Kinsey just smiled at her father and nodded.

"You nailed it there, Daddy," Kinsey said. "Too much pussy for the SEALs." She grabbed her crotch and thrust towards her father. "The Navy couldn't handle this pussy, so it fucked my blood work up to kick me out. Yeah, I'm the pussy. Whatever."

"Glad you brought her," Darren said as he patted Thorne on the shoulder and pushed past him to the stairs leading to the upper deck. "Let me know how it works out."

Everyone else followed Darren, even Thorne, leaving Kinsey up on the helipad alone with Darby.

"What is wrong with you?" Darby asked.

"Oh, you know," Kinsey shrugged, "just a junkie making her way in life."

"Fuck that," Darby said, moving in close to Kinsey. "That's just surface bullshit. What's really wrong with you?"

"You aren't known for your interpersonal skills, are you?" Kinsey said, uncomfortable with the invasion of her personal space as Darby kept moving in closer.

"I don't care for them," Darby said. "I don't care for excuses either. Get rid of yours and we'll be fine."

Darby leaned forward and tapped her forehead to Kinsey's, then turned and left the helipad.

"What the fuck...?" Kinsey whispered. "Nice rabbit hole you fell through, Kins. How are you getting out of this one?"

"Ms. Thorne?" Popeye asked from the upper deck. The sun was in his face and both eyes were squinted until almost shut, his massive forearms folded across his chest. "I've been sent to make sure you get to the briefing room."

"Briefing room?" Kinsey asked. "Oooh, that sounds important."

"It's a room," Popeye said, "where you get briefed. Not as important as the head, if you ask me."

Kinsey smiled at the man that looked like a cartoon character. It was her first genuine smile in days. And as she thought about it, probably the first genuine smile in months.

"Point me in the right direction," Kinsey said as she descended the steps and planted her feet on the deck.

She took a deep breath and felt better as the salt air filled her lungs. The swaying of the ship wasn't as noticeable as it had been, and she started to feel something so unfamiliar she wasn't sure what it was at first. The she realized it was comfort; the comfort of the sea all around her. She hadn't realized how much she'd missed the water.

"You okay, Ms. Thorne?" Popeye asked.

"Just fine," Kinsey said, "and call me Kinsey, not Ms. Thorne. Ms. Thorne was my mother and she was a better woman than me."

"Not from what the captain says," Popeye replied. "I mean, I don't know what your mother was like, but the captain thinks highly of you. So does Doc."

"Doc?" Kinsey asked as she followed Popeye to a hatch that led down to the main deck. "Who's Doc?"

"Gunnar," Popeye said, "Doctor Gunnar Peterson. Guy seems to like you and was pretty excited to find out you were coming aboard."

Kinsey couldn't even respond to that she was so stunned.

The ship was a maze that Kinsey knew she'd learn at some point, but she didn't bother memorizing the turns as she followed Popeye. He brought her to a well-lit briefing room, rimmed with several portholes that brought in the light being reflected from the water below. Everyone was seated around a long conference table, including a few faces Kinsey didn't recognize.

One of the faces she did recognize belonged to a man she hadn't see in so long, she couldn't remember the last time they'd been in the same room together.

"Gunnar…?" Kinsey asked quietly as the man wrapped his arms about her and lifted her into the air. "I didn't…I didn't know you'd be here." She found her father looking at her. "No one told me."

"Would it have made a difference?" Gunnar asked. "I'm a trained doctor, you know. I'm very aware of the mental state of those going through withdrawal."

"You know what?" Kinsey answered honestly. "I think it would have made a difference. It's so good to see you."

"And it is good to see you, Ms. Thorne," Mr. Ballantine said from the head of the table, a space usually reserved for the captain, but Darren sat to the man's right. "I have heard many things about you and look forward to hearing more. But I'm afraid I have to break up this reunion and get down to business."

Darby started passing out folders to each of the new arrivals.

"Inside these, you will find your contracts and all forms needed to begin your employment," Mr. Ballantine said. "I'll give you a few minutes to read over them. Then I expect you to sign them so we can begin. Captain Chambers has assured me that all of you are exactly what we need for this mission, so I'd like to not waste any more time, if that's possible."

"Yeah, sure," Kinsey said as Gunnar led her to a seat next to him, "whatever."

"I applaud your enthusiasm," Mr. Ballantine said, giving her a wink, "now, let's please continue."

Kinsey sat and watched as everyone started to read what was in their folders. The puzzled looks on her cousins' faces piqued her interest, so she opened her own folder and began studying the documents.

"Hold on," Kinsey said, "I'm sure I missed a lot on the plane, but what is this about 'post-mission research'?"

"That is the true heart of this operation," Mr. Ballantine said. "The company I work for solves problems. The main mission is to raid the pirate compound where the kidnapped crew of a container ship belonging to one of our clients are being held. That pays the bills. It is a new direction we are taking and success is crucial to the rest of the operation."

"But what is the rest of the operation?" Shane asked. "That's not explained in here."

"No, it is not," Mr. Ballantine smiled.

They all waited.

"Uh, so…?" Max asked. "What is the rest of the operation?"

"That will be revealed after our main mission is finished," Mr. Ballantine said. "If you are successful, then we will proceed, if you fail, then there is no point in explaining any of it since you'll either be dead or in a Somali prison."

"Did you know any of this?" Shane asked Thorne.

"I only know what he told me," Thorne said, nodding at Darren.

Max and Shane turned to Darren, and then shook their heads in unison.

"No way, Ditcher," Shane said, "are you kidding?"

"Is this a fish hunt, Ditcher?" Max asked.

"Whales aren't fish," Darren replied, "and don't call me Ditcher. I fucking hate that."

"I love it," Kinsey said, "because it's true."

Bobby snorted and Kinsey focused her attention on the pilot.

"Got something to share with the rest of us?" Kinsey asked.

"Pretty sure you served him with divorce papers," Bobby said, "not the other way around. Who ditched who?"

"No," Mr. Ballantine said, placing his palms on the table. Something about the slow way he spread his fingers out and pressed down grabbed everyone's attention. That and the dark look on his face. "This will not devolve into a battle of wills and personalities. You are professionals, even you Ms. Thorne. Act it."

"But what about the fish hunt?" Max asked.

"Whales aren't fish," Darren snapped.

"We'll discuss the fish hunt after the mission, Mr. Reynolds," Mr. Ballantine said. "Please finish reading the file and then sign all accompanying documents."

"And, just for clarification, what happens if we don't sign?" Shane asked.

"You will," Mr. Ballantine replied, smiling.

"But what if we don't?" Max asked.

"You will," Mr. Ballantine said.

"Got it," Shane replied, giving a thumbs up. "Who's got a pen?"

One was slid across the table to him and he signed the many documents in the file, shut the folder, and slid it and the pen to Mr. Ballantine.

"You want to pay me for one night's work and a pointless vacation of a fish hunt, then more power to you," Shane said, "I can use the rest. Gives me time to work on my tan while you all stare at the horizon and hope Moby Dick shows up."

"I'm just looking forward to visiting a new, exotic place and killing people," Max said as he slid his folder over. "I don't like to tan as much as my brother does. Anyone play poker? I'm up for a few weeks of cards."

"As long as I get to fly that bird, I'm in," Bobby said, adding her folder to the pile.

"Me too," Lucy said, "plus I get to show these SEALs how a real shooter does it."

"Oh, no she didn't!" Max laughed.

Thorne silently slid his folder over and looked at Kinsey. Her head was down and she was busy reading the documents. Or busy trying to look like she was reading them. He could see the sheen of sweat on her brow and cheeks. Despite her bravado, he knew his daughter was still suffering greatly and was using all of her willpower to keep from collapsing.

Just as he was about to say something, Gunnar leaned in and whispered in her ear. She looked over at him, her eyes wide and then turned back to the file and began to sign the paperwork. She finished and tossed the folder on the pile, giving her father a quick glance.

"Excellent," Mr. Ballantine said. "I have to sort through these, scan and get them to headquarters. The captain will take over from here. You have a lot of work to do, but I'm sure we can allow time for a tour of the Beowulf II and possibly a chance to clean up and eat before the first briefing."

"Hey," Max said, "what happened to the first Beowulf?"

"We don't talk about that," Mr. Ballantine said, "please don't ask again."

Then he left, followed by Darby, and Max looked down the table at the rest of the crew that had sat there quietly.

"What the fuck was that about?" Max asked. "Is he joking? They don't talk about it?"

"We don't know," Lake said as he stood up. "He says he isn't. Doesn't matter to me. I have to relieve Jennings on the bridge."

Lake left and Darren stood up. "That was my CO, Marty Lake. I may be Captain, but he's in charge, trust me. Do whatever he says and you'll be fine. You aren't crew, but you are subject to the rules of the ship. Pay attention and don't step on toes."

Darren introduced the rest of the men seated at the table: Popeye, Cougher, Beau, and Gunnar.

"There are twenty others below deck running the ship," Darren said, "but honestly, I don't know them yet. They came with the Beowulf II and Ballantine has said that there is no need to make personal connections. Apparently, they'll be swapped out as often as possible so that no unauthorized crew knows too much about our operation."

"What is the operation, Captain Ditcher?" Max asked. Darren gave him a cold look. "What? I said Captain?"

"Let's focus on the mission," Thorne said, "like Mr. Ballantine explained, there will be time for the rest of the operation after we free the hostages."

"So we get to kill pirates?" Shane said. "Sweet, sweet, sweet. Do we get to use the mini-sub?"

"How about a tour first?" Darren said. "Then you guys can grab some chow and take a quick nap. We'll gather after supper and begin to plan. We have about eight days to get ready. I don't want to lose a minute."

***

To say everyone was impressed with the Beowulf II would be an understatement. They were floored by it.

It was similar to the RV Falkor that was part of the Schmidt Ocean Institute, and funded by Google, but it had some major differences. Such as a reinforced double hull. Not standard on a simple research vessel; mostly used for military vessels that expected to see battle. That brought some questions, but Darren just smiled.

The shaft and diesel generators were also much more powerful than the Falkor, which gave the ship a maximum speed of 25 knots, not the usual 20 knots. Cruising speed was 15 knots, while survey speed was a steady 10 knots. The Team was impressed.

The best part for them, besides the well-equipped crew lounge full of snacks, beer, and video games, was the mini-sub attached to the stern of the boat. It was locked into two large deployment arms and held in place by large claws that could fold out and place the sub right in the water, and then pick it up when done. They all, except for Kinsey, wanted to go inside and check it out. But Darren said there'd be time for that as he led them to the mess and put them in the hands of Beau.

"Grab a tray and fill it up," Beau said. "Eat what you can and all you can. There's plenty."

The Team did as instructed and were soon stuffed. Beau showed them to their quarters where their gear was stashed. They were surprised to find that they each had their own cabin. But being a ship, there was barely enough room for gear and the cot they were each to sleep on. Max had to crawl over his gear to get to the cot and didn't even bother to pull off his boots before crashing out.

Before any of them knew it, the dinner bell rang.

Instead of joining the others, Kinsey made her way to the upper deck. She took a couple of wrong turns, but eventually found her way topside. The sun was setting and she found that the upper deck had an open lounge complete with plush deck chairs. She settled into one and watched the orange light play across the small waves.

"What did Gunnar say to you to get you to sign?" Thorne asked as he sat down next to Kinsey.

"Couldn't just let a girl enjoy the sunset, huh Daddy?" Kinsey sighed. "Couldn't give me that?"

"Why I should give you anything, I don't know," Thorne replied, "from what I've seen, you don't deserve any of this."

Kinsey turned and looked at her father and smiled. "He said he had something close to methadone that will ease me through the withdrawal, and he'd make sure I was part of the Team during the mission."

Thorne watched her for a minute, studying her face, looking for the joke. But he didn't find it because she wasn't joking. He stood up quickly and started to walk away.

"We'll see about this," Thorne said.

"Too late, Daddy," Kinsey smiled, "he gave me the shot while you all were eating. I'm already starting to feel a little clearer. Clearer than I have in a long time."

"Motherfucker," Thorne said. "I don't know who he thinks he is. I'm the Team leader and I decide who is on the mission. Not that faggot."

Kinsey sat there and shook her head. "Oh, Daddy, really? Faggot? What is this, the 20th century?" She stood up and got in her father's face. "You know who the first person was to call me when Darren left for BUD/S and I knew my marriage was over? Gunnar. I have known that man most of my life, Daddy, and he is nothing but kind and generous. Is he gay? Yeah, but so fucking what? Don't ever call him that again."

"Fine," Thorne said, "I didn't mean it. I know the kid is a good guy."

"He's not a kid, Daddy," Kinsey laughed. "He's the same age as me and Darren, which means he'll be thirty next year."

"Jesus," Thorne said, rubbing his face, "Thirty? Already?" He looked out at the water. "Doesn't change the fact that you aren't going to be on the mission."

"It does," Kinsey said, backing away from her father and sitting back in the lounge chair. "I am going to be on the mission. Mr. Ballantine already approved it. Gunnar said Darren balked, but had to agree that I have a skill set needed."

"What's that?" Thorne laughed. "You know we'll be killing people, not bottles of whiskey, right?"

"Funny," Kinsey said. "You have two snipers, a Coast Guard gunner and yourself. You'll probably put Shane on overwatch, the gunner will be on the helo for cover during extraction, which leaves you and Max to clear and rescue the hostages. Two men. Not possible."

"We'll have Darren and Darby," Thorne said, "that's four."

"Nope," Kinsey said, "Darren and Darby have a side mission they have to attend to simultaneously."

"What? That's news to me," Thorne said, taken by surprise. "Who told you that?"

"It's amazing what you learn when you don't call someone faggot," Kinsey said. "You need me, old man. Plus, I'm the best close quarters fighter out there. I nearly took all three of you while high and shit faced. Did you know I'd just shot up like ten minutes earlier and had finished about four bottles of whiskey in the last twenty-four hours? And I kicked your ass."

"You didn't even come close to kicking my ass," Thorne said, but he couldn't help but smile. She had come very close. "We'll talk about this. I'm now more worried about why Darren and that Darby woman won't be part of the mission."

"You'll find out now," Darren said as he came around the corner. "Wasn't eavesdropping, just coming to find you for the briefing. If you want to follow me, we'll get started."

Instead of going below deck, they just walked a few meters to a glass enclosed meeting room. It was obviously a room designed to impress visitors and not for general purpose use. Expensive chairs ringed a table made from what looked like a single piece of mahogany. Kinsey was almost afraid to put her boots on the polished wood floors.

Seated around the table were the Reynolds, Lucy, Bobby, Darby, and Mr. Ballantine. This time Ballantine didn't take the head of the table and was actually seated towards the end. They all faced a large video screen that slowly unfolded from the ceiling.

"Have a seat," Darren said. He waited for Kinsey and Thorne to sit before he began. "Welcome to Team Grendel. It's an honor to have all of you here."

"Team Grendel?" Max asked. "Who came up with that?"

"I did," Mr. Ballantine said, "it fits the theme."

"Right," Max nodded.

"I get it," Shane said. "Beowulf. Grendel. Wyrm. Are you like completely obsessed with ancient Anglo-Saxon epic poetry?"

"No," Mr. Ballantine replied, "just the one poem."

"It doesn't matter," Darren said, "I like the name and we're keeping it. Team Grendel it is." Shane raised his hand. "What?"

"What's the sub's name?" Shane asked. "Is it named after Grendel's mom?"

"It's named after your mom," Lucy smiled.

"Hey, that's my mom too," Max said. "And Dorothy is a shitty name for a mini-sub."

"The sub is named Wiglaf," Mr. Ballantine answered.

They all stared at him.

"After the kid that helps Beowulf slay Wyrm?" Shane said. "Seriously?"

"I like Dorothy better," Max said.

"Me too," Lucy replied.

"It's Wiglaf," Mr. Ballantine said, "and that's the end of it."

"I'm still calling it Dorothy," Max whispered loudly.

"Does that mean the sub and the helo have to fight?" Shane asked.

"The helo will kick that sub's ass," Bobby replied.

"Don't count Dorothy out," Max said, "she's one tough broad."

"Okay, okay, enough," Darren said, "business time."

A man's picture came up on the video screen.

"This is Daacad Khalid Shimbir," Darren explained. "He is the leader of one of the most notorious pirate gangs in the Darood tribe. He is one tough motherfucker and his men almost worship him." The picture changed to an aerial view of a small compound. "This is his stronghold. The compound is two miles inland in the Somali city of Hilweyne. There isn't much between the coast and the compound, just residential buildings. We'll hit the coast at 0200 hours and make our way on foot to the compound."

"Hit the coast?" Max asked. "Who's driving the boat?"

"I'll have Jennings pilot the Zodiac," Darren said, "he's the best at it and won't panic if things go south."

"Go south?" Shane asked. "How? You just said it's only residential buildings between the water and the compound."

"Right," Darren replied, "but this is pirate territory. Armed men could be anywhere. Unfortunately, there is no way to know when or where. Think of these guys like the insurgents in Iraq or the militias in Afghanistan. They aren't trained like the Taliban, they have no discipline except to listen to their leaders. They are thugs that walk around with AK-47s and intimidate whoever they come across. If they see us, they will start shooting. At that point, we go in hard and hot and fight our way to the compound. Instead of waiting for extraction, Bobby and Lucy will bring in the Wyrm and lay down some cover, letting us do our thing."

"So, no sat cover?" Max smiled.

"Not this time," Mr. Ballantine answered, "but if this mission is successful, then the next one will have drone cover. We'll be able to relay an overview to your goggles."

The Team just stared.

"I'm sorry," Thorne said, "relay to our goggles?"

"I'm still stuck on the 'not this time' part," Shane said.

"Who flies the drone?" Bobby asked.

"There's no drone yet," Darren said. "The funding for this Team will be staggered. For every successful mission, you will be paid handsomely, and our budget increases. The company Mr. Ballantine works for has pretty deep pockets."

"Bottomless," Mr. Ballantine smiled.

"Get back to the goggles," Thorne said. "What do you mean relayed?"

"Each of us will have the latest generation of night-vision goggles," Darren said. "Instead of four tubes, there is one long visor. The great thing about the goggles is they are basically high-def monitors. Any visual you need can be sent to you, including aerial visuals from drones. You can even see what your teammates are seeing."

"That could get messy," Shane said.

"It has to be switched from the ship," Mr. Ballantine said, "and upon request. You can't accidentally switch visuals. If there is a malfunction, then the goggles go black so they don't send a wrong visual or fry your eyes."

"Oh, okay then," Shane nodded. "Can we have a robot dog too? I've always wanted an assault dog, but never wanted to clean up the mess. A robot dog would be perfect."

Mr. Ballantine smiled at Shane; it didn't make him feel comfortable at all.

"That's scheduled for 2020 at the earliest," Mr. Ballantine said, "sorry."

"He's kidding," Darren said. "So let's get back to the mission."

"How many fighters are we looking at?" Thorne asked.

"Depends," Darren said. "It varies. We hope to hit them while they have some of their men out on raiding parties. If that's the case, then the compound will be all but deserted. They'll have guards on the hostages, guards at the main gates, but very few on patrol."

Thorne studied the photo of the compound.

"Which building are the hostages in?" Thorne asked. "I count, what, three main buildings and a couple sheds?"

"Yes," Darren said. He directed a laser pointer at a building on the east side of the compound. "This is where the hostages are being kept, if our intel is correct."

The whole Team laughed at that, all having had their own experience with "correct" intel. Darren smiled at them, liking how the negatives brought them together. It made for a stronger Team. If they were successful, then he couldn't wait to see what they were like after the mission. Battle always brought soldiers even closer.

"Right, if our intel is correct, then the hostages are in there," Darren continued. "The building next to it is the barracks and kitchen/mess. The last building is Daacad's personal residence. He has several children by multiple wives."

"Multiple wives?" Max asked.

"Yes," Darren said, "Daacad, like many Muslims, believes he honors God by procreating."

"Watch out for the sister wives," Shane said, "they bite."

"You will have to watch out for them," Darren said. "We can't have any non-hostile casualties on this mission. That is a stipulation by the company. And you only engage when engaged."

"Wait...what?" Shane asked. "If I'm on overwatch and I see a hostile coming towards the Team with an AK-47, you're saying I can't take him out until he starts shooting?"

"Blast him," Max said, "who's gonna know?"

"Your goggles," Thorne said, "they'll know, right?"

"Very good, Mr. Thorne," Mr. Ballantine said. "I was wondering who would figure that out first. I'm pleased it was you."

"Oh, shit," Lucy said, "the goggles record and transmit too?"

"Yep," Darren nodded, "so do all the scopes and sights on your rifles."

"Whoa, whoa, whoa!" Max and Shane said at the same time.

"No one messes with my rig," Shane said.

"Mine either," Max said. "You hired us to do a job and part of that is we bring our own tools."

"Your tools are being retrofitted right this moment," Mr. Ballantine said. "There is an armory below deck with three techs. You dream it, they build it. Trust me, you won't know your gear has been touched."

"Uh, they weren't part of the tour," Shane said. "Where are they?"

"Below deck," Darren said, "that's all you need to know." He sighed and then sat down. "Okay, listen up, because I'll only say this once. This mission is your audition. You nail it and you get the keys to the theater. You bomb and you get the hook."

"Why the theater metaphor?" Max asked.

"I'd personally prefer some type of medical metaphor," Shane said.

"Like what?" Max asked.

"Like you get one chance to keep the patient alive," Shane said, "you screw up and the patient dies and you lose your license. How's that?"

"That wouldn't work," Lucy said, "Doctors don't lose their licenses because a patient dies. That's stupid."

"Sure they can," Shane argued, "if it's their fault the patient dies."

"Yeah, but there's a whole review process," Max said, "they don't just get fired right then."

"Oh, and we will?" Shane asked. "Is Mr. Ballantine going to be standing on the beach like Donald Trump yelling, 'You're fired!'? Is that what's going to happen?" Shane looked at Ballantine. "That's not what's going to happen, is it?"

"Shut up," Kinsey said, quiet until that point. "Let Darren speak, please. I'd like to get this briefing over and get back to sleep. I have a feeling the next few days are going to be grueling. More so for me than for all of you."

"Thank you, 'Sey,'" Darren said. Bobby visibly bristled at the use of the nickname. Kinsey smiled at that.

"Fuck you, 'Ren,'" Kinsey said, "but please, go on."

Darren stood back up. "I wouldn't have picked any of you if I thought you'd fail." He glanced quickly at Kinsey. "So don't fail."

"And where will you and Ms. Darby be?" Kinsey asked.

"Darby," Darby said, "just Darby."

"What are your qualifications exactly?" Kinsey asked, turning the focus on the woman seated by Ballantine. "You can fly a chopper, so good for you. Where'd you learn that? What's your training?"

"Darby doesn't need to explain herself to you, Ms. Thorne," Mr. Ballantine said. "She is well qualified. That's all you need---"

Darby held up her hand. "I was Mossad for a while then switched up to Sayeret when I got bored with the paperwork."

"Wait," Max said, leaning forward, his eyes locked on Darby, "you just 'switched' to the Sayeret because you were bored? That's like the fucking Israeli Special Forces, right?"

"Yes," Darby nodded. "I was with Sayeret 13 at first, and then moved up to Sayeret Matkal. Similar to your Delta Force and SEAL Team Six. Is that qualified enough?"

"Will you marry me?" Max asked.

"No," Darby said, "not a chance."

"Is it because of my face?" Max asked.

"It's because you are breathing," Darby replied.

"I will keep asking," Max smiled.

"He will," Shane agreed.

"I'll keep rejecting you," Darby replied.

"Now that we've settled that," Darren said, "can I continue?"

"Can you?" Shane asked.

Mr. Ballantine laughed. "You SEALs are nothing, if not entertaining."

"There is other intel we need," Darren said, "on the other side of town. Darby and I will be obtaining that while you free the hostages."

"Uh, can we address the 100 ton elephant in the room?" Lucy asked. "Not that I want to stir anything up."

"Don't you mean the 100 ton sea elephant?" Max asked. "Because that's part of why we are here, is to find Ditcher's white whale."

"No, no," Lucy said, "I don't care about that. That's after the mission and I'll have been paid by then. Who cares if Ahab wants to hunt a whale?"

"It's not white, and I'm not Ahab," Darren said. "This thing is real. I bet my life on that."

"You're betting our lives on that," Thorne said, "because if it wasn't dangerous, you wouldn't need us."

"I need you for the hostage extraction," Darren said.

"Yes, you do," Thorne said, "but that could have been a one and done operation. Paid us and let us go on our way. But you want us on board to help find this whale."

"Mr. Ballantine insisted on a security Team while we are researching," Darren said. "I don't know if you heard, but there's pirates in these here waters."

"Uh, that's not what I was talking about," Lucy said, glancing over at Kinsey.

"Oh, right," Darren said.

"Yeah, right," Bobby said, "why is she part of this?"

"Because I want her to be," Mr. Ballantine said. "I've read her file and I believe she was a political casualty. She should have made it through SQT and been the first woman SEAL. The fact she wasn't is a shame and since Mr. Thorne insisted she come along, I decided we should actually have her work for the large sum of money she is to be paid."

"But she's a junkie," Lucy said. "No offense, Kinsey."

"None taken," Kinsey said as she looked everyone in the eye, one by one, "I'm the first to admit it."

"So?" Bobby said. "You want a medal for that? Having you on the op will jeopardize everyone. You may have come close to being a SEAL, but you aren't one. That's a liability in of itself."

"Says the Coast Guard pilot," Kinsey laughed. "How dedicated are you? I heard you wouldn't even suck a cock to keep your job. I would have sucked ten cocks to become a SEAL. Fuck knows I've sucked more than that being a junkie."

The room went still and quiet. The only sounds were the waves slapping against the ship and the slight hum of the motors. Other than that, a mouse could have farted and it would have sounded like a fog horn.

"Oh, Jesus, Kins," Thorne said finally, "really?"

"Fact of life, Daddy," Kinsey said. "I fucked a few guys too. Kept me in smack and booze. But none of that shit matters since there isn't a pinch of heroin on this ship. I can wish all I want, but I'm getting clean. Gunnar has me on some new cocktail which will keep the worst side effects at bay and allow me to train. Which is what I plan to do until the mission. I plan on training."

"You're still a junkie," Bobby said, "which means you can't be trusted. And even if you do have an eight day training montage that whips you into super perfect shape, at the end of it all, you can't be trusted. You're useless to the Team."

"Care to step outside and let me show you how useless I am?" Kinsey asked.

"Seriously?" Bobby laughed, looking around the table. "Is she serious?"

"She sounds like it," Max said as he stood up. Shane joined him.

Thorne stood up too. "I'd like to see this. Where should we do this? Is there a gym?"

"There is," Darby said, "below deck. But the empty helipad will work also."

"Let's go," Kinsey said, standing and gesturing to the door, "or are you afraid a junkie will beat you?"

"D? Are you going to let this happen?" Bobby asked. "I don't want to fight her!"

"Yeah, D? Are you going to let this happen?" Kinsey laughed. "You were a SEAL, right? You know once a challenge is thrown down you can't back off. If she can't take care of herself, then how can any of us trust her to take care of her job? Or us on the mission? She chickens now, and she'll chicken then."

"Fucking A," Darren said, looking to Mr. Ballantine. The man just shrugged and smiled. "You went after her, B. You called her out. I'm sorry, but you made your bed. That's just how it works on a Team."

"But this isn't the SEALs!" Bobby protested. "And I'm not a SEAL. I don't have to play by old macho rules!"

"You're not a SEAL?" Kinsey laughed. "Isn't that part of the argument against me? You come outside and take your beating like a woman or I have a feeling we'll be using Darby as our extraction pilot while you take a row boat back to Cape Town."

Bobby scanned the faces and found no one, not even Lucy, backing her up. She had called Kinsey out and even though she detested the arcane boys' club rules, she knew she had to put her money where her mouth was.

"Fine," Bobby said, stomping out to the deck, "come take your fucking beat down."

"You wish, bitch," Kinsey laughed, following close behind.

"Now we're talking," Max said.

"Hooyah!" Shane hooted.

"Don't let them get too hurt," Mr. Ballantine said as he took Darby by the arm.

She looked down at his hand and he released it. "They'll get as hurt as they get," Darby said. "You wanted to play with toy soldiers and I warned you what could happen. This will not be the last grudge fight you witness. Men and women trained at this level will let off steam however they can, even if it means beating each other bloody."

"She's right about that," Thorne said as he pushed past.

They all hurried out into the sea air and over to the second helipad. It was smaller than the one the Wyrm sat on, which told all of them it was designed for lighter choppers such as maybe a MH-6 Little Bird. Kinsey and Bobby stepped up onto the helipad, watching each other closely.

"I blame you for this," Thorne said. "You should have told me one of the Team members was your girlfriend."

"She's not my girlfriend," Darren said. "We have a very loose, casual thing. I honestly didn't expect this."

"But you knew I was bringing Kinsey," Thorne said, "and you know how Kinsey gets."

"Which is why I protested from the start," Darren replied. "I'm sorry I didn't give you details, but would it have mattered if I did?"

Thorne shrugged. "Probably not."

"It'll be good for them," Max said, eavesdropping. "They'll get a chance to stretch their claws and maybe get some of that estrogenic rage out."

"You're a pig," Lucy said, "I thought I was going to be away from guys like you."

"It wasn't intended to be derogatory," Max said. "I would have said the same thing if two guys were up there, except I'd have substituted testosterone for estrogen." Max smiled at her. "What's its name?"

"Excuse me?" Lucy asked.

"The chip on your shoulder," Max answered, "have you named it?"

"Asshole," Lucy said and moved to the other side of the helipad as Kinsey and Bobby squared off.

"Making friends?" Shane asked.

"You know I am," Max said. "I just have a way- OH, DAMN!"

Everyone gasped as Kinsey came in fast and low and punched Bobby right in the gut, doubling the woman over so Kinsey could then land a hard uppercut to the jaw. Bobby's entire body rocked back and she fell on her ass hard.

"There," Kinsey said, "satisfied?"

She didn't get another word out as Bobby swept her legs from under her. Kinsey tumbled to the helipad, but was back up on her feet before Bobby could get up and close the distance. The women squared off again.

"She's sweating hard," Darby said.

"Which one?" Shane asked.

But they all knew which one. Kinsey was already looking tired even though the fight had barely begun. On the other hand, Bobby was not even winded and had recovered from the gut shot quickly. They began to circle each other and Darby sighed.

"This is boring," she said, "I'll be in the armory."

"I'll escort you, my lady," Max said.

"No, you won't," Darby said.

"The armory is off limits until after the mission," Mr. Ballantine said. "Once you prove yourself, then the rest of the Beowulf II will be opened to you."

"That sucks," Max said.

They all groaned as Bobby jabbed with her right, feinted with her left, then came in with two body blows that sent Kinsey reeling. She tried to recover, but Bobby didn't waste her momentum and pushed forward, landing blow after blow until Kinsey was down on her knees.

"Done?" Bobby asked.

Kinsey tried her own leg sweep, but Bobby jumped over it and then came down with a punch to Kinsey's face. The combination of strength and gravity sent Kinsey to the deck, laying her out flat on the helipad.

"And that's that," Shane said. "Help me carry her to the infirmary."

"I think we need to add this job to our resume," Max said, "wounded cousin carriers."

"Fuck you all," Kinsey mumbled.

***

"Couldn't help yourself, huh?" Gunnar asked as he swabbed the deep gash that split Kinsey's left eyebrow. "I shouldn't be surprised. You were always in more fights than any of us growing up."

"Because I was always rescuing your asses," Kinsey said, "especially yours."

"You, your brother, Darren, even the Reynolds," Gunnar said. "I never was too much of a brawler."

"Still have mad knife skills?" Kinsey asked. "Or did you give up on those when you joined Darren's snipe hunt?"

"I'm even better with a blade now than I was then," Gunnar said. "Not much else to do on a ship. Actually saved our butt in Manila one time. I'd cut three guys before they got the picture that Darren and I were leaving that bar unharmed. Well, almost unharmed. Darren had already had a tooth knocked out. Luckily, I found it under a table and he was able to get it put back in."

"Ow! Watch it!" Kinsey snapped as Gunnar started to suture the gash.

"Oh, sorry," Gunnar said. "Did you want a shot of anesthetic? I know you don't like needles, so I figured you'd just take the pain." Kinsey gave him an exasperated look. "What? You always hated needles when we were younger. I know I gave you a shot earlier, but you were pretty desperate for that."

"Yeah, I've since gotten over that fear," Kinsey said.

"Oh, right," Gunnar smirked, "my bad."

They sat there in silence until Gunnar was finished stitching her up.

"You still in love with him?" Kinsey asked.

"Don't, Kins," Gunnar said, "I don't need to be teased."

"I'm not teasing," she replied. "I'm asking. Are you still in love with him?"

"I'll always love him," Gunnar said.

"Not what I'm asking."

"I don't know," Gunnar answered. "I gave up on that a long time ago. I had to push it down and bury it. So I don't really know how I feel."

Kinsey slid off the exam table and smiled weakly. "I know exactly how you feel."

"Yeah, I guess you do," Gunnar said. "How about you?"

Kinsey shrugged. "When I'm not busy hating him, I guess I do still love him."

"Between Darren and getting kicked out of SQT, no wonder you started using," Gunnar said.

"I started using because I was a weak pussy and didn't want to face that," Kinsey said. "Now I guess I have to."

"Speaking of," Gunnar said, "I'll give you another shot. We'll do two more tomorrow then wean down to one a day. It'll keep you steady. We'll work on a full detox after the mission."

"Thanks, Gun," Kinsey said and hugged him, wincing at the pain in her body. "I know I love *you*."

"You too, Kins," Gunnar said. "Now, try not to get your ass kicked tomorrow, okay? Doctor's orders."

"I'll try, but no promises," Kinsey said.

She left the infirmary and wound her way to her quarters, grateful she only ran into some of the crew and not anyone from the Team. She locked her door, stripped down, and crawled into her bunk. Despite the fifty billion thoughts rushing through her head, she drifted off to sleep in just a few minutes.

It could hardly be called a restful sleep, as her mind continued to race, just on a subconscious level. She found herself back at SQT and being called into the command office. Her dream self didn't know what was about to happen, but the real Kinsey did and she tried to fight it. She didn't want to step through those doors again and see the stern disappointed faces staring at her from across the table.

Her subconscious must have heard her plea, because instead of the SQT command seated across the table, ready to hand out its disciplinary action and expel her from the training, she found herself face to face with several versions of her old dealer. "Old" dealer, because he had died a horrible death by castration months earlier.

"You need a fix, sunshine?" the men said in unison. "We got what you need."

They were in Navy dress, but when they stood up, Kinsey could see they didn't have pants on. They were all naked from the waist down and bleeding from ragged holes in their crotches.

"Come on, sunshine," the men droned, "just give it a kiss. Ain't nothin' you haven't done before. Just open wide and blow!"

Dream Kinsey ran from the room, shoving past people that she thought were fellow trainees, but as she looked closer, she could see that all of them had faces of her dealers. Dealers that were dead; all having been found mutilated in alleys, in their apartments, their cars, on the sidewalk. Dream Kinsey, as well as Dreaming Kinsey, realized that her dealers didn't live long.

She ran and ran, shoving the dead dealers out of the way, in a mad dash for the door to the outside. Just as she reached for the handle, something clicked in her brain; a realization that---

"WAKEY WAKEY, NEWBIE!"

"GET YOUR ASS OUT OF BED AND ON DECK NOW!"

Kinsey bolted upright, her head screaming as all the blood rushed there, compounding the hangover feeling she had from withdrawal.

"What the fuck?" she shouted as she saw two figures silhouetted against her hatchway. "Fuck off!"

"NO FUCKING OFF TODAY, NEWBIE!"

"GET YOUR SHIT TOGETHER!"

It was her cousins, both armed with bullhorns that were rousting her. She flipped them off then turned over and yanked her blanket up over head. Hands grabbed her, wrapped her tight in the blanket, and yanked her from her bunk.

"Fuckers!" Kinsey yelled as she tried to kick free, but the blanket was too secure.

"Don't even try, newbie," Max said. "This isn't the first time we've done this."

"Feel lucky we woke you and are only using your blanket," Shane added as they dragged her from her quarters and into the hallway. "We could have duct taped you in your sleep."

"Then shaved your head," Max said.

"Which we may still do," Shane continued. "That multi-colored rainbow spiky haired thing gives me a headache."

"I am so going to kick your fucking asses when I get out of here!" Kinsey shouted as the brothers hauled her up the stairs and out onto the upper deck. "Do you hear me? Do you?"

"We all hear you," Thorne said, when the Reynolds dropped her on the deck. "We also all know you aren't even close to ready for the mission. So we're going to get you ready. Together as a Team."

"This is bullshit," Bobby said, "why are we punished because she's out of shape?"

Thorne and the Reynolds turned to Bobby and smiled.

"You think you're in shape?" Thorne asked.

"I'm in way better shape than she is," Bobby said, pointing to Kinsey as the woman struggled to get free of her blanket.

"Not going to argue that," Thorne said, "but just because your shit doesn't stink, doesn't mean it ain't still shit."

"Still using that line?" Darren laughed as he walked up to the group with a mug of coffee. The sun had just started to crest over the horizon and the world was illuminated in pink and blue. "I thought you'd have changed it by now."

"No need to retire a good thing," Thorne said.

"So why'd they retire you, Uncle Vinny?" Max asked.

"Nice one," Shane said.

"Ha fucking ha," Thorne said. "Push-ups. One hundred. Now."

"Shit," Max said, but complied, as did his brother.

"I'll be on the bridge if you need me," Darren said.

"Where the fuck do you think you're going?" Thorne said as he pushed up his sleeves and dropped to his hands. "We're all doing push-ups. Then sit ups. Then pull ups. Then push-ups. Then laps. And we'll start it all over again until lunch."

"Yeah, well, I'm the captain and I'm needed on the bridge," Darren said.

"I got it covered, Captain," Lake said, as he leaned against the bridge hatch and looked down at them all. "You keep playing with your friends. Don't worry about us."

"Sorry, I'm late," Darby said as she sprinted up to them and began doing push-ups. "Won't happen again."

"I appreciate that, Darby," Thorne huffed between pushes. "Captain Chambers?"

Darren looked at Bobby and Lucy and shrugged, then dropped. The two women joined, which left only Kinsey, still struggling with her blanket.

When she was free, she started to get up and walk away, but the image of her old dealer's face on the SQT brass's heads made her stop. The thought of going back to her life of blowing losers for junk didn't sit well. The revelation surprised her. Not that she loved being a junkie, just that the need to get high wasn't what was at the forefront of her mind. As she watched everyone start to struggle and grunt, that old feeling she had when she first started BUD/S came to her.

She had something to prove.

"Fuck this shit," she said and got down on the deck, "fuck all if I'm going to let you fucking losers beat me."

She didn't know if it was because she weighed so little, or because she began to think of each push-up as a hit of smack or shot of booze, but soon she was pacing everyone else. When her arms began to scream, and the track marks started to itch and burn, she used that to keep her going. Every ounce of discomfort became fuel for her need to prove that she was more than what they all thought she was.

Before she knew it, she was on her back doing sit ups. Then up and grabbing one of the many bars that spanned parts of the ship. Pull ups almost defeated her as she barely eked out ten. But she regained her confidence on the run, easily lapping her father before they were all back down on the deck and pushing up and down.

When the mess bell rang for lunch, Team Grendel nearly had to crawl below deck to the mess. Drenched in sweat, their chests heaving, desperate for oxygen, the Team basically fell into the room.

"Chow's there," Popeye grinned as he sat at one of the tables munching on a granola bar. "Get in line. Ain't no table service here."

"We know the drill," Max gasped, barely able to hold the lunch tray as one of the cooks slapped various foods upon it. The smell made his mouth water, but the thought of running on a full stomach after lunch nearly made him gag.

Which is what they all did as soon as their trays were tossed in the wash tubs and they were back above deck. There was plenty of gagging and puking to go around. Even Thorne did his fair share, while also barking at them all to push, push, push to the limit.

And that is what they did for the next seven days.

They did physical training, ran mock assaults using the various decks of the Beowulf II, fine tuned techniques, and competed against each other at everything, trying to push someone over the edge. But none broke, not even Kinsey. She just grew gradually stronger and stronger, which built some confidence in the rest of the Team.

But just some. They all knew she was the weak link.

On the eighth day, they did not rest. Instead, they sat in the conference room on the upper deck and went over the plan again and again.

"Jennings brings us in here," Thorne said, pointing to the intended destination on the beach nearest their target. "We come in wet and hump it to the compound. This is residential area, so we'll have to be quiet as shit, but I don't expect much resistance."

"The area has been terrorized by Daacad's men for years," Mr. Ballantine said. "They see your guns and they'll duck and cover. No one wants trouble. This isn't Afghanistan. There aren't Taliban sympathizers everywhere to mess with the mission."

"But we can't take that for granted, right?" Max asked.

"Exactly," Thorne said. "With these guys, we can't take anything for granted. We go in quietly and hit hard. We keep to the schedule and we'll be on the Wyrm in under sixty minutes. Then we pick up Darren and Darby at the rendezvous point."

"Still not sure why they're hitting a different target," Shane said. "Why wouldn't they be with us? What's at the other target?"

"It's something that will be shared after the op is complete," Darren said, "but not before then."

"Whale," Max whispered to his brother.

"More like whale shit," Shane whispered back.

"Gentlemen? Care to share?" Thorne asked.

"Nope," Max replied.

"I'm good," Shane said.

"Then let's go over it again," Thorne said. "After that, I want everyone to hit their bunks and get some sleep. We'll need all of our energy for this op. With our small numbers, there is no room for error."

CHAPTER FIVE: THE OP

As the sun set over the Indian Ocean, the peaceful quiet and calm of the sea was broken by the sound of helicopter rotors. Just having awoken from a day's sleep, Kinsey stretched on the upper deck, working out the kinks in her muscles, as she searched the sky for the source of the noise.

"Good," Mr. Ballantine said, coming up behind her, "they're here."

Kinsey smiled at the tone of his voice which belied the fact he didn't think it was good at all.

"Company?" Kinsey asked.

"You have no idea how right you are," Mr. Ballantine said, giving her a tired smile, "we all have our hoops to jump through."

The chopper –a MH-6 Little Bird- began to circle the ship and drew the attention of the others. Mr. Ballantine gave a short wave as the helo put down on the second helipad and three figures hurried away from the rotor wash and down the steps to him.

"What's with the suits?" Max asked, a mug of coffee in his hand as he stepped up next to Kinsey.

"Don't know," she replied, "but boss man isn't happy."

"Watchers," Darby said, her own coffee to her lips.

Kinsey looked over her shoulder and could see quite a few members of the crew either on the upper deck or peering out of windows from the bridge. Everyone looked surprised by the arrival of the helo.

"What do you mean?" Kinsey asked. "Watchers for what?"

"For us," Darby said, "for the op."

"What does that mean?" Shane asked, joining the rest.

"It means that everyone answers to someone else," Darby said.

"Yeah, that's about what Ballantine said," Kinsey added.

As soon as the visitors were clear, the helo lifted into the air and took off. Everyone noticed it was headed further out to sea and not towards land.

"We have a sister ship out there?" Shane asked.

"Company ship, probably," Darby said. "Hard to say. Nothing is ever consistent or repeated. Keeps things under wraps that way."

"Huh," Shane replied. It was a sentiment they all shared.

"Fuck," Darren said as he walked past everyone. "Not looking forward to this." He reached Mr. Ballantine and the visitors and extended his hand. "Captain Chambers, welcome aboard the Beowulf II."

"Interim captain," a woman, dressed in an expensive silk shirt, black slacks, and shoes not even close to appropriate for ocean work, said. "How your op goes tonight will dictate if you are to remain the captain of this ship."

"Uh, what?" Darren asked, looking at Mr. Ballantine.

"Not here, Darren," Mr. Ballantine responded.

"Where shall we set up?" a diminutive man asked. He clutched a leather briefcase to his chest, rumpling his suit considerably. By the pallor of his skin, it was easy to see he didn't enjoy the helo ride. "We have work to do before the demonstration."

"I'll show you the way to the command center," Mr. Ballantine said.

The third person, tall and immaculately presented as if he'd just stepped out of Barney's, nodded to the Team as they walked by. They all nodded back, turning and watching as the visitors went below deck and disappeared from sight.

"What was that happy horse shit?" Thorne asked as he joined the Team. "What did I miss?"

"Apparently we have a command center," Max said.

"Anyone else turned on by the ball buster?" Shane asked.

Kinsey turned to Darby. "Spill it. Who are they?"

Darby looked at them and sighed. "The woman is Diane Horace. She's in charge of Finance. The small guy that looked like he pissed himself is Jeremy Longbottom. He's Insurance."

The Reynolds couldn't help but laugh.

"Yes, I am sure he regrets his name also," Darby said. "The tall man is Stefan Perry. He's Legal."

"Finance?" Thorne asked. "Insurance? Legal? What the fuck does any of that mean?"

"They head up those departments in the company," Darby said. "Since the company is in the business of solving problems, they are here to watch our op and make sure we aren't creating any new ones."

"The audition," Max smiled, "now I get it."

"Way better than the stupid medical analogy," Shane said.

"Much better," Max agreed.

"Are you going to let them just watch and judge us?" Kinsey asked her father.

"Doesn't fucking matter to me," he shrugged. "There's always someone watching ops in the SEALs. I could give a shit. We have a job to do and we'll do it. They like to watch, then good for them."

"I like to watch," Max said to Darby.

"Yes, I guessed as much," Darby responded, "it explains a lot."

"Because he's a sniper, right?" Shane said.

"Because he's a douche," Darby said and walked away.

"I will marry her one day," Max said, "as God is my witness, I will!"

"Masochist," Shane said.

"Enough crap," Thorne said. "Go over your gear, triple check everything. I'm going to meet with Jennings and make sure he's up to the task tonight."

"Got it," Max said.

"Will do," Shane replied.

"I didn't like that Darren seemed to be in the dark," Kinsey said.

"Me either, but nothing we can do about it," Thorne responded. "It's his ship, he has to deal with the red tape and bullshit that comes with it. We just have to kill bad guys and rescue good guys."

***

The cold spray invigorated Kinsey as the Zodiac bounced across the waves just off the Somali coast. She sat at the bow, her modified M-4 cradled in her arms. The rest of Team Grendel sat behind her, all eyes on the few twinkling lights of the city they were about to infiltrate.

It was 0213 when Jennings cut the motor and let the Zodiac drift through the surf and onto the rocky beach. The Team silently jumped out of the boat and then pushed it back into the waves so Jennings could race back to the Beowulf II before being spotted. Everything from there on depended on them not being found out and targeted.

They sprinted up the beach and took cover in a thatch of thorny bushes close to a small gravel road. Each of them were outfitted with their NVGs (night vision goggles), a modified M-4, a Sig Sauer P220 pistol, body armor, and pouches filled with their various kits that covered almost every contingency from cash they could use to buy their way out of town if the extraction went bad to morphine and med kits. The only variation in gear was Shane's sniper rifle, which he had strapped across his back.

They had thought of everything they could and it was all up to fate at that point.

"We slide through those houses," Darren said, "then Darby and I split off."

"Stay on schedule," Thorne said. "We'll be bringing some heat with us when we come for you."

"We know," Darren said.

Thorne looked around at each member of the Team, making sure they were set. Confident they were as ready as they ever would be, he slowly moved towards the buildings in a low crouch. Once they hit the houses, which were just glorified shacks, they straightened up and made their way slowly through and around the trash and detritus of the small African city.

It didn't take long for them to realize they were in a Third World country. The smells, the garbage, the scavenged materials used for the housing, all of it was indicative of a people living a life of subsistence. That was good for the Team. It meant less loyalty to the pirate gang. There would be tribal ties, but on a deep level, no one wanted to help those that didn't like to share the spoils.

When they made it past the first set of shacks, Darren and Darby split off, moving from shadow to shadow off to their target. The Team watched them go, their bodies illuminated clearly in the NVGs, and made sure they made it to their route without trouble, then continued on to the compound.

It took them longer to get to the compound than they would have liked, and Thorne felt the pressure of their timetable. Keeping to com silence, he gestured for everyone to pick up the pace and started to hump it double time through the maze of shacks and mud houses. They gained some of their lost time, but not much, by the time they reached the compound.

The objective was to get in through a side gate undetected, so Shane could get onto the roof of the first building and set up an overwatch to cover the rest of the Team. The compound had the only multistory buildings other than the city municipal buildings, so they had to get inside first before Shane could get a good position. Having him watching their backs was key to the success of the op.

When they got to the side gate, they were surprised to find it unlocked and open. They quickly glanced around, scanning the area for guards or a gang member that was out for a night walk. They saw nothing and quickly entered the compound, glad for their luck. A locked gate would have meant having to blow the lock and risk detection right away.

Once inside, Shane hurried to his position, as the Team crouched in the shadow of the large wall that surrounded the compound. There was no fire escape on the building, but that wasn't a problem for Shane. He was able to find foot and hand holds in the window sills and exposed bricks of the building. Its lack of upkeep made it easily scalable.

"Position," Shane said over the com, the first words any of them had uttered since Darren and Darby split off.

"Good luck," Mr. Ballantine's voice said over the com, "stay safe."

Thorne chuckled at that last part. Easy for Ballantine to say, all safe out at sea, miles from the action.

The Team headed for the building where the hostages were kept. Or where they thought they were kept. They only had company intel to go off of, and if that intel was as good as what the military had always provided, then who knew where the hostages were kept.

Max tried the door, hoping the knob was unlocked. It wasn't.

"Breaching charge?" Max asked.

Thorne nodded and Max pulled a strip of explosives from his pack. He pulled off the adhesive, pressed the charge right next to the lock, turned, and ducked his head. Kinsey and Thorne turned away also as two seconds later, there was a small blast and the door swung inward.

Max was first in and he swung his rifle to the right as Kinsey followed, covering the left. Two men stood there in the small room, AK-47s in their hands, their eyes wide with shock and surprise. Kinsey took down one as Max took the other, the suppressors on their rifles keeping the sound of the shots down to a quiet cough. Thorne came in behind them and pushed forward towards a door at the back of the room; Kinsey and Max were right on his heels.

"You have four hostiles heading your way," Shane said, "take them?"

"Not unless they engage," the voice of Stefan Perry said over the com.

"Get off my line," Thorne growled. "Any of you interrupt or give orders again during this op and I'll personally give you an M-4 enema when we get back aboard."

"There's hardly a need for threats," Jeremy Longbottom said.

"Let's respect Commander Thorne's request, shall we?" Mr. Ballantine said.

"Gee, thanks Ballantine," Thorne said.

"Any time, Thorne," Mr. Ballantine replied.

"Hostiles have spotted the breached door," Shane said. "Heading your way fast."

"I consider that engagement," Thorne said, "light 'em up."

Shane tracked the first man, aiming for the center of the man's back. He gently squeezed the trigger. When the break came, he shifted targets, repeating the shot three more times. All four hit the dirt, massive holes in their torsos from the .338.

"Clear," Shane said, "but they know we're here now."

Even with the suppressor on his sniper rifle, the .338 was too powerful to be quiet. Unsuppressed, it would have sounded like a small cannon, but with the suppressor, it sounded like a .22. That was still loud enough to attract attention. The door to the barracks opened and several men came rushing out. As soon as they saw their fallen comrades, they began shouting and cursing.

The compound was instantly flooded by light.

"Fuck," Shane said, flipping up his NVGs, almost blinded by the sudden light. "No one said anything about those!"

"What the fuck, Ballantine?" Thorne growled. "It's Friday Fucking Night Lights out there!"

"We didn't know," Mr. Ballantine replied, "the lights must be a new install."

"Fuck," Shane said again. "One of them has a brain. My hide is blown. Engaging with extreme prejudice."

"You've always wanted to say that, huh?" Max said as he tried the door at the back of the small room. Locked also.

"I have always wanted to say that," Shane agreed.

They could hear the .338 go fully active. AK-47s responded quickly. Men were shouting and screaming. And sounded like they were dying too.

The door in front of them was obviously cheap laminate and Max gave it a hard kick next to the jamb. It burst open and he moved inside quickly.

"Jesus fuck," Max said as he saw the scene before him, "they're fucking dead."

They were. Every hostage in the room lay in congealed pools of their own blood, their throats slit from ear to ear. Each corpse had handcuffs on their wrist and ankles, securing them to bolts in the concrete floor.

The Team could hear gagging from the command center.

"Get off the fucking com if you can't handle it!" Thorne barked. "Don't you fucking puke in my ear!" The gagging noise was cut short. "Bug out! Command, we need immediate extraction! The op is a bust!"

"I only count eleven hostages," Diane Horace said over the com. "There should be twelve. The captain must be in the main building with Daacad."

"You don't know that," Thorne said. "We don't know that. Mission is off. Get us the fuck out of here."

"Your job is to rescue the hostages, Mr. Thorne," Ms. Horace said. "There is still one more hostage."

"Is she serious?" Max asked as the sounds of AK-47s from the compound increased. "It is getting hot as shit out there. She wants us to wade through that and take another building?"

"That's exactly what I want you to do, Mr. Reynolds," Ms. Horace replied, "or no extraction."

"You fucking cunt," Kinsey snapped, about to say more, but stopped when her father shook his head.

"We're on it," Thorne said. "Shane?"

"I got it covered out here," Shane said, "but don't come out the front door. You'll walk right into a six pack of fuckers."

"Window," Max said as he pointed to a barred window at the back of the room.

He quickly set explosive strips on all four sides and then waved Kinsey and Thorne back. They each unceremoniously flattened themselves out next to a corpse, taking whatever cover the bodies would provide. The concrete and brick around the window exploded and showered them with debris. The barred grate covering the window slammed against a wall and clattered to the floor.

Max and Kinsey hopped out through the hole where the window used to be, landing in a small alley between the building and the compound wall. It was barely wide enough for them to move and their gear kept getting hung up on chunks of the wall, as they hurried towards the end of the building. Thorne was right behind them, covering their six.

Max checked the corner and gave a thumbs up. All three sprinted in a crouch to the wall of the next building, which according to intel, should have been Daacad's quarters. Each laughed internally, knowing how the intel had turned out for them so far that night.

Out in the courtyard of the compound, men were falling everywhere as Shane put round after round in their chests, their bellies, their heads.

"Gonna run out of ammo soon," Shane said. "How's that extraction coming?"

"The extraction is not---" Ms. Horace began to say, but was instantly cut off.

"Inbound," Bobby called over the com. "ETA five minutes."

"Who authorized that?" Ms. Horace said. "I specifically told you to find and rescue the hostage first!"

"Mr. Ballantine?" Thorne asked. "If you don't mind."

"Of course," Mr. Ballantine replied.

The audio connection to the command center was severed.

"Good," Thorne said. "We proceed into the building, but if we haven't found the hostage by the time the Wyrm is here, then we are gone. This has gone south fast."

"So we quit?" Kinsey asked.

"We aren't quitting," Thorne said as he squeezed the trigger and put two rounds in the head of a hostile that had turned and was about to fire. "We're living."

"Feels like quitting," Kinsey said. She dropped two hostiles then turned as Max tapped her shoulder.

"Back here," he said, nodding towards an alcove at the end of the building.

They hustled back to the alcove, which covered a side door, and all took a knee, their rifles aimed towards the courtyard. Each of them dropped two hostiles. Max shouldered his rifle and tested the door knob, while Kinsey and Thorne covered him. Instantly, gunfire erupted and Max fell onto his back as bullets punched holes in the door and flew over his head, just missing his skull.

"Fuck!" he yelled.

Thorne turned and fired into the door then stood and kicked it in, continuing his fire as he rushed into a kitchen.

"Ah, shit," Thorne said, his rifle covering the body of a boy that couldn't have been more than eleven years old. The boy held an AK-47 against his bleeding chest, a photo of Kanye West on his t-shirt, his mouth opening and closing like a dying fish. But he wasn't a fish, he was a young boy. It wasn't the first time Thorne had killed a child combatant, but that didn't make it any easier.

"He fired first," Kinsey said at his shoulder, "you had no choice."

"There's always a choice," Thorne said, "just not always a good one."

"I doubt they have him in here," Max said, looking past the dying boy at the rest of the kitchen. "We need to get to the courtyard."

"Hold on," Kinsey said, eyeing a small walk-in cooler at the back of the room. "That would the perfect place to stash a hostage."

"And your holiday ham," Max said.

"They're Muslim," Shane said over the com.

"Oh, right," Max said.

The three stepped to the door, Kinsey taking one side, Thorne taking the other, as Max crouched and grabbed the handle. He gave the door a smack and ducked to the side, waiting for shots to be fired. But there was nothing. He held up three fingers, then counted down and pulled the handle.

Kinsey stepped in first, the flashlight on her rifle illuminating the empty wire shelves. And a still body, face down on the concrete floor.

"Got him!" Kinsey said as she slung her rifle and moved forward.

She pulled her pistol, keeping the body covered as she nudged her foot under the man and rolled him over. Kinsey barely had time to notice that the man was dead before something rolled out from underneath him.

"GRENADE!" she yelled, kicking the metal avocado aside as she leaped back, shielding Max and her father from the blast.

BOOM!

The concussion and heat sucked the breath from her, knocking her off her feet and into Max, and she felt a sharp pain in her right calf, but most of the blast was contained inside the cooler. The whole world was nothing but a loud ringing and she looked down into Max's face and could see him talking to her. Hands grabbed her from behind and got her on her feet.

"Kinsey!" Thorne shouted as he spun her about. "Are you hurt?"

"Hostage is dead," Max said over the com. "We're coming out, bro. You got us covered?"

"Got ya," Shane said.

"We are thirty seconds out," Bobby said.

"Get to ground, Shane," Lucy said, "I have this. Cover them down there."

Shane pulled back from the edge of the roof, secured his rifle, and sprinted to the other side of the building. He affixed a line and rappelled quickly down the side. When his boots hit the ground, he immediately put his M-4 to his shoulder and rounded the corner.

Pop. Pop, pop.

Two guys down as he made his way to the others' location.

Pop pop popopopopop.

Four more down.

He felt the heat of a bullet whiz by his cheek and he spun to the left, taking out a young man that was running at him, his AK-47 barking fire. The young man was shooting wild, screaming as he ran, and Shane placed two rounds in his chest, dropping him quickly. He heard the door behind him bang open and whirled about, coming barrel to barrel with his brother.

"Duck," Max said.

Shane didn't even think, just did. Max squeezed off three shots as Shane turned on his heels in a crouch to see two men fall as they sprinted across the courtyard.

The sound of the Wyrm filled the air and dust and dirt began to swirl as the rotor wash sent anything not nailed down tumbling about. The Team didn't need any prompting and sprinted to the Wyrm. Shane grabbed the skid and pulled himself up into the cabin as Lucy laid down a stream of cover fire. Hostiles dropped as she sprayed them with the M-240 mounted machine gun.

"Even out the weight!" Bobby yelled into the com as Shane swung around to help Max into the cabin.

The brothers took opposite sides, distributing their weight so the helo didn't list to one side. Kinsey jumped up and crawled in, then helped her father after her.

"Go!" Thorne shouted. "Go, go, go!"

Bobby took the Wyrm up and out of the compound as Shane and Max joined Lucy in sending round after round back at the hostiles. In seconds, Bobby cleared the closest building and put some distance between the Wyrm and the hostiles that were still firing.

"Time to get my boy and Darby," Bobby announced as she took the Wyrm higher above the city. "Darren? Come in. Darren?"

Thorne couldn't help but notice how the "my boy" comment rankled Kinsey.

"We don't have com with Darren and Darby," Bobby said. "Command? Are their coms down?"

"Coms are active," Mr. Ballantine responded, "they've switched channels."

"Switched channels?" Thorne asked. "What channel are they on?"

Mr. Ballantine didn't respond.

"Command?" Thorne asked again. "I repeat, what channel did they switch to?"

"Just be ready to grab them," Mr. Ballantine replied. "Don't worry about their com right now."

"What the fuck?" Shane said.

"You know, we really need call signs," Max said.

* * *

"Captain Chambers," Mr. Ballantine announced over the com. "Your ride is on the way."

Darren had just finished disassembling the third desktop and yanked the hard drive, stuffing it in his pack as Darby kept watch over the homeowners.

"Almost ready," Darren said.

"Just a heads up, Captain, they are not happy you and Darby are on a different channel," Mr. Ballantine said.

"And how did they find out?" Darren asked as he double checked the work bench the desktops had been sitting upon.

"I may have let it slip," Mr. Ballantine said. "I couldn't lie to them. They'll find out soon enough why."

The family that huddled against the wall watched Darby closely, their eyes focused on the barrel of her M-4. She showed zero emotion, keeping her face a blank slate. The father looked past Darby at Darren.

"How did you find me?" the man asked. "I wiped that iPhone."

"Don't know anything about an iPhone," Darren said. "Tracked your IP address from the YouTube video despite the proxies you have set up."

"YouTube?" the man asked. "What YouTube?" He looked over at his wife and children. One of his boys would not meet his eyes. "What did you do? What did you upload?"

"The whale," the boy whispered.

"No," the man shook his head, "how could you be so stupid? Do you know where that video came from?"

"I'd like to know where it came from?" Darren said. The man went silent. "And that's why we are taking your hard drives."

"Helo inbound," Darby said as she cocked her head. "One minute."

"Where was the video taken?" Darren asked as he secured his pack and pulled his pistol. "Can you tell me the coordinates?"

"The coordinates?" the man asked, watching the pistol carefully. "I do not know."

"Are you sure?" Darren asked, turning the pistol on the man's children. "I'm not asking again."

"I do not know," the man said, his face a mixture of fear and anger. "I would tell you if I did! But I cannot tell you what I do not know!"

Darby glanced at Darren, then at the pistol.

"Fine," Darren said, holstering the weapon. "Thought I'd try. I'll be able to get the coordinates off the geotag on the video."

The hut shook as the Wyrm hovered close by.

"Time to go," Darby said.

"Thank you, folks," Darren said, "it's been a pleasure."

Darren opened the door and Darby was right behind him, keeping her rifle trained on the family until they were out of the hut and the door was closed. She turned to follow Darren as he sprinted down the street to an open crossroads big enough for the Wyrm to come down low.

"You have some serious explaining to do," Thorne said as Darren hopped into the Wyrm.

"I know," Darren said then looked about the cabin. "Where are the hostages?"

"Dead," Kinsey answered, "all of them. They knew we were coming."

"A leak?" Darren asked, voicing a concern they were all considering.

"Maybe," Thorne said, "or they suspected a rescue and killed the hostages to set an example."

"Did we miss a ransom deadline?" Max asked.

"We missed two," Mr. Ballantine said over the com. "We thought they were bluffing. The hostages are no good to them dead."

"They're no good to us dead," Thorne replied. "Daacad just proved he will go all the way if pushed. Those corpses are now worth millions to him. He just invested in death."

The Team let that sink in for a minute. Mr. Ballantine didn't respond.

"Find what you needed?" Kinsey asked Darren.

"I did," Darren replied.

"Care to share with the rest of us?" Shane asked.

"Later," Darren said, "not yet."

"Whale," Max said.

"Whale," Shane agreed, smirking.

"Leave my boy alone," Bobby said as the Wyrm passed over the last building and headed out over the water towards the Beowulf II. "Let him have his whale."

"Your boy," Thorne said, "broke protocol and changed com channels. He can have his whale, but not at the expense of the mission."

"It didn't compromise the mission," Darren said, "and you'll get all the info back on the ship, once I've had a chance to go over it."

"I say we toss him out of the helo," Max said. "Make him swim back as punishment."

Shane leaned over and looked out the door at the dark water that passed below them. "I'm cool with that."

"Funny," Darren said, "but I'm not just the Team Leader, I'm the captain of the ship. That's mutiny and sedition." He matched Shane's smirk. "Just kidding."

"Better be," Thorne said, "because I'm Team Leader. Your com stunt proved that. Anyone disagree?"

"I say cage fight decides," Max said.

"Two douches enter," Shane laughed, "one douche leaves."

"So you two will be doing the fighting then?" Kinsey smiled.

"Good one," Lucy laughed and offered a high five which Kinsey obliged.

"Thorne is Team Leader," Mr. Ballantine said over the com. "The money decides."

"One financier enters," Max said, "everyone shuts the fuck up."

"ETA ten minutes," Bobby said.

"Too bad the op failed," Lucy said.

"Did it?" Darby asked then leaned back and closed her eyes, letting everyone know she didn't expect an answer.

***

Daacad stood on the beach, a cigarette in his hand, as he watched the Wyrm disappear across the water. His phone rang and he answered casually, seemingly unconcerned about the night's events.

"Yes?" he answered.

"They took all the drives," the caller said, "like your source said they would. I will have their ship's location shortly."

"Excellent, Kowtame," Daacad replied, "you did right by telling me Tarabi brought you the phone. I won't forget that."

"Tarabi never came to get the phone," Kowtame said.

"No, he didn't," Daacad said, "it is yours. He won't be needing it."

"Oh," Kowtame responded quietly, "thank you, Daacad."

"What are friends for?" he asked as he hung up.

He slid his phone into his pocket, took a drag on the cigarette, then turned and walked back towards the city. He had another son to say goodbye to. At least there was a whole body to bury and not just an arm.

Before he reached his compound, he pulled out a different phone and sent a text message. He tossed the butt of his cigarette away and joined the bloody chaos that his compound had become.

***

The whine of the Wyrm's rotors died down as Team Grendel made their way to the briefing room to report. While they would have rather dumped their gear and grabbed some chow and showers, Thorne wanted them to debrief immediately. He was pretty fired up over the failure of the mission, and he planned on speaking his mind to Mr. Ballantine and the rest of the company folks.

"Congratulations, Commander," Mr. Ballantine said as he came into the briefing room with Perry, Horace, and Longbottom in tow. "That was a great success."

"A what?" Thorne snapped. "A success? Are you out of your mind?"

"No, no," Max said, "he's out of his *fucking* mind. Use the proper terminology, Uncle Vinny."

"They were all dead," Kinsey snarled, "they'd been dead for a couple of days, by my guess."

"By the smell," Shane said. "Kind of a waste of a mission."

"On the contrary," Mr. Ballantine said as he gestured for everyone to take a seat.

They looked to Thorne and he nodded for them to sit. They all did, except for Darren, who was busy emptying his pack onto the table. The company folks all sat at one end by Mr. Ballantine, while Team Grendel, including Darby, sat at the other end. Kinsey didn't let the look Ballantine gave Darby slip her attention.

"We had a feeling the hostages were already dead," Mr. Ballantine said. "A source alerted us to this a few days ago. We never believed Daacad would uphold his end of the bargain if we paid him. According to our source, he wanted to kill the hostages as a warning to every shipping company out there. The man means business and any hesitancy will result in deaths."

"Then why send us?" Thorne asked as he tried to keep from exploding and rushing Ballantine. "Any one of us could have lost our lives."

"Came close a few times," Max said.

"Did it?" Mr. Ballantine said. "The video and audio we received from your NVGs told a different story. What I saw was a brand new Team on its first mission acting like a well-oiled machine. That was the real reason for the mission. I needed to see if you could be effective."

"*We* needed to see that," Ms. Horace said, nodding towards her colleagues. "Mr. Ballantine has showed us that an extraction Team on the payroll can be highly beneficial."

"Even with all of the expenses," Mr. Perry added, "Team Grendel is still cheaper than paying ransom every time a crew is taken hostage."

"And knowing you are out here could deter future attacks," Mr. Longbottom said, "and will help with the insurance underwriters."

"This really was an audition," Thorne said, shaking his head, "you didn't expect us to succeed at all."

"It would have been nice if you had," Mr. Ballantine responded, "but we didn't think that was likely. Our source assured us the crew was already dead."

"Then why keep them chained up?" Max asked. "Why didn't Daacad dispose of the bodies?"

"Like I said before," Mr. Ballantine replied, "he wanted to send a warning."

"Then he knew we were coming," Shane replied.

"You specifically?" Mr. Ballantine said. "No. But he suspected we would try something. We left hints for him to figure out. Little strategic breadcrumbs that would give him the impression that he would be raided."

"Did you leave hints before or after the hostages were killed?" Kinsey asked. "If it was before, then you killed those men, not Daacad. He saw an opportunity you dangled in front of him and he took it."

"That is possible," Mr. Ballantine said, "but highly unlikely. Something happened when they took the crew hostage. Something that changed Daacad's mind on how he would proceed. Darren?"

Darren had been busy with the hard drives, connecting them to a terminal in the corner of the briefing room. He looked up as his name was called and nodded.

"I have it here," Darren said, "it was on the first drive."

He typed a few commands and a large monitor flipped down from the ceiling. The video of the giant whale breaching started, and everyone instantly saw it was raw footage and not the YouTube video that had been circulating on the various social networking sites.

"That's that crazy whale video!" Max said. "I told you this was all about a whale."

"Not quite," Mr. Ballantine said, "this is about securing the seas for our clients and also having an extraction Team in place for when the seas are not secure enough. And trust me, they are not secure."

"And that is a whale there, yes," Darren said, "but it's nothing like anyone has ever seen. That whale shouldn't exist."

The video kept playing and went longer than what had been edited and uploaded on YouTube. They heard young Abshir yelling to his shipmate, then they saw the whale breach again. And the chunk bitten out of its tail. All hell broke loose and no one could figure out what was happening as the camera was jostled every which way.

Mr. Ballantine leaned forward, his eyes studying the screen. A large smile crept across his face.

"What the fuck was that?" Shane asked.

"A whale did that?" Max asked.

"No, didn't you see the whale's tail?" Lucy said. "Something got it."

"Yes, something did," Mr. Ballantine replied, "and what that something is, is our next mission."

"Mr. Ballantine," Ms. Horace said, "that was not what was agreed upon."

"You were to demonstrate the Team's effectiveness and then proceed with Mr. Chambers' scientific mission of finding the whale," Mr. Perry said.

"Any deviation from the original plan makes me very nervous, Mr. Ballantine," Mr. Longbottom said. "That looks like danger, not research. Danger can be very expensive."

Thorne looked at his Team and frowned.

"Anyone care to tell me what is going on?" Thorne said. "And tell us all of it, not this need to know bullshit."

"I'll tell you, Commander Thorne," Ms. Horace said. "Mr. Ballantine proposed a permanent extraction Team be part of the services we offered as a company. He was very persuasive. But part of his proposal was to hire Captain Chambers and Captain Chambers would only take the job if he could continue his research."

"Why Ditcher?" Max asked. "I mean, why *Captain Chambers*, specifically?"

"Like I said, Mr. Ballantine was very persuasive," Ms. Horace said. "He said a research vessel would be the perfect cover for an extraction Team. And Captain Chambers had gained a certain reputation that kept him off the private security, and also the oceanic research communities' radar. Also, any profits that could be made would go to the company."

"Don't remember that part," Darren frowned, eyeing Mr. Ballantine.

"You can't expect the company to foot the bill and not get some recompense, can you?" Mr. Perry smiled. "Which is why the change in direction of the research is troubling, Mr. Ballantine. And I am sure I speak for my colleagues when I say I am unsure what *exactly* that change *is*."

"How about we all get a good night's sleep and talk about this in the morning?" Mr. Ballantine proposed, holding up his hand before anyone could respond. "That will give me more time to go over the video and offer some surprising details. This change could be way better than a whale."

"Well, just as good, at least," Darren said.

"Yes, of course," Mr. Ballantine nodded. His smile betrayed the fact that he didn't quite believe that.

"Fine," Thorne said as he stood up, "I'll let you bureaucrats duke this out. I'm exhausted. You want to give us a slide show in the morning about big fish? Great. I'm going to bed."

Team Grendel all stood, grabbed their gear, and left. Kinsey looked back and saw the look of worry on Darren's face. He obviously had gotten a little more than he bargained for. She couldn't help but smile.

Good, she thought. Let him sweat it for a while.

***

"Hey," Thorne said to Kinsey as she was about to close the hatch on her quarters, "good job tonight."

"Thanks," she said.

"I mean that, Kins," Thorne said, "you performed like a true professional. You would have made a great SEAL. I'm sorry someone felt a woman shouldn't be included. If I ever find out who tampered with your blood work, I'll gut them myself."

"So tonight I proved myself, but during BUD/S and SQT, I didn't?" Kinsey asked, instantly on the defensive. "Good to know you had my back."

"Hey!" Thorne shouted. "I resigned because of what happened to you!"

"No, Dad, you resigned because it would have looked bad if you didn't," Kinsey said. "If another woman that wasn't your daughter had the same thing happen to her, you wouldn't have resigned. I was your daughter, you felt the duty to protest, and you did. Don't dress it up as something it wasn't."

Thorne started to respond then closed his mouth and shook his head. He turned away, turned back, then turned away again and walked down the hall to his quarters.

"You know what?" he said, stopping after a few feet. "You're probably right. But that doesn't detract from the fact that you did a great job tonight. That can't be denied or debated. Goodnight, Kinsey."

He rounded the corner, leaving Kinsey standing in the hatchway of her quarters. She almost thought of going after him to apologize, but didn't, and shut the hatch instead. She was beyond exhausted and needed some sleep before she messed things up more than they were.

She began to get undressed when there was a knock at the hatch.

"Hold on," she said as she threw on a robe that had been provided along with some towels and toiletries. She opened the hatch, thinking she would be giving that apology after all. "Dad, I'm sorry. I didn't mean---, Oh."

"Uh-oh," Gunnar said, "what did I miss?"

"Just daddy/daughter stuff," Kinsey smiled. She saw the small black case in Gunnar's hand and frowned. "You think I need that? The op is over. I can probably detox like a normal addict now."

"Unfortunately, that isn't true," Gunnar replied as he stepped inside and closed the hatch behind him. "While my formula helps diminish and mask the withdrawal side effects, it doesn't mean you aren't still addicted. I stop this, without a proper weaning process, and your symptoms will be ten times worse than if you had just quit cold turkey."

"You forgot to tell me that part," Kinsey said as she sat on her bunk and offered Gunnar her arm.

"Would it have made a difference in your decision?" Gunnar smiled as he swabbed the injection point, and then tied a rubber tube around her upper arm.

"No," Kinsey admitted, "I'd have agreed anyway."

"Exactly," Gunnar said, "and then there's the fact you may not have come back from the op. No need to wean then."

"Wow, thanks for the vote of confidence," Kinsey laughed.

"Any time," he grinned.

Gunnar prepared the syringe and injected Kinsey. Instantly, she started to feel more relaxed, like a weight from her shoulders, veil from her eyes, and fog in her brain were all lifted at the same time.

"Oooh, that's the stuff," she sighed, suddenly even more tired than before. "Do I have to wean off this shit?"

"Uh, yeah," Gunnar said as he untied Kinsey's arm, "especially when you respond like that. Tonight's dose was slightly less than this morning's. We'll keep doing this until I am certain you are clear."

"Really?" Kinsey asked. "For how long?"

"A week, maybe two," Gunnar said, "hard to tell. I'll monitor your reactions as I lessen the dose. As long as you don't show withdrawal symptoms, then I'll know we're on the right track."

"Oh, you hit the right track," Kinsey said, yawning as she slapped the inside of her arm with two fingers. She yawned again and had a hard time keeping her eyes open. "Damn. I need to shower, but I don't think I'll make it."

"Don't worry about it," Gunnar said. "Get some sleep. You can shower when you wake up. It's a brand new day for everyone on this ship."

"Hey, Gun?" Kinsey asked sleepily as she pulled the covers back on her bunk. "Why weren't you in the briefing room tonight? You are Chief Science Officer. Shouldn't you have been in there?"

"I wasn't invited," Gunnar said. "Mr. Ballantine likes to keep his cards close to his chest. He hasn't quite figured out what to do with me yet. Darren is Captain and could put together an extraction Team. I, on the other hand, am just the gay Science and Medical Officer. And I have been studying whales with Darren for years. Mr. Ballantine isn't exactly looking for whales."

"What is he looking for?" Kinsey asked, her voice sleepy and her eyelids very heavy.

"I'm not sure," Gunnar replied, "but we'll know soon. I ran into Darren and he was bordering on excitement and fear. Whatever it is Ballantine is cooking up, it won't be boring, I can say that."

"Good," Kinsey replied, "I hate…boring…"

Her breathing slowed, and in seconds, she was snoring. Gunnar smiled and turned out the light before closing the hatch and leaving her to her dreams.

CHAPTER SIX: A DIFFERENT KETTLE OF FISH

Team Grendel, the representatives from the company, and Darren's original crew all sat in the large conference room below deck and stared at the video screen, as Mr. Ballantine stood before them, a laser pointer outlining a shadow on the screen.

"Right there," Mr. Ballantine said, "this is why we needed the hard drives. I wanted the original raw footage so it could be enhanced and filtered."

"You're saying that's a shark?" Cougher asked. "Not a whale?"

"Not a whale, Mr. Colfer," Mr. Ballantine replied, "and yes, it is a shark."

"Ballantine," Mr. Perry said, "this is highly irregular. A prehistoric whale is one thing; that can be spun into all kinds of goodwill and feel good press for the company and our clients, if needed. What a discovery. But this? It's Jaws nonsense."

"Yeah, how'd that work out?" Max whispered to his brother.

"I understand your reluctance, Mr. Perry," Mr. Ballantine said, "but science isn't always about goodwill or feel good press. Sometimes it's about facing fear and looking into the abyss. Then when something looks back, you punch it in the face."

"Can't argue with that," Shane said.

"Shut it," Thorne snapped.

"I would almost say the same thing to Mr. Ballantine," Ms. Horace said. "You are jeopardizing your career here. I agree with Mr. Perry that a whale is one thing, but a shark is completely different."

"How is this even a conversation?" Kinsey asked, looking over at Gunnar. "Come on, Gun, a prehistoric whale? A prehistoric shark?"

"We don't know if either are prehistoric," Gunnar replied. "They could be entirely new species. As for the whale, I'd like to find out, that's why I'm here." He looked over at Darren who was sitting close to the head of the table. "But a shark? One that can go after our whale? That's not something we're prepared for."

"On the contrary, Doctor," Mr. Ballantine responded. "The Beowulf II is completely prepared. Double hull, the Wyrm, the Wiglaf---"

"Wiglaf?" Mr. Longbottom asked. "What is that?"

"The mini-sub," Bobby said.

"Oh."

"If I may continue? Thank you," Mr. Ballantine said. "The Beowulf II is prepared. I have all the current research ready for you below, Doctor. Everything I've compiled over the years. You'll know everything I do."

"Why?" Lake asked. "Why chase some monster shark that may or may not exist?"

"It exists," Mr. Ballantine said, "trust me."

"And that's where I have a problem," Lake said, "I don't trust you. I trust Captain Chambers, and he seems to trust you. That's why I signed on. But if you'd told me back in Cape Town we'd be chasing some imaginary shark, then I would have laughed and walked away."

A few of the other crew members nodded in agreement.

"How is this creature more imaginary than the whale you were chasing?" Mr. Ballantine asked.

"Because Darren saw the whale," Gunnar said, "and Darren wouldn't lie about something as important as that."

Kinsey snorted then frowned at the looks she got.

"Whales, sharks, I could give a fuck," Thorne said. "I was hired to put together an extraction Team. I did that. But if you are chasing sea monsters, then why am I still here?"

"Security, Commander Thorne," Mr. Ballantine said. "These are dangerous waters. A ship like the Beowulf II would be a prize for pirates. It looks expensive because it is. Pirates would love to get their hands on this ship as well as the crew and all of you. They see us and all they see are dollar signs streaming by."

"So we're here to babysit while you play mad explorer?" Thorne asked, folding his arms across his chest. Kinsey smiled at that, knowing her father was getting ready for a fight.

"If we get an assignment from the company, then we drop the research and do our jobs," Darren said. "That's why we are being funded. We've proven we can go in and do a job. We'll just use our 'down time' to continue my research." He smiled weakly and looked at the screen. "And Mr. Ballantine's research also."

"When did you first see it?" Kinsey asked.

"On the Beowulf I," Mr. Ballantine said. "I had just hired Darby. She saw it also."

Darby nodded.

"So…what happened to the Beowulf I?" Max asked.

"Yes, Mr. Ballantine," Mr. Longbottom asked, "I would like to know that as well. The company has the file sealed, even from me."

"Me as well," Ms. Horace said, "which is highly irregular. I do not like irregular."

"They don't talk about it," Kinsey said, "might as well stop asking."

"I don't believe we can finance this, Ballantine," Mr. Perry said as he stood up. "I'll call for a helicopter to pick us up. We'll report to the Board; they'll make the final decision."

"Oh, I believe you'll be persuaded otherwise," Mr. Ballantine said, "Captain Chambers?"

"We have been at a steady cruising speed since Team Grendel returned," Darren said, "and we've actually pushed that speed once I had coordinates."

"Coordinates?" Ms. Horace asked. "For what? For where?"

"That," Darren said as he pointed at the screen. "The raw video was geotagged. We are going to that exact site. We'll be there in about twelve hours."

"Wait a minute," Mr. Longbottom protested, "you are taking us away from land? Further into the ocean?"

"Once you see the evidence in person, Mr. Longbottom," Mr. Ballantine said, "you'll be a supporter of the entire mission. Seeing is believing. Remember, Team Grendel will save the company's clients possibly billions of dollars. Any expenses for our scientific endeavors will be minimal compared to the profits made and saved."

"This is ridiculous," Ms. Horace said. She stood up and pulled a phone from a briefcase. "I am calling for a helicopter once I get up on deck and have a clear satellite signal. I will need our exact coordinates, Captain Chambers."

"Lake?" Darren said. "Will you get those for Ms. Horace?"

"Sure thing," Lake said as he got up and followed Ms. Horace out of the conference room.

Mr. Ballantine gave the room a smile. "Any other questions?"

***

"You son of a bitch," Ms. Horace snarled as she stood with Perry, Longbottom, and Ballantine on the upper deck. "All long range company helicopters are in use on other business. The soonest one will be available and in range to get us is in two days."

"How unfortunate," Mr. Ballantine said.

"Not unfortunate as much as underhanded," Ms. Horace said. "The business they are being used for was authorized by you, Ballantine. You knew we'd want to leave and shut you down, so you arranged for us to be stuck here."

"That's quite an accusation," Mr. Ballantine said, "and if it were true, I'd be offended."

"Are we the hostages now, Ballantine?" Mr. Perry asked.

"Stefan, please," Mr. Ballantine said, "of course not. Two days until the helicopter can get here. Enjoy your time. Relax, soak up some sun. Go for a swim."

The three looked out at the water, the looks on their faces not ones of confidence.

"I'll stay on the boat," Mr. Longbottom replied.

"Good," Mr. Ballantine said, "we can use these two days to go over projected revenue for Team Grendel. We'll need to be exact when offering cost quotes to clients."

"Drones are online," Darby said as she walked up to the group.

"You tasked company drones?" Ms. Horace asked. "Who authorized that?"

"I did. But only for a short time, as I know how precious they are to the company," Mr. Ballantine said. "Thank you, Darby. I'll join you in the command center soon. Please let Captain Chambers and Doctor Peterson know. They'll want to be present as the drones do a couple runs over the coordinates."

"Yes, sir," Darby said and left.

"You are a piece of work, Ballantine," Mr. Perry said.

"A piece of something," Ms. Horace said.

"Now, now, no need for disparaging comments," Mr. Ballantine said. "If I fail, then yes, you can disparage me all you want. But even if I don't find what I am looking for, the Beowulf II will be invaluable to the company just because of Grendel."

"We'll see," Mr. Perry said. "How about we go over those figures starting now? I don't intend on wasting the company's funds relaxing, Ballantine."

"My pleasure, Stefan," Mr. Ballantine said, gesturing towards the above deck briefing room. "This way."

Max and Shane watched as Ballantine and his colleagues left the deck for the briefing room. They were set up in the top most crow's nest above the observation deck, their sniper rifles resting on the rail.

"This is some crazy shit," Max said. "Not exactly what Uncle Vinny advertised."

"Giant sharks as well as Darren's whale? What the fuck?" Shane said, shaking his head. "Are we in the fucking Twilight Zone?"

"More like X-Files," Max said.

"Bermuda Triangle shit, bro," Shane said. "How crazy do you think Darren and Ballantine are?"

"Oh, they're full on batshit," Max said, "but that doesn't mean they're wrong."

"Are you buying this crap?" Shane laughed.

"Not at all," Max said, "I'm just not closing my mind to the possibility." He put his eye to his scope and scanned the ocean, gauging distances between white caps. He squeezed off a shot and watched the spray as the bullet hit the water 800 yards off. "I mean, come on, how awesome would it be to see a fucking whale that isn't supposed to exist?"

"It would be awesome," Shane said, "but I'd rather not come face to face with a fucking giant whale eating shark. That I can do without."

"Is this a boys only tree house or can a girl join too?" Lucy called from below, her .50 caliber in hand.

"Come on up," Max said, "you looking to kill some waves? Because this is the spot for killing waves. We done kill 'em dead up here."

"Actually," Lucy said as she climbed up into the crow's nest with Max and Shane, "I may have mentioned I was probably a better shot than both of you."

"Oh, really?" Shane laughed. "You talking to yourself?"

"Nope," Lucy smiled as she lay down on her belly and settled the .50, "talking to them."

"Okay, everyone!" Bach shouted as a crowd gathered on the deck below. "No bets over fifty! We aren't trying to break each other, just have a little fun!"

"My money's on the smart brother," Popeye said.

"Fuck you!" Max shouted down.

"I was talking about you!" Popeye yelled back.

"Oh, cool. Thanks!" Max smiled as he looked at his brother. "You're the dumb one."

"That's like deciding which turd stinks the most," Lucy said. She squeezed the trigger, killing a wave instantly. It never stood a chance. "Still just two turds."

"Nice," Shane said. He looked down below. "Can we get in on the action?"

"You bet," Bach said.

The three snipers were surprised to see Jennings in a Zodiac speeding well away from the ship. Soon, he started to drop debris into the water so pieces floated out there at different distances. He came zipping back, and with a little help, was up on deck and placing bets with the rest.

Beau and Cougher stood to the side of the group, each with a spyglass to their eye, and raised a hand into the air.

"Spotters are ready," Bach announced, "Snipers, are you ready?"

"Ready," Max said.

"You bet," Shane said.

"Born that way," Lucy said.

"I am so calling you Lady Gaga from now on," Max said.

"You will each get one shot per target," Bach said. "Ladies first, then Lucy can go."

"Oh, God," Shane laughed, "the jokes! Heeee-larious!"

"Shane then Max then Lucy," Bach said. "You can't take more than thirty seconds to set up your shot. Keep your hands to yourself and no sabotaging the other shooters. We'll start targets left to right. Shoot, shoot, shoot, then move to the next one. Beau and I will announce a hit or miss. Ready?"

"Let's kill some trash!" Shane bellowed. "Die fucking trash! DIE!"

"I'm just regular ready," Max said, "not crazy ready."

"Hold on," Shane said and pulled a joint from his pocket.

"No way," Lucy said. "No performance enhancing drugs."

"What?" Max asked. "Just some harmless weed."

"I've heard about you two and weed," Lucy said, "it's like Popeye and spinach."

'What?" Popeye shouted from below.

"Nothing," she yelled down, "just fucking shoot."

Shane squeezed the trigger and a five gallon plastic bucket spun in the water 500 yards out. Max followed, then Lucy. The bucket sank quickly.

"Three hits," Beau said.

The crowd groaned since there wasn't a miss.

"Better hurry," Bach said, "the current and wind are taking your targets further out."

There was a good sized piece of orange foam rubber bobbing in the waves about 900 yards out. Shane took aim and squeezed. Beau and Bach watched a chunk of foam fly into the air. Max hit it also, as did Lucy.

The crowd began to get bored.

"I think we're losing our audience," Max said.

"What were they expecting?" Shane said. "For us to do back flips and shoot from the hip?"

"Let's move it along," Lucy said. "Five second rule."

"We're moving it up to five seconds," Shane announced. "Get this party rolling."

The crowd gave a weak cheer and some of them started to walk away.

"Tough room," Max said.

Shane, Max, Lucy. Shane, Max, Lucy. It went that way for several minutes until there remained only one target they hadn't shot: a beach ball that had drifted at least 1,400 yards out.

Shane put his scope to his eye, sighted on the target, then began to squeeze the trigger, but stopped. "Do you guys see that?"

The other two snipers had been watching through their scopes, gauging the target for themselves. Once the ball was punctured, it would sink quickly, so they knew they had to be ready.

"See what?" Max asked.

"Wait...I think I see something," Lucy said. "What is that?"

"You two seeing that down there?" Shane yelled to Bach and Beau.

"I see it," Beau replied. "Is it a boat? Looks like a Zodiac or raft torn to shit and upside down."

"Do seagulls eat rubber?" Lucy asked. "Don't you see them all?"

Everyone had been so busy watching the contest that they didn't even notice the flock of seagulls circling the mystery item. More and more kept diving down, grabbing chunks and flying off.

"Must be pretty fucking tasty for those gulls to be all the way out here," Max said. "We're a long way from shore."

"I'm going to check it out," Bach announced. "Who wants to come?"

"It's probably a dead whale," Jennings said. "It happens out here."

"But what if it's *the* dead whale?" Bach said. "Worth checking out."

"I'm going," Shane said as he climbed down from the crow's nest. "Should we get Ditcher?"

"I got it," Bach said as he grabbed a radio clipped to his belt. "Captain? This is Bach. We have something you'll want to see."

"What is it?" Darren replied, obviously groggy from sleep.

"Are you taking a nap?" Bach asked.

"Shut up," Darren replied. "What's up, Bach?"

"Maybe a whale carcass, sir," Bach said. "I'm taking a Zodiac out with Shane."

"I'm going," Jennings said. "I pilot the Zodiacs better than you."

"We'll cover you up here," Lucy said.

"We will?" Max said. "From what?"

"Look at how the carcass is moving," Lucy said. "Sharks. A lot of them. They're having a buffet."

"Good eye," Max said. "Yep, gotcha covered."

"I'll be right up," Darren said. "Tell Lake to change course and get us closer."

Beau took off and headed for the bridge while Bach, Jennings, and Shane got the Zodiac ready. It was only a couple minutes before Darren was up on deck, pulling a t-shirt on and shaking the sleep from his head.

"Alright, let's go see some rotten flesh," Darren said.

"Captain," Lake called from the bridge window, "I object. I'll go. You should stay on the bridge."

"Not happening, Lake," Darren said, "if it's my whale, then I want to be one of the first to see it."

"Fine," Lake scowled, "you're the Captain."

"He's the Riker to your Picard," Shane laughed.

"Shut it, nerd," Darren smiled as Popeye worked the power winch and lowered the Zodiac to the water below.

***

The knocking woke her slowly and she had to fight to get her eyes open. Kinsey wondered if Gunnar hadn't put a little extra in her formula.

"Wha...uh...what?" Kinsey croaked, her throat dry. "What?"

The hatch opened and Darby looked in. "You'll want to see this," she said. "There's a bunch of the crew, including Captain Chambers, taking a Zodiac out to a carcass that was spotted."

"Good for them," Kinsey said. "Let them."

Darby stepped fully into Kinsey's quarters. "I'll let you think it through for a second."

"Think what through?" Kinsey asked, annoyed that Darby wouldn't let her go back to sleep. Darby just waited. "It's going to be like that, huh? You stand there and let your big announcement sink into my brain and then all of a sudden, I'll understand what you're getting at? Is that it?" Darby didn't respond. "Listen, Darby, you seem cool and all, but I---"

Kinsey stopped. Darby smiled.

"Carcass?" Kinsey said. "Things like to eat carcasses."

"Yes, they do," Darby said, "and your ex is too focused on whales to think what might want to eat a whale carcass."

"Ah, fuck," Kinsey said as she hopped from her bunk and grabbed her pants, tugging them up over her bare legs. She got a tank top over her bra and then pushed past Darby, grabbing her boots on the way.

"Ah, Ms. Thorne," Mr. Ballantine said as he hurried up the passageway, "news travels fast."

"A Zodiac won't be much against your giant shark," Kinsey said.

"No, it won't," Mr. Ballantine said. "Maybe we should talk some sense into the captain before he gets hurt?"

"Oh, I don't care if he gets hurt," Kinsey said, "I just don't want to miss it if it happens."

"Ouch," Mr. Ballantine smirked.

They all rushed up onto the upper deck, joining the rest of the crew that weren't busy with duties and tasks to keep the ship working.

"Mr. Ballantine," Ms. Horace nodded, her hand shielding her eyes from the glare of the sun off the water. "I believe the captain has left the ship and is chasing his whale."

"Chasing his tail, more like," Mr. Perry said from her left. "Whatever is out there is dead. No good use to anyone."

"I'm sorry, Mr. Perry," Mr. Ballantine said, "did you think I was going to let the shark live?"

"Didn't think much about it," Mr. Perry replied, "because I don't believe in your shark, Mr. Ballantine. I do believe in Captain Chambers' whale, though. And I am 100% against killing whales. My parents gave me a subscription to Greenpeace magazine when I was little. Save the whales."

"I had no idea you knew what compassion was, Mr. Perry," Mr. Ballantine said.

"Only for whales, Mr. Ballantine," Mr. Perry smiled. "People, I can care less about."

"Delightful."

Kinsey left Mr. Ballantine and his colleagues and made her way up to the crow's nest, followed closely by Darby.

"Hey, my fiancé is here," Max said. "Hey, sweetie. Having a good day?"

"Not going to happen, rifle jockey," Darby replied.

"Give me that," Kinsey said, as she took Max's rifle from him and put her eye to the scope.

"Hey, bad form, Sis," Max said. "You never take a sniper's gun from them."

"Not if you want to live," Lucy said giving Max a quick high five.

"They think it's a whale?" Kinsey asked. "Whatever it is, it's huge."

"See how the sharks are gnawing on it?" Lucy asked. "Even if we aren't talking about Ballantine's super shark, there are still some big fuckers out there. They need to watch themselves in that Zodiac."

***

"*C. Megalodon*," Darren said to Shane, "that's the shark Ballantine is chasing. I'm chasing what I believe to be *Livyatan Melville*, which would have been a contemporary of Megalodon. But I highly doubt a shark the size of Megalodon could go undetected for decades, if not centuries."

"And your whale can?" Shane asked as the Zodiac bounced across the waves.

"Do you know how many blue whale sightings there are each year?" Darren asked.

"Not a clue," Shane said.

"Except for off the California coast," Darren said, "there are less than a dozen sightings a year."

"What's so special about the California coast?" Shane asked.

"Of the close to 10,000 blue whales left alive, almost a quarter of them show up on the California coast each summer and fall to breed. The rest are scattered throughout the oceans."

"So that leaves about 7,000 blue whales that almost never get spotted?" Shane asked. "Is that what you're getting at?"

"Exactly," Darren replied as the Zodiac got closer to its target, "and blue whales can be 100 feet long. The *Livyatan Melville* doesn't get quite that long."

A smell began to fill the air, even with the wind whipping past them, as the Zodiac sped over the waves.

"Damn," Bach said, "whatever it is, it's been dead a while."

"Why give a shit about a whale that isn't even the biggest?" Shane asked.

"Because of its jaw," Shane said. "It's like a sperm whale, with carnivorous teeth, but top *and* bottom. Unlike the sperm whale, which has a smaller lower jaw, *Livyatan Melville* has a lower jaw that matches the upper jaw. The crushing power is unbelievable. Theory is, it was the reason that Megalodon went extinct, among other things."

"Damn," Shane said. "So we're talking Jonah's whale then? This thing is all biblical and shit?"

"Could be," Darren said as he brought his hand to his nose to cover the stench. "Damn."

Jennings cut the engine and let the Zodiac drift close in to the carcass. Several of the feasting gulls protested and flew up into the air. Shane looked over the side of the Zodiac and saw a sight that sent his balls up into his throat.

"That's a lot of sharks," Shane said. "Fun."

"Fucking A," Darren whispered, ignoring the sharks and focusing on the whale. "Can you get me closer?"

"Not without gumming up the motor," Jennings said. "Too much guts and shit floating about."

"Paddle," Bach said, grabbing the paddles from the floor of the large raft. "We'll get in closer that way."

Darren and Bach paddled, taking the Zodiac in as close as possible. Everyone in the boat just stared at what they saw. Even if over two dozen sharks weren't tearing hunks of the beast off, it would have still been impressive because of the jaw.

"That's your whale," Shane almost whispered. "Holy fuck, Ditcher. You found your whale."

"It's not very long," Jennings said. "What is it? Thirty feet? I've seen orcas that big."

"It's only part," Bach said, pointing the paddle at where the tail should have been. "Quite a bit is missing."

"About another twenty feet," Darren said, "but it's not the size, man. Look at that jaw. That anatomy doesn't exist anymore. Or shouldn't."

"So you found it?" Jennings asked. "You found Moby Dick?"

"God, I'd wish you'd all stop saying that," Darren said, "but fuck yeah, I found it!"

Shane studied the carcass, but kept coming back to where the tail should have been. He wasn't a marine biologist, but he was a SEAL sniper and trained to observe every tiny detail. Sure, he and his brother played the fools, it helped let them stay under the radar when they wanted to. But the truth was, as with most SEALs, he could shame a MIT grad if he wanted to.

"What do you think bit the tail off?" Shane said. "Great white?"

Darren tore his eyes away from the decomposing jaw and looked back at the tail. He did some quick calculations and frowned. "Bite radius is too big."

"Too big?" Bach asked. "What has a bigger bite radius than a great white?"

"Ballantine's shark does, I bet," Jennings said. "How big does that fucker get?"

"Not much bigger than fifty feet," Darren said, "which makes it very possible that it attacked this whale."

"You mean the whale we're next to?" Jennings frowned. "The one attracting sharks for miles?"

They all let that sink in.

"What now?" Shane asked. "How do we get this back to the ship? Which I assume is what you want to do."

"Ship is on its way," Bach said, turning around and waving to the Beowulf II as it slowly came towards them. The ship gave two quick horn blasts. He could see quite the audience on deck. "Let's paddle around it and see what else there is to see."

"I'm guessing it will be more stinky, rotten whale," Shane said. "Just a guess."

They paddled around and everyone gasped.

"What's the bite radius of that, Cousteau?" Shane asked Darren. "Still saying fifty feet?"

Darren did the math and shook his head. "That can't be," he said. "That has to be a double bite. It's an illusion."

"A double bite? Is that a thing?" Jennings asked.

Shane suddenly had an urge to start scanning the waters, ignoring the smaller sharks that swarmed below the boat, bumping against the hull now and again as they jostled for position. No, he was looking for something bigger, deeper, deadlier. For the first time since leaving California, Shane's gut warned him that he was not safe. SEALs were trained to ignore fear and pain, but also to listen to it.

Shane's fear was screaming at him to get the fuck out of there.

A shadow. Deep below.

"We need to fucking go," Shane said. "Jennings? Get us out of here."

"What?" Bach asked. "What do you see?"

"I don't know," Shane said. "But that's the problem. We need to get up on the ship."

"I can't," Jennings said. "See all the fucking sharks? I'll chop them in half and it'll break the motor."

"The Beowulf II is on the way," Darren said. "See? It's almost here."

"I think I see it," Bach said, his eyes studying the water below. "Big shadow?"

"Yeah," Shane said. "Why'd we take a Zodiac out to an all you can eat shark buffet? I think we just created a new level of stupid."

"We're fine," Darren said, "just hold steady. We'll need to be here to help get the carcass loaded up onto the Beowulf II."

"What?" Jennings said. "We're taking that onboard?"

"How else will we study it?" Darren asked. "Gunnar is going to need space to move and dissect. He can't do that in the water."

"Not with a monster shark circling us," Shane said. "Seriously, Ditcher, there's something big down there."

***

"How will we get it up on deck?" Gunnar asked.

"Simple," Mr. Ballantine said, pointing to the stern, "the Wiglaf clamps are designed to grab any large object, not just the mini-sub itself. They have precision calibration so they don't crush soft flesh and destroy the specimen. I'll operate them and get that bloated carcass on deck easily. I practiced on dead cows for weeks."

"Hey, Gunnar?" Lake called from the bridge. "Will you come up here?"

"I'm a little busy, Chief," Gunnar replied.

"You'll want to see this," Lake said. He turned his head and peered up at the crow's nest. "All of you will."

Gunnar and Ballantine exchanged glances; so did Kinsey and Darby up in the crow's nest.

"You go," Mr. Ballantine said, "I'm going to prep the clamps."

Gunnar nodded and headed for the bridge, while Kinsey and Darby climbed down to it.

"What?" Gunnar asked.

Lake pointed at the sonar station.

"That look normal?" Lake asked.

Kinsey was amazed at the detail of the sonar. Most deep scanning devices just created blobs on the screen, but the Beowulf II's sonar showed way more detail. Enough that you knew if you were looking at a shark or a dolphin or tuna. She was impressed. And a little frightened as she saw what was beneath them.

"What's the scale?" Kinsey asked. "How big is that?"

"Jesus Christ," Gunnar said, looking at the sonar, then out the window at the carcass. The Beowulf II was getting closer, but so was what was on the sonar. "That's gotta be fifty feet, at least. And moving fast."

"That's a shark?" Kinsey asked. "Right?"

"It is," Gunnar said, "a big one. Probably the largest great white on record."

"Not a great white," Darby said.

"Fuck," Kinsey said, "it'll devour that Zodiac."

"It's going for the dead whale," Gunnar said. "It wants nothing to do with the Zodiac."

The sonar started to beep loudly.

"What is that?" Kinsey asked.

Darby sat down at the station and watched the screens. "It's a movement alarm. It was triggered because of all the sudden activity. See those there?" Darby pointed at the outlines of the hundreds of smaller sharks. "They're leaving."

She was right. Everything quickly left the area; they all watched as the only thing left on the screen was the big outline, still going straight for the Zodiac.

"We have to get them out of there," Kinsey shouted as she rushed out of the bridge.

"Pilot this ship as fast you can," Darby said, following Kinsey.

"What about the helo?" Gunnar asked.

"Bobby won't get it powered up in time," Lake said. "Fuck. I should have been watching that."

"Well, your crew is all out on deck watching the show," Gunnar said, "no one was prepared."

"They will be next time," Lake said.

"If there is a next time," Gunnar said as he took off after the ladies.

***

Shane placed the forestock of the .338 on Bach's shoulder. "Sorry, man. I have to steady this thing. Cover your ears and don't move."

Shane stood up, very aware of the constant movement of the Zodiac, and began to track the shadow below as it circled the carcass and the boat.

"Hey!" Kinsey called from the deck. "You have company!"

"We know!" Shane shouted, watching the shadow's every move. "We see it!"

"No, you don't!" Kinsey yelled. "Whatever you see is not what's coming!"

"Not what's coming?" Jennings asked. "What the fuck does that mean?"

Bach looked back at the Beowulf II, which was only about twenty yards away.

"Don't move," Shane snapped, "Jesus."

"We can paddle now," Bach said. "Darren? Jennings? Get us back to the ship."

Neither man argued, and started to paddle. The shadow below changed directions, its movements showing it was tracking the Zodiac. Then it was gone.

"What happened?" Shane asked. "Where'd it go?"

"It left," Bach said. "I saw it take off. It was so fucking fast I would have missed it if I wasn't looking right at it."

"Why'd it leave?" Shane asked. "Why now?"

"Fuck," Jennings said, "it's so going to come up at us from below. Like that Shark Week video."

"Just paddle," Bach said.

***

Ballantine guided the clamps up and over the Wiglaf, getting them down close to the water.

"Bring the ship around, Lake!" Mr. Ballantine shouted. "We need to get the carcass close to the stern!"

"We need to get the men out of the water," Darby said from his side. "There's something else down there."

"That's what they keep shouting about," Mr. Ballantine said as he worked the controls.

"No, there's something else," Darby said.

Mr. Ballantine turned his attention from the clamps and to her. He saw the look in her eye and he smiled.

"Do you think?" he asked.

"I think," Darby replied.

"Then what were they shouting about before?" Mr. Ballantine said.

Darby shrugged. "Possibly a great white."

"Hmmm," Mr. Ballantine mused, "possibly."

***

Lake cut the engines, hoping the Beowulf II would coast close enough to the Zodiac. He didn't want the engines going and miss the Zodiac, allowing it to get caught in the wake of the ship. He needed to limit the variables that already complicated everything.

***

The water below was a deep blue and just got darker as he looked deeper and deeper. Shane put his eye to his scope and couldn't see anything. There just wasn't enough light to pierce the deep blue of the ocean.

"They're passing us!" Jennings shouted.

"They're getting us to the stern," Darren said. "See Ballantine up there? He's going to use the clamps."

"Huh," Shane said, taking his eye away from the scope then putting it back.

"What?" Bach asked.

"I don't know," Shane said. "What do you see down there?"

"Nothing," Bach replied. "No...wait...what is that?"

"Oh...FUCK!" Shane screamed just as they saw the massive jaws coming up at them.

Shane couldn't see anything before because his scope had been looking right down the throat of the giant shark. A giant shark that was rushing up to them at close to fifty miles an hour.

"What?" Darren asked. "What is---"

His words were cut off as the Zodiac was lifted up into the air.

***

"COCKSUCKING MEGASHARK!" Max yelled as he watched the Zodiac launch into the air, gripped in the jaws of a beast he couldn't even wrap his head around. "HOLY FUCK!"

Instinct kicked in and he started to fire, sending round after round into the belly of the giant shark. Lucy's .50 barked next to him, matching him shot for shot. They both went Winchester and their rifles clicked empty. They dropped their magazines and slammed in new ones, almost in perfect synch.

Then started firing again.

The monster had barely crested and started to fall back to the water before it already had close to twenty massive holes in it.

But when it did fall, it took the Zodiac with it. The boat, and the men inside, were lost from sight in a splash that launched water twenty feet into the air.

"SHANE!" Max shouted.

***

Water filled Shane's nose and mouth, and he lost the grip on his .338 as he slammed into the ocean's surface, then was dragged under as the Zodiac collapsed around him. All he could see were clouds of bubbles and a darkness spreading. Blood.

He didn't know if it was human or shark blood.

He didn't really care.

All his SEAL training kicked in and he instantly sought the surface, knowing that if he didn't right himself, he'd drown fast. But something clamped onto his leg and pulled at him, making him lose his sense of direction. He yanked a large knife from its sheath on his belt and was about to cut some serious shark flesh when he realized it was Bach clinging to him.

Bach's eyes bulged and Shane could see that the man had run out of air and was about to inhale seawater if they didn't get to the surface. Shane dropped the knife, reached down, and pulled Bach's hand from his leg, taking the man with him as he swam to the surface.

Their heads broke the surface and Bach gasped so hard that he swallowed half a wave that slapped him in the face. He choked and gagged, but managed to stay above water.

"Thanks," he gasped as he smiled weakly at Shane.

"No problem," Shane said. "Now fucking swim."

The two men looked around and realized they had surfaced further away from the Beowulf II, not closer. They started to stroke, swimming as fast as they could to the ship.

"Hey! Over here!" Darren shouted at them from the whale carcass. He and Jennings had climbed on top of the rotted corpse.

"Fuck...that!" Shane shouted back as he kept swimming. "We're going for the ship!"

"You won't make it!" Darren shouted, pointing into the water. "It's fucking coming back!"

Shane risked a glance into the water and almost froze; if he hadn't been conditioned to ignore fear, he would have stopped swimming and just pissed himself. Instead, he pissed himself as he kept swimming.

But Bach did stop.

"Holy fuck!" Bach screamed as the shark came up at him from below.

It breached the surface, Bach clutched in its jaws, and started to twist and dive.

The thing had launched itself so fast that it rocketed over Shane and he watched in terror as Bach was crushed in the monster's massive jaws. But the man didn't go down without a fight. Over and over, Bach slammed his stump into the creature's nose, hoping it would let him go. He put every ounce of strength he had into each blow, but the shark didn't care. And in less than two seconds, they were both underwater.

Shane shook off the shock and kept swimming towards the Beowulf II. The water around him bloomed red with blood. He wasn't a shark expert, but he knew the big ones had saw-like teeth and shook their prey back and forth, ripping them to pieces. He tried to shove the thought away, but all he could see in his imagination was Bach being cut in half.

Shane was almost overtaken with gratitude when Bach burst to the surface ahead of him. He swam to the wounded man and grabbed him around the neck, ready to swim with him the last few yards to the Beowulf II. But he quickly realized the weight placement was all wrong.

He held only the top half of Bach in his arms.

"Fuck!" he shouted as he let go and back stroked away from the half-corpse as fast as possible. He could hear the shouting from the deck, but didn't look back or change his stroke. He just kept swimming backwards, his eyes locked on Bach as the top half of the man's body bobbed up and down in the waves.

Every nerve in his body felt like live wires. He knew the thing was close and getting closer; he didn't have to look, his instincts told him he had maybe two or three seconds of life left. But he was a SEAL and he didn't give up; SEALs never quit.

"SHANE!" Max screamed from above and he took the time to look up just as a rope and lifesaver was tossed overboard.

The ring smacked Shane in the face, but he shook it off and looped his arm inside as Max and the others started to pull. He was out of the water and swinging against the boat, his feet planted on the side, trying to gain some traction so he could help his ascension to the upper deck.

Rifle fire filled the air and Shane could see Lucy with her .50 caliber at the rail, aiming just behind him. She went Winchester twice, putting fresh magazines into the rifle each time it clicked empty. She had just put a third one in when Shane was yanked up over the rail.

"Give me that!" he yelled.

Lucy didn't argue as Shane took the hot rifle from her hands. He spun about and placed the rifle on the rail, his finger on the trigger. Later, when they all sat about to discuss the shot, Shane would say he had no clue how he knew where it would be, just that at that hyper-aware moment, it was like he knew where every fish in the ocean was.

He squeezed the trigger just as the shark came bursting out of the water. Blood exploded from the monster's forehead and its mouth slapped shut. The beast tilted and fell back into the ocean on its side. It floated there for a minute then began to sink.

"Holy fuck, bro," Max said at Shane's elbow. "That was fucking crazy."

"Get us turned!" Mr. Ballantine shouted. "I want that shark!"

"Fuck you," Kinsey said. "We're getting our crew first." She looked up at the bridge and could see Lake looking from her to Ballantine. "Who are you going to fear most when you close your eyes, Lake?"

He kept the Beowulf II steaming towards the whale carcass.

"Lake!" Mr. Ballantine screamed. "I will throw you overboard if you don't obey me this instant!"

"You're not the captain," Darby said at his side, "back off, sir."

"Who's team are you on, Darby?" Mr. Ballantine snarled, whirling on her. "Be careful you don't pick the wrong one."

Darby watched him for a minute then moved over to the Wiglaf and opened the hatch. Mr. Ballantine gave her a quizzical look and she just sneered at him.

"I'll get your shark, sir," Darby said, and then turned. "Kinsey! You're coming with!"

Kinsey looked over and frowned, then saw what she was doing and smiled.

"Fine by me," Kinsey said as she climbed on top of the Wiglaf. "Max? Make sure Ballantine gets Darren and Jennings on board. We'll go get his shark." Max nodded as Kinsey followed Darby through the hatch.

Darby locked the hatch in place and started up the sub, checking systems and gauges.

"Gonna show me how to pilot this?" Kinsey asked.

"I am," Darby said. She turned on the com. "Ballantine? Shove us in the water."

The response was a loud thud against the side of the sub and then the two women could feel the Wiglaf being lifted into the air. In seconds, they were plunged into the ocean and the sub began to dive as Darby piloted away from the Beowulf II.

"I'll circle around," Darby said, "go deeper and scan as we come up. The shark couldn't have sunk too far."

"Why didn't it float like the whale?" Kinsey asked as she studied the inside of the mini-sub.

"It will once it starts to break down," Darby said, "when gasses are generated. But for now, it will sink."

"Let's get it and get the fuck out of the water," Kinsey said. "I'm running on adrenaline right now, otherwise, I wouldn't have gotten in this thing."

"Afraid of tight spaces?" Darby asked as she studied the sonar readings.

"I don't like to be confined in the water," Kinsey said. "I like to swim in it."

"Not the most hospitable ocean today," Darby said. "You will want to think twice before going for a swim."

The sonar bleeped and Darby changed trajectory and aimed the Wiglaf at the source.

"There it is," Darby said. "I'll pilot and you can manipulate the arms. They aren't as strong as the ones on the Beowulf, so try not to tear the body too much. Mr. Ballantine is already pissed off."

"These controls here?" Kinsey asked as she put her hands on two large joysticks in front of a small video screen. "I got this."

"Play with the claws a little, get the feel," Darby said as she aimed the nose of the sub at the blip on the sonar. They were quiet for a minute as they each performed their tasks. "Did you know Bach?"

"What?" Kinsey asked. "Bach? No, not until I got aboard."

"Me either," Darby said, "seemed like a nice fellow. It's a shame."

"Yeah," Kinsey said. "How close are we?"

"Ten meters," Darby said, "I have it in view."

Kinsey saw it also on her screen and manipulated the claws and arms in place.

"Steady," Darby said. "Steady. And…grab!"

The claws grabbed onto the massive shark, one close to the tail and one by the gills. The mini-sub strained with effort to turn itself as Darby pointed it back towards the Beowulf II; the shark was longer than the sub by a good couple meters.

"Is it secure?" Darby asked.

"As far as I know," Kinsey said.

"Good," Darby replied, "then lock it and come here. I'll show you the basics."

Kinsey made sure the claws and arms were locked into place, then sat down in the seat next to Darby's.

"Basic joystick controls here, also," Darby said. "Up, down, left, right. This lever accelerates, pull back and it decelerates. Don't forget that you're in water. There's no instant braking. Plan for your stop and change of direction. Be ten steps ahead."

"And the gauges?" Kinsey asked.

Darby pulled a plastic coated manual from a slot next to the pilot's chair. "Read that. Study it, know it. We'll take this out in the morning again and you can show me what you learned."

"Why the sudden urge to teach me how to pilot this?"

"Because the men won't show you," Darby said, "trust me. They'll either want to play with it themselves or just won't bother to learn. Lucy is a shooter and Bobby has the Wyrm. That leaves you to teach."

The manual was thick and heavy and Kinsey dreaded the reading, but she got what Darby was saying. The woman had made it further than most men in her field and she knew that even that amazing accomplishment meant nothing to the dicks and balls topside. To them, she was tits that could fight.

"Got it," Kinsey said, "thanks."

"Don't thank me," Darby said. "This thing is used when shit gets crazy. It's not the safest place to be when that happens. The boys know that and despite their bravado and chivalrous fronts, they'll send you down in this every time. They'll think they're showing equality, but they're just showing how chicken shit they are to take this baby down 3,000 feet."

"It goes that deep?"

"More," Darby said, "5,000 is the maximum, but Ballantine has hinted it can withstand more. I don't want to be the one to find out if that's true."

The Wiglaf approached the stern of the Beowulf II and the two women saw the ship's claws plunge into the water and move towards them.

"What's your story with Ballantine?" Kinsey asked while they were still alone.

"Nothing sexual," Darby said, "if that's what you're asking. I don't know if Ballantine even has sex."

"Okay, wish I hadn't asked," Kinsey smiled, "now all I can picture is my old Ken doll and his smooth place."

There was a jolt and a crunching sound, and then the Wiglaf was lifted from the water and swung about until it was docked. Darby went to the arm controls and positioned the shark carcass onto a loading deck just feet away. She smiled at Kinsey and then reached up and opened the top hatch.

The ocean breeze that blew in pushed out the stale, canned air of the mini-sub and Kinsey breathed deeply. Darby went first and Kinsey followed. The sweet scent of the ocean air was quickly replaced by one of rotten flesh and death. The whale carcass covered the empty helipad.

"Damn," Kinsey said.

"There it is!" Mr. Ballantine shouted as he jumped to the loading deck and hurried to the shark. "Fifty feet, easy!"

"Yeah," Shane said, Lucy's .50 caliber in the crook of his elbow, "easy. Real easy. Just one crew member dead."

"Super. Fucking. Easy," Max said at his shoulder.

Ballantine looked up at the faces of the crew that peered down at him from the deck above. He tried to think of something inspirational, but nothing came to mind. He nodded and then looked back at his shark.

"That's what I thought," Shane said and turned away.

"Team Grendel," Thorne said, "briefing room in five. We need to talk."

"I'll say," Bobby said and walked over to where Darren stood staring at the bloated whale carcass. "Bach died for this."

"Bach knew what he signed up for," Darren said.

"Seriously?" Bobby snapped.

"What?" Darren asked, then looked at her. "Sorry, sorry, shit. You're right. It's just that I didn't think I'd see this again. I lost sight of priorities."

"I have to meet with Thorne and the others," Bobby said, "you play with your fish. We'll talk later."

"It's not a---"

"Fish," Bobby interrupted, "I know."

Darren watched her walk off with the rest of Team Grendel. He saw the crew staring at him. They all had duties to attend to, but none were moving.

"You have about five minutes to straighten things out," Kinsey said as she came up behind him. "Better get control before you have a mutiny on your hands."

"They've been with me a long time," Darren said, "they knew it could happen."

"No, they didn't," Kinsey said, "not until it actually happened. Look at them."

Darren did, then looked at Kinsey.

"They aren't scared," Kinsey said, "they trust you. They just need to know they won't be next. Give them that."

She walked off to join her father and Team Grendel in the briefing room, leaving Darren to stand there by himself, his crew watching from various decks above.

***

"That was shit," Thorne growled once everyone was seated. "That was fucking chaos. Reactive chaos, which is the worst. It won't happen again."

"It all happened so fast," Lucy said.

"It always happens fast," Thorne said, "but we are professionals. Our job is to slow that shit down. Next time, we don't let a single fucking crew member off this ship until every last motherfucking duck is in a row. A man died today. Why? Because everyone got all amped about a dead fucking whale."

Thorne took a deep breath then continued.

"A whale is not more important than a human life," he said. "I don't fucking care how much they pay us or the crew. Next time, we take control just like any other op. We assess and then plan accordingly. Tell me what we could have done better."

"Not take a Zodiac into deep waters when there's a fucking shark frenzy," Shane said. "We use the Beowulf II."

"Exactly," Thorne said. "There's a reason we have a big fucking ship like this. What else?"

"We don't listen to Darren or Ballantine," Max said, "we listen to you."

"Hey, Darren is captain," Bobby said, "we have to listen to him."

"No, we don't," Thorne said. "Understand this, pilot. Darren is Captain, and that is all. He isn't Team Grendel. I lead this Team. And that's all that matters. You don't want to be a part of this Team? Fine, you can be a chop jock. We'll use you when it's time to fly. Other than that, you can sit on your thumbs."

"Darren's an ex-SEAL," Bobby said, "he knows what he's doing."

"No, he doesn't," Kinsey said, "no more than I did."

"What the fuck does that mean?" Bobby asked.

"The way he looked at that carcass," Shane said, "Junkie."

"Junkie," Max nodded.

"Yep," Kinsey said. "Same look in his eye. I know that look well. He found his fix and he was willing to sacrifice everyone for it."

"Bullshit!" Bobby snapped. "He is not some junked out whore like you!"

Thorne slammed his hands on the table, his eyes red with anger.

"Pull your head out of your twat!" Thorne shouted. "And stop fighting this! Your boyfriend is in it. He is deep in it. I don't give two tons of fuck if he's shooting heroin or jonesing for his whale discovery, he's in it. And that means his thinking is compromised."

He rubbed his face and suddenly looked ten years older.

"Which is why we are here," Thorne said. "Did you think we were just along to save some random hostages now and then? Did you think those company people out there were here for that only?

Think. Think! Ballantine had to have us here to handle security or he wouldn't have gotten the funds for this ship.

"He knew Darren wouldn't be able to think straight once he had sight of his precious whale. How did he know? Because he can't think straight when it comes to his shark. Two obsessive personalities in a pod."

"So we're babysitters?" Max asked. "For the science junkies?"

"What about Gunnar?" Shane asked. "Do we need to watch him?"

"Gunnar doesn't call the shots," Kinsey replied. "He can get as lost in the science as he wants."

"Just like we have to get lost in the security of this crew and this ship," Thorne said. "From now on, no one makes a move without clearing it with me. And you all will back me up on that. No more dead."

"But---" Bobby started to protest then stopped. She saw the looks on everyone's face, even Lucy's. "Okay. You're right."

Thorne got nods from everyone seated at the table. He nodded in return.

"Now, let's go see what the fuck this was all for," he said, "and don't cut them any slack. Darren or Ballantine. They say something stupid, then let them have it. If we have to punch some perspective in their heads, then we will."

CHAPTER SEVEN: DISCOVERIES

The top half of Bach's torso was wrapped in linen and sent overboard as the entire crew stood on deck and saluted towards the sun setting on the horizon. Darren stood by the rail and turned to address them all.

"It was my fault," Darren said, "I know that. No one has to remind me of that." He looked at the steel gaze of Thorne. "I lost sight and Bach paid the price. It won't happen again."

"Said that a few times," Kinsey whispered.

"Shhh," Gunnar said at her side, "not the time."

"Sorry," Kinsey said as a few crewmembers glanced at her.

"I have had a long talk with our Chief Security Officer," Darren said, "and starting tomorrow, we will be running drills and putting protocols into place for new events."

"But we have the whale?" Popeye said. "Why bother?"

"We'll discuss that tomorrow," Darren said, "right now, I just want you to know I am making a promise that what happened to Bach, won't happen to you. I won't fail you again. His death will forever be a reminder to me that some things aren't worth the price that can be paid."

A barely perceptible huff came from the back of the crowd and Kinsey looked over her shoulder at where Ballantine stood. The slight smirk he had on his face disappeared as he saw her looking at him. He nodded to her, but she didn't nod in return, just turned back to look at Darren.

"And so that Bach's death isn't a waste," Darren said, "you'll be getting new assignments to be handed out by Gunnar. We have a lot of dead meat and no way to get it below deck into the freezers and coolers without some labor. If you aren't on regular duty or training with Team Grendel, then you'll be handling a saw and a hook so we can dissect these animals as fast as possible before they rot completely."

"Oh, dude," Cougher said, "that's gonna suck."

"Better than being dead," Jennings said, "don't ya think?"

"Yeah," Cougher replied quietly.

"Unfortunately," Darren said, "that means we start tonight. We'll light up the bodies so Gunnar can begin his work. I'll assign a crew of five to him so that he has plenty of hands to help. You do as he says when he says it. We need to get as much information from these bodies as we can. For Bach."

The crew all nodded.

"Get some chow first," Beau said, "Galley line is up and ready. I'll have chow going all night for the crews."

"Thanks, Beau," Darren nodded. He looked each person in the face, "Dismissed."

***

"That ain't gonna study itself," Jennings said as he set a tray of chow down next to Kinsey. He nodded at the manual open in front of her and then followed her gaze. "He's not all that, you know."

"Huh? What?" Kinsey asked, looking away from where Darren and Bobby sat in a corner of the mess. "Who's not studying what?"

"Nice," Jennings smiled as he jammed a forkful of mashed potatoes into his mouth. "What the hell did he do to you?"

"Who? Darren?" Kinsey said. "Nothing. Just divorced me."

"Hmmm," Jennings said as he took another bite.

"Hmmm, what?" Kinsey asked. "What the fuck does that mean?"

Jennings held up a hand in defense. "Not trying to start a fight," he replied after swallowing, "it's just that the captain has a different story."

"I bet he does," Kinsey laughed. "Let me guess, the way he tells it, I left him without any warning, right? He came home and I had packed up all my shit and was gone."

"Something like that," Jennings nodded. "Not how it happened?"

"Oh, I packed all my shit and was gone when he got back from his last deployment," Kinsey said, "but he shouldn't have been surprised. I'd quit the Marines for his ass. I could have signed back up, but decided it would be better for the both of us if I didn't. We'd been in the military our entire marriage. It was time for *us*, as far as I was concerned. You know what he did?"

"What?" Jennings asked, smiling.

Kinsey wasn't sure if she liked the smile, but she kept talking. "He re-enlisted. Didn't say a word to me. Just re-upped and that was that. I got the message. His priority was the SEALs and the Team. Not our marriage. I had almost left him once before when he started BUD/S and joined the SEALs. He pissed away his second chance."

"Then he left the SEALs for a whale," Jennings said, "that must hurt, knowing that he didn't leave them for you, but for a giant fucking dolphin."

"There's giant dolphins?" Lucy asked as she sat down with them. "Great. Just what we need."

"Nah, I was just exaggerating," Jennings said. "So when did that happen?"

"What?" Lucy asked, then saw Darren and Bobby. "Oh, that. Last year sometime. You didn't know about it?"

"None of us did," Jennings said.

"You didn't?" Kinsey asked, surprised.

"Nope."

"They were both at some marine biology symposium," Lucy said, "Bobby was looking for research vessels that needed a helo pilot. Darren was looking for more funding. They found each other instead."

"Don't make me puke," Kinsey said.

"She's a nice woman," Lucy responded. "I've known her for a decade. Worked with her for almost that long. You two would get along."

"Don't see that happening," Jennings smirked.

"Me neither," Kinsey said and turned her focus to the manual in front of her.

"What's that for?" Lucy said.

"Darby wants me to train on the Wiglaf," Kinsey said.

"God, I hate that name," Jennings said. "What the fuck is a Wiglaf?"

"One of the guys that fought with Beowulf," Shane said as he joined them.

"Great, it's a party," Kinsey said, slamming the manual closed and standing up. "Enjoy your slop. I'm going to my quarters."

She stepped from the table and hurried out of the mess.

"What the fuck did I say?" Shane said.

Jennings pushed his tray to the side and got up to follow Kinsey.

"Seriously?" Shane called after him.

"Hey," Lucy said, "great shooting today."

"Thanks," Shane said, "you too."

"You guys seen my wife?" Max asked as he walked by.

"I think she's on deck with Ballantine," Shane said.

"You really should stop calling her that," Lucy said, "it pisses her off."

"Did she say that?" Max asked.

"No," Lucy said, "she doesn't have to."

"Whatever," Max shrugged.

***

"Hey," Jennings called out, "Thorne!"

Kinsey turned around and frowned. "Thorne is my dad. Call me Kinsey or call me nothing."

"Well, Nothing," Jennings smiled, looking at the manual tucked under Kinsey's arm. "You want some help with that."

"Funny," Kinsey said, "you know how to work the Wiglaf?"

"I do and so does Lake," Jennings said. "We learned as soon as we came aboard. Darren does because of SEAL training and shit, but I don't think he's taken it out for a spin yet. You want to?"

"I've been," Kinsey said.

"Right," Jennings nodded. "To catch a dead fish. How about without the trauma and pressure? Just you, me, and the deep blue sea."

"At night? It'll be dark."

"It's always dark down below," Jennings shrugged. "So…you game?"

Kinsey watched him for a second and cocked her head. "Are you trying to pick me up?"

"Yes," Jennings said, "nothing sexier than a cramped mini-sub. Come on. That manual will put you to sleep. Come out with me and I'll have you proficient with every inch of that machine before you know it."

Kinsey watched him. She studied the way he held himself, how he stood with one leg bent, his arms folded across his chest, his muscles pressed against his t-shirt. He wasn't anything special, just a guy with a receding hairline, but he had style. He smirked at her the entire time until she met his eyes.

"Done?" Jennings asked. "Need me to turn around? Do a little spin for ya?"

"What? No. Shut up."

"Then…?"

"Sure, fine, let's go," Kinsey said, "what'll it hurt?"

"I like the enthusiasm," Jennings said.

They stepped topside and the night air felt incredible after the stifling stuffiness of the mess below deck. The darkness was beaten back by row after row of blazing Klieg lights aimed at the dead whale and the dead shark. Gunnar was busy shouting orders as men hurried about.

"Damn," Jennings said, "that thing just won't stop stinking."

"It'll get worse the deeper I cut," Gunnar said, his clothes covered in gunk. "And I still have a lot of cutting to do." He looked from Jennings to Kinsey and back, then raised an eyebrow.

"Shut up," Kinsey said, "he's going to show me how to really operate the mini-sub."

"I didn't say a word," Gunnar said. "But don't be gone too long. You're on next shift."

"What? When did that happen?" Kinsey asked.

"When I put your name on the next shift list," Thorne said as he walked up to them. "You and Max are security."

"Security? For what?" Kinsey asked.

"For whatever," Thorne said. "Where are you going?"

"Mini-sub training," Jennings said. "I've gotten pretty good with it so I said I'd help her study."

"Right," Thorne nodded. "Darby said she wanted you to be the other trained pilot on the Team. Didn't know you were so gung ho about it."

"Ex-Marine," Kinsey shrugged, "I'm gung ho about everything."

"I know," Thorne said.

"What does that mean?" Kinsey asked.

"Nothing," Thorne replied, "don't be late for your shift."

Kinsey watched her father walk away then turned to Jennings. "Let's get this done. I guess I have to work next shift."

"After you," he said, motioning towards the Wiglaf.

"I should have some interesting findings when you get back," Gunnar said, "I'll tell you all about them during your shift."

"Looking forward to it, Gun," Kinsey said.

"Sure you are," Gunnar said quietly as Jennings and Kinsey got into the mini-sub.

Popeye worked the arms and lowered the Wiglaf into the dark water. Once Jennings had the motors going, he gave the all clear over the com and Popeye released the mini-sub, letting it speed down into the deep.

"I'll take us a good distance so you have room to move around," Jennings said.

"So I don't crash us into the ship?" Kinsey asked as she tucked the manual back into its slot.

"Yep," Jennings said.

"Thanks for the vote of confidence."

"Anytime."

They were quiet during the few minutes Jennings took them down and away from the Beowulf II. Kinsey studied his movements and the adjustments he made as the mini-sub descended. It wasn't hard at all; easier than some of the video games she played on her PS3 back home. Or did before she hawked it for dope money.

"You going to let me drive?" Kinsey asked after they'd been down below for at least fifteen minutes.

"Sure," Jennings said, getting up from the pilot's seat and squeezing past Kinsey. The mini-sub technically could fit four, but that was cheek to cheek, knee to knee. It was barely comfortable for two. "All yours."

Kinsey sat down and put her hands on the controls. She understood the basics and turned the mini-sub to port, angling it deeper.

"Not too much," Jennings said, "this baby is electric. No diesel engines to pull us out of a sharp dive. No more than twenty-five degrees."

"Got it," Kinsey said, getting a feel for the way the Wiglaf responded. "Don't kill us."

"Yep," Jennings said.

"Anything I should be watching for?" Kinsey asked as she leveled out the mini-sub.

"Fish," Jennings said, "don't hit any fish. It's a bitch to get the guts off the windshield."

Kinsey smiled as she looked out the thick plastic window in front of her. It revealed nothing but the dark. "Where're the lights?"

"I was waiting for you to ask," Jennings said. "I've gotten good at piloting by instruments."

He reached past her and flicked two switches. As he pulled back, their cheeks brushed and he gave her a sly smile.

"Training," Kinsey said, "that's what we're here for."

"What? I didn't do anything," Jennings said. "It gets cramped in here. Not my fault I touched you and got cooties all over my face."

"Cooties from me?" Kinsey said. "You're the sailor. I don't even want to know what cooties you've picked up from port to port."

"Clean as a whistle," Jennings said. "My dad died of syphilis, so I pay attention."

"Jesus. Really?" Kinsey asked.

"That's what my mom said," Jennings replied. "I don't know for sure since I never met the guy."

"Damn, aren't you just the classic sea going story," Kinsey said. "Two hundred years ago and there'd be one-eyed pirates and treasure chests in that story."

"Not buying it?" Jennings smiled.

"Not a word," Kinsey said.

"Okay," Jennings said, "my mom was a hooker and died of HIV. I always use protection. How's that?"

Kinsey looked over her shoulder at him and studied his body language.

"Fuck," she said finally, "your mom was a hooker."

"And died of HIV," Jennings said. "She worked the Long Beach pier. When she died, I had no place to go so I hopped on the first freighter that would take me."

"How old were you?"

"Thirteen," Jennings said.

"Christ."

"No need for one-eyed pirates or treasure," Jennings said. "I've had plenty of fucking adventure without them."

"I bet," Kinsey said.

"What about you?" Jennings asked then pointed. "See that! Damn, I love it when they school."

A group of iridescent fish swam past the mini-sub, taking up the entire view out the small window.

"Look here," Jennings said, pointing to the sonar, "this thing cost a million dollars, but can't pick up a school of fish if it's too close."

"Serious flaw,' Kinsey said, "but it'll pick up something bigger, right?"

"Until it gets right on us," Jennings said. "If it's closer than a meter, we won't see it. Unless we actually see it."

"Huh," Kinsey said. "Good to know."

"So?" Jennings asked.

"So what?"

"What about you? What's your story? With a daddy like that, you have to have a story."

"Everybody has a story," Kinsey replied.

"Yeah, but not everyone's story has a SEAL for a dad," Jennings replied, "spill it."

"I barely know you," Kinsey said, "I'm not spilling my life story."

"Come on," Jennings protested, "I just told you that my mom was a whore and died from AIDS."

"You said HIV," Kinsey replied.

"Same thing."

"No, not technically," Kinsey countered.

"Well, *technically*, dead is still dead, so it doesn't really fucking matter, Thorne," Jennings said.

"I said not to call me that," Kinsey said, swatting at him.

"Oh, Thorne, Thorne, Thorne," Jennings said, "the way you protest about your name makes me really want to hear your story. Come on, Thorne, out with it."

"Knock it off," Kinsey said.

"Not until you tell me your story, Thorne," Jennings said.

Kinsey's face went red and she turned around and took a swing at him. But she banged her elbow then her head as she rocked back from the pain.

"Son of a bitch!" she cried. "That is so your fault!"

"Gotta watch how you move in here, Thorne," Jennings laughed.

She threw a jab with her left and Jennings caught her fist in his palm. Kinsey's eyes went wide.

"Yep. I know how to fight," Jennings said. "I've had a lot of practice. A lot."

"Can I have my hand back?" Kinsey asked.

"Nope," Jennings said, "Spill it."

Kinsey tugged, but Jennings held his grip.

"Are you kidding?" she said.

"Spill. It."

She tugged harder, but Jennings just pulled back. They kept at the fist in palm tug of war until they both started laughing.

"Okay, okay," Kinsey said, "I'll spill it."

She told him about growing up a Navy brat. About going to high school with Darren and Gunnar. About her brother joining the Marines. About how she married Darren right out of school even though he'd joined the Navy. She talked about joining the Marines as a way to follow her brother and also get at Darren. She talked about losing her brother then losing her mother. She said how pissed she was when instead of being there for her, Darren had re-enlisted.

She started to talk about joining BUD/S to prove that she could beat him, but her voice faltered and she stopped.

"Sorry," Jennings said, "I didn't mean to make you cry."

"I'm not crying," Kinsey sniffed then wiped her cheeks and found them to be wet, "Son of a bitch."

Jennings reached out and wiped a tear from her chin. "Let's head back. That cool?"

"Not yet," she said, "just a little longer."

She got out of her seat and pulled Jennings down onto the floor.

"Hey, you don't have---" he started, but she shut him up with her mouth on his.

"I can't drink or shoot up," Kinsey said, "and I could really use an endorphin boost right now."

"So I'm just another fix, is that it?" Jennings laughed.

"Do you care?"

"Nope," he said as she pulled his shirt up over his head. He fumbled at her pants and undid the belt and then the zipper. "I don't care at all."

***

The com beeped as they struggled to get dressed in the tight space.

"Where the fuck are you?" Lake asked when Jennings finally answered. "It's been two hours, god dammit."

"Sorry, Chief," Jennings replied as he got the Wiglaf turned about. "Just got lost in the beauty." He looked over at Kinsey and gave her a wink. She rolled her eyes, but smiled at him. "We're on our way back now."

"Not so fast," Thorne said, suddenly on the com, "have you been checking your radar?"

"No," Jennings admitted, "we're about fifty meters deep. Running on sonar."

"Surface slowly and watch your radar," Thorne said. "We have a blip that keeps going in and out. We need you to get a visual and see if it's a threat."

"Got it," Jennings said. "We have enough power to go have a look and still make it back safe."

"You better make it back safe," Thorne said, "you have my daughter."

"Not a mermaid that needs saving, thank you," Kinsey snapped then turned off the com. "What an ass."

"He just cares," Jennings said.

"A caring ass is still an ass," Kinsey said. "Now show me how to take this up and surface slowly."

***

"It's an adolescent," Gunnar said, his face nearly beaming with excitement. "Not even fully grown!"

"How can you be sure?" Darren asked, trying to mask his own excitement at the discovery.

"Bone structure," Gunnar said. "Reproductive organs. This female hasn't hit sexual maturity."

"Female?" Darren asked. "Don't they usually stay close to the matriarchal pods?"

"Some do," Gunnar said. "Depends on the species. And we know nothing about this species since it's been extinct for thousands of years!"

"Calm down, man," Darren smiled. "What about the shark?"

"You can't tell a shark's age," Mr. Ballantine said from the deck below, "not accurately. There could be sharks in the ocean right now that are hundreds of years old. We don't know."

"This has been fascinating," Ms. Horace said, covering her nose and mouth. "But I am going to bed. You gentlemen have fun with your fish. I'll speak to you in the morning, Mr. Ballantine. We still have many details to work out."

"Yes, yes, of course," Mr. Ballantine said, dismissing the woman with a wave of a blood covered, gloved hand. "In the morning."

"Be careful, Ballantine," Mr. Perry said. "She holds a grudge."

"Does she?" Mr. Ballantine asked. "Then she can join the club. Turning in too, Stefan?"

"No," Mr. Perry said, "I'm going to enjoy a cocktail on the observation deck. Hopefully away from this smell."

"And Mr. Longbottom?" Mr. Ballantine asked.

"He has turned in," Mr. Perry said as he walked away. "He didn't have the stomach for any of this."

"Of course not," Mr. Ballantine said.

"You didn't put us on a sinking ship, did you Ballantine?" Darren asked, standing at the edge of the helipad.

"Sinking? No, of course not," Mr. Ballantine said. "But we may be adrift for a tad longer than I anticipated. At least until our discovery is legitimized. Then the company will see the benefits of an extraction Team under the cover of a true research vessel. A rouse would have been found out eventually. But this?" Ballantine spread his arms. "This couldn't be more perfect."

"Captain?" Lake called from up on the bridge. "You should get up here."

"What's up, Lake?" Darren asked.

"I just need to see you, please," Lake said.

Those that had been with him from the beginning all looked up at Lake then back at the captain.

"Please?" Popeye muttered. "When does he say please."

Gunnar looked up at Darren. "We okay?"

"I'll find out," Darren said, "be right back."

Lake and Thorne both stood with their arms crossed, looking at a video screen on the control board.

"Well?" Darren asked. "What's up?"

"That," Lake said.

"Video from the Wiglaf," Thorne said. "Kinsey just sent it to us. Then it went black. But not after seeing this."

The video was dark and grainy, and hard to make out as the camera kept bobbing up and down, but the subject was easy enough to make out. A ship was front and center.

"Audio?" Darren asked.

"Didn't come through," Lake said, "keep watching."

Darren sighed then his eyes went wide as a bright flash came from the ship and shot towards the camera. At that point, everything went black.

"Play it again," Darren said. They did. "Fuck me. RPG?"

"That's my guess," Thorne said.

"No word from the Wiglaf," Lake added. "We can't get them on the com."

"Radar? Sonar?" Darren asked.

"If they submerged, then no radar," Thorne said. "They are well out of sonar range."

"What now?" Darren asked, looking out of the bridge and down to the carcasses being worked on. "Which way are they headed?"

"Towards us," Lake said, "at a good clip."

"Fuck," Darren muttered, rubbing his tired face.

"We need to send the Team in the Wyrm to go get them," Thorne stated.

His tone of voice said there was no argument in there, but Darren had to argue. Everything he'd worked for was sitting on the second helipad below.

"We can't do that," Darren said. "We don't know if they are dead or alive. There are RPGs in play. We send the Wyrm and it could get shot out of the sky."

Thorne watched Darren for a second then smiled. He reached out slowly, put his hand on Darren's shoulder and squeezed.

"I used to think of you as my son," Thorne said. "I've known you since you were a teenager. Before you and Kinsey started dating. You've always been a good kid, Darren. But I will not hesitate to put a bullet between your eyes if it means saving my daughter."

"Whoa!" Lake protested. "No need for that!"

"It's cool, Marty," Darren said. "I get where he's coming from. I just don't think he gets where I'm coming from. We send the Wyrm and it gets shot down with the Team inside and then where are we? Undefended. We need Grendel here to fight off these bastards when they engage."

"I need my daughter to be alive," Thorne said.

"How about a compromise?" Lake said. "Send one of the Zodiacs with a couple people. Just to scout things."

"And lose them too?" Darren said. "We need to hold tight. Gunnar is working as fast as he can. We'll get as much data as possible, then get the specimen stored below. At that point we'll see where we are. It could be a freak thing."

"That wasn't a freak thing, Darren," Thorne snarled. "That was an RPG aimed at my little girl."

"Vincent, listen," Darren said. "I'm the captain of the Beowulf II. When all is said and done, you work for me. I have made my call. We aren't risking more lives to go after Kinsey."

"And Jennings," Lake added.

"Right, and Jennings," Darren said. "They'll make it back. I know Kinsey and she isn't going to die in a fucking mini-sub."

"Have you checked the damage transponder?" Darby asked from the hatchway.

"We don't have a signal at all," Lake said.

"Good," Darby said as she went to a screen on the control board. "If the Wiglaf is damaged so that it can't operate, then a transponder automatically kicks in and sends a signal here. It has a three hundred mile radius."

"Three hundred?" Darren said. "That would alert pretty much everyone."

"That's the point," Darby said. "It's a last resort only. And doesn't come on unless the Wiglaf has been nearly destroyed. Allows any company allied vessel to go after it and retrieve it quickly. There's a good sized reward for obtaining the remains of that mini-sub."

She typed at a keyboard for a couple minutes as the three men watched. Thorne frowned at every key stroke while Darren just stood there and rubbed his face; his fatigue was showing. Lake kept glancing from Darby to the radar and out at the dissections on the decks below.

"There," she said. "I hacked it. Not an easy thing to do, but I know most of the codes."

A beeping began to echo through the bridge. Lake looked at the radar and the sonar, but saw nothing.

"Won't that bring ships to it?" Darren said. "Which is the opposite of what we want?"

"No," Darby said, "I set it to test mode. Any ship picking that up will either not know what it is or decode and realize it's just routine maintenance."

"Then let's go get my daughter," Thorne said. "Mr. Lake, please take us to the heading of that signal."

"That will put us right in the path of the other ship," Lake said.

"So we don't go," Darren said. "In fact, we need to move the opposite direction. Get as far away from that ship as possible."

"They'll run out of power," Lake said.

Thorne started to move towards Darren, but Darby stepped between them. Despite her size, she was an imposing figure.

"I will take a Zodiac with one of the brothers," Darby said. "We'll scout them out. If they need help, we'll ditch the Wiglaf and bring them back in the Zodiac."

"Fine," Darren said, "do it."

"Smartest thing you've said all night," Thorne said.

***

"We have lost it on the sonar," Abuukar, one of Daacad's ensigns, said as Daacad stared out of the bridge and into the darkness of the night.

"Did anyone confirm a hit?" Daacad asked.

"No, sir," Abuukar replied.

"Not a one? How many rockets did we send?" Daacad asked.

"Three, sir."

"Send me the men that fired the rockets."

Orders were called out and Daacad waited patiently, his face blank, for the men to arrive.

"These are the three men that fired, sir," Abuukar announced as three scared looking men were escorted onto the bridge. "It was dark and the target was moving---"

Daacad pulled out his pistol and shot all three men in their head. Brains and blood splattered the glass windows of the bridge. No one dared move until Daacad had holstered his pistol.

"We proceed as planned," Daacad stated. "Follow the tracker. They know where that monster is. I will kill that beast or die trying. And all of you will be coming with me."

"Yes, sir," Abuukar said. Everyone else nodded, shocked at the sight of the corpses at their feet.

***

"We are taking on water too fast!" Kinsey yelled. She put her hand up to block a spray of sea water that was aimed right at her face as she sat at the controls, trying to get the Wiglaf to respond. "Any thoughts?"

"We have to just keep going," Jennings said, "and hope we have enough power to get back to the Beowulf II."

"Brilliant," Kinsey said, "just brilliant."

"What else do you want?" Jennings said. "We can't surface or they'll start sending rockets again. Look at the radar! They are almost right on top of us!"

"This is just perfect," Kinsey said. "I just wanted to get laid and now I'm going to die for it."

"Wanted to get laid?" Jennings said. "I took you out here to show you how to work the controls."

"Do you think I'm that stupid?" Kinsey said. "I knew you were hitting on me. Plus, Darby showed me the basics and I'd already gone through the manual three times. I could pilot this piece of shit in my dreams. It's not rocket science."

"You're saying you knew we were going to fuck?" Jennings laughed. "I didn't even know that. What if I'd said no?"

Kinsey smirked at him.

"What?" Jennings protested. "I might have."

"No you wouldn't have," Kinsey said. "Stop wasting your breath. Actually, stop wasting our breath. Look at the O2 meter."

"Shit," Jennings said, "the tanks must have been hit. We're running out of air fast."

"Which means we have to surface," Kinsey said.

"You think?" Jennings replied, slamming his hand against the controls. "Ow."

"It's dark, right?" Kinsey said. "Maybe they won't see us."

"We could play the maybe game all night long," Jennings said.

They sat there, each trying to work out what their next move would be.

"What if we ditch?" Kinsey suggested. "We bail when we're almost to the surface. If they blow the Wiglaf away, then they'll think we're dead."

"Which means we're stranded in the middle of the ocean," Jennings said. "I think you forgot to think your plan all the way through."

"No, I didn't," Kinsey said. "While they're dealing with the mini-sub, we'll sneak aboard their ship. We've already figured out that they're headed for the Beowulf II, right? That's their obvious heading. We just stay low and hitch a ride. Might do everyone some good to have us onboard that ship if things get tense."

"Yes, because they aren't tense now," Jennings said. He took a deep breath and let it out. "Sure. Let's do it. Just one problem."

"What's that?" Kinsey asked.

"How do we get aboard their ship?"

"That's not a problem at all," Kinsey said. "I was almost a SEAL. I'm trained for this."

"You realize the weakness in your plan is the use of the word 'almost', right?" Jennings said.

***

"Off port bow!" a sentry shouted.

Daacad hurried from the bridge, picking up an RPG launcher as he descended the stairs to the deck below. He put the weapon to his shoulder and looked out where the sentry pointed.

"This is how it is done," Daacad said as he fired the rocket at the surfacing mini-sub.

The explosion lit the night and sent fire raging into the sky. Daacad handed the spent launcher to the sentry.

"Reload that," Daacad said. "Job well done."

***

Her breath held, Kinsey tossed the hook and rope up as high as she could, saying a silent prayer that no one would notice or hear the noise. She gave the rope a tug and was confident the hook was secure on the railing above. She hadn't had to scale a ship's hull since SQT, which didn't exactly bring back happy memories.

She pulled herself up and over the rail, a knife in her hand. She should have brought a pistol with her into the Wiglaf, but she didn't think she'd be engaging hostiles. Lesson learned.

A sentry was about fifteen feet away and began to turn towards her, but she closed the distance and had the knife buried to the hilt up in the soft flesh under his chin, through his palate and into his brain. The man's eyes widened in surprise then glazed over in death. Kinsey lowered the body to the deck quietly and dragged it over to a lifeboat. She pulled back the cover and shoved the body inside, then crouched low and took a look about. It was clear.

"Come on," she whispered down at Jennings.

The man was winded by the time he reached the rail and Kinsey gave him a reproachful look.

"What?" Jennings said. "That wasn't exactly easy."

"I'm detoxing from alcohol and junk," Kinsey said, "and I barely broke a sweat."

"Fuck you, supergirl," Jennings said. "What now?"

"In here," Kinsey said as she opened the cover to the lifeboat.

"No way," Jennings said, seeing the dead body.

"Don't be a pussy," Kinsey said, "get in."

Jennings muttered and swore, but climbed in. Kinsey followed and let the cover fall back down.

"Now we sit tight," Kinsey said. "We reassess when this ship gets to the Beowulf II."

"What if we're wrong?" Jennings said. "What if this ship isn't going after the Beowulf II and changes course? Then what?"

"What else would they be doing out here?" Kinsey said. "And why would they have RPGs? They're going after the Beowulf II."

***

"Gone? What do you mean gone?" Thorne asked. "What the fuck happened to the signal, Darby?"

"It stopped," Darby said over the com. "I'm not getting a reading anymore. Unless you guys have something there, we've lost it."

"Shit!" Thorne shouted. He looked at Lake then Darren. They both shook their head.

"Something I could help with?" Mr. Ballantine asked as he stepped onto the bridge. "I saw Darby leave with one of the Reynolds. I assume she is doing something important?"

"Kinsey and Jennings took the Wiglaf out for training and there has been an incident," Darren said. "Show him."

"Show him?" Lake said. "Are you talking to me? What am I, you're A/V specialist?"

"Just play the fucking video!" Thorne shouted.

Mr. Ballantine raised his eyebrows in surprise, but said nothing as Lake started the video. Mr. Ballantine only watched it once then nodded.

"And what were you hoping to accomplish by sending Darby out?" Mr. Ballantine said.

"We were hoping to rescue my daughter," Thorne snapped.

"And Jennings," Lake added, "let's not forget Jennings."

Thorne just glared.

"Commander Thorne wanted to have Bobby take the Wyrm up, but I said that was too much of a risk," Darren said.

"You're right there," Mr. Ballantine agreed, "but there may be another option."

"And that is?" Thorne asked.

"I have just received word that the long range helicopter is available and tasked to pick up my colleagues a day early," Mr. Ballantine said. "It is on the way now. It can pick up Mr. Perry, Ms. Horace, and Mr. Longbottom, then look for Ms. Thorne and Mr. Jennings. How does that sound?"

"It should look for them first," Thorne said, "that's how that sounds."

"It won't," Mr. Ballantine said. "The pilot is under orders from the company. I can't influence the objective until I get face to face with the man."

"But what would happen to Kinsey and Jennings?" Lake asked.

"They'd be taken to a company ship," Mr. Ballantine said. "Then back to the mainland. They'd miss the rest of the mission, but we'd pick them up in a month or so."

"They…what? A month?" Thorne fumed. "You have got to be shitting me."

"I shit you not," Mr. Ballantine said.

"Darren? You know about this?" Thorne asked.

"Of course he does," Mr. Ballantine said. "Well, the continuing of the mission part. You see, Commander, with the discovery that the whale is an adolescent that means Captain Chambers hasn't found exactly what he was looking for. And neither have I, for that matter."

"Are you two fucking nuts?" Thorne roared, pointing out of the bridge and at the decks below. "You have two motherfucking prehistoric sea creatures on this motherfucking ship! And you aren't satisfied?" He turned on Darren. "Is Gunnar satisfied? I have a feeling he has enough work to last him years! And you greedy motherfuckers want more?" Thorne began to pull his sidearm. "Fuck you!"

Lake grabbed Thorne's hand and got right in his face. "No, sir. Just no."

Thorne nearly went for Lake's throat, but he saw the look in the Chief's eyes and knew the man was just saving him from making a big mistake.

"I'm cool," Thorne said to Lake. When the Chief finally backed off, Thorne turned to Ballantine. "What about the pirates? You think they'll stick with your new plan?"

"Pirates?" Mr. Ballantine asked. "What's this?"

"Presumed pirates," Darren said, "we don't have confirmation."

"Yes, we do," Darby said over the com, "or did you forget about us?"

* * *

The Zodiac bobbed in the small waves about one hundred yards from Daacad's ship. Darby and Shane, both wearing their NVGs, watched the ship carefully, counting as many men on deck as they could see.

"You catching this?" Shane whispered. "Are the NVGs transmitting?"

"Crystal clear," Max replied. "Full Team is here in the command center. Well, except for all of you out there on the high seas. We're watching what you're watching."

"Definitely pirates," Darby said. "Any face rec coming in?"

"Give us a second," Darren replied. "The satellite uplink is slow."

"Switch to the manual database," Darby said. "I have a hunch."

The ship kept moving and Darby turned the Zodiac to follow, staying well back out of the ship's lights and to the side of the wake. The ship's engines were loud enough to drown out any noise the Zodiac's motor was making, but Darby still wasn't happy with how close they were. She would have preferred to tail from a couple hundred yards further back. But they needed the close proximity for the NVGs to pick up information.

"Bingo," Max said, "we have a winner."

"Care to let us in on the good news?" Shane asked.

"Sure thing, bro," Max said. "We have at least three faces the NVGs picked up during our attempted rescue the other night. Those pirates are *our* pirates. I think they missed us."

"How did they find us?" Darren said over the com.

"Who says they did?" Lake countered. "Maybe they're just out looking for another target. And we happen to be the only suckers out here."

"Doesn't feel right," Darby said.

"Well, not to copy Ditcher, since I'd rather drink my own pee, but how did they find us?" Max asked.

"That would be my fault," Darby said, "I didn't scan the hard drives."

"No, we both scanned them," Darren replied. "That's how we got the geotag coordinates."

"I mean I didn't scan for bugs or tracking devices," Darby said. "I would wager if you scanned them now, you'd find something that has led them right to us."

"I count two RPGs," Lucy said. "Is that what you're seeing?"

"I see two now," Shane replied, his eye to his scope, having taken Lucy's .50 caliber with him. "But there were at least two more earlier. They must have gone below."

"You sure they didn't hand off the weapons?" Thorne asked.

"I'm sure," Shane said. "You can check the footage. You'll see. That makes a minimum of four RPGs."

"Mr. Ballantine?" Darby asked. "Don't you think it's time the Team met the Toyshop?"

"It could be, Darby," Mr. Ballantine said. "But I was hoping to wait until my colleagues had departed the ship."

"Toyshop? What the fuck is that?" Thorne asked. "And why wait until the suits are gone?"

"Some of the items below are not sanctioned by the company," Mr. Ballantine said. "They could possibly violate more than a few international arms treaties."

"I like the sound of that," Max said.

"Darby? You and Mr. Reynolds should return to the Beowulf II immediately," Mr. Ballantine suggested. "Since there is no sign of Ms. Thorne or Mr. Jennings."

Darby and Shane flipped up their NVGs and looked at each other.

"You want to tell them?" Shane asked.

"The man is your uncle," Darby said, "you should tell them."

"Tell us what?" Thorne asked. "What did you find?"

"At first we didn't know what we were seeing," Shane said. "Then we realized we were floating through debris. It was the Wiglaf. Looks like it took a rocket."

"Fuck," Thorne whispered.

"Even more reason to get back here," Mr. Ballantine said. "We'll need all hands on deck. Especially Team Grendel hands. Copy that, Darby?"

"Copy, sir," Darby said.

"As do I," Daacad's voice interrupted over the com. "Hello, friends."

A spot light flared to life from the stern of the ship, lighting up the Zodiac.

"You have impressive technology," Daacad said. "But so do I. You should work on your communication encryption algorithm. It was painfully easy to break."

"I got it," Shane said. He squeezed the trigger and the spotlight went dark just as Darby scrambled to the motor controls and started to turn the Zodiac around.

"Please stay where you are," Daacad said as another spotlight illuminated the Zodiac. "You are well in range of my rockets. And as you have seen, I have more than enough to blast you out of the water."

"Ah, fuck," Shane said, "what now?"

"Killing com, Darby," Mr. Ballantine said, his voice cold.

"Understood," Darby replied.

The com went dead in Shane and Darby's ear. It cut off their communication with the Beowulf II, but it also cut communication with Daacad and his ship.

"So?" Shane asked. "What now? Options?"

"Run or don't run," Darby said.

"Run and we may get a rocket or two up our asses," Shane said. "We could bail and last in this warm water for a long time. But…"

"But we've had a glimpse of what is in these waters," Darby said. "Prehistoric or not, there are many predators below."

"Okay, then don't run and we let the pirates pick us up," Shane said, "the company can pay our ransom."

"First, we are expendable," Darby said. "They will not pay ransom for anyone on the extraction Team. That was made clear in your contract."

"Yeah, I saw that," Shane said. "I was hoping it was a standard clause and might be overlooked."

"The point of standard clauses is to avoid things being overlooked," Darby said. "We will be on our own. But that isn't the problem."

"What is?" Shane asked. "I'd really like to hear this."

"Normally, I'd say this was a revenge mission on the pirates' part," Darby said, "but that wouldn't explain why they put a tracker in one of the hard drives. They knew we would come. Which means they were given a heads up."

"A heads up?" Shane said. "You mean like a spy? What the fuck?"

"Do not attempt to flee!" a voice boomed from a bullhorn on the ship. "You will bring your boat to us! Steer to the starboard side and you will be brought aboard! Leave all weapons in the boat! If a weapon is seen in your hand you will be killed! Comply now or you will be killed!"

Darby adjusted course and aimed for the starboard side of the ship.

"So, not running?" Shane asked.

"No," Darby said, "we need more intel on who is working with the pirates and why."

"Can we call this a new mission?" Shane asked. "That is a way bigger boost to the ego than just being captured."

"Tell yourself what you need," Darby said, "but I have never been captured before and don't intend to be now. I'm always in control."

"I like the positive attitude," Shane said as the Zodiac approached the side of the ship. "I can see why my brother wants to marry you."

"Never going to happen," Darby said.

"I keep telling him that," Shane replied. "He's not right for you. Me, on the other hand---"

"Never going to happen," Darby said. "Shut up and get ready for the new mission. Keep your eyes and ears open. I'm relying on you to get as much intel as possible."

The Zodiac came alongside the ship and two rope ladders were dropped from the rail.

"Take a hold of the ladders!" the bullhorn blared.

Shane reached for one and grabbed on, lifting up from the boat. Darby struggled to keep the Zodiac steady next to the moving ship. She sped up and kept one hand on the controls while reaching for a ladder with the other.

"Just hold it still!" Shane shouted. "I'll grab on to you!"

The Zodiac slammed up and down on the ship's wake and Darby lost her grip on the controls. She screamed as the boat slammed into the side of the ship then ran up the hull and flipped.

"Darby!" Shane cried. "DARBY!"

He dangled from the ladder, smacking against the side of the ship, as he searched the churning waters below for any sign of her. But she and the Zodiac were gone, lost under the ship, taken below by the pull of the water.

"Keep climbing or you will be shot!" the bullhorn screeched.

"Fuck you!" Shane shouted up at the rail.

He looked up, but could see nothing above as he was blinded by several high-powered flashlights. He thought about saying fuck it and dropping from the ladder, but a warning shot pushed that thought from his head. He realized he wanted to live. Plus, he had a new mission to accomplish: find out who sold out the Beowulf II and Team Grendel.

Whoever it was would pay dearly.

CHAPTER EIGHT: BAD BOYS AND BAD TOYS

"Carlos, Ingrid, Moshi," Mr. Ballantine said, "they are the elves of the Toyshop."

"Don't call it that," Carlos said. Short, squat, with a thin, black Mohawk, the man stood at a caged in counter, his arms crossed against his flabby chest. He wore a stained t-shirt with a faded TMNT logo on it. "And we're not elves."

"Nice shirt," Cougher said from the back of the group that Ballantine had brought down to meet the weapons specialists tucked away in the hidden armory. "That an original Eastman and Laird version?"

"Of course," Carlos said. "I stopped reading the series when it went all afternoon cartoon and Archie blech."

"Sweet," Cougher said, then saw everyone looking back at him. "What? Fuck you guys."

"Hey," Ingrid said. She was tall, skinny, had long, bright (not natural) red pigtails that were braided up around the back of her head, and she wore a bright yellow jumpsuit. Her eyes were almost white they were so blue. "Welcome to the Toyshop. I like it to be called that. Makes it fun."

Moshi, the third tech, stood almost directly behind Ingrid. Each time the tall woman shifted, Moshi matched her and stayed obscured. She peeked out a little and gave a small wave, then brushed the black bangs from her forehead and ducked back behind Ingrid.

"Moshi doesn't talk," Ingrid said, "like never ever. But her fingers are the most dexterous I have ever seen in a weaponsmith. Or, like anyone, not just weaponsmiths. But I'd have to say that weaponsmiths are the most dexterous of craftspeople. See how I said craftspeople? You'll notice there's only one guy here. And he can be a total---"

"Thank you, Ingrid," Mr. Ballantine said, cutting her off, "but we are short on time."

"We need heavy artillery that can handle pirates armed with RPGs," Thorne said, standing next to Mr. Ballantine at the head of the group. Behind him were Darren, Max, Lucy, Bobby, and Cougher. "And we have only a couple hours before they get here."

"You want counter artillery?" Carlos asked. "Are you looking to stop the rockets before they hit the B2? Or looking to take out the launchers at the source? First strike?"

"Whatever you can give us," Thorne said.

"B2," Max said, "it's so much easier than saying Beowulf II all the time. B2. Wish I'd thought of that."

"Well, you didn't," Carlos grumbled, "I did. I call copyright."

"Uh, okay," Max said, "you have copyright. Good for you." He looked over his shoulder at Lucy and Bobby and mouthed, "What the fuck?"

"Carlos has what you need, Commander Thorne," Mr. Ballantine said. "I'll leave you to work out the details." He tapped his ear. "I am being called by Doctor Peterson. He has something interesting to tell me about our specimens."

"Don't you think there's more important issues to deal with?" Thorne asked. "I'd say the science can wait."

Mr. Ballantine just smiled and left the room.

"This is so cool," Cougher said.

"Why are you here again?" Bobby asked him.

"I'm First Engineer now that Bach is dead," Cougher frowned. "It's my job to know about all of the equipment on the ship."

"I don't work for you," Carlos said, pointing a finger towards Cougher. "I don't work for anybody. This is my shop, what I say goes."

"Shut up," Thorne said, "both of you. I need firepower and I need it now. What have you got?"

"I'll bring up some samples," Carlos said.

"Can't we just come back there?" Darren asked. "I am the Captain of the ship."

"No," Carlos said, "you're captain of dick down here. My shop."

"Just fucking hurry," Thorne snarled, "or I'll turn *you* into captain of dick. Captain of my dick up your ass!"

"Not sure who that insulted more, Uncle Vinny," Max said, but shut right up when Thorne turned a deadly glare on him.

***

"Gunnar," Mr. Ballantine said as he stepped into the main research lab, "what could be so urgent at this time?"

"Everything," Gunnar said, his voice slightly cold. "I know we will have company shortly, but I thought I'd have a word with you before we possibly die."

"We won't be dying today, Gunnar," Mr. Ballantine said, "or tomorrow or the next day. That's why I hired Commander Thorne. He'll keep us safe."

"From who?" Gunnar asked. "Because I'm having trouble figuring out who the bad guys are?"

"I'm sorry, Gunnar, I'm not following you," Mr. Ballantine said, "have I missed something?"

"No, you don't miss a thing," Gunnar said as he stepped to a keyboard and started typing. A large vid screen came to life. "Unfortunately for you, I don't either."

"That's a lot of data on that screen," Mr. Ballantine said, grabbing a stool and taking a seat, "I should get comfortable."

"Are you armed?" Gunnar asked.

"Am I what?"

"Armed," Gunnar repeated. "With a pistol or any type of weapon you could use to kill me once I reveal what I've found."

Mr. Ballantine grimaced. "I'm really not liking where this conversation is going, Doctor Peterson. Please explain yourself immediately."

"I will," Gunnar replied. He pulled a small pistol from his pocket and held it loosely at his side. "I just want to make sure I have your undivided attention."

"That, Doctor Peterson, you have," Mr. Ballantine said, "completely undivided."

***

"Chopper incoming!" Popeye shouted. "But we ain't got the helipad cleared!"

Lake watched out the bridge windows as the company helicopter –a large, grey helo that was almost twice the size of the Wyrm- circled the Beowulf II. He tapped the com.

"This is Chief Officer Martin Lake of the Beowulf II," Lake announced over the com. "Can you put down on the carcass?"

"Are you joking?" the helo pilot replied. "You want me to set down on that pile of guts? Please tell me you're joking?"

"The alternative is to circle for a couple hours while we clear the space," Lake responded. "You have the fuel for that?"

"Listen, Chief," the pilot said, "I can set down on that thing, sure, but it won't be pretty. You know what my bird is going to do to that? It'll destroy it. And not in a good way."

"Is there a good way to destroy something?" Lake asked. "Just set down. We'll deal with the mess as best we can."

"Okay, but I warned you," the pilot said as the helo came in close.

It hovered over the whale carcass for a minute then slowly landed. Even with the rotors still at full power, everyone on deck heard the crunching of bones and the loud pop as the spine of the whale split and the carcass burst open from the back.

"Fuck me," Popeye swore as he stood on the deck covered in rotten whale guts. The thing had exploded right at him and he didn't have a chance even to duck. "This shit ain't ever coming out. Gonna have to burn these damn clothes."

***

"Name," a large, muscled brute asked, then slammed a fist into Shane's gut before he could answer.

His hands strung up over him, Shane hung from a large hook, his toes just able to touch the rusted floor of the dark, dank room he had been thrown into. His face was a patchwork of cuts and bruises which matched his torso as he hung there naked, shivering, and glared at the pirate before him that had been tasked with making his life hell.

"I already told you," Shane spat. "My name is Inigo Montoya. Prepare to die."

"That is a funny movie," Daacad said as he came into the room, "Princess Bride, yes? Very funny movie."

Daacad motioned for the brute to move and the man did immediately. In his hand, Daacad held an ice pick. He twirled it around his fingers and Shane couldn't help swallowing hard at what that implied.

"Do you like watching movies?" Daacad asked Shane, the ice pick twirling and twirling.

"Yeah," Shane replied, "everyone likes watching movies. My favorite is La Femme Nikita. Ever see that one?"

"No, I have not seen that one," Daacad said, "please tell me about it."

"Uh, well, it's about this street girl that gets a chance to become this bad ass assassin instead of being put to death for killing a cop," Shane explained, his eyes watching as the ice pick twirled, twirled, twirled. "But, of course, shit gets fucked up and things don't turn out how she wants. Especially when she falls in love with a normal guy that can't know what she does."

"Shit gets fucked up?" Daacad laughed. "Americans and their vernacular. Shit gets fucked up. I like that. Very appropriate for your situation, yes? Your shit has gotten fucked up."

"I'd like to unfuck it," Shane said. "How about you just let me go?"

"No, I do not think so," Daacad said. He motioned at the brute and the man brought over a metal folding chair. Daacad took a seat. "But I want to hear more about your favorite movie. Start from the beginning."

"Uh…you want me to tell you all of it?" Shane asked.

"Yes," Daacad replied, "and when you are, done I will ask you one question."

"And what is that question?" Shane asked.

"No, no, no," Daacad said, "as the internet likes to say that would be a spoiler. Tell me the story of La Femme Nikita. Then I will ask my question."

Shane took a deep breath, his eyes on the ice pick that never stopped twirling, twirling, twirling.

***

"I matched the DNA profile of the whale with what was in the database I compiled of all known fossil samples found," Gunnar said as he pointed at the video screen. "This carcass we found matched to 98%. Which is disappointing."

"You were hoping for 100%?" Mr. Ballantine asked, his eyes going from Gunnar's face to the pistol the scientist held at his side. "Perfection is always the goal, right Doctor Peterson?"

"Yet unobtainable," Gunnar replied. "We are talking a million years of evolution here. The fact that there is a 98% match is remarkable. But, this means we may not have actually found *Livyatan Melville*, just its direct descendant."

"Congratulations," Mr. Ballantine said, "Your discovery will be lauded in the marine biology field, if not the scientific community as a whole."

"I found a dead whale," Gunnar said. "Well, *we* found a dead whale. Nothing to be lauded there. I may get credit for finding a new species, but not for finding an extinct species still alive."

"Yes, well, we can't have everything," Mr. Ballantine said. "Still quite an achievement."

"It is," Gunnar said, "I will admit that. It will take months, maybe years to fully write this up and verify my findings. But I'm not going to have the time to do that, am I?"

"You're being very cryptic today, Gunnar," Mr. Ballantine said, "and more than a little unstable. I've played your game and would really appreciate an explanation as to why you feel it necessary to keep me sitting here at gunpoint."

"I'm not pointing a gun at you," Gunnar said. "Just keeping some insurance on hand."

"Insurance? Do I need to fetch Mr. Longbottom? He is the expert in that field," Mr. Ballantine grinned. Gunnar didn't. "Ah, not up for levity, I see. Well, I am your captive guest. Please continue. I want to hear why you won't have time for your research."

"Because you'll probably have me killed," Gunnar said, "for what I found."

"Kill you over a whale?" Mr. Ballantine asked, obviously puzzled. "You have truly lost me, Gunnar."

"Not over the whale," Gunnar said, "that was just to lure us out here. Give you a smoke screen for what you really wanted."

"And what do I really want?" Mr. Ballantine asked.

"The shark," Gunnar said as he closed one window on the screen and brought up another.

"Yes, I have said I was after the shark," Mr. Ballantine nodded. "I have made no secret of that."

"Yeah, but you weren't exactly forthcoming about the true nature of the shark," Gunnar said. "Your shark. The one you made."

Mr. Ballantine looked at the screen and then at Gunnar. And smiled. It was probably the most genuine smile he'd shown anyone since leaving Cape Town. It took Gunnar aback and he gripped the pistol tighter.

"Oh, put that away, for Christ's sake," Mr. Ballantine laughed, "I'm not going to kill you. I'd rather hug you right now. You have exceeded my wildest dreams, Gunnar. At no point did I expect you to come to that conclusion so quickly."

"Expected me?" Gunnar said. "What the hell does that mean?"

"It means you have passed your audition, Doctor Gunnar Peterson," Mr. Ballantine said. He got up from the stool and held out his hand. "Welcome to the company."

***

"Then she opened the box and it was a gun with two extra magazines...or three magazines?" Shane said. "No, two, I'm pretty sure."

"Oh, it wasn't a celebration, was it?" Daacad said. "She was set up?"

"Yeah, her handler set her up," Shane continued. "Turns out, she was there for a job. She had to kill a guy sitting at the table close to them."

"That must have broken her heart," Daacad said. "To be lured in and tricked like that. I would have shot the handler, if it was me. I don't like to be played with."

"No, she went through with the job," Shane said. "It was what she was trained to do."

The ice pick twirled, twirled, twirled.

"And then what?" Daacad asked. "She got away?"

"Sort of," Shane responded.

***

"I'll need that shit cleared off this pad before I take off," the helo pilot shouted as the rotors powered down and he opened the cockpit door. "Look at that crap! I have fucking bones jammed up around the skids."

"We aren't doing anything until I get the okay from Gunnar," Lake said as he stood by the helipad. "That's his specimen. I'm already going to catch hell for letting you destroy it."

"I don't care what hell you catch," the pilot said. "Get someone to clear that crap off so I can pick up my passengers and leave this ship. Or I'll start kicking some ass until it gets done."

Lake furrowed his brow. "Uh, kick some ass? You need to lighten up. Let me get Gunnar up here and we'll go from there."

***

The pistol shook as Gunnar lifted it towards Mr. Ballantine. "Fucking explain what the fuck you're talking about. Now."

"Now? Right now?" Mr. Ballantine smiled. "Not until you put the pistol down, Gunnar. You aren't a killer. You aren't going to shoot me. And after what I tell you, you won't want to."

"Then tell me," Gunnar said.

"First, I want to know what you found," Mr. Ballantine said, "to make sure I'm not mistaken in my praise for you."

Gunnar sighed and nodded back at the video screen. "At first, after running the DNA, I thought that my great find was the shark. Your shark. For all intents and purposes, it matches perfectly the DNA for *C. Megalodon*, the prehistoric monster shark. That's what the database said. I tested it again and got the same result. Except for a strange anomaly that kept coming up."

"Which was?" Mr. Ballantine said.

"Something in the sample kept crashing the sequencing process," Gunnar said, "which is impressive considering the equipment this lab has. I'm able to do analysis in a twentieth the time it would normally take."

"A hundredth," Mr. Ballantine corrected. "You just haven't learned to use it all properly."

"A hundredth? Really?" Gunnar asked as he looked about the lab. Then he shook his head and focused back on Ballantine. "Whatever. I had to reboot the system over and over. Each time I'd reboot, I'd get more of the result until *C. Megalodon* was the answer the computer spit out."

"Incredible," Mr. Ballantine said. "Couple that with your new species of whale and your legend is secured in the annals of scientific discovery."

"Yeah, except that the computer lied," Gunnar said. "That isn't *C. Megalodon* up on deck, that's something different. Right?"

"You tell me, Gunnar. Is it?" Mr. Ballantine asked.

***

"I can't feel my legs," Jennings whispered. "They have gone completely fucking numb."

"You'd make a shitty SEAL," Kinsey said. "SEALs have to hold a position for days sometimes without moving. You just think past the pain and discomfort."

"And I have to piss," Jennings said, "bad."

"Then piss," Kinsey responded, "and shut the fuck up about it. They'll hear us."

"Don't you have to piss?" Jennings asked.

"No," Kinsey said, "I already did."

"Oh," Jennings said, "gross."

"Shut. Up," Kinsey said.

The sun had just crested the horizon and the lifeboat they were hidden in had started to warm up. The air under the canvass cover had become stifling. Kinsey wasn't sure how long they would last under there once the sun was fully beating down on them.

"We can't stay here," Kinsey said, "we're going to cook."

"Maybe I'll sweat out the piss," Jennings said.

"Dream big, stud," Kinsey said. "Hold tight. I'm going to have a look."

Kinsey gently lifted the cover and had a peek at the ship. She waited for the movement to be detected, but no alarm went up. There was no one in her limited field of vision, so she carefully hooked a leg over the lifeboat's side and stepped onto the ship's deck. She crouched down as she got out and scanned her surroundings.

No one was in sight.

"Come on," Kinsey said, "we'll see if we can work our way below."

"And do what?" Jennings whispered as he followed Kinsey out of the lifeboat.

"Sabotage the ship," Kinsey said. "We'll take it down from the inside."

"Works for me," Jennings replied. "Show me the way."

"You're the sailor," Kinsey said. "After you."

"Great," Jennings said. He studied the ship. "Okay, I know where the engine room is on this thing. I worked a ship like it when I was a kid."

"Maybe it's the same ship," Kinsey said, "we are dealing with pirates."

"Nope," Jennings said, "that ship sank. It was an unlucky piece of shit. Fucking thing was cursed. The crew barely made it off."

"Let's hope we have better luck," Kinsey said as they cautiously moved across the deck towards a hatch that stood partially open.

***

"Will someone tell me why Gunnar isn't answering the com?" Lake asked. "Anyone?"

"Lake, this is Thorne," Thorne's voice replied over the com, "how long have you been trying to reach him?"

"For a few minutes," Lake said. "We have a situation up top that he'll want to know about."

"Ballantine was going to see him," Thorne said. "They both should be in the lab. I'll go see what I can find out."

"Thanks," Lake said as he stood there and glared at the helo pilot.

"Hey, Chief?" Popeye asked, pointing over the rail down at the water. "You see that?"

"I'm standing over here, Popeye," Lake said. "I can't see anything except for the big cluster fuck in front of me."

"Right back atcha," the pilot said.

"Huh," Popeye said, "never mind. Don't see nothing no more."

***

"All data suggests that what we caught is *C. Megalodon*, a monster shark that was the apex predator of its time," Gunnar said, "and that's where the problem is. The DNA match is *too* perfect."

"That's a problem?" Mr. Ballantine replied. "I guess my understanding of scientific findings isn't the same as yours. Aren't you trying for perfection?"

"No," Gunnar replied, "you see, the DNA matched one of the samples 100%. That was what kept gumming up the analysis. Or that's what I thought. So I looked deeper. The DNA matches 100% because it was designed to. That shark up there isn't a descendant of the Megalodon in the database sample, it's a fucking clone of it."

"Clone? That's just crazy talk, Doctor Peterson," Mr. Ballantine smirked. "No one would believe that."

"Yeah, not even the computer," Gunnar said, "but I found the genetic markers. I found the identical mutations that every single living thing on Earth has. No two creatures can be exactly alike, but this one is. How'd you do it?"

"I didn't do anything," Mr. Ballantine said.

"Then how'd the company do it? I assume that's who created the creature?" Gunnar asked.

"Now that's disappointing," Mr. Ballantine said. "You were doing so well up until that point. The company doesn't create anything. Except solutions to problems."

"So a client created the shark, is that it?"

"That is it."

"And what? It got out of its tank?"

"Oh, it didn't get out," Mr. Ballantine said. "It was never in a tank. That shark was born in the ocean. Or birthed is more like it. There would have to be conception actually to be born, am I right? I'm hazy on that science. Maybe you can tell me the difference."

"What? That can't be right," Gunnar said, "this shark is a clone. Unless you are saying a different shark was impregnated with this shark and that was the shark that got loose? Is that what you are telling me?"

"I'm not telling you anything," Mr. Ballantine said, "I'm listening to you discover. And it's very entertaining."

"God dammit!" Gunnar yelled. "Cut the crap! Just give me a straight answer!"

"To what?" Thorne asked from the hatch to the lab. His eyes instantly zeroed in on the pistol in Gunnar's hand. "What the fuck is this, kid?"

"Oh, nothing to worry about, Commander," Mr. Ballantine said. "Doctor Peterson is a little jumpy because he has found out some very sensitive information. What he still doesn't understand, is that I wanted him to find it out. If I had just told him, then the truth would have been buried under disbelief."

"Disbelief in what?" Thorne asked, moving into the lab, his eyes never leaving Gunnar's pistol. "What the hell is going on?"

"Doctor Peterson was explaining how the shark we caught is not a real shark at all," Mr. Ballantine said. "Does that answer your question or just bring up more?"

***

"Back, back," Kinsey hissed as she grabbed Jennings by the shoulders and yanked him into an open hatch.

They both nearly tumbled into the dark room just as a man with a rifle walked past. Kinsey instinctively covered Jennings's mouth with her hand as she pulled him further into the shadows. The man with the rifle paused at the hatch. He looked into the room, cocked his head and listened, then shrugged and pulled the hatch closed, plunging them into pitch blackness.

Kinsey waited a couple minutes, and then took her hand away from Jennings's mouth.

"You almost suffocated me," Jennings said. "I know how to be fucking quiet."

"Neither of you do," a voice said from across the room. "Your whispers carry across the whole damn ship."

"What the fuck?" Jennings jumped.

"Darby?" Kinsey asked. "How the hell did you get here?"

"Good ears, Kinsey," Darby said. "I came with Shane to find you two."

"Shane's here?" Kinsey asked. "Hey, cuz."

"He's not here with me," Darby replied, "he was captured. I wasn't. Now I have to rescue him as well as you two."

"We don't need rescuing," Jennings said. "Do we?"

"No," Kinsey replied, "but now plans change. We were going to sabotage the engines. I guess we should rescue my cousin first."

"That would be a good idea," Darby said, "since I'm certain he's being tortured for information. And sabotaging the engines would be a bad idea since this ship is heading for the Beowulf II as we speak. No point in wrecking our ride."

***

"Clones?" Thorne asked. "Is this a joke?"

196

"In a twisted way, Commander, yes," Mr. Ballantine said, "because the clone shouldn't exist. There were never meant to be duplicates. Just the one."

"Why?" Thorne asked.

"Did you find him?" Lake asked over the com.

"Hold on, Chief," Thorne replied, "I found him, but I have a situation on my hands right now."

"Who are you talking to?" Gunnar asked.

"Lake," Thorne replied, "he needs to talk to you. Something about the company helicopter landing on your whale body."

"IT WHAT?" Gunnar shouted. He started to move towards the hatch, looked at the gun in his hand, and then looked at Ballantine.

"Go ahead," Thorne said, "I'll keep an eye on Ballantine until you get back. Maybe he can catch me up on what I've missed."

"Oh, I'd prefer to go with Doctor Peterson," Mr. Ballantine said. "I should probably speak to the pilot. And my colleagues who must be itching to leave this ship as soon as possible."

"Give me that," Thorne said as he took the pistol from Gunnar. "Get up there and see what's going on."

Gunnar looked at Thorne then back at Ballantine.

"Go!" Thorne shouted. "Jesus."

Gunnar took off running.

"Are we going to have a problem?" Thorne asked.

"We never have and never will," Mr. Ballantine said. "Despite Gunnar's suspicions, I am fully on your side. Can I explain as we walk?"

"You fucking better," Thorne said as he slipped Gunnar's pistol into his pocket.

"How trusting," Mr. Ballantine observed.

"Just confident," Thorne replied. "I know you have training, but I have more. It may be a fight if you try something, but it won't be a long one."

"Fair enough," Mr. Ballantine said. "Let's see…where do I start?"

"At the beginning," Thorne said as he motioned towards the hatch.

***

"And she just leaves him?" Daacad asked, standing up from his chair. "She's gone?"

"Gone," Shane said, "on the run."

"What about the sequel?" Daacad asked. "Where does she turn up in that?"

"There is no sequel," Shane replied. "That's one reason I love that movie so much. It stands on its own."

"Well," Daacad said as he moved up close to Shane, the ice pick ever twirling, "then it is time for my question."

"I could tell you about my second favorite movie?" Shane said.

"And what is that?" Daacad asked.

"Ghostbusters," Shane said. "You ever see Ghostbusters?"

"Everyone has seen that movie," Daacad said, "and you are out of time to talk movies. Now I ask my question."

Daacad got right up next to Shane and pressed the tip of the ice pick close to Shane's left eye. Shane started to struggle, to swing himself away, but Daacad grabbed him by the throat and held him still.

"Ready for my question?" Daacad asked.

"No," Shane admitted, "can I take a rain check?"

"No," Daacad replied. "My question is: do you ever want to see a movie again? Answer honestly, please, Mr. Montoya."

"Ha. Funny," Shane said, "and yes, I do want to see another movie. I'd like to see lots of movies."

"Then you will answer every new question I ask from now on," Daacad said. "Understand me? You will answer truthfully and without hesitation. Or no more movies for you."

Daacad slid the ice pick into Shane's eye slowly. Blood and fluid spurted from the orb and onto Daacad's hand. The scream that came from Shane's mouth was ear splitting.

"Stay still," Daacad said as he pushed the ice pick in further, "or I may slip and hit your brain."

Shane continued to scream, drowning out the boy that stood at the hatch, calling to Daacad.

"Sir! Sir!" the boy shouted. "You are needed on the bridge, sir!"

"What?" Daacad asked, pulling the ice pick from Shane's eye. "Speak up, boy!"

"The bridge, sir," the boy said, his eyes drawn to the bloody mess that used to be Shane's left eye. "You are needed. We have spotted the other ship."

"Very good," Daacad said, slapping Shane on the cheek. "I will be back so we can talk some more. But first I have to kill your friends."

A whimper was all the reply Shane could muster.

Daacad followed the boy from the room and closed the hatch behind him. As soon as the hatch's wheel stopped turning, Shane burst out crying. He sobbed and sobbed at the pain and the loss. His eye was gone, he could feel the deflated husk of it stuck inside his socket. His body began to shiver and on some level, he knew shock was going to set in.

But fear pushed that away when he saw the wheel turn again and the hatch start to open.

"No," he begged, "no, please, no."

"Shane?" a voice whispered. "Shane?"

He looked at the hatch with his one good eye and thought he would die right then. Kinsey. There she stood. And with Jennings and Darby.

"Oh…God," Kinsey cried as she rushed to her cousin. "Oh, fuck, Shane! What did they do?"

"What happened to your face?" Jennings asked. "Your eyelid is all fucked up."

"They punctured his eye," Darby said as she watched the hatch while Kinsey and Jennings lowered Shane to the floor. "That's why his face looks like that. Easy to spot."

"Jesus Christ," Kinsey said, as she cradled her cousin in her arms once his hands were free. He gripped her and pulled himself closer to her as he wept on her chest. "I'll kill the fuckers."

"Me…first," Shane said as he tried to pull himself together.

"We have to move," Darby said. "No time for sympathy or revenge plans." She looked down at Shane. "Can you walk?"

"I can," Shane said. "I almost had them, Darby. A couple more minutes and they would have spilled it all."

Darby smiled and nodded. "I'm sure. We'll just have to figure out who the traitor is another way."

"The what? What did I miss?" Kinsey asked.

"Tracking device in one of the hard drives we secured," Darby said, "that's how the pirates knew where to find us."

"And that means someone sold us out? Why?" Jennings asked.

"Because, why else would they put a tracker in the hard drives?" Darby said. "Unless they knew someone was coming to take them?"

"We'll deal with that later," Kinsey said, "we have to get off this ship first."

"You? What are you doing?" a man said from the hatch as he raised his rifle.

Darby sprang at him, her fists connecting with his face before her feet touched the ground. He stumbled back, but she was able to grab him and pull him into the room. She grabbed both sides of his head and twisted, snapping his neck. His body crumpled to the floor and she started to search him.

"9mm," she said, handing it back to Kinsey, "Machete. And the rifle. One extra magazine." She put the rifle to her shoulder and moved to the hatch. "Let's go."

"Where?" Jennings asked as he helped carry/drag Shane. "They'll see us if we try to use a lifeboat."

"Maybe," Darby said, "maybe not. They'll be busy dealing with the Beowulf II in a few minutes. That could be distraction enough."

"I still think we should disable the engines," Kinsey said. "We're here now. Let's sink this fucker."

"We need to get off first," Jennings said. "As much as I admire the take one for the Team attitude, I signed up to find a whale with Darren, not die fighting pirates."

"But...that'd be a pretty cool way to go," Shane said, "death by pirate. I wouldn't mind."

"You almost got that wish, man," Jennings said, "how'd that feel?"

"Good point," Shane said.

"Take him," Kinsey said. "You get them up top and into a lifeboat. I'll turn this thing into a floating paperweight."

"That's the best you could come up with?" Shane chuckled weakly. "You've gotta hang with Max and me more. We'll get your wit whipped into shape."

"I doubt that," Darby said. She looked at Kinsey. "Are you sure? You may not make it."

"I'm sure," Kinsey said.

"Stop," Jennings said, "this is stupid."

"Probably," Kinsey replied, "but it has to be done."

"No, I mean you going is stupid," he said as he took Shane's arm from around his shoulders. "Here. Go with your cousin. I told you I worked on a ship like this before. I know where the engine room is and I know how to disable it. I'll go."

"Kinsey has a better chance of getting there," Darby said, "she would have a fighting chance."

"I may not look like much," Jennings said, "but I can hold my own. You don't spend a life at sea and not learn how to fucking scrap."

The women looked at each other, then Kinsey nodded.

"Fine, you go," Darby said and handed him the machete, "this may be useful."

"I hope not," Jennings said, "but thanks."

"Good luck," Kinsey said. She leaned in and kissed him hard. Jennings matched the kiss then pushed her away.

"Go," he said. "Get the fuck off this ship."

"We'll wait for you," Kinsey said.

"Don't," Jennings replied. "I'll get off the ship on my own. If I have to jump and swim over to the Beowulf II, then I'll do that."

He nodded to them and then turned and ran down the passageway. He rounded a corner and was gone.

"That was touching," Shane said.

"You want to get left here, asshole?" Kinsey asked.

"No."

"Then not another fucking word about it," Kinsey snarled. "Come on."

**

"This is all some fucking joke," Thorne said as he and Ballantine stepped onto the upper deck, "right? This is science fiction shit, not reality. You're making it all up."

"I'm not," Mr. Ballantine said, "wish I was, but it is very real."

"Jesus," Thorne said.

"I know," Mr. Ballantine replied, "it is a lot to swallow."

"No, not that," Thorne said, "that."

He pointed at the two men fighting in the whale guts below the helo. Thorne hurried over to where Lake and most of the crew were standing around watching the pilot and Gunnar go at it.

"No one thought to break them up?" Thorne asked.

"And get that shit all over us?" Lake said. "No thanks."

"Woo hoo!" Max said as he came up on deck, a matte black rifle over his shoulder. "Daddy got a new toy!"

"Don't call yourself daddy," Lucy said as she followed behind with her own rifle.

The weapons looked like highly modified .50 calibers. Max slapped a magazine home and looked around the deck.

"Gimme something to shoot!" he laughed.

"Shit," Lake said as he looked over at Max and Lucy then past them, "fuck."

He sprinted away and up to the bridge. Everyone turned and looked out at what he saw.

"Huh," Max said, "guess that snuck up on us."

Thorne rubbed his forehead then pointed to the rifles.

"We need something to take out rockets!" Thorne said. "We need our own rockets and that's what they gave you?"

"Smart rounds," Max said. "Fucking heat seeking cartridges."

"The way Ingrid explained it," Lucy started.

"Because Carlos is too much of a pompous cocksucker to do the talking," Max interrupted.

"The rifle shoots a cartridge instead of a bullet," Lucy continued. "The cartridge has a microprocessor that senses heat and then fires a bullet at the target. Designed specifically to take out RPGs that have already been launched."

"This is all too much Star Trek shit for me," Thorne said. "Self-directing bullets and cloned fucking sharks. Max, Lucy, get your asses up in the crow's nest. I want scopes on that ship. You fire when you have to. Don't hesitate."

"You got it, Uncle Vinny," Max said as he started to hurry off then stopped. "Wait? Cloned sharks?"

"No time!" Thorne barked. "Go!"

"Someone really should separate them," Mr. Ballantine said, as it looked like Gunnar and the pilot were just slipping and sliding in whale guts more than actually landing any punches. "This isn't the time for rough housing."

"Popeye!" Thorne shouted to the man as he stood by the far rail, his attention turned to the water below. "Break that shit up!"

"What?" Popeye asked. "Commander, you should come look at this."

"I don't want to look at anything right now," Thorne said, "just go pull those morons apart!"

"But you should see---," Popeye said.

"I'll see your ass tossed overboard if you don't fucking go grab them!" Thorne roared.

The crew scrambled away and hurried off to their posts, leaving just Ballantine, Thorne, Bobby, and Popeye on deck. And the gore covered pilot and Gunnar.

Popeye smacked Gunnar upside the head and pulled him away from the pilot. The pilot tried to get a couple kicks in, but Popeye socked him in the gut and shoved him away.

"There," Popeye said, "broken up."

Gunnar looked like he would go after the pilot again, but Popeye grabbed him by his shirt and shoved him from the helipad. He landed on his ass hard, as he fell a couple feet down onto the deck proper.

"Fuck, Popeye," Gunnar complained, "you didn't have to do that."

"Got your attention," Thorne said as he helped Gunnar to his feet.

"I still need this shit cleared away!" the pilot shouted. "Or I can't take off!"

"You aren't going anywhere!" Thorne shouted back, pointing at the ship that was steaming towards them. "Those are fucking pirates, you idiot! And until we get out of this mess, that bird is grounded!"

"No, actually, Commander," Mr. Perry said from behind them all, "it isn't."

Thorne turned around and his face fell. "What's this happy horseshit now?"

"I have to agree with Thorne, Stefan," Mr. Ballantine said. "I am a little confused by this turn of events."

Mr. Perry stood there, one hand holding Ms. Horace's throat while the other held a .45 to her temple. Mr. Longbottom stood directly behind Mr. Perry, looking sheepish, but obviously part of what was going on.

"While I didn't expect this to turn out this way," Mr. Perry said, "I can't say I'm surprised. It changes a few things, but not by much."

"Perry, what the fuck?" Thorne said and stepped towards him.

"Stay where you are, Commander," Mr. Perry said, "or the beautiful Diane Horace stops being so beautiful. Or alive."

"What do you want?" Mr. Ballantine asked. "What is your end game?"

"First, I want you to listen to that pilot and clear that pad so the helicopter can take off," Mr. Perry said. "Then I want you to secure the shark carcass to the helicopter. It's coming with."

"Hey," the pilot said, "I know you're the guy with the gun, but there isn't enough fuel in my bird to carry us all and that dead shark back to land."

"I don't need it to go to land," Mr. Perry said, glancing towards the approaching ship, "just need it to go to my ride."

CHAPTER NINE: TAKE OFF

The man's throat spurted blood as Darby slashed with the knife. She caught him before he could fall, while also catching quite a bit of blood to the face, and let the man slump against the wall. She hurried beck to help Kinsey with Shane.

"That's four," Darby said. "They are bound to notice the loss of numbers."

"They aren't exactly professionals," Kinsey said. "They may not notice anything."

"I'm not willing to bet my life on that," Darby said, nodding towards the stairs that would take them up top. "You going to be able to get him up those?"

"Aren't you going to help?" Kinsey said.

"Tactical nightmare," Darby said. "I get tangled in him and someone comes down, then we are dead. I need to take point."

"Fine, sure," Kinsey said, looking at her cousin. "I'm going to need you to dig deep, Shane. I can't carry your weight all on my own up those stairs."

"If it means staying alive, then I can do it," Shane said. "Just make sure I don't fall backwards. My balance is off with only one eye."

"Depth perception is shot," Darby said, "that'll play havoc with your shooting. You'll have to retrain yourself."

"Looking forward to it," Shane said. "See what I did there? I said looking. But I'm missing an eye."

"Hilarious," Kinsey said, "now shut up and pay attention to each step."

"Stay close," Darby said. "Stay right on me. When we hit that hatch, we'll have seconds to move."

"Roger," Kinsey said.

***

The truth about the elbow being the hardest part of the human body was very apparent to Jennings as he took one to the cheek. His head exploded with stars and whirls of light. He fell to a knee and thrust blindly with his machete. A grunt told him he hit his mark. The warmth of blood just reinforced that.

Jennings yanked the machete free from the man's belly and shoved him away. The man stumbled back against the wall and stared at Jennings, as he tried to keep his intestines from slipping out of the hole in his gut.

"You...you...," the man muttered as he slid to the floor. Then his eyes glazed over and he was silent.

It wasn't a man at all, Jennings realized, but a boy of maybe sixteen.

The roaring sound of the diesel engines drew Jennings's attention from the dead boy. He knew he didn't have much time, that Kinsey was relying on him, so he shook off the pain in his head and moved as quickly as he could down the hall and towards his goal.

***

"Want me to take him?" Max asked over the com. "I have a clean line."

"No, Mr. Reynolds," Mr. Perry said, "I would prefer you didn't. And yes, I have a com in my ear also. It is open to all channels. A perk of being in management. So don't bother trying to coordinate my takedown."

Popeye, as well as the pilot, Gunnar, Bobby, and some of the crew, all struggled to cut up and remove the whale carcass and detangle it from the helo's skids. There was a good deal of gagging and possibly some vomiting as the stench nearly overpowered them all.

Mr. Perry, still holding a pistol to Ms. Horace's temple, with Mr. Longbottom close at hand, stood at the base of the helipad and kept his eye on Thorne, Darren, and Mr. Ballantine.

"Where can this possibly lead, Stefan?" Mr. Ballantine said. "The company won't stand for it. You'll be hunted down and killed no matter where you go."

"The company won't know a thing about any of this," Mr. Perry replied, "no witnesses, no problems."

"There will be plenty of witnesses," Thorne said.

"No, there won't," Mr. Perry said, "my partners will make sure of that."

"Saying you're going to kill us anyway undermines your leverage," Thorne said, "you're not very good at this, are you?"

"Oh, I have leverage, don't I, Mr. Ballantine?" Mr. Perry smiled.

"Yes," Mr. Ballantine said, "she'll live? You promise?"

"It's part of the deal," Mr. Longbottom said, finally speaking up, "she lives or I don't corroborate."

"Exactly," Mr. Perry said, "plus, you are a SEAL, Commander Thorne. Never say die, never give up. I know deep down you actually think you can survive this. Even with the overpowering threat coming towards us."

"Yeah," Thorne smile,. "take the shot, Max."

"No!" Mr. Ballantine shouted. "Do not take the shot!"

"Vinny?" Max asked. "Your call."

"Please," Mr. Ballantine said, "don't. There is another way. You'll think of it. It's why I hired you."

"Ha!" Mr. Perry barked. "The reason I let you hire Thorne and his misfits is for the opposite reason! They are washouts. Each one of them flawed and subpar. You just keep thinking of a way to beat me, Commander Thorne. I'm counting on it."

Thorne just glared.

"May I ask why?" Mr. Ballantine said, gesturing towards the cleanup crew. "Since we have some time before you can leave us. Why are you doing this?"

"Money," Mr. Perry said, "a better life than just a company stooge."

"The shark? Is that it? Who's buying it? Which biotech company bought you?" Mr. Ballantine asked.

"Does it matter?" Mr. Perry replied.

"To me, yes," Mr. Ballantine said, "I'll cross them off the possible client list."

"Ever the optimist, Ballantine," Mr. Perry said. "How you rose in the company I'll never figure out." He glanced at Darren. "You can stop that, Captain. Hand signal to your Chief up on the bridge all you want, it makes no difference in today's outcome."

"Just flexing my hand," Darren said, "getting it loose so it doesn't hurt as much when I beat the shit out of you."

"Another optimist," Mr. Perry laughed, "a true ship of fools."

"Stefan," Ms. Horace croaked.

"Shut up, Diane," Mr. Perry said, and squeezed her throat tighter, "don't complicate this. You may get out of this alive."

"Then you'll have a witness," Thorne said.

"But a well-paid one," Mr. Longbottom said.

"She'll live comfortably for the rest of her life," Mr. Perry said, "but in a quiet part of the world, having retired from the company due to her grief stricken state at your death, Ballantine."

"And knowing she has a target on her head until she dies," Mr. Ballantine said. "Yes, I understand."

"Good," Mr. Perry nodded, then looked at the cleanup crew. "How close are we, pilot? The other ship has about arrived. I'd like to be gone soon, if you don't mind."

"Then you come clean some of this shit up," the pilot snapped, "Asshole."

***

"Not too close," Daacad said as he stood on the bridge, "we do not want to be right next to it when we blow it out of the water."

"Yes, sir."

He left the bridge and pulled a radio from his pocket, adjusting the channel before putting it to his mouth. "Perry? Do you read me, Mr. Perry?"

"I do, Mr. Shimbir," Mr. Perry's voice responded over the radio, "but I would prefer if you maintained radio silence. There are ears listening."

"We will be in range shortly," Daacad said as he looked down at the deck below and the eight men that held RPGs over their shoulders. "Do you have the shark that killed my son?"

"That is quite enough, Mr. Shimbir," Mr. Perry said, "please do as I ask and go silent."

Daacad didn't like to be ordered about like that, but he let it slide and turned off the radio. He would deal with Mr. Perry's disrespect when the man stood before him.

***

"Aaah!" Darby hissed as the blade slid into her shoulder. "Fuck!"

She spun about, twisting the arm attached to the knife around her own arm and then dropped to her knees. Her weight and momentum snapped the arm, and she stood quickly and broke the man's neck before he could cry out.

"Shit," Kinsey said, "you hurt bad?"

"Not bad," Darby said, exploring the wound with her fingers, "it won't slow me."

"Good," Kinsey said, "the lifeboat is this way."

"No," Darby said. "The ship is turning. That side will be facing the Beowulf II. We need to be on the other side."

"Boats on both sides," Shane said, "boats for all."

His head sagged and Kinsey gave him a quick slap.

"No going into shock," Kinsey said, "you stay awake, Shane. Dig deep, frogman! This is the real shit!"

"You don't have to tell me how real it is," Shane replied, "I can see for myself, thank you." He chuckled weakly.

"God," Kinsey said, "it'll be eye puns for the rest of your life, won't it?"

"Yes, yes it will," Shane replied, "but since we'll probably die soon, you won't have to deal with them much longer."

***

He tried to listen at the hatch to the engine room to hear if anyone was inside, but the noise was too much for Jennings to sift through, so he just opened the hatch and hoped for the best.

He got the worst.

"Who are you?" a man asked as he picked up an AK-47 that had been leaning against some machinery. "Where did you come from?"

"Shit," Jennings said, "I, uh, well. I'm the new guy."

"No you are the dead guy," the man said, gesturing for Jennings to move to the side. "You stand there. Do not move."

Jennings set his machete down, moved to the side of the hatch and stood there, his hands raised. He looked about the engine room and was glad to see that he knew the engines pretty well. If he didn't get his ass blown off, he could shut them down permanently, and fairly easily.

But first he'd have to deal with the man with the rifle. And the six other men that started to appear from around the engines as they heard their comrade's voice. Lucky for Jennings, the first man was the only one armed. With a rifle at least. The others had various tools in their hands that could prove quite lethal if needed.

"I know, I know," Jennings said, "this is the hazing part, right? Give the new guy a hard time. Push him around a little."

The man with the rifle moved closer, gripping his weapon tighter with each step.

"You shut up," the man said, "you are not part of this crew. I know everyone on board and they do not look like you."

"Oh, right, because I'm white?" Jennings asked. "That's kind of racist, don't you think?"

"Shut up!" the man yelled. His audience cringed and Jennings had to wonder if maybe the man was in the engine room not to guard the engines, but to guard the men working on the engines.

"You guys like this guy?" Jennings addressed the mechanics. "Is he a pal of yours? Or is he a dick that gets his kicks from threatening you with his little rifle?"

"I said to shut up!" the man shouted and closed on Jennings quickly. He spun the rifle and smashed the butt into Jennings's face. "There! See! You shut up now!"

Blood spurted from Jennings's nose and his hands went to his face as he fell to one knee. He looked up, but only saw the end of the rifle again as the man slammed it into his cheek right where the elbow had connected before. He felt the skin split open and tried to avoid the next attack, but he wasn't fast enough as he was nailed once more with the rifle. The blow sent him sprawling on the floor.

The man laughed and kicked Jennings in the ribs.

"New guy, yes? That you?" the man laughed again, kicked again. "Why you down on the ground, new guy? You don't like to work? That it, new guy?" He kept laughing, kept kicking. "New guy…you must think I'm stupid."

The blows to his head had him dazed, so at that moment, Jennings didn't know what he thought.

***

"There!" Gunnar shouted. "It's clear enough! The helicopter can take off just fine! Leave me something!"

"More optimism," Mr. Perry said as looked to the pilot. "Can you lift off now?"

"Yeah," the pilot said, "not that I want to. You'll probably just kill me."

"I promise I won't," Mr. Perry said. "I'll need you to take us from the ship to land. Can't exactly come into port on a pirate ship, now can we?"

The pilot eyed the shark carcass on the loading deck below. "Uh, how much does that weigh?"

"Several tons," Gunnar said.

"Several tons?" the pilot said and then laughed. "That's not coming with."

"I assure you the weight rating on your helicopter will allow us to fly the short distance to the other ship," Mr. Perry said.

"At like five feet above the water," the pilot said.

"Tow it over," Popeye suggested, "net it, tow it through the water, and then winch it up on deck with the two loading cranes on the back of that ship."

Everyone looked at Popeye.

"What?" he asked. "I'm the boatswain. I figure this shit out."

"Thank you, Mr. De Bruhl," Mr. Ballantine sighed, "that was very helpful."

"Make it happen," Mr. Perry said, "now."

***

"I so want to blast a hole in that guy," Max said as he kept his scope on Mr. Perry. "Come on, I can do this."

"Hold," Lucy said, "if we…"

"If we…what?" Max asked.

"Check your three," Lucy said. "Ditch the scope and go eyes on."

Max looked away from his scope and off to his right. "What am I looking at?"

"In the water," Lucy said, "see that shadow moving?"

"Yeah," Max said, "it just went under the B2. Looked big. Probably a shark coming to check out the all the chum we've been tossing in the water. I'll bet we'll see quite a few more soon."

"That was a big shadow," Lucy said, "and where are all the others? There should be a feeding frenzy down there with all those whale guts."

"The little ones are hanging back," Max said.

"Not even great whites command that respect when there's this much blood and guts."

"So, what? Another monster shark?"

"I don't know," Lucy replied, "but one of us should keep an eye on the water and one on the pirates incoming."

***

The crew had the shark carcass netted and strapped tight. The pilot made sure the two lines were placed correctly on the hooks up under the belly of the helo.

"That's as good as it gets," the pilot said as he hopped into the helo. "I'll get us started up and we can take off in a minute."

The rotors began to spin as the pilot started the engines.

"Good bye, Ballantine," Mr. Perry shouted over the noise. "It was good working with you. I mean that. Sorry to rain on your parade."

"Go fuck yourself, Perry!" Thorne yelled.

"Couldn't have said it better myself," Mr. Ballantine said, "thank you, Commander."

Mr. Perry backed up to the helo and waited as Mr. Longbottom opened the side door. He took the pistol as Mr. Perry climbed in with Ms. Horace following right behind. The door slid closed and the helo started to lift from the pad, bits of whale sinew and offal dripping from the skids.

The helo angled and began to fly slowly out over the water, the lines connecting it to the netted shark going taught. Everyone could hear the engines strain as the helo pulled the shark from the ship and into the water. Water splashed everywhere and the helo bucked before regaining stability, and headed for the incoming ship. The shark was almost completely submerged making for very slow progress.

"Come on, Uncle Vinny!" Max yelled over the com. "One in the gas tank! Boom, done!"

"No," Thorne said, "we are still alive for now. Let's see how this plays---"

"Holy shit!" Lucy shouted over the com.

Everyone jumped and more than a few members of the crew screamed as the water exploded around the shark carcass. Massive jaws, larger than any of them had ever seen before, larger than the dead shark, chomped down on the carcass and pulled it below.

"Jesus H. Christ," Thorne said, "what the fuck was that, Ballantine?"

"That would be the original," Mr. Ballantine said. "I had a feeling it was still hanging around."

The shark carcass was lost below the churning water, but the tow lines were still visible. And still attached to the helo. The machine began to strain and fight as the pilot put all the power into the rotors, trying to gain some lift and fight the drag of the carcass. But it was too late. The helo was pulled down into the water as the monster shark dove deep.

There was a massive fireball and the sound of wrenching metal as the helicopter exploded on impact.

"Told you there was something in the water," Popeye said, "but none of ya would listen."

***

"What the fuck was that?" Kinsey asked.

"Take him," Darby said as she helped Kinsey lift Shane into a lifeboat. "I'll go for a look. If I'm not back in a minute –one minute- then you lower this into the water and get out of here."

"That was a big boom," Shane said, his face flushed and feverish, "big. Boom."

"You get your ass back here," Kinsey said, "we don't need to see what it was, we need to get off this ship."

"One minute," Darby said as she held up a finger.

She took off running, ducking behind crates and random junk piled on the deck, able to avoid detection as she made her way to a clear spot by the rail. The water below was filled with debris and flaming fuel. Then the shark carcass bobbed to the surface, most of it bitten in half, held together only by twisted ropes and netting. Darby could see a distinct shadow below the carcass, circling, circling.

"Oh crap," Darby said. "Kinsey. She can't go into the water."

She turned about, ready to run and warn Kinsey and Shane, but came face to face with Daacad instead.

"Little lady," Daacad said, "you should not be here."

***

"No more waiting," Max said as he turned his scope to the pirate ship, "time to go to work." He squeezed the trigger and the man's head that had been in his crosshairs was turned to a bloody mist. "Motherfucker! Nailed it!"

Lucy didn't argue that time and joined right in. Anyone holding an RPG was quickly dropped. And anyone standing next to them were dropped as well. The air above the pirate ship was filled with smoke from the helicopter and blood from the dead.

The two snipers didn't stop firing until they'd gone full Winchester and emptied every magazine they had.

***

Darby went low.

She didn't reply to Daacad or wait for the man to make the first move, just dropped to her knees and sent two jabs into his crotch. He cried out in a high pitched voice, grabbed his balls, and fell to his knees, coming face to face with Darby. She slammed her forehead into his nose, knocking him onto his back, and leapt to her feet as three of Daacad's men sprinted towards her.

The first man to reach her swung high and Darby easily ducked the swing, landing a hard hit to the man's ribs. The crack of bone was like a gunshot, adding to the cacophony already filling the air. She grabbed him by the back of the neck and brought her knee up, while bringing his face down. The man's cheekbone shattered and he screamed as half his face caved in.

Without missing a beat, Darby spun the man about and shoved him into the two others coming at her, giving her time to grab the rail, shove herself up into the air, and spin about. Her legs whipped about, catching one man in the temple and the other across the jaw. The first contact was a dead shot, killing the man instantly. The second hit crushed the other man's jaw, nearly ripping it from his face. He screamed, but it came out as a pitiful, choked cry.

Darby landed on her feet and went in for the kill, but she was tripped up by Daacad as the man grabbed her ankle and pulled her off her feet. He scrambled on top of her and his hands were around her throat, strangling, crushing, killing. The blood in her head began to pound, sending sharp, stabbing pains to a space right behind her eyes. She could feel them bulging out of the sockets as her throat was crushed, cutting off the air flow to her lungs and the circulation to her brain.

"Little ladies shouldn't be fighting with big men," Daacad said, "only whores try to do that."

Darby jammed her thumbs up into Daacad's armpits, nailing pressure points that would have taken down men twice his size. But the pirate clan leader wasn't giving up; he shouted, roared, screamed in pain, yet his hands remained clamped to Darby's neck. She brought her hands up to his face, her thumbs finding his eyes, and she pressed with every last ounce of strength she had.

Daacad screeched. His voice went up two octaves as Darby squashed his eyes into pulp. Jelly and blood squirted from under his lids and ran down his cheeks. He shook his head back and forth, but Darby had her thumbs hooked inside his sockets. With his eyes nothing but mush, she focused on his orbital bones. She wanted to literally rip his face off. But she was losing oxygen to her brain. It felt as if his hands were crushing her throat all the way back against her spine. She knew she had seconds and she gave one last effort, but it wasn't enough.

She was done.

Her vision went red as the blood vessels in her eyes burst and she took one last look up at the man that had beaten her. His face was a rictus of pain and rage, his mouth open in a scream she couldn't hear over the thudding of trapped blood behind her eardrums. The red started to turn to black, and she wished she could close her eyes so Daacad's wicked face wouldn't be her last sight in life.

Then the vision of his head split in two. Literally. And the pressure on her throat eased. Daacad wavered in her vision, and then toppled from her. Standing there, in Darby's damaged vision, was Kinsey, a machete drenched in blood hanging from her hand.

"Come on," Kinsey said, "we're getting out of here."

Darby was pulled to her feet as Kinsey basically carried her across the ship to the lifeboat. She wanted to protest, to argue, to warn Kinsey that they couldn't get into the lifeboat and drop to the water. Something was down there. But the words wouldn't come out. All her vocal efforts produced, were strangled croaks and groans.

"Hush," Kinsey said, "I've got you. We're gonna be fine."

The lifeboat, with Shane's naked, prone, battered figure slumped inside, was feet away and Darby was powerless to stop Kinsey from dropping them to their doom.

***

"That's not good," Lake said as warning claxons blared on the bridge. "What the fuck?"

He checked his gauges and screens and found the source: hull breach below water level.

The Beowulf II was taking on water. And fast.

"I need eyes on the damage!" Lake shouted into the com. "All hands below deck, I need a report now!"

He waited a minute and then Cougher's voice came over the com.

"I can't get all the way to it," Cougher said, "the bottom two decks are already filling with water."

"What the hell happened?" Lake asked, doing the math and realizing that they had maybe five, possibly ten minutes, before the Beowulf II started to go down. "This thing has a double hull!"

"I'm sealing off compartments and decks," Cougher shouted. "Reports I've gotten from the crew is that something sliced right through both hulls. Like a fucking giant knife."

"What the---" Lake said then realized what had happened. "The fucking helo. A rotor blade must have hit the ship when the damn thing exploded."

Lake slammed his hand down on the emergency alert and all claxons were drowned out by one single one: the abandon ship warning.

***

"Everyone to the lifeboats!" Darren shouted. "Abandon ship!"

"I can take a few up in the Wyrm," Bobby said, "land us over on the other ship and take that."

"Good," Mr. Ballantine said, "because we may not have enough room in the lifeboats."

"What?" Thorne yelled. "How the hell is there not enough room? This thing is supposed to be state of the art?"

"It is," Mr. Ballantine replied, "but corners may have been cut to make room for other equipment. The Beowulf II was designed to take a direct hit from a torpedo and still stay afloat."

"And how's that working out?" Thorne shouted.

"Not so well, Commander," Mr. Ballantine responded.

"Max, Lucy!" Thorne yelled into the com. "Get down here! Team Grendel is taking the pirate ship! We need to secure that vessel so we can evacuate our crew over there!"

"Taking a pirate ship?" Max replied. "I've waited my entire life to hear those words!"

***

Jennings crawled away and tried to put some distance between himself and his attacker. The man just followed casually behind him, laughing his head off.

"Where you going to go, new guy?" the man asked. "You think you can hide in the corner? That you tuck your face away I won't see you? Like a little child?"

Jennings reached up, his hand finding a valve just above him. He turned it until it stopped.

"What have you done?" the man said, still laughing. "Turned off the hot water? Now we cannot take comfortable showers. That is a great plan, new guy. When I cannot wash myself properly tonight, I will curse your soul."

Jennings rolled onto his back and smiled at the man.

"Why are you smiling, new guy? What do you find so funny?" the man asked. "You are happy to die? Is that it?"

"No," Jennings said, "that's not it."

He reached behind him and pulled a lever that was tucked between two pipes. Scalding steam escaped from four vents to the side, blasting the man's head and torso. He screamed and brought his hands to his face, which had already started puckering with nasty blisters that burst open and oozed bloody fluid.

Jennings pushed the lever back into place and turned the valve back to its original position. He ignored the pain in his palm as he pulled himself up by a hot pipe. The man before him had fallen to his knees, his screams echoing in the engine room. His face was a melted mess as strips of boiled skin hung from his cheeks and chin.

As he limped over to the man, Jennings brought his fist back then let it fly, connecting with the man's face. The man's screams cut off with a wet crunching noise as he fell backwards, unconscious.

Jennings shook his head to clear his thoughts and almost passed out. He fell to one knee and took a deep breath, then mustered the strength to get back up. His body felt broken and nearly done for. The man had given him the beating of his life. The mechanics that had watched the entire fight without doing anything, just stared at him.

"A word of advice?" Jennings said. "Run."

The men didn't need to be told twice and they hurried out of the engine room, as Jennings began to twist and turn every valve and handle he could find. Gauges crept towards their redlines. It would only be minutes before the pressure built enough to blast the engine room right through the side of the ship.

Jennings smiled as he leaned against a wall and slid to his ass. He felt like death, and knew he wasn't going to live long, but he couldn't help but smile. He'd done what he could and it was only a matter of time before the pirate ship was sent to the deep.

***

"Stop struggling," Kinsey yelled at Darby, "what the hell is wrong with you?"

Kinsey had to move from one drop line to the other in order to the keep the lifeboat from tipping and dumping them into the ocean, as she slowly lowered it to the waves below. Darby tried to grab her hands and pull them from the lines, but Kinsey just swatted her away.

"Knock it off," Kinsey said, "you're going to make me flip this thing!"

But Darby wouldn't stop. When she couldn't stop Kinsey from releasing the lines, she just tried to stop Kinsey from moving all together, and grabbed her about the waist.

"What the fuck, Darby?" Kinsey shouted. "We have to get off this ship and back to the Beowulf II! Have you lost your mind?"

Darby tried to speak, but the pain was excruciating as air struggled to get through her crushed larynx. She'd never wanted to communicate with someone so badly in her life. She slapped at Kinsey's side and back, desperate to get the woman to pay attention.

"Darby!" Kinsey yelled and shoved her away. "Stop!"

But Darby came back at Kinsey and left the woman no option. Kinsey let go of the line she was working on, dropped down behind Darby, and wrapped her arms about Darby's neck. The woman let out a weak screech and pounded at Kinsey's arms, but she just didn't have the strength left in her. In seconds, Darby was choked out and left unconscious on the bottom of the lifeboat next to Shane.

"Sorry about that," Kinsey said, "but you were going to get us killed."

She went back to the systematic back and forth with the drop lines, and the lifeboat slowly lowered into the ocean.

***

"What the hell?" Popeye shouted as Team Grendel hopped into the Wyrm. "You're leaving us here, Captain?"

"We're going to secure that ship!" Darren shouted over the noise of the rotor blades, an M-4 in hand. "We'll take the bridge and get the ship as close to us as possible. In the meantime, you need to get everyone into the lifeboats! Lake is in charge. Ballantine and Gunnar are below trying to secure as much data as possible. I am counting on you, Trevor, to keep things orderly on deck and fill those lifeboats. Bobby will come back and get everyone that can't fit. Got it?"

"You never call me Trevor," Popeye said.

"That's how fucking important this is," Darren said, "you up for this?"

"Born for it, sir," Popeye said, giving a sturdy salute.

Darren returned it as the Wyrm lifted off and angled towards the pirate ship.

Popeye watched it go, then turned to start shouting orders at the crew members that were streaming up from below. Then he realized one thing: the lifeboats would go into the water. It was a simple realization that wouldn't have mattered much any other time, since the lifeboats were covered and basically like small watercrafts in of themselves. But that was the problem. They were small. And what was in the water wasn't small. Not small at all.

***

"Hard drives, flash drives, any specimens that we can carry!" Gunnar yelled as he scrambled about the lab and shoved whatever he could grab into cases and dry bags. "I'm not losing all of this data!"

"I have satellite uplink established," Mr. Ballantine said from a computer terminal. "Everything you have compiled is being uploaded to the company database as we speak."

"Is that good?" Gunnar said. "After Perry and the others, I'd have a hard time trusting anything to do with the company."

"I agree," Mr. Ballantine said, "but we have no choice. I've initiated top level encryption on the data, but that won't keep it secure for long. If someone in the company wants to hack in and study our findings, then they will. All I can do is hope Mr. Perry and Mr. Longbottom were working alone."

"But they weren't," Gunnar said as he struggled to get an overstuffed case closed, "Perry was working for someone that wanted that shark." Gunnar stopped and looked at Ballantine. "How many more are there?"

"Like I said, Gunnar," Mr. Ballantine replied, "I am hoping none. Mr. Perry was respected in the company, but not well liked. He was---"

"No, no," Gunnar said, "not that. I mean, how many sharks are out there. We caught one and there's another one, a big motherfucker, stalking us. How many more? What are we looking at?"

Mr. Ballantine stopped what he was doing at the terminal long enough to give Gunnar a hard, honest stare. "I don't know."

"You don't know?" Gunnar asked. "How can you not know? The outfit that hired the company to solve its little shark problem didn't tell you?"

"They didn't know," Mr. Ballantine said, "that is the problem."

"Fucking come clean, Ballantine!" Gunnar shouted. "The Beowulf II is going down! Stop being so fucking coy, you bitch!"

"Fine," Mr. Ballantine said as he left that terminal and moved to another one, "there was only one shark to begin with. A creature cloned from prehistoric DNA…and enhanced. It escaped and it wasn't until after it had escaped into the ocean that its creators discovered an anomaly they couldn't have predicted. No one could."

"Fucking out with it," Gunnar snarled.

"The shark was pregnant," Mr. Ballantine replied.

"Impossible," Gunnar said, "a clone couldn't just be pregnant."

"Apparently it could," Mr. Ballantine said. "They don't know how, they don't know why. But it happened."

"How many are we talking?" Gunnar asked. "A great white can have anywhere from two to ten pups, but some have been known to birth clutches of up to 15."

"We don't know," Mr. Ballantine said, "but it has happened."

"And these sharks being born? Are they clones also?" Gunnar asked. "Because if they are…"

"Then they could also be pregnant," Mr. Ballantine answered for him, "making the threat exponential."

"Holy fuck," Gunnar said, "how many are down there?"

"No clue," Mr. Ballantine said, "but the one that we know of is problem enough."

He tapped at the keys and then left the terminal to help Gunnar pack. Video screens began to flash and then go blank across the lab.

"What did you do?" Gunnar asked.

"Fried the servers," Mr. Ballantine said, "wouldn't want any information to survive and be salvaged by unknown entities."

"Nah, wouldn't want that," Gunnar smirked, "the known entities are dangerous enough."

***

"Cougher? Report!" Lake shouted into the com.

"All hands below deck are accounted for," Cougher said, "but we had some casualties. Six men didn't make it before I sealed off the second deck."

"Six?" Lake asked, rubbing his face. "Jesus."

"We are taking on water fast, sir," Cougher said. "Bilge pumps three, seven, nine, and twelve have burned out. How is it going up there?"

"Popeye has things under control up on deck," Lake said, "but we still have too many crew members to fit on the lifeboats."

"I'll stay behind," Cougher said, "I'll go down with the ship."

"Not going to happen," Lake said. "Grendel is about to land and take the pirate ship for us. Anyone not on lifeboats will transfer over there as soon as Bobby brings the Wyrm back. You do another sweep below, make sure you haven't missed anyone then get your ass up on deck."

"Roger," Cougher said.

***

The RPG came at the Wyrm with blinding speed, fire spewing from its tail.

"You got that?" Lucy shouted at Max. "Max? Do you have that?"

"Hush," Max said, his eye to his scope, "I got it."

"Those the special rounds?" Darren asked.

"No," Lucy said, "we spent all of those."

"What?" Thorne shouted. "He's going to take---"

His protest was cut off by a loud explosion that rocked the Wyrm as it flew over the pirate ship's deck.

"Bingo," Max smiled, "good old fashioned shooting. No heat seekers, no bells, no whistles, lots of bangs."

"Good shooting," Lucy said and high-fived Max.

"Yeah," Darren said, "nice shot."

"How about you do it again?" Bobby yelled over the com. "Got another on our two o'clock!"

It was Lucy's turn to take aim. She centered the rocket in her sights then led it by a few feet. She exhaled slowly and squeezed the trigger. The entire process from rifle to shoulder and trigger squeeze was less than a second. The bullet hit the RPG, but the rocket had gotten too close. It exploded and shrapnel peppered the Wyrm. Alarms rang out and the helo started to dip fast.

"Hold on!" Bobby shouted. "This is going to hurt!"

Everyone braced themselves, grabbing onto whatever they could as the Wyrm started to spin out of control. It dropped quickly and slammed onto the deck of the ship, but Bobby was able to keep the rotors from dipping and slicing through the deck. Several cables and posts were sent flying as they were severed, and more than a few men on the deck were split in half by the carnage.

"That's one way to land," Max said as he jumped from the helo and opened fire on anything that moved.

The rest of the Team followed him, rifles to their shoulders, ice in their veins.

***

"That ain't good," Popeye said as he watched the Wyrm crash land on the pirate ship. "That was my ride."

"Come on!" a crew member shouted from the last lifeboat as Popeye was about to send it down to the water.

The vessel was about fifteen feet long and looked like a small pleasure craft that would be happy on any recreational lake in America, but it was completely enclosed and was built for safety, not fun or speed. Popeye could see desperate faces looking at him from the portholes in the side. He'd already jammed it over capacity and knew that even one more body could jeopardize the craft, though it was only going a dozen or so yards to the other ship.

"No! Go!" Popeye said as he waved off the crew member. "Close that hatch! I'm dropping in three, two, one!"

The hatch closed just as Popeye hit the release, sending the last lifeboat down to the water in a massive splash that sent water shooting up over the rail. Popeye wiped the seawater from his face and turned towards the bridge. He could see Lake looking across the water at the damaged Wyrm on the other ship. The Chief glanced down and locked eyes with Popeye. They knew the fix they were in.

***

"What the fuck are you two still doing down here?" Cougher shouted as he rushed into the lab. "You need to get your asses up on deck now! Do you see the fucking water at your feet?"

Both Ballantine and Gunnar looked down and seemed to realize for the first time they were standing in six inches of seawater.

"That was fast," Mr. Ballantine said.

"Here!" Gunnar yelled, shoving cases and bags at Cougher. "Help me get these up top!"

Cougher just stared at Gunnar. "Are you fucking nuts? The Beowulf II is going down, man! It's fucking sinking right now! You need to be worried about yourself, not some fish guts and hard drives!"

"If I don't save this, then everything will have been for nothing!" Gunnar yelled. "And I can't live with that!"

"You can't live with half the ocean filling your fucking lungs either, dumbass!" Cougher yelled.

"Take what you can," Mr. Ballantine said, as he grabbed two bags and slung them over his shoulders, then picked up two cases that were floating on the rising water. "At least make an effort."

"Holy fuck," Cougher said, "you two are nuts."

He picked up a bag and two cases and turned towards the hatch, but was knocked off his feet as the ship shuddered and lurched to the side.

"What the fuck was that?" Cougher asked. "Did something hit us?"

Gunnar and Ballantine looked at each other.

"What exactly was the shark designed to do?" Gunnar asked. "You said it was enhanced, but never told me how."

"Yes, about that," Mr. Ballantine frowned, "it may have been designed for warfare. Specifically as a hunter killer."

"Hunter killer?" Cougher asked as the ship shuddered once more. "Of what?"

"Oh, you know," Mr. Ballantine said, "oil platforms, submarines, ships. That sort of thing."

"You have got to be fucking kidding me," Cougher said. "You fucking people."

"I didn't design it," Mr. Ballantine said, "and I resent that you'd think me so careless."

"But your clients designed it," Gunnar said, "and you knew what it was and didn't tell us."

"Yes, I'll admit to that," Mr. Ballantine said, "but we can have this discussion at a later date. I think our priority should be to get up above to whatever rescue is awaiting us."

The ship rocked and shook again and again and then started to cant to starboard, sending the men reeling into the wall of the passageway as they hurried from the lab. The water at their feet rose faster and faster and by the time they reached the stairs, it was up to their knees.

***

"The B2 is going down fast!" Max shouted as he put two bullets into a man's chest, then one in the head as the guy came at him with nothing but a steel pipe. "Lifeboats are in the water, but there's still crew on deck!"

"I can see that!" Darren yelled as he blew the kneecaps off a pirate and then shot the man in the throat as he fell. "Get high and cover this deck! Kill anyone that comes up from above! Bobby and I will go drop whatever lifeboats this thing has and get over to the Beowulf II!"

"Down!" Thorne yelled and Darren hit the deck. He heard a bullet whiz past his ear. Thorne opened fire and dropped two pirates before spinning and taking out two more that were rushing at them from the bridge.

"Frag out!" Lucy yelled, as she tossed a grenade through a hatch and down into the deck below. She ducked to the side and covered her ears as the thing blew. Smoke and flame shot out of the hatch and she waited, but no shots came. "I'll check below!"

"I have this deck!" Max shouted. "You take the bridge, Commander!"

Thorne didn't wait. He took off up the stairs to the bridge, cutting down more men as he went. He saw their faces, saw the fear and desperation in their eyes, saw how young they were. But he didn't stop. They held AK-47s and pointed them towards him. That meant they were old enough to die.

He got to the bridge hatch and threw in a flash bang. Anyone still inside would have been both deaf and blind for a while. His ears ringing, Thorne turned and rushed the bridge. A stunned man reached for a rifle, but Thorne put two bullets in his chest. Another man stumbled towards him, but appeared to be unarmed, so Thorne slammed the butt of his rifle into the man's face. The man cried out, then fell to the floor, reaching for his leg and a long knife in his boot.

"Too bad," Thorne said as he shot the man in the head, "I would have let you live, you idiot."

The bridge secured, Thorne slammed and locked the hatch, then turned to the controls. It had been a while since he'd piloted a ship of that size, but he had no time to get familiar. He grabbed the wheel and spun it hard to port and pushed the engines to full in order to bring the ship closer to the sinking Beowulf II.

***

The engines began to groan and shriek as the pressure built. Jennings smiled as he realized someone on the bridge had pushed them to full. They were just hurrying up the inevitable. He took a breath and tried to stand, thinking that maybe, just maybe, he could make it up top. He was able to get to his feet and slowly lurched and stumbled his way to the hatch.

His ribs screamed at him, his face felt swollen and stiff, and he was pretty sure one of his legs were busted. But he couldn't tell which one, since his whole body was nothing but a field of pain.

The engine room hatch was open, which Jennings was thankful for since he wasn't sure he had the strength even to turn a wheel. He gripped the edge of the hatchway and slowly worked his way out into the passage. He rested his hand against the wall and concentrated on each step, putting one foot in front of the other as carefully as he could. He knew that if he fell, he didn't have it in him to get back up.

"Let me see your hands, motherfucker!" Lucy screamed as she came around the corner, her rifle at her shoulder and pointed right at Jennings. "Holy fuck…Jennings?"

"Hey," Jennings said, "how's it going? What the fuck are you doing here?"

"We're securing the ship," Lucy said, "the B2 is going down. This ship is our only chance."

Jennings's already pale face went completely white and he leaned his back against the wall.

"That's going to be a problem," he said.

"Why? What's wrong?" Lucy asked.

"I've got the engines set to blow," he said, "the pressure is building right now."

"What? Why?" Lucy yelled.

"Because I thought I was stopping pirates," Jennings said. "I was going to be the sacrificial hero. People would write songs about me."

"People don't write those kinds of songs anymore, dipshit," Lucy said. "Commander? Do you read me? Commander!"

"What?" Thorne replied over the com.

"Shut down the engines!" Lucy said. "They are damaged and going to explode! If you don't power down we'll lose this ship too!"

"Jesus!" Thorne yelled. "Roger that!"

The sounds from the engine room lessened, but it was still apparent that everything was not good in that room.

"Help me get back in there," Jennings said, reaching for Lucy, "I'll see if I can fix the mess I made."

"Fuck, Jennings," Lucy said, "you're Second Officer, not an engineer."

"Can't hurt to try," Jennings said, "it's the only shot we have apparently."

"Fuck," Lucy snapped and shouldered her rifle. She draped Jennings's arm over her shoulders and turned him back towards the engine room.

***

"What the hell is that?" Lake yelled as he rushed down the stairs from the bridge to the upper deck just as Gunnar, Cougher, and Ballantine came up from below. "What is ramming us?"

"Shark," Cougher said, "that motherfucking shark."

Lake blinked in disbelief. "Are you fucking joking?"

"No," Gunnar said, "what's the plan?"

"Yes, Chief, what is the plan?" Mr. Ballantine asked as he dropped the gear he was holding and looked across the water at the pirate ship. He saw the damaged Wyrm and frowned. "I do hope that wasn't the plan."

"Sure was," Popeye said, "we're stuck."

"Looks like they're dropping lifeboats," Cougher said as he shielded his eyes from the sun and stared at the other ship. "I think that's Darren and Bobby over there."

"Well, I can certainly say that Team Grendel knows how to do their jobs when asked to," Mr. Ballantine smiled.

The Beowulf II pitched further to the side, and the cases and bags the men had brought up top started to join loose equipment and slide across the deck.

"Grab that!" Gunnar yelled. "We can't lose those cases!"

Lake grabbed Gunnar's arm as the man started to dive for the sliding gear. "We can't lose you, idiot!" he shouted. "Get a hold of yourself, Gunnar! Grab onto the rail and hang on! This ship is about to flip!"

"Do you feel that?" Cougher asked.

"What?" Popeye replied. "I don't feel nothing."

"Yeah," Cougher said, "exactly. Nothing's ramming us anymore."

"The shark is gone?" Popeye asked.

"But where did it go?" Mr. Ballantine wondered.

The men, holding onto the rail as the Beowulf II slowly rolled, looked over the side and down to the water below.

"The lifeboats," Gunnar said, "it's going for the lifeboats!"

"Son of a bitch!" Lake yelled.

CHAPTER TEN: ALL HELL ON DECK

The lifeboat was old, made of wood planks, and to Kinsey, it looked like it hadn't been serviced in years. She guessed pirates didn't have to deal with maritime inspections very often as she struggled to row the large boat by herself. With each stroke, she worried that the weathered oars would snap in half; they were already bending at angles she was not comfortable with.

She had heard the shooting and yelling from up above, and wondered what the source was, but it didn't deter her from her mission of getting the lifeboat clear of the pirate ship and over to the Beowulf II.

"Hey," Shane croaked as he opened his eyes, "wouldn't happen to have any sweat pants or something, would you? My junk is taking a beating from this sun."

Kinsey looked over at her cousin, and for the first time, really realized he was stark naked. In the heat of the rescue, she hadn't even registered it. She frowned and shook her head.

"Just hold your hands over yourself," she said, "it'll give you a funny tan line, but will keep your nuts from frying."

"Thanks for the effort," Shane said. He rolled his head and saw Darby next to him. "What's her story? She dead?"

"No," Kinsey said, "but she wouldn't cooperate. I had to choke her out."

"Damn," Shane said, "she's gonna kill you when she wakes up."

"Probably," Kinsey said as she turned the boat around past the pirate ship's stern.

"Oh…fuck," Shane said, "I may have only one eye, but that doesn't look good."

Kinsey looked over her shoulder and stopped rowing. Behind her she saw the Beowulf II listing heavily to its side. In the water were the ship's lifeboats, as well as two more from the pirate ship.

"What the fuck?" Kinsey asked. "How did that happen?"

"Guess we missed all the fun," Shane said. "Leave it to Max to start the party without me."

"Hey!" Max shouted from above them. Kinsey and Shane looked up and could see him peering over the stern rail. "Get to the lines! We'll pull you up! Darren and Bobby are going for the others!"

"What happened?" Kinsey yelled.

"Shark met helo and went boom," Max said.

"What the fuck are you babbling about?" Shane called.

"Dude!" Max yelled. "Why are you fucking naked?" He gaped. "Whoa…what's wrong with your face?"

"Get us up there and I'll regale you with my sordid tales of torture and despair," Shane shouted.

"We're coming around!" Kinsey said as she started rowing again. It was easier just to go to the other side of the ship than turn the boat around.

"What happened to the shark?" Shane yelled up to his brother. "Did you kill it like the last one?"

"No," Max said, "it's still down there."

"Oh, fuck," Kinsey whispered and looked at Darby. She gave a jump as she saw that the woman was conscious and staring right at her. "Hey. Sorry. You were trying to tell me, weren't you?"

Darby just glared.

"I'll take that as a yes," Kinsey said, "fuck."

***

The passengers on the first of the Beowulf II's lifeboats all rushed to the portholes as the craft shuddered. Their eyes wide with panic, they watched as an unbelievably large shadow passed by under the surface of the water.

"Somebody do something!" a man shouted.

But none of them knew what to do except keep going towards the pirate ship in hopes of being taken aboard in time.

**

"Anyone else do the calculations?" Gunnar asked as the men held onto the rail and watched the shadow circle the lifeboat. "I'm really hoping I just went stupid and my math is wrong."

"It's almost four times the length of the lifeboat," Lake said. "You may be stupid, but your math is right."

"It's gotta be thirty yards," Popeye said, "that possible? Can something be that big?"

"It's not natural," Cougher said.

"You are correct there, Mr. Colfer," Mr. Ballantine replied, "it is not natural. But there it is. In the water. Where we shall be shortly."

"Fucking great," Lake said.

"What are we going to do?" Popeye asked. "Hey, where'd it go?"

They all saw that the shadow was gone, no longer circling the lifeboat. They turned their attention to the other lifeboat, and the smaller boats that were being rowed by Darren and Bobby. There was no sign of the shark.

"Did it leave?" Popeye asked. "Maybe the ship is leaking something it didn't like? Sharks are sensitive to smells, ya know."

"That's true," Gunnar said, "but I don't think that's why it's gone."

"Why then?" Lake asked.

"It's moving to attack," Mr. Ballantine said.

"From below," Gunnar added.

"I can't watch this," Cougher said, but didn't turn away. None of them could.

"Get out of the water!" Lake shouted to Darren and Bobby. "Go back, you idiots! GO BACK!"

***

Darren looked over his shoulder at the sinking Beowulf II. He could hear men shouting at him, but he was too far away to understand what they were saying. He looked to his side and saw Bobby pacing him, her arms digging hard to row the lifeboat to the Beowulf II. They didn't need both lifeboats, but considering that his was already taking on water, he was glad they had a redundancy. Classic SEAL training was always to double up, never rely on just one of anything.

He turned back and concentrated on steering around the lifeboat that was motoring past him towards the pirate ship. He nodded to the men that stared out of the portholes at him. He heard them shouting and since he was only feet away, he could make out some of the words. His blood went cold.

"Shark!"

"Get out of the water!"

"Captain! Look out!"

Darren tensed and waited for the hit. He knew what the shark could do. He let the oars fall into the boat and grabbed up his M-4. If it came for him, he'd leap from the boat and start firing. It would probably do nothing, but he didn't plan on dying without a fight.

But to his incredible shock and horror, the shark didn't come for him. It came for the lifeboat next to him.

The craft shot into the air as massive jaws clamped around it. Even filled with pure terror, Darren still had the training to estimate the jaws at fifteen feet across. That was wide enough to grab the lifeboat, lift it into the air, and crush the middle.

"Holy fuck," Darren whispered.

The lifeboat split and the front half fell back into the water while the shark came down and took the back half under with it. Men screamed, blood flowed, and a huge wave came right at Darren.

"Holy fuck!" No whisper that time.

The wave hit the lifeboat and flipped it over, sending Darren into the water. He caught an oar to the head, was momentarily stunned, and floated beneath the surface of the ocean, his head bleeding and his eyes trying to make sense of what he saw.

Under him a shark that was easily 90 feet long, had half of a lifeboat in its jaws as it dove deeper and deeper. It took the broken craft, and the men inside, down into the darkness and was quickly lost from Darren's sight. He felt his lungs start to burn and he snapped out of his daze.

His head broke the surface and he gasped, taking in air that smelled of diesel fuel and blood.

"Darren!" Bobby yelled. "Swim here!"

He turned about and saw the lifeboat she rowed only a few feet from him. His lifeboat was nowhere to be seen, having sunk quickly. He swam hard and reached up to her as he got to the side of her lifeboat.

"Thank God for two, right?" Bobby said.

"We could use God's help right about now," Darren said, as he climbed into the boat, "because we are fucked if we don't get a miracle. Did you see that?"

"The international space station could see that thing," Bobby said. "I didn't think a shark could be that big. It was larger than a whale."

"Not quite larger," Darren said, "but close."

"You're really going to argue with me right now?" Bobby said. "You're a piece of work, Chambers."

"Sorry," Darren said, "can't help it."

"We can't get any closer to the Beowulf II," Bobby said, "it's going down fast and it'll pull us under."

Darren looked up at the ship and saw the faces of Gunnar, Mr. Ballantine, Lake, Popeye, and Cougher, staring down at him. He looked around and saw men trying to swim towards them, and towards the last Beowulf II lifeboat left. He calculated the space and realized they were going to be at capacity.

"Jump!" Darren shouted up at the men still on the Beowulf II. "Get down here now!"

"Shark!" Popeye yelled.

"It dove!" Darren replied. "Took the boat down with it! Hurry before it comes back!"

He could see the men struggle with their reality. Even with the ship sinking, it was still several meters from the rail to the water. The ship was rolling, so they could at least slide along the hull part of the way, but still… The alternative was to wait until the ship sank further and they could just hop right in the water, but the pull of the sinking ship would easily drag them under. He doubted any of them had the strength to fight that.

"Now!" Darren yelled. "MOVE!"

Lake was the first to go. He swung his legs up over the rail and pushed off. His ass bounced along the hull, then he was airborne, flying out over the water, his arms flailing. He slammed into the waves and went under.

"Where is he?" Bobby yelled. "Do you see him?"

Lake came up sputtering and immediately began to swim towards the lifeboat. Darren grabbed him and yanked him up inside. Voices calling out made Darren turn his head and he saw five men swimming towards the lifeboat.

"Come on!" Lake shouted up at the others. "Don't be pussies!"

Cougher and Popeye both jumped quickly. They hit the water, went under, then came back up and swam as fast as they could to the lifeboat. They reached the craft just as the other men in the water did. In seconds, the lifeboat was nearly full.

"We're taking on water," Bobby said, "we can't wait here."

"GOD DAMMIT, GUNNAR!" Darren shouted. "JUMP!"

He did, followed right behind by Mr. Ballantine. The two men were hauled into the lifeboat, pushing the waterline almost to the top edge of the craft.

"I think we have some help coming," Cougher said as he pointed at the other lifeboat that had turned around and was motoring to them.

" Idiots," Lake said, "they need to save themselves and get to the ship. It's the only safe place."

"I'll take their stupidity right about now," Mr. Ballantine said. "The craft we are in doesn't have long to last."

They all looked at the water that was spilling up over the sides and came up through the old, weathered planks.

***

"Even powered down, the pressure is too much!" Jennings yelled to Lucy over the whining and whistling of the massive diesel engines. "I really fucked these things!"

"How?" Lucy said. "I don't understand. If the engines are off, then how can there still be pressure?"

"This ship is old, probably from back in the sixties," Jennings said. "To maximize power, the diesel engines are used as the fire to fuel the boilers. For all intents and purposes, this ship is still run on steam."

"Then release the pressure!" Lucy said. "There has to be a release valve, right?"

"Yeah," Jennings said, "you're looking at it." He pointed at a twisted hunk of metal. "Like I said, I did a job on this. I didn't know we'd need it."

"Crap," she said, "crap, crap, crap. What do we do?"

"I may be able to get some of the pipes loose and release the pressure that way," Jennings frowned. "So you should get out of here."

"What do you mean?" Lucy said. "I can help."

"I know," Jennings said, "and I could use the help. But…"

"What?"

"This room is going to turn into a sauna from hell once I open the pipes," Jennings said. "The steam that is going to be released will boil the skin right off you."

"That means it'll boil you too!" Lucy said.

"I know," Jennings replied, "but that's my lot. I got this. Get topside and fill everyone in. Help with what you can up there. Prepare them if I fail."

"Jesus, Jennings," Lucy said, "you can't be serious."

"I am," Jennings said as he painfully bent down and picked up a large wrench one of the mechanics had dropped. "Go. Please. I can't do this with you here. I'll lose my nerve."

Lucy just stood there.

"Lucy?" Thorne called over the com. "What's the status?"

She kept standing there, her eyes on Jennings as he limped to a large pipe and started working at the coupling with the wrench.

"Lucy! Come in!"

"Sorry, sir," Lucy replied, "I'm coming up. Jennings has this in hand."

"Good," Thorne said, "because we have a situation up here and need you on your rifle."

"Be right there," Lucy said.

She walked over to Jennings and grabbed him by the shoulders. He turned to her and she hugged him tight, then quickly let go as he winced in pain.

"Thank you," she said.

"Don't thank me yet," Jennings said, "I could still totally fail."

***

The water below was coated in a sheen of red. Body parts were everywhere and Kinsey shook her head as she watched the two lifeboats that were left, rendezvous with each other. The lifeboat she was in stopped moving as it was winched into place. She was more than surprised by the faces that helped her, Shane, and Darby out onto the deck.

"Uh, hi," Kinsey said to the men that stood before her.

"They're cool," Max said from a few feet away, his rifle trained on a group of pirates that were bound. "Those guys were conscripted against their will. Paying off debts or just kidnapped into service. Mechanics, cooks, slaves."

"Damn," Shane said, "think they could kidnap some clothes for me?"

"Here," a man said as he took his shirt off and handed it to Shane.

"Thanks," Shane said.

Another man took off his pants and handed them over.

"Uh, what about you?" Shane said as Kinsey helped him get dressed.

The man nodded at the many corpses that littered the deck.

"Why isn't the ship moving?" Kinsey asked Max. "I don't feel the engines."

"Right, about that," Max said, "There's a little snag in that plan."

"What kind of snag?"

"Max!" Thorne yelled from the bridge. "I need guns on the water before it comes back!"

"Right!" Max said. "What about these guys?"

Darby moved to him and grabbed the AK-47 he was holding. She leveled it at the men and nodded to Max.

"You sure?" Max asked. "You're looking a little shaky." Darby glared. "Fine. You got it." He reached down and picked up his sniper rifle, then saw Lucy as she came up on deck. "Come on. We've got an overwatch to man."

"On it," Lucy said. "Hey."

"Hey," Kinsey said, "good shooting. Wait…where's Jennings?"

"Below," Lucy said, "working on the engines."

"Good," Kinsey said, "maybe he can get this thing moving."

Max and Lucy shared a look.

"Probably not," Lucy said, "we'll see."

"Keep your eyes peeled, Sis," Max said, "you spot anything give a shout."

"Will do," Kinsey nodded. She went back to the rail and scanned the water, her eyes drawn to the two lifeboats.

***

The two lifeboats pushed up against each other and the smaller one nearly sank as men began to climb from it and clamber up the side of the other. Darren shouted for them to stop and calm down or they'd sink them all, but the men didn't listen. The air was ripe with panic and Mr. Ballantine shook his head.

"I believed myself a better judge of character," he said, "I thought I'd hired top notch sailors, not selfish cowards."

A few men slowed down, a few gave Ballantine the bird, but most kept rushing out of the boat. Bobby grabbed a tow line that was tossed to her and tied it to the bow of the lifeboat. The larger craft began to sink as it took on weight, but the water line was well below dangerous. Its motor surged and it turned and headed for the ship, towing the smaller lifeboat behind it.

Darren looked back at the Beowulf II, as did the others, and watched it slowly sink further and further until it was lost from sight. Churning water filled with debris was all that was left. Gunnar made a low groan and Darren turned to him.

"Sorry, buddy," Darren said, "I know you lost everything."

"*We* lost everything," Gunnar said. "Without the samples and that data, no one will believe us."

"Don't lose hope, Gunnar," Mr. Ballantine said, "the satellite uplink did save some data. At least what you were able to log and analyze."

"Which was a fraction of what was needed," Gunnar said.

"I think we have bigger things to worry about," Lake said, "we're still in the water with a monster."

"Not for long," Bobby said, "look."

They turned and saw lines being thrown down to the Beowulf II's lifeboat and smiled. Safety was so close. So close.

But others turned back towards the open water and saw different lines. Lines in the water. Lines that formed the wake of a huge dorsal fin.

"Oh, fuck me," Cougher said.

"Lift! Lift!" men started shouting up at the ship. "Pull us up!"

"I could really go for one of those RPGs right about now," Popeye said.

"Thorne!" Darren shouted into the com. "The RPGs! Blast that fucking shark out of the water!"

"On it!" Thorne replied.

The fin grew closer and closer as it rose in the water. Then the nose broke the surface and the massive mouth opened. It scooped up body parts that floated here and there and was gone.

"Where'd it go?" Lake asked.

"There," Cougher said as he looked over the side of the boat.

The shark passed right below them and its dorsal fin scraped the bottom of the boat before it dove deeper and was lost from sight.

"Man, I hate that thing," Cougher said. Everyone looked at him. "What? It had to be said."

"No, it didn't," Lake said.

"We don't have a visual any longer," Max said over the com, "it dropped deep."

"Shit," Darren said, "then get us out of here."

***

"The winch isn't designed to bring up a lifeboat that size," Kinsey said, as she watched the lines grow taught and strain with the weight. "The lines are going to snap!"

As soon as she said it, the winch motors began to buzz loudly and a line did snap. It whipped up over the rail, slashing a man in half as he stood on deck, just waiting and watching. Blood sprayed everyone that stood there and sent them into a state of panic.

"Stop!" Kinsey yelled. "We still have to get the lifeboat up here! Someone help me!"

She ran to the winches and shut down the motors. One was obviously fried, but the other was still functional. She leaned over the rail and saw the lifeboats below. And the terrified looks on the men's faces.

"Hold tight!" she yelled, her hands cupped to her mouth. "We are going to have to bring you up in shifts in the smaller boat! Motor to the next set of winches!"

She could hear the protests and pleas from below, but there was nothing she could do. The winches couldn't handle the strain. The men would have to be brought up in shifts, eight at a time was her guess. Any more than that would snap the lifeboat itself.

She hurried to the next set of winches several yards away and motioned for some of the men on deck to help. The brave ran to her immediately; the less than brave backed away, their eyes on their dissected comrade.

"If you cowards aren't going to help with this, then grab those RPG launchers and take them up to the professionals!" Kinsey yelled and pointed at the crow's nest. "Move!"

"Way to motivate, Sis," Max said over the com.

"Shut it, cuz!" she snapped.

"Roger that. Shutting it."

***

Max grinned from ear to ear as he set his rifle aside and picked up a RPG launcher. He looked over at Lucy and she just shook her head.

"You aren't going to have the accuracy that you think you'll have," Lucy said.

"I know how to fire one of these," Max replied.

"Really? At a moving target in the water?" Lucy asked.

"Did you see the fucking size of that thing?" Max asked. "If I miss, I'll eat my boxers."

"You wear boxers?"

"Will you two shut up," Thorne barked over the com. "Get those rockets ready!"

Lucy and Max shut up quickly and stood up in the crow's nest, the launchers across their shoulders. They scanned the water, watching for the monster, waiting for the next attack.

"If it comes straight up from below, then we won't have much of a chance," Lucy said. "We could hit the crew down there."

"If it comes up from below, there won't be anything of the crew left," Max said.

"The com is on, assholes!" Darren yelled. "You want to keep the gloom and doom to yourself?"

"THERE!" someone screamed from the deck.

The dorsal fin was back. It looked as if it could slice the lifeboats in half just by itself; it didn't even need fifteen foot jaws or razor sharp teeth the size of a person's hand.

"I got it," Max whispered as he sighted just ahead of the shark. "Come on, baby. Come on."

The beast was a hundred yards out, but considering its size, that meant it was pretty close. Men from the lifeboats began to shout and scream, pleading to be pulled up. Kinsey was screaming back at them that they needed to shut the fuck up, and she was working as fast as she could, but it made no difference, fear ruled the day.

"Tag," Max said, "you're it."

The rocket shot from his shoulder and down at the shark just as the fin started to sink. Everyone held their breath and watched, desperate for some good luck. Only the tip of the fin could be seen when the rocket hit the water. The explosion sent a shock wave across the water, knocking some men from where they were perched on the Beowulf II's lifeboat. The sea churned from the explosion and waves rocked everything and everyone in the water.

"Get them back up on that boat!" Darren yelled as the men called out for help. "Get them out of the water!"

"Did you just say 'tag, you're it'?" Lucy asked.

"Shut up," Max said, "I hit it, didn't I?"

"Did you?" Thorne asked from the com. "I don't see any blood. No sign of shark chunks."

Max and Lucy studied the water, looking for any sign of success. Success wasn't what they saw, though.

"Holy fuck!" Lucy and Max yelled together as the shark burst from the surface, swallowing the men in the water in one gulp.

It rocketed up into the air like it was a massive, grey RPG itself. Everyone stared as it came fully out of the water, twisted, and fell back down. The wave it produced was ten feet high and slammed into both lifeboats, knocking everyone back into the sea.

"Shit!" Max shouted.

***

Darren fought to get to the surface. He could see the thing down under him, only yards away. He pushed any and all fear from his mind, his only thoughts were on getting up so he could take a deep breath of air. His lungs burned and he couldn't figure out why he wasn't making progress.

Then he looked down and saw the hand clamped to his ankle. Bobby. She had a hold of his leg and her eyes were wide with terror. She reached for him with her free hand and he bent in the water and reached back, hoping to pull her up with him. All he had to do was give her a boost, just something to get her momentum going. But he couldn't get to her. Even with her hanging onto his leg, they were worlds apart as the water continued to churn about them.

He looked up at the surface that was so close and wondered if he could get his head above water and take a gulp of air, then dive and grab her. But when he looked down, that fear he had suppressed, roared to life and he froze.

The shark was right there, its gargantuan body just feet from him, its mouth wide open. Everything slowed and he could see hunks of bloody clothes and pieces of men wedged in the shark's teeth. The leg from a pair of jeans flapped in the water, stuck in the corner of the shark's mouth.

Then it took Bobby from the side.

It hit so hard that Darren could hear the bones cracking even under the water. Blood and air bubbled out of Bobby's mouth as she screamed. Half of her was inside the monster's jaws while half was still hanging out, joining the pair of jeans. Her eyes went wide and Darren had to stop himself from calling to her as the shark turned and dove. The last thing he saw was her fingers reaching, searching, longing for his help, but it was too late.

He whipped his head up and swam as hard as he could for the sunlight that sparkled above. When he broke the surface, he gulped almost as much water as air, but just puked it back out and swam to the Beowulf II's lifeboat. Above him, the other lifeboat was taking up the first shift of terrified men.

"Captain!" Mr. Ballantine shouted, from the Beowulf II's lifeboat. "Here!"

Darren took the extended hand and was pulled up onto the lifeboat. He looked about at the faces that stared back at him.

"How many did we lose?" Darren asked.

"At least six," Lake said.

Gunnar, Popeye, and Cougher nodded.

"Then we are on the next shift up," Darren said, "if we last that long."

***

Darby and Thorne climbed up into the crow's nest and each picked up a RPG launcher.

"I want you to send it all the next time it comes up!" Thorne shouted. "You fire, reload and keep firing! This time we don't miss!"

"You okay?" Max asked as he saw the state Darby was in. Her throat was nothing but black and purple skin, covered in bruises that were obviously finger shaped.

She nodded and turned towards the water.

"Cool," Max said, "thank God."

Darby gave him a quizzical look then smiled slightly. Just slightly. She was back to business before Max was even sure it had happened.

"Thank God," Thorne said, "later today, we put our prayers in portable artillery."

***

"Oh shit, oh shit, oh shit, oh shit," Cougher said as the fin appeared once more.

"I think a year gets taken off my life every time that fucker shows up," Lake said.

Rockets fired from above and everyone watched them race to the water, right at the dorsal fin. Just before the impacts, the men ducked and covered their heads with their arms. Four almost simultaneous explosions sucked the oxygen right out of the air, and Darren felt his lungs fill with the stink of sulfur and copper. He gasped for air and found it a split second later.

"Blood!" Popeye shouted. "You hit it!"

A cheer went out from the lifeboats and from the deck above.

But Darren wasn't convinced. There was blood in the water, more than there had been, but if even one of the RPGs had made a direct hit, there would have been shark steaks for everyone. He didn't see shark steaks.

Then they heard it. A loud, deep banging noise. It reverberated around them, coming from everywhere.

"I was afraid of this," Mr. Ballantine said, "the shark knows it is being threatened."

"Ya think?" Lake said.

"I do," Mr. Ballantine replied, ignoring the sarcasm, "it is hurt and is going to take out the threat."

"Are you saying it knows the rockets came from the ship?" Darren asked. "Sharks aren't that smart."

"Sharks have been a top ocean predator for millions of years," Mr. Ballantine said. "I may not know marine biology like you do, Mr. Chambers, but I know predators. They're all smart. Every damn one of them."

"He's right," Gunnar said, "and if this thing has been genetically programmed and altered, then who knows what it's capable of?"

"It's capable of making me piss in my pants," Popeye said, "I'll admit it."

"Get in line," Cougher said.

The banging sounded again and they all turned to look at the source.

"But why?" Darren asked. "It's huge, but it's not big enough to take out the ship. There's no way."

"Not quite accurate," Mr. Ballantine said, "Gunnar is closer than he knows. The program included the possibility of actually designing the shark to go after key weaknesses in a ship. Such as the engines."

"How the hell would it know where the engine room is?" Cougher asked.

"It knows," Mr. Ballantine replied.

The other men began to cheer and cry out and Darren looked up to see the smaller lifeboat just above them.

"Climb in!" Kinsey yelled. "Hurry!"

"I'm not convinced the ship is the safest place," Lake said. "Great."

***

The room shuddered and Jennings stopped whacking at the pipe with the wrench. He had tried to uncouple the pipe at the junction point, but the pressure was too great, so he said screw it to finesse and began to beat the pipe with the heavy wrench. All he needed was for one pipe to come loose and vent the steam pressure that was building faster and faster.

But then the room began to shake and he stared in disbelief as the hull on the far side of the room started to buckle.

"What the fuck?" Jennings asked.

"Jesus," Max said from the hatch, a RPG launcher in his hands, "Ballantine was right. The fucking thing is trying to get at the engines."

"It's what?" Jennings asked. "What's getting at what?"

"Mega shark," Lucy said from behind, "we pissed it off."

"Why the fuck would you do that?" Jennings shouted. "That's a fucking stupid thing to do!"

"We didn't do it on purpose!" Max yelled back.

The ship shook as the shark rammed it again and then again.

"God damn," Jennings said, "it must be huge."

The hull buckled even more. Max put the launcher over his shoulder.

"What the fuck are you doing?" Jennings said.

"I'm going to fucking kill it if it breaks through!"

"You'll kill us all!" Jennings yelled. "I've been down here ready to sacrifice myself to save all your asses and now you want to fucking blow a hole in the ship? Fuck you!"

"It's coming in," Max said, "and there's nothing we can do to stop it. We can't dive in and punch it out. The thing fucking swallows people whole, man!"

"So the ship is going down no matter what?" Jennings asked.

"Looks like it," Max said.

"We're fucked if we do and fucked if we don't," Lucy said. "At least if we kill it, we won't have to deal with it coming after us as we all tread water."

"Jesus," Jennings said, "then if it's all gone to shit anyway…"

He limped over to the engine controls and flipped every switch, pulled every lever, and turned every knob. All to full.

"Let's do this right," Jennings said. "Get everyone up top to the bow. They need to be ready, because when this goes, it'll rip this ship apart. Life preservers, whatever rafts are ready, anything that'll help people float and keep them from being sucked below."

Max lowered the RPG. "Alright. Now we're talking. Let's go."

"Nope," Jennings said, "I'm still stuck here."

"What do you mean?" Lucy asked. "It'll blow without you."

"It will," Jennings said, "eventually." He put his hand on a large lever by the side of the controls. "But this will make sure it blows when it's supposed to. Someone has to stay here and time this right. When it comes through the hull, I'll take it out."

"Dear God," Lucy said, "you are the bravest man ever."

"No shit," Max said and offered his hand. Jennings shook it quickly. Max slapped the RPG. "I'll have this up top if it doesn't work."

"Good to know," Jennings said. "Now get the fuck up top. This place is not going to be fun." He looked at Lucy. "Remember that steam?"

"Yeah," she nodded.

"It's still coming," Jennings said. He pulled his belt loose from his pants and wrapped his hand to the large lever. "Better go before it hits cooking temperature in here."

Lucy and Max nodded and turned away, leaving Jennings to his continued fate of self-sacrifice.

***

"Put on whatever you can!" Kinsey yelled at the men. Even the pirates were dragged to the bow, their bonds cut so they stood a chance of survival. She didn't agree with the choice, but her father insisted.

"We're all in this together now," Thorne had said, "might as well give them a shot at living. Then we'll deal with them."

She still didn't agree, but she understood.

The small lifeboat had been dragged up on deck and the wounded, which included Shane, were put inside and strapped tight.

"You know if this capsizes, I'll drown, right?" Shane said.

"If it capsizes, you're totally fucked anyway, bro," Max said. "How long do you think you can tread water?"

"All of thirty seconds," Shane replied, "but they'd be *my* thirty seconds."

"That doesn't make sense," Lucy said.

"He never does," Max replied.

"Sorry about Bobby," Kinsey said as Darren stepped to her side and helped hand out life preservers and lifesavers.

"Thanks," he nodded, "it still hasn't sunk in."

"It will," Kinsey said. "When it does, I'll be here."

"Good," Darren replied, "that's good to know."

"Touching," Mr. Ballantine said. He looked at Darby. "You should be in the lifeboat."

The ship shook and everyone stood stock still. It shook again and they all heard a distinctive groan.

"It'll breach the hull any second," Lake said, "from the sound of that metal stress."

"Hey!" Cougher shouted from the bridge. "I have the Navy! The fucking US Navy is on the radio!"

Thorne sprinted from where he was helping and up the stairs to the bridge. He was gone for several minutes and everyone waited, each becoming hopeful for a brief second. When he returned the optimism level dropped considerably at the look on his face.

"There's a destroyer due south," Thorne said, "they've been authorized to come get us."

"But…?" Kinsey asked.

"But they're two hundred miles off," Thorne said.

"Five hours," Lake said, "it'll take them five hours to get here."

"Keep working!" Kinsey shouted, not letting the news sink in with anyone. "We have to stay alive for five hours! You hear that? Five hours, people!"

***

The steel buckled further and rivets popped, ricocheting about the engine room. Jennings cried out as one slammed into his leg and ripped his kneecap off. He only had one hand free and he clamped it to his leg, feeling the blood flow through his fingers. The hull buckled further and water started to spray in with all the pressure of the ocean behind it.

Jennings's eyes were locked on the hull as he watched the steel begin to fold in on itself, letting in more and more water. He found himself holding his breath and he let it out and started to breathe deeply. Even though everything smelled of steel, salt, and diesel fumes, he wanted to taste it all in the last few minutes of his life.

But he didn't get minutes.

The hull crumpled as the entire ship shook from the shark's impact. It hammered at the ship, ramming it over and over. Jennings was waist deep in water when he saw teeth; teeth so big he didn't know what he was seeing at first. The hull ripped apart and Jennings's stared into the maw of a monster only known in nightmares. The ocean came at him fast and he didn't hesitate. The water made it hard to pull the lever, but he put all of his weight on it and yanked.

It went down and the diesel engines that had started to sputter from the sea water, whined to a new pitch that made Jennings's teeth vibrate. The shark must of felt the change, because it tried to back out of the hole it had made.

Jennings's took a lung full of water, but managed to smile as a bright flash filled his vision; the last thing he ever saw.

***

Those on deck were thrown off their feet as fire erupted from pipes across the ship. The vessel began to pitch immediately, as the stern cracked off from the rest of the ship. Everyone grabbed what they could and braced themselves as the bow was lifted into the air; air that was filled with the sounds of metal ripping and people screaming.

"Hold on to each other!" Kinsey yelled. "Do not let go! Just hold on!"

Her words were lost in the chaos and she reached out to find Darren by her. His arms encircled her as the bow tilted higher and higher.

"Come on!" Thorne shouted from what would have been in front of them moments earlier, but was then above them as the ship sank fast. He hooked his arm through Darren's and pulled hard, bringing the man and his daughter up to the railing that lined the bow. "Grab this!"

They each held onto the railing and watched the death about them. Men fell as they lost their grips on whatever they had tried to use to brace themselves. Their screams were cut short as they smacked into equipment, their bodies snapped in half, crushed, contorted.

Smoke billowed into the air and enveloped everyone, making them choke and gag. For a split second, Kinsey believed she'd die from asphyxiation, but the ocean breeze came along and spared her that indignity. She tried to peer through the smoke below her to see how fast they were sinking, but her eyes stung and watered and she couldn't make out a thing.

Then the water hit and she was under.

She knew Darren and her father were close, but she couldn't search for them; she had to get to the surface. That was her one duty, then she could worry about the ones she cared for. She looked up and saw the surface just within reach. The drag from the sinking ship pulled at her, but the life vest she had strapped around her chest countered that. With all her might, she reached for the light, the muscles in her arms burned and strained with the effort.

She surfaced to the sound of dozens of lungs gasping and filling with air. All about her, heads bobbed. The lifeboat with the wounded was dozens of yards away from her, but she didn't care. It hadn't been destroyed and she said a quick prayer of thanks for that. The Beowulf II's lifeboat bobbed in the churning water in the opposite direction. She made the decision to head for it, along with many others, even though it had proved to be less than safe from the shark.

But the beast was dead, right? She thought. It had to be.

She got to the lifeboat and was helped up into it. It soon filled up inside as well as on top, and she quickly worried it would capsize, or just sink from the weight.

"Hey," Max gasped, appearing at the hatch, "you made it."

"Darren? My dad?" Kinsey asked.

"Up here," Max said. "Lucy?"

"I don't know," Kinsey said. "Who else do you see?"

"Lake and Cougher," Max replied, "but I can't find Gunnar or Popeye. Or Ballantine."

"Fuck," Kinsey said.

***

"Hey," Gunnar said as he slapped Popeye's face, "you alive?"

"Huh?" Popeye muttered as he floated on his back next to Gunnar. They both had life preservers on and bobbed lazily in the water. "What?"

"Good," Gunnar said, "we need to swim."

Popeye came out of his daze and looked about, and then frowned.

"How the hell'd we get over here?" Popeye asked as he saw they were over a hundred yards from everyone else. Bodies floated about them in various states of dismemberment. "Ah, shit and shite."

"We must have been pushed this far by a wave when the ship went down," Gunnar said. "Can you swim? Are you hurt?"

"I think I can- Ow! Fuck!" Popeye cried out. "My leg!"

Gunnar took a deep breath and put his head under the water for a look. He didn't like what he saw.

"What? How bad?" Popeye asked when Gunnar came back up.

"Not good," Gunnar said, "you have a foot long hunk of steel sticking out of your thigh and you're bleeding bad."

"Can you get it," Popeye said, "tie off my leg?"

"Jesus," Gunnar replied, "maybe."

"I ain't swimming nowhere with that metal in me," Popeye said. "So if you think you can't do it, then just leave me, okay? No need for both of us to die, Doc."

"I'm not leaving you," Gunnar said, "just hold on."

Gunnar pulled his life preserver up over his head.

"Hey! You'll need that!" Popeye protested.

"I can't dive under with it on," Gunnar said. "You hang onto it. Maybe bite down on it. This will hurt."

He pulled a strap from the preserver then dove under. He tied the strap tight above the wound then went back up for air. Popeye was screaming like a banshee.

"Oh, sweet Lord!" he yelled. "Thank God you're done!"

"I'm not," Gunnar said, "that was just the tourniquet."

"No," Popeye said, shaking his head, "Dear Lord, no."

Gunnar dove again and wrapped his hands around the hunk of metal and pulled. It wouldn't budge. He pulled at it over and over, but it was stuck tight. His lungs started to burn and he surfaced to gulp some air. Popeye, his head resting on Gunnar's life preserver, was passed out. He decided he'd try one more time then leave the metal in. It was probably better if he did, but it would be hard for Popeye to swim and they needed to get to the lifeboats.

He filled his lungs then dove under one more time. The second he did, the air was forced from his lugs in a fit of panic.

"Oh, fuck," he said when he came back up sputtering water.

Gunnar looked at the shadow that swam a dozen feet below them. Hunks of white flesh and blood started to pool about him and Popeye, adding to the human chum that they treaded in. Gunnar could see a huge, gaping divot was blasted in the beast. But it was still going.

"It fucking lives," Gunnar said.

He turned towards the lifeboat and waved his arms over his head. Without the life preserver, his head went under and he splashed to the surface, coughing and gagging. He grabbed onto Popeye with one arm and waved the other.

"It's alive!" he shouted. "The shark is still alive!"

***

"What's that?" Cougher asked, nudging Lake and pointing towards Gunnar. "You hear that?"

"That's Gunnar," Lake said and shouted to those inside the lifeboat, "we can see Gunnar!"

"And that's not all," Cougher whimpered. "Ah, come on, man!"

Lake saw it, as did everyone up on top of the lifeboat. A dorsal fin so large that even over a hundred yards away it was easy to spot. And it headed straight for where Gunnar was shouting and yelling.

***

He heard the voices shouting back to him, but he couldn't make out what they were saying. He could see arms waving and moving, so Gunnar waved back at them harder. He hoped the lifeboat was operational and they could just motor to him. But it had been a day of hopes dashed and he knew better.

He was afraid to look down in the water, but he forced himself to and was pleased to see absolutely nothing. Gunnar knew that didn't mean a thing, since the monster could be anywhere. It could be down deep ready to rocket up at him; it could be off to the side, circling him, ready to scoop him up with the bloody mess he was stuck in; it could even be right behind him, swimming fast and ready to chomp.

He looked over his shoulder and struggled not to cry.

***

"Do we have anything that can take it out?" Thorne asked. "Someone tell me we have something!"

"This," Lucy said as she tossed up a RPG launcher from the water below, "I fucking held onto this the entire time."

"You're insane," Max smiled at her, "I would have let it go."

"Yet, another reason the Coast Guard has more guts than the Navy," Lucy said as she was helped up onto the overcrowded surface of the lifeboat. "So who's going to fire the thing?"

"At this range?" Darren said.

"I got it," Max said, "I'll put it right down the throat of that fucking shark."

"Then do it," Darren said.

Once more, Max found himself with a RPG launcher on his shoulder. He actually wondered if he'd chosen the wrong profession as a sniper. Despite the circumstances, he found he liked blowing shit up.

***

"Popeye," Gunnar said, smacking the man, "Popeye! Wake up, man!"

But Popeye didn't wake up.

The fin was still a long ways off, but at the speed it was moving, it would be to him in seconds. He nodded in resignation and his whole body relaxed. He had rejected human medicine for a life as a marine biologist. It was a fitting end, he thought.

He felt lighter knowing he would be gone soon. He just hoped it would be quick and as painless as possible. The shark closed rapidly. The feeling of lightness increased, like he was being lifted on bubbles. Then he looked down and saw that actual bubbles were coming up from below, pushing at his body.

"What the fuck?" he said as his eyes widened. "WHAT THE FUCK?"

The ocean churned and roiled about him, and he and Popeye were lifted out of the water and up into the air. He had no clue what was happening to him, how any of it was possible.

He was on top of a huge, floating rectangle of steel, just inches from a large hatch. The wheel on the hatch began to turn and Beau's head popped out.

"You fuckers totally forgot about me," he said. "Now get your ass inside."

Gunnar grabbed Popeye and was helped down into the whatever the hell it was. He was stunned at what he saw about him and shook his head over and over.

"No fucking way," he said.

"You're the scientist guy, right?" Ingrid said. "How's it going?"

"I've been better," Gunnar said, "what the hell is this?"

"The armory," Carlos said from a bank of controls, "now shut up. We're busy."

"The Toyshop?" Gunnar asked, looking at Beau. "What the fuck?"

"I said shut up," Carlos snapped, "and don't call it that."

"Ten meters and closing," Ingrid said, as she turned and pressed her face to what looked like a periscope. Moshi sat right next to her, her hands on two joysticks. "Nine meters. Eight, seven, six."

"Fire," Carlos said casually, looking over at Moshi, "let's finish this. I have a season of Grimm recorded at home. I'd like to get back and watch that sooner than later."

"No fucking way," Gunnar repeated as Moshi, still silent in all the chaos, squeezed the triggers that were on the joysticks she held.

Two loud clanking noises rang out and Ingrid pushed on Gunnar's shoulders, forcing him to the floor.

"Cover your ears," she said.

He did just a second before the sound of one, then a second explosion nearly deafened him. The Toyshop (or Toyship? Gunnar wondered) shook and shuddered. Then all was quiet.

"Direct hit!" Ingrid shouted as she looked back into the scope. "Killed that bastard!"

"Let's get visual confirmation," Carlos said and shoved past Gunnar as he climbed the ladder and opened the top hatch.

"What the hell is going on, Beau?" Gunnar asked. "How is this possible?"

"I was running from the mess when the Beowulf started to go down," Beau said, "water rushed about me and I was swept off my feet and down the stairs to the deck below. I thought I was dead when hands grabbed me and pulled me in here."

"My hands," Ingrid smiled.

"Yeah, hers," Beau nodded. "As soon as I was inside the Toyshop, the walls started closing about and Carlos was yelling at me to help, while Moshi was busy pushing buttons and pulling levers. The whole fucking room turned into a sub, man."

"More of a tactical escape pod, really," Ingrid said. "It was something Carlos insisted we incorporate into the design. Especially after the Beowulf I went down and we lost everything."

"What the hell happened to the Beowulf I, anyway?" Gunnar asked.

"Oh, we don't talk about that," Ingrid said. "Hey, you thirsty or hungry? We have soda and chips over there."

"Get up here!" Carlos shouted from above. "You'll want to see this!"

Gunnar left Popeye passed out on the floor of the Toyshop/escape pod and climbed the ladder. His eyes went wide as he saw the swathe of blood and guts that floated everywhere.

"I think we got it," Carlos smirked.

"I'll believe it when I see it," Gunnar replied.

"You are seeing it," Carlos said. "I guarantee it's gone."

"Hopefully it's the only one left," Gunnar said. "If smaller sharks come to feed, then we'll know the area is clear of any big ones."

Realization hit him and he turned about and looked towards the others that were far off in the distance and getting further away as the current pulled them in the opposite direction.

"Does this thing have motors?" Gunnar asked. "We need to go help the others get out of the water!"

"Motors?" Carlos grumbled. "Don't be an idiot. It's an armory. Motors…"

He was still grumbling as he went below. In a minute, he was back up and tossed two cases overboard. As they flew down to the water they burst open and inflated into rafts.

"Better start paddling," Carlos said, "before they turn into shark bait."

"Where are you going?" Gunnar snapped as Carlos descended back inside the Toyshop.

"I want a Pepsi," Carlos said, "and I don't paddle."

Gunnar looked at Beau, then at the rafts that had started to float off. "You have got to be fucking kidding me."

CHAPTER ELEVEN: THE GIG IS ON

The sharks did come. Small compared to the monster, but large enough to make many of the Somali crew and the others uneasy, as they watched them feast on the remains of their fallen comrades.

But Gunnar, with the help of Team Grendel, was able to get the survivors to safety. After some time, Cougher even got the Beowulf II's lifeboat motor to work, albeit at a severely reduced efficiency level, and ferried over to the small lifeboat and the wounded. There they found Ballantine and Darby clinging to the side, Darby's arm clamped around the man's shoulders, keeping him from slipping off and sinking into the water.

With everyone secure, or as secure as they could be in the midst of a shark feeding frenzy, Ballantine sat inside the Toyshop, a cold can of soda pressed to a huge knot on his forehead, and his eyes focused on Carlos with laser intensity.

"All of this behind my back," Mr. Ballantine stated, "I don't know whether to be grateful or extremely angry with you, Carlos."

"Doesn't matter to me," Carlos said, his face showing almost no expression, as if he hadn't been part of destroying a nearly 100 foot shark that shouldn't have existed. "I'm alive. I could give a crap how you feel."

Team Grendel (except for Shane who was resting inside the Beowulf II's lifeboat), Gunnar, Lake, Darren, and Darby, all sat on the floor or stood against the walls of the Toyshop, watching the two men spar.

"Enlighten me, if you will," Mr. Ballantine said, "you have obviously proved to be the more prescient of us."

"After the loss of the Beowulf I---" Carlos started.

"What did happen to that ship?" Max asked.

"We don't talk about it," Mr. Ballantine, Carlos, and Ingrid, said in unison. Moshi nodded her head in agreement. Darby rolled her eyes.

"Oh," Max nodded, "gotcha."

"As I was saying," Carlos said, giving Max a quick glare, "after the Beowulf I was lost---"

"Which you don't talk about," Max said. Kinsey smacked him in the back of the head and he shut up.

"Yes, that," Carlos said, "I added some refinements to the design of the Beowulf II. Just enough to get us started and wouldn't alert you to what I had planned."

"Because I would have said no," Mr. Ballantine said, "it would have looked weak in the eyes of the company."

"Admitting disaster was imminent," Thorne said, "I get that."

"Yes, whatever," Carlos said, "it was fairly easy. And as we sat in port, waiting for you to approach Mr. Chambers, I put my team to work. We had the armory retrofitted before we left Cape Town."

"It is remarkable," Mr. Ballantine said as he looked about the space, "but next time, you'll seek my approval before making adjustments."

Carlos just shrugged.

"Next time?" Darren asked. "You're joking, right?"

"Am I, Captain?" Mr. Ballantine replied. "Of course, there are many hurdles to jump before I can even answer that, but we'll see."

There was a rapping at the top hatch and Max climbed up and opened it. Beau peeked his head through and looked about until he found Thorne and Darren.

"They're here," Beau said, "the Navy. They found us."

"Good," Mr. Ballantine said, "I'll do the talking."

"Better let me," Thorne said, "I know the lingo."

"I was the captain of the Beowulf II," Darren said, "it would make more sense if I spoke to them."

"I'll let you two work it out," Mr. Ballantine said, "but remember that the Beowulf II was a research vessel that was attacked by pirates. No mention of oversized sharks."

"Genetically manipulated oversized sharks," Gunnar added.

Mr. Ballantine nodded as Thorne and Darren ascended the ladder.

***

The USS Hopper took everyone aboard quickly. The wounded were tended to and the rest were fed and given what they needed to be comfortable, as the destroyer steamed to the African coast. A diplomatic ship was sent out by the Somali government to obtain its nationals, so the indentured Somali crew could be returned to their tribes and the pirates could be dealt with as the government saw fit.

Neither Thorne nor the Commander of the Hopper had any illusions that the pirates would end up anywhere but out raiding again in a few week's time, once they reestablished their leadership.

Team Grendel and the Beowulf II's crew were scrutinized and questioned thoroughly by US government officials when they were taken to the Gulf of Aden. No one broke, everyone stayed on message. And despite the fact that no one from the US consulate believed a word of what they said, they were all put on planes and sent to their homes. They were even individually escorted to their respective houses, apartments, condos, dive bars, and observed until their doors closed.

It would be weeks before any of them heard from Mr. Ballantine. Although each one was glad to see a sizeable sum of money had been wired to their bank accounts.

When the text came, Kinsey just stared at it, unsure of whether to answer or not. She had used the weeks to get completely clean. With Gunnar's help, she was weaned off even his formula, and the text from Ballantine made her itch like she needed a fix. She didn't like that feeling, not anymore, and she tossed her phone onto the café table where she sat.

"Bad news?" Gunnar asked as he sipped coffee across from her. Then his phone chimed and he frowned. "Oh."

With her apartment serving only as a reminder of a life she wanted nothing to do with, she had moved in with Gunnar, staying in the guest room of his spacious condo in the La Jolla area of San Diego. It was certainly a step up from the ghetto crack hell she'd lived in before.

"Can I get you anything else?" the waiter asked as Gunnar and Kinsey stared at each other, unsure of even what to say.

"No, thank you," Kinsey said, "the check will be fine. We have to go."

"Do we?" Gunnar asked. "I'm not super keen on the idea."

"What else are we going to do?" Kinsey asked. "I can't live off you the rest of my life."

"There are security jobs," Gunnar said. "I'm looking into taking a research position with a non-profit. I'm sure I could get you something there."

"Not with my background," Kinsey said. "The dishonorable discharge alone pretty much bars me from using my skills for anything except paintball."

"But that discharge was crap," Gunnar insisted, "there has to be a way to get it cleared up. You were obviously sabotaged."

Kinsey smiled weakly and looked out into the sunny street that ran next to the outdoor café's tables. Her eyes misted up and she quickly wiped at them.

"Kins? What's up?" Gunnar asked, leaning across the table to take her hand.

She pulled her hand back and took a deep breath, laughing at her sudden break.

"I have to tell you something, Gun," she said, "but you have to promise not to tell anyone. Like doctor- patient promise, got it?"

"Got it," Gunnar frowned.

"It wasn't crap," she said, "the discharge. I deserved it."

Gunnar just stared for a minute then sat back in his chair. He rubbed at his face and shook his head.

"Why?" Gunnar asked. "What did you do?"

"What they said I did," Kinsey admitted. "I took speed. I wasn't going to make it, Gun. I'd spent every bit of energy I had in BUD/S and didn't have an ounce more when I hit SQT. I was about to wash out."

"Can you do that?" Gunnar said. "I thought once you hit SQT you were a SEAL."

"You aren't a SEAL until you get assigned to a Team," Kinsey said. "They pushed me hard, harder than any of the men. It pissed me off. They tried to break me at every move. And it worked. I broke, but I thought I could hide it."

"Jesus, Kins," Gunnar said, "have you told your father? He retired because of you. You have to tell him."

"No way, not going to happen," Kinsey said, "and you better not tell him. You promised to keep this between us. You promised, Gun."

"Yeah, yeah, I know," Gunnar said, "I won't say a word." He looked up at the bright blue, California sky and sighed. "So we're doing this?"

"We're going to see what he wants," Kinsey said, "listen to his pitch. Maybe it won't be monster sharks that can eat ships this time?"

"Maybe," Gunnar said and looked back at her, "might be time for my own admission."

"What do you mean?" Kinsey asked.

"I'll tell you on the way back to the condo," Gunnar said, "you drive."

"About?"

"Monster sharks."

***

The cabin was the unassuming, two-story modular log construction seen throughout the Northern California coast. Max leaned against it as Shane held the sniper rifle to his shoulder and carefully squeezed off six shots, obliterating the apples that had been perched on a fence three hundred yards away. Once the echoes of the shots dissipated, the sound of the ocean came up over the cliff the cabin was perched near and joined Max's clapping.

"Bravo, one-eye," Max said, "six for six. That fruit never stood a chance."

Shane got up from the ground and leaned his rifle up on his shoulder. The eye patch he wore had a large pot leaf on it, which went nicely with the joint that hung from the corner of his mouth.

"I am Shane Reynolds," he said, "and I kill apples. I'm not proud of what I do, but it's a job, and if I don't do it, then someone else will."

"Good to see you back in action," Lucy said as she came from around the side of the cabin.

"Hey there," Max smiled and hurried over to give her a big hug, "how the fuck are you?"

"Dealing," Lucy said, "it's been crazy since I got back. It wasn't easy lying to Bobby's family."

"I bet," Shane said, "anyone else with you?"

"Not yet, but I think I hear someone," Lucy said.

The three walked to the other side of the cabin where the Reynolds's Jeep was parked as well as a compact rental Lucy drove. A black Land Rover pulled up and Thorne, followed closely by Kinsey and Gunnar, hopped out.

"Gang's all here," Shane said, "but why's the fish doctor tagging along? Thought this was a Team Grendel reunion only."

"I'm not part of the Team?" Gunnar smiled. "Why you gotta be so mean?"

"To compensate for my handicap," Shane grinned, "I'm bitter."

"You're stoned," Kinsey said as she walked up, gave him a hug, then took the joint from his mouth and tossed it to the ground.

"Hey!" he complained. "That's medicinal! I have a prescription now, ya know?"

"So that means Ditcher is coming too?" Max said.

In answer, a pickup truck came speeding out of the tall fir trees that lined the property around the cabin. Dust trailed behind it and then clouded around everyone as it came to a stop.

"Way to make an entrance, dude," Max coughed.

"Sorry," Darren said, "I thought I was going to be late." After hugs, handshakes, and all the greetings, he looked about. "Where's Ballantine?"

"Been waiting here the whole time," Mr. Ballantine said as the cabin door opened. Darby stood directly behind him, her throat covered in a wide bandage. "Could have taken all of you with ease. Makes me wonder if I'm talking to the right people."

Everyone turned and looked at Shane and Max.

"You didn't go inside?" Kinsey asked.

"Not our cabin," Max shrugged, "would have been rude."

"And neither of you thought to knock?" Thorne said. "How are you related to me?"

"No vehicle," Shane said, "and I didn't really care. So there's that."

"We were dropped off by associates," Mr. Ballantine smiled, "which is why I brought you here."

"You're supposed to ask us if we were wondering why you brought us here," Max said, "don't you know anything about dramatic affect?"

"I'm going to go for the direct approach," Mr. Ballantine said. "I've cleared it with the company and I want to hire you again. Come in so we can discuss it."

"Nope," Max said.

"Don't think so," Shane responded.

"Not interested," added Lucy.

"Before everyone declines," Mr. Ballantine said, "hear me out. Please?"

"We'll hear you out, Ballantine," Thorne said, "but we have quite a few dead reasons to decline, so do not get your hopes up."

"Wouldn't think of it," Mr. Ballantine said as he gestured for them to come inside.

***

The sunset filled the sky with deep reds and glowing oranges. The air was chilly compared to San Diego, and Kinsey wrapped her arms about herself as she stood on the edge of the cliff, watching the waves far below crash against the coarse sand of the beach.

"Hey, 'Sey," Darren said as he walked up to her, "am I interrupting a private moment?"

"Nope," Kinsey said, "I can share the sunset with you, 'Ren."

They stood there silently until the sun was almost lost to the horizon.

"Thoughts?" Darren finally asked.

"On Ballantine's offer?" Kinsey replied.

"No, on the 49ers' chances at the Super Bowl," Darren said.

"Lame joke."

"Yeah, it was. But…?"

"He makes a good point," Kinsey said. "There's more danger out there and we have the experience needed to deal with it. Throw another Team into the fray and they could end up as broken as us."

"Are we broken?" Darren asked. "The way everyone was glad to see each other, I'd say we're pretty well put together."

"Could be," Kinsey said, "what about your crew? Are they onboard with it?"

"They will be," Darren answered, "I've been feeling them out the last week. I knew this would be coming from Ballantine."

"How are they?"

"Good. Popeye is being fitted with a prosthetic leg. They just couldn't save it, too much blood loss. Lake is always ready to get out on the water and Cougher is stoked that he'll be First Engineer. Beau could go either way."

"I thought they'd turn you down flat after losing Bach," Kinsey frowned, "and Jennings."

"I know you and Jennings had a connection, so to say," Darren smiled, "I'm sorry."

"It was casual," Kinsey said, "a way to let off steam. But he was a good guy."

"He was," Darren agreed, "and that wraps that up. The dead are remembered and the living mentioned. What are you going to say to Ballantine?"

"Is Gunnar in?" Kinsey asked.

"He is," Darren said, "as is your dad."

"The boys are still deciding," Kinsey said, "I think they'll make Ballantine sweat before they answer."

"Lucy's in," Darren said, "she didn't want Bobby's death to be for nothing."

"Is that why you're doing it?" Kinsey asked.

"No, not at all," Darren replied, "well, sort of. It's a factor. But the main reason is I still have a quest to finish."

"Your whale," Kinsey stated.

"My whale," Darren nodded, "it's out there, 'Sey. I know it is. The one we found wasn't big enough."

"And we lost the hard evidence that it even existed," Kinsey said, "I'm sure Gunnar pointed that out."

"He did," Darren said, "he also pointed out the dangers of what is loose in the ocean. He knows there are more sharks. Big ones, like what we dealt with."

"That's what Ballantine said," Kinsey said.

"He also hinted that there may be more anomalies," Darren said.

Kinsey finally turned from the picturesque sky and looked Darren full in the face.

"What does that mean?" she asked.

"The company, the one Ballantine works for, solves problems," Darren said. "I guess there are a lot more problems than even Ballantine knew about. Despite what we all may think, the company considers what we accomplished a success. They need us."

"The company, the company," Kinsey laughed, "what the fuck is this company? They solve problems? Whoopty shit. We all have problems. They should learn to solve theirs on their own like the rest of us."

"Do we really?" Darren asked. "Do we solve them on our own? I think you've had some help with yours. And I know I haven't gotten through mine without backup."

Kinsey was quiet for a while.

"I don't know yet," she finally said, "I'm going to need some time to think about it."

"Good," Darren said, "that's better than a flat no."

"Hey!" Max yelled from the cabin. "Come on, you two! We have several bottles of whiskey and a deck of cards! OW! Hey! Why'd you hit me?"

"We also have non-alcoholic drinks, Kinsey," Lucy yelled.

"And we're going to play some strip poker!" Max added. "Darby said she'd totally play! OW! OWOWOW! Okay, okay, Darby is *not* playing! Jeez." The cabin door shut, but they could still hear Max complaining.

"You coming in?" Darren asked. "Ballantine said the cabin is owned by the company and we can stay all weekend."

"I'm going to hang out here for a bit," Kinsey said, "go ahead. I'll be in soon."

"Okay," Darren said, and squeezed Kinsey on the shoulder. She patted his hand and gave him a smile. "Don't stay out too long. It gets cold fast up here."

"You bet, dad," Kinsey laughed.

"I'm the dad," Thorne said from behind them, "not him."

"Jesus," Darren said, "damn you're quiet."

"Occupational hazard," Thorne said.

"I'll leave you two," Darren said, "play nice."

They waited until Darren had walked into the cabin before speaking.

"Play nice?" Thorne said. "I think we know how to do that."

"We do," Kinsey said, "just don't ask if I'm in or not. I don't know."

"I don't want you to be in," Thorne said. "I know we haven't talked a lot since we got back, but Gunnar has assured me you are making progress. I don't want that to get screwed up."

"You mean you don't want your daughter to end up relapsing and turning back into a junkie whore?" Kinsey laughed.

"Something like that," Thorne replied. The smile on his face surprised Kinsey.

"Not the reaction I expected," Kinsey said.

"You thought you'd shock me?" Thorne asked. "After surviving a 100 foot mega shark, I think I'm all surprised out."

"Oh, I don't know about that," Kinsey said. When her father gave her a puzzled look she just shook her head. "Never mind. It's all good."

"Okay," Thorne said, "but if you're going to tell me you're pregnant, at least wait until I've had a few shots first." His shoulders slumped. "Dammit. Sorry."

"Nothing to be sorry about," Kinsey said, "I may join you." She held up her hands. "Kidding! Don't go ballistic on me."

"Funny," he nodded, "I do want to say that if you decide you want in, then you have my support. I'd rather you didn't, but it is your life. And, well, I liked being around you again. I missed that."

"Missed almost dying on the high seas? I think you may need to be the one that walks away from this."

"Probably," Thorne agreed, "but you can't teach an old frogman new tricks. And being a frogman is all I know, really."

"I know that," Kinsey said, "okay. Enough sappy crappy. How about we play some cards and just enjoy life for the night?"

"Good idea," Thorne said as he reached out and took her hand. He was glad she didn't pull away.

"Who'd have thought we would end up here," Kinsey said.

"In Northern California? Not me. Too many damn hippies."

"No, smart ass. I meant where we are in life."

"You mean talking to each other?"

"Yeah."

"Honestly? I didn't."

"Me neither," Kinsey said, "but I like it."

"Good," Thorne said as they reached the cabin door, "me too."

"I'm still going to kick your ass at Hold 'Em," Kinsey said.

"Only if I let you," Thorne said.

A cheer went up as they walked into the cabin and then shut the door behind them. Laughter echoed out into the evening air. It was the type of overly honest laughter reserved for warriors and survivors.

And the cabin was filled with both.

THE END

About The Author:

A professional writer since 2009, Jake Bible has a proven record of innovation, invention and creativity. Novelist, short story writer, independent screenwriter, podcaster, and inventor of the Drabble Novel, Jake is able to switch between, or mash-up genres with ease to create new and exciting storyscapes that have captivated and built an audience of thousands. He is the author of the horror/military scifi series the Apex Trilogy (*DEAD MECH, The Americans, Metal and Ash*) and the bestselling suburban zombie apocalypse series, *Z-Burbia*, allavailable from Severed Press. He is also the author of *Bethany and the Zombie Jesus, Stark- An Illustrated Novella* and the YA horror novel *Little Dead*. Jake Bible lives in Asheville, NC with his family. **Find him at www.jakebible.com**.